MORODA

To Kerry,

Never give up
on your dreams.

25·5·19

MORODA

L. L. McNeil

First published in Great Britain in 2017

Moroda © 2017 L. L. McNeil
ISBN: 978-0-9957922-0-3
Cover by: Book Beaver

Printed and bound in Great Britain by Clays Ltd,
Elcograf S.p.A.

www.llmcneil.com

DEDICATION

For Pipkin, who brought me out of the darkness and gave me the confidence to follow my dreams.

ACKNOWLEDGEMENTS

I would like to thank so many people for their unending support, patience, and help, but in particular: Ian, who was my alpha and beta reader, first editor, producer of fantastic ideas and greatest fan, and without whom this novel would not exist as it does; Eve and Michael, who offered me their unalloyed critique to help strengthen the book and my writing; and everyone in the *Fab Marketing Team*, for giving me the push when I wanted to procrastinate.

To anyone who purchases my book, I am eternally grateful. It would mean the world and more if you would be kind enough to review *Moroda*.

Chapter One

Morning dew flavoured her skin with the taste of autumn. Pale sunlight filtered through the steel barred window, and Moroda shivered in the dank cell of Rosecastle Dungeon. She shifted her position to ease the cramp developing in her aching back and legs. She was not in chains, thank Rhea, but it did not take away the fear and uncertainty which plagued her.

She wouldn't be beheaded, surely? It had been an idle threat to keep the crowd from retaliating at her sudden arrest, hadn't it? Murderers were beheaded. Or traitors to the crown. Surely they wouldn't kill a woman who had voiced an opinion?

Goose bumps rose on the flesh of her legs and arms after brushing the cold stone floor and she flinched, a light clink sounding within her skirt. Reaching carefully into the deep pocket, she grasped three coins. 'I'd forgotten about you,' she said, smiling down at the silver florins.

She did not have the chance to enjoy finding the forgotten money; the door to the dungeon rattled, and muffled shouting carried through from the other side along with grunts from the guard restraining a new, aggressive-sounding prisoner.

Eyes wide, Moroda looked for somewhere to hide her treasure. Surely if she put it back in her pocket, the coins would jingle when she moved. The window, perhaps? No, they would be too easily seen between the bars.

Scrabbling to the corner of her cell, Moroda spied a cracked floor slab. She could hear the steel hinges of the oak door creak as it was heaved open, and she had no time to look for an alternative hiding place. Shuffling over on her knees, one fist clenched around her coins, she wedged the fingers of her free hand under the stone slab. It was rough against her skin, but Moroda lifted it just high enough to slide the coins into the gap. The door of the dungeon slammed shut, the slab dropped back into place, and the new prisoner entered the chamber.

The same guard who brought her to the cell barely an hour ago was now wrestling with another prisoner, a woman, and a lowborn one from her insults and the rasp in her voice. She spat and kicked, trying to bite and wriggle out of the guard's hold, and Moroda pressed herself to the back of the cell.

She watched, anxious, as the guard frog marched the new prisoner to the cell. Pressing her against the metal, he took the keys from his waist, unlocked the gate, slid it open, and threw the woman into the cell.

Blood spattered the floor from an open gash on the woman's shoulder, bringing a splash of colour to the drab grey dungeon. She immediately whirled round and threw herself at the gate, reaching between the bars and scrabbling for the guard's face with chipped nails. 'You pig! Bastard! Get this gate open now, or I swear to Rhea herself you'll pay!'

'Amarah, you're done. You know we've been after you for years. No threat will change that,' he replied with a shrug, out of reach of her flailing hands and at ease.

'Morgen, I'll kill you for this!' she spat back, one hand reaching up to cover the wound on her left shoulder. Blood trickled through her fingers as she tried to stem the flow. 'At least get me a medic! You don't want me to bleed to death in here do you?' Her eyes narrowed on the young man as he glanced over her wound.

'You're not going to die, calm down. I'll see what I can do. Try not to cause too much disruption,' he sighed, walking back towards the door.

'What about Khanna? I hope you're not going to destroy that ship! She's faster than anything the Imperial fleet has!' Amarah called, walking along the gate of the cell, keeping as close to Morgen as possible. 'Be of some use, won't she?'

'I don't know, it's not my decision. She's locked up safe and sound, just like you,' he answered, ignoring her glare as he heaved the dungeon door open and slammed it shut behind him. As the sound of his footsteps echoed away, Moroda remained still. Amarah hadn't noticed her, and she was keen to keep it that way. Who knew who she was, or what she had done to warrant being locked up. Moroda had no intention of finding out, preferring instead to keep away from the uncouth criminal. She slid slowly down the wall, until she was half-sat, half-crouched on the floor, heart racing and breath held. Perhaps if she stayed quiet enough, Amarah would not spot her before Morgen returned to take one of them away.

After a moment, Amarah turned and looked round the cell, pausing to glare at Moroda when she spotted her. 'What do you think you're looking at, little girl?'

Moroda was lost for words. 'I...I didn't mean...'

'Good, shut up and keep out of my fucking way then,'
Amarah interrupted, looking over the rest of the cell, scowling at the
floor, walls, and windows. 'Damned if I'm staying in here long
enough to be executed.'

Moroda said nothing, remaining crouched and watching her
carefully. She tried to keep out of Amarah's way as the she stepped
towards the window. The new prisoner released her hand from her
shoulder and grabbed onto the bars, letting go after giving each of
them a short pull, leaving the metal slick with blood. 'Damn.'

Amarah glanced at Moroda again, who met her gaze
defiantly, before she looked to the steel bars of the cell door.
Despite the castle's age, the cells seemed well kept. An escape plan
was not forthcoming. Amarah swore again and leaned her back
against the metal gate, her arm returning to cover the wound on her
twitching shoulder.

'What happened?' Moroda dared, expecting to be insulted
again.

Amarah shrugged, 'Too much haste. Got sloppy. Made a
mistake. Never again, I tell you.' The older woman closed her eyes,
allowing silence to fill the cell once again.

Moroda took the opportunity to study Amarah's face. She
had short, dark hair, roughly cut and in no way styled, in contrast to
Moroda's longer, messy brown tresses. She wore no powders on her
face or oils in her hair. A thin scar lined her left cheek, just below
her dark eyes, and she looked grubby, as though she hadn't bathed

for months. Moroda dropped her gaze every time Amarah moved, lest she caught her staring. She guessed the injured woman to be in her thirties; but wounds and dirt did a lot to age a person, so Moroda couldn't be sure. All she knew was she feared her aggression, and hoped she would keep her distance while they were locked up together.

'That fool Morgen is no more fit to be in the Imperial Guard than you are to be in here,' Amarah said, breaking the silence after watching Moroda for several minutes. 'I heard what you did this morning, standing up to that foreign bastard.'

Moroda flinched as Amarah swore again, but was flattered her deed that morning had not gone unnoticed. Then again, she had been arrested very publicly, so she supposed word of her actions, a Goldstone's actions, no less, would spread like wildfire. Not that she was really considered a Goldstone anymore, her heart sinking as she thought to the three florins she had hidden, her only money in the world. It was all that remained of a vast inheritance which should have ensured she and her sister were well-kept until the end of their days. Moroda nodded. 'Thank you.'

'That the only reason Morgen arrest you? Or you do something else? Sleep with some other Goldstone you shouldn't have, or something?' Amarah pressed.

'What? No…nothing like that! I would never!'

Amarah's cackle filled the room, echoing off the stone. 'Ah you Goldstones are all the same, aren't you? Little goody-goody rich girls who never get in trouble or do anything wrong.'

'I'm not a Goldstone…not anymore,' Moroda replied softly.

'Yes, well I can see that, can't I,' Amarah grinned, licking her lips and shifting her hold on her injured shoulder. 'Can't buy yourself out of this one, can you?'

'Do you want me to help with that?' Moroda asked, 'I can use some cloth to stem the blood? At least, until help comes?'

Amarah paused for a moment before nodding, 'Yeah, if you can.'

Moroda tore a strip of fabric from the bottom of her skirt—it was thick, dark cotton—and carefully shuffled over to Amarah. When the other woman dropped her hand from her shoulder, Moroda wrapped the length of cloth around Amarah's wound as best she could. 'It won't stop the bleeding completely, but it might help a little?' Moroda said, wiping her bloodied hands on her skirt.

Amarah inspected the bandage for another long moment, before approving it with a nod. She glanced back through the cell bars to the dungeon door and sighed, and it did not take long before her gaze drifted to the rest of the cell. 'Oh great, not a Varkain, too,' she said, her voice taking on the same edge as before.

'But I'm not…?' Moroda began, before following Amarah's gaze to the back corner of the cell, set in shadow.

Confused, Moroda looked back to Amarah and back to the corner, squinting in the darkness as she tried to make out what Amarah could see. Her heart began to race again when she spotted the silhouette of another person sat in the shadows. Had someone else been there all the time and she hadn't noticed? How could that have happened? She had been locked up almost an hour.

'I do love the sound of a panicked heartbeat.'

Moroda stood up, her breathing quickening as she realised there was someone there—someone who was far more of a threat than Amarah could ever be. Stumbling backwards, Moroda tried to put as much distance between herself and the dark corner as she could.

'Ah yes, and there is the accompanying scent of fear…such a nectar.'

'Shut up you filthy creature,' Amarah growled, on edge, but without the anxiety of Moroda. 'What in Rhea's name we're doing in the same cell as you, I don't know! What happened to enforced segregation?'

'Perhaps they forgot. Being invisible is our specialty.'

Moroda's heart continued to pound, but she couldn't quite make out the features of the Varkain—the cell was too poorly lit, and he was keeping too still. She could have sworn she had checked the cell over when she was first thrown in, and found it empty. Then again, she had never before come across a Varkain face to face, and was terrified.

'Come out from the shadows, Varkain. Show yourself,' Amarah ordered, her hand returning to cover the wound in her shoulder. Moroda wanted to object, but her voice had left her.

'No. I am chained.'

Amarah's shoulders dropped as she visibly relaxed, and Moroda followed suit. Perhaps that was why she hadn't been attacked earlier. She had grown up on stories of brutal Varkain killings, and did not wish to be the centre of the next one.

'Ah, well you're just a worm then, aren't you?' Amarah

cackled, straightening her stance and wandering over to the edge of the shadow. 'Tied up and left for dead. It's all you're worth.'

'Be quiet.'

Amarah crouched down, a sneer on her face. 'I don't think so. I don't take orders from anyone, not least the likes of you. Tell me, Varkain, were you given a name at birth? Or just abandoned along with the thousands of others?' she asked, head tilted slightly to one side. 'Dumped in a hole in the ground and left to rot like the maggots you are.'

Moroda did not know what might come of taunting such a dangerous creature, but Amarah clearly thought he posed no threat.

'Sapora,' he answered. 'I know you are Amarah, a sky pirate and thief, and a murderer, just as much as I am.'

Moroda remained quiet as her companion ignored Sapora and took to pacing around the cell. With her good hand, Amarah grabbed one of the bars on the gate and shook it furiously. 'Morgen! Where the hell is my medic!'

Silence responded. She stepped away from the gate, looked around the cell again and tapped her fingers against her arm, clearly rattled by Sapora's words. It did not take long for Amarah to notice the cracked stone slab, and she paused.

'Oh? What's this?' She dropped to one knee and picked at the cracked stone. Within seconds, she had lifted the slab and was rewarded with the glint of silver. 'Every cloud,' she said, snatching up the coins and examining them. 'Three florins. Perfect!'

Amarah pocketed them as quickly as she found them, leaving Moroda to clench her fists in response. She had no desire to get into a conflict with Amarah, especially if she was a murderer, as Sapora claimed, despite those simple coins being the only thing of any worth she had left. All her fight had gone out after that morning.

Why she even bothered to stand up to that man, she had no idea. He was obviously a guest of the royals. He had been invited into Rosecastle and was surrounded by Imperial Guards, with a following of soldiers of his own. But she could not accept the words he spewed to the crowd. Others may have, and that was their choice as far as Moroda was concerned, but she would not allow her family to be dictated to by anyone, especially a war-mongering bully like this foreigner. Her immediate arrest only proved she'd touched a nerve. Imprison or behead enough people, and folks soon stop standing against you.

Closing her eyes, Moroda exhaled, resigning herself to her situation. Beheaded or left to rot in a cell with two murderers, she couldn't tell which fate was worse.

It took only a few minutes before the dungeon door was forced open once again, but it was not Morgen who walked down the corridor—it was a woman of twenty years, clutching a ring of bronze keys close to her chest as she tiptoed across the cold stone in soft leather shoes.

'Eryn!' Moroda gasped, leaping to her feet and clutching at the bars. 'What in Rhea's name are you doing here? How did you get into the castle?'

'Sshh, never you mind about that. I'm getting you out, now!' Eryn replied, glancing over her shoulder. The sisters shared a similar look: dark brunette hair and hazel eyes, but Eryn's face was soft and round in contrast to Moroda's leaner features.

Amarah narrowed her eyes at the newcomer, unconcerned with the hows and whys. 'Get on with it, then! Hurry up!'

Eryn nodded and tried each key quickly, breathing a sigh of relief as the successful one clicked and the door lifted off the lock.

Before Eryn could move, Amarah wrenched the door open and shoved past. 'Get out now if you know what's good for you!' she called over her shoulder, before racing down the corridor and through the door.

Unfazed by Amarah's brusqueness, Eryn turned to her sister. 'You heard her, let's go!'

Moroda paused at the door, and looked back to the corner of the cell. 'Do you have all the keys? There's someone else back there…chained up,' she said.

'Moroda, this isn't a jailbreak! I'm here to get you and get out!' Eryn replied, looking back to the door. 'They'll be here any minute, and I'll be locked up too! Let's go!'

Shaking her head, Moroda grabbed the keys and ran to the dark corner, before hesitating. 'You…you won't attack me…if I let you out?' she asked, feeling meek and small once again.

'No.'

She took another step forward, trying to make out his features in the poor light. 'How do I know I can trust your word?' Moroda asked, crouching down and thumbing through the keys.

'The promise of a Varkain is known throughout Linaria as truth.'

She could feel him smiling in the darkness, and it made her

more uneasy than ever. Ignoring Eryn's frantic calls, she took a deep breath. She couldn't leave someone behind, she just couldn't—and should he ever escape, she did not want to incur the wrath of the Varkain for having left him in the cell. Perhaps the reason for her actions were not so noble after all. 'Okay. I'll leave the keys with you, are your hands free?'

'Yes.'

Moroda dropped the keys on the floor and ran back to the gate.

'There's a Varkain in there? Why did you release him! We should be locking the gate, not letting him out!' Eryn cried, incredulous.

By the time Moroda had turned around to check, Sapora had unlocked himself and was on his feet, racing through the door faster than she could blink.

'Thanks very much,' Sapora said, grinning. Both rows of dagger-like teeth flashed white as ivory from his dull, grey skin. He was thin, shorter than a full grown man, but lean and supple. Dried blood covered his clawed hands and the clothes he wore were faded black. A mop of dark, greenish hair matched his eyes, and he watched the two girls with vertical-slit pupils widely dilated in the dim light of the dungeon.

Before either sister could respond to their first sight of a Varkain, he, too, raced off without another word.

'Ugh, those creatures are vile,' Eryn shivered. 'Come on, before that guard realises what's happened!' She grabbed Moroda's arm and led the pair out the dungeon and into the lower halls of the castle. 'There's a servant's entrance just along here, by the back of the kitchens. If we hurry, they won't know you're gone for hours!' Moroda's heart soared as they ran through empty halls; she could practically smell the sunlight bursting through the windows as they raced along. The nightmare was going to be over! She wasn't going to die! Thank the dragons above for family and the resourcefulness of her sister!

As they ran, Moroda smelled bread baking. 'The kitchens are on the other side of this wall,' Eryn panted. 'The door's…just at the end…of the corridor!'

Moroda readied herself for a final sprint, when a door burst open to their right and Morgen hurtled through it, tackling her to the ground. 'Not so fast!' he yelled, grabbing at her legs as she wriggled out of his hold.

'Get off her!' Eryn screamed, circling back to kick at his hands.

Between the two of them thrashing around, Morgen's hold loosened, and Moroda managed to get back on her feet. Without pausing for breath, the two sprinted to the end of the corridor and straight out into the bustling street. The afternoon sunlight was dazzling after so long in the darkness, and Moroda took in a deep breath.

'Stop right there!' Morgen shouted, only a few paces behind, but the escaped prisoners raced into the crowded market streets.

Chapter Two

'Stop where you are!' Morgen yelled, shoving past the crowds mingling on the cobblestones of Niversai's market streets, which were filled with buskers, artists and actors vying for attention. Laughter and shouting filled the air, a cacophony of noise, colour, and light. Noblemen and women—Goldstones and Silverstones from throughout Corhaven and beyond—spilled over the grounds of Rosecastle into the bustling market square. Vendors bartered across one another from their stalls, or pushed carts overflowing with food and silks, sacks of spices and materials, through the city. Courtesans cloaked in red and yellow silk lingered near the edges of the market, looking for the attention of any Goldstone who glanced their way, while people of high standing wandered through the crowds, one of the few times of the year they enjoyed Niversai's festivities alongside the common folk.

The low wall that surrounded Rosecastle was unmanned, and Morgen cursed as he raced through the open gate and into the street. The Imperial Guards stationed at Rosecastle were short due to two main reasons; the annual airship races currently underway, and Aciel, the foreign visitor, whose sudden, unplanned arrival had thrown the entire castle into disarray. Aciel and his small retinue had, in the space of a few hours, somehow agreed with the king to take on two hundred Imperial soldiers, and had left the capital that morning, following an address to the citizens. It left the remaining officers stretched so thin they could work every hour of the day and night and still not patrol the entire city. What remaining guards could be spared were posted at the city gates to try and balance the flow of Linarians coming to visit and stay in Niversai for the races. It meant Morgen alone was in charge of prisoners, and the only one in pursuit of Moroda, Eryn, and the other two escapees.

Though not suited in full armour, his steel boots, greaves and gauntlets made him considerably heavier than the much more lightly dressed girls he was trying to chase down. When coupled with the busy streets, the young soldier had hardly any chance of keeping them in sight, much less apprehending them. He knew Amarah and Sapora would have also escaped from the cell, but if he could at least bring one prisoner back, it might start to make up for the mistake of allowing the escape in the first place. Of course, the other two were far more dangerous, but Morgen wasn't about to try and hunt down a Varkain or a sky pirate by himself. He didn't know if they had allies in the city, and wasn't keen on finding out.

In truth, it hadn't been his plan to put all the prisoners in one cell to begin with—he was only following his captain's orders—but that had backfired, and he was sure his colleagues would somehow find a way to pin it on him, as they always did. He had actually been trying to seek out a medic for Amarah's injury. So much for having some compassion.

Morgen came to a halt, doubled over and panting, trying to catch his breath and will away the stitch which had developed in his side. He shook his head, angry at himself. He was a young, fit man who could outrun his captains with ease—why was he having such a hard time trying to chase down two prisoners? Wiping his brow with the back of his hand, Morgen shook his head before looking back in the direction they had raced off. Among the crowd of bartering townsfolk and market stall traders, he could not see them.

Setting off again, Morgen turned his attention to the traders, taking a sly glance into every tent and behind every stall he could, hoping to discover them by searching methodically.

*

Moroda and her sister sat at an empty table by the door of a small tavern near the back of the market they'd ducked into a couple of streets ahead. It gave them excellent views of Rosecastle and its grounds, and provided much needed sanctuary. Both had been born and raised in Niversai, and knew this part of the city like the back of their hands. At twenty-five, Moroda had frequented the tavern for several years, and had brought Eryn along with her when she developed the taste for hot wine.

'He won't even realise there's a tavern here,' Eryn said, once she had her breath back, resting her arms on the table, and putting her face into them. 'It still looks like the old blacksmith's.'

'If it weren't for you, I'd have died,' Moroda replied, a little more sombre. 'Even if you think the beheading sentence was just a threat, there were two...real criminals in there,' she shook her head and thought back to her cell mates. 'That Amarah is obviously a thief and a fighter, and has her own airship to boot...and the Varkain, Sapora...I don't even want to think about him.'

Lifting her face from the table, Eryn shook her head, 'but

nothing happened, so don't worry. We just need to lie low for a bit. I'll get us something to eat.' Ever positive, she got up and made her way past the other patrons to the bar.

Moroda decided to take better notice of her surroundings so as not to be caught unawares again. Perhaps she wouldn't come upon another Varkain for years, but anyone could be dangerous if you got on the wrong side of them.

She took the time to observe the other patrons, trying to figure out who to potentially be wary of. She was impressed Amarah had spotted the Varkain after only a minute or two of being in the cell; Moroda did not aspire to be a thief, yet she had to admire Amarah's observation—she even managed to find the florins she had hidden away!

Perhaps that was her next move? To try and find that sky pirate and demand her florins back. She had helped her with the injury, after all, and they had only escaped thanks to Eryn. Surely one good turn deserved another? What were three florins to a notorious pirate, anyway? Moroda supposed she had entire chests full of silver florins and gold crowns hidden away somewhere secret.

As her mind wandered, Moroda's gaze fell on a cloaked man sat at a tall table near the window at the front of the tavern. The thick glass windows were dirty, and let in only a little light which illuminated his face, showing scars criss-crossing his pale cheeks and lips. He was hunched over a steaming mug, and his heavy travel cloak fell to the floor, covering his limbs. He wore a wide-brimmed hat, brown like his cloak, which covered his dark blond hair and sagged with age.

Moroda tried to note more about the man, when he blinked and turned, his bright grey eyes meeting hers. Caught staring, Moroda hurriedly looked away, and was relieved when Eryn returned to the table a moment later with two mugs of tea and a bowl of cloudberries.

After waiting a few, long seconds, Moroda risked another glance at the man, who had thankfully returned his attention to the window.

'What are you staring at?' Eryn asked, looking over the other tables in the tavern and handing her sister one of the mugs.

Moroda took it, careful to take her time before glancing up again, 'that man sat at the table by the window...No, no, don't look now...He's...a bit odd.'

'Odd?' Eryn questioned, popping a cloudberry in her mouth and chewing, trying to look over her shoulder inconspicuously. It didn't take her long to pick him out, and she whipped back round to her sister. 'I bet he's an Ittallan,' Eryn said, her eyebrows raised. 'The airship races bring all sorts. He's not a trader or a pilot, he can't be, otherwise he'd be out there with the others. Maybe he's here supporting someone? I wouldn't worry. Eat!' Her haughty tone belied her concern for her sister. Eryn shoved the bowl of food towards Moroda. 'Just think how close we are to the castle! We're hiding right under their noses and they'll never realise!'

Moroda smiled at her sister's words, and drank deeply from her cup of honeyed tea before saying slowly, 'I can't help but worry. Not about that guard Morgen, but about my arrest this morning...

Some stranger from a foreign land who can take hundreds of our soldiers, treat the townsfolk as though they were all beneath him…I had to say something. If he's going from city to city doing this…soon, all of Corhaven, all of Linaria, might be following him! I really don't like it.'

'With everything else going on, Ro, I think you need to stop worrying about Linaria's politics. You go and get yourself arrested the moment my back is turned! Like some common criminal! I'm sure I should have been the older sister!'

Moroda remained quiet as the two resumed their meagre meal, a far cry from the fine meats and wine they had grown accustomed to, while they observed the comings and goings of the tavern.

'I also lost the coin I had,' Moroda added in a small voice, once they had finished eating.

'What?'

'In the cell…I tried to hide the florins under a loose slab, but that woman, the other prisoner, Amarah…she found them,' Moroda sighed, leaning forward and pressing her face into her folded arms on the table. 'Today has been so awful, and I worry if this is what happens the first time Aciel shows up, what's going to become of me?'

'Ro, stop it,' Eryn said sharply. 'It's nothing to do with that man. Just your bad luck, that's all. We'll get through this! I still have a crown saved and a few half florins, too. With all the trade going on right now, I'm sure we'll be fine. No more worrying about Aciel or politics, agreed? It's nothing to do with us, and he's already left the city, so stop thinking about him.'

'No worrying about Aciel or politics,' Moroda echoed. 'I honestly don't know where I'd be without you, Eryn.'

'Back in that dank cell with a dirty snake, I expect!'

The man by the window pushed his chair back as he stood up, and the scrape of wood on wood caught the girl's attention. Moroda watched him walk towards the door from the corner of her eye, noting a slight limp in his stride.

The man took his final swig from his mug, emptying the contents completely, before wiping his mouth with the back of his sleeve and placing the empty container on the sisters' table. 'Aciel should be the least of your concerns. You wanna worry about something? You ought to worry about the dragons,' he said, watching them closely.

'What about the dragons?' Moroda asked, half getting out of her seat to address the man, emboldened.

'Speaking as a dragon hunter, you see. You ought to take shelter if you know what's good for you, and soon.' He lightly tapped the edge of his hat to them and headed out into the late afternoon sun.

*

The market stalls were less than appealing to Amarah as she navigated the busy streets. Shouts of fresh fruit and vegetables, expensive jewellery, bags of coffee beans, sacks of potatoes, strips of cloth and jewels of every colour were directed her way, but she disregarded them all. It was a shame—she had come to Niversai this time of year specifically to take her pick from the traders and finance her way through winter, but her arrest and the seizure of her weapons and airship had put her plans out of order for the moment.

Ever resilient, Amarah knew her next step was to re-arm herself before stealing Khanna back. She never felt more vulnerable than when she was without her weapon, and it was without question the first thing she had to do. The airship races would be on for another few days, yet—she might still have time to win some coin from arrogant pilots as the excitement dwindled.

As she left the busier inner market and started to peruse the smaller stalls offering steadily more exotic goods and spices, she finally came upon something worth looking at: a weapons trader.

'Finest weapons in all Linaria,' the trader called, noting her interest had been caught. 'None better.'

Amarah glanced up at him, and a smile crept onto her face—he was an Ittallan trader, no doubt about that. The man was huge, bordering on seven feet tall, with broad shoulders, a bald head, a wide girth, and hands that looked like they could crush boulders. His eyes were a soft brownish-orange, gentle and smiling, matching the rich baritone of his voice and his deeply tanned skin.

'The best in Linaria? That's quite a claim,' Amarah said, a hand on her hip as she played along.

'Yes. But a true claim,' he replied, selecting a dagger with an ornate handle. 'You see the work here,' he pointed with his little finger, 'the detail in the hilt is by Anahrik,' he gestured to another man with his top half in a barrel at the back of the stall.

'Silver?' Amarah tilted her head, taking the offered blade to examine it closely. It was not something she had seen on a real weapon before—usually they were made for display in the homes of Goldstones and royalty.

'Yes, silver. For beauty and strength, and our trademark. No-one else does this for their weapons or armour.'

Amarah nodded, stepping to the side to better look at the rest of his options. 'I don't see my weapon here, though,' she said, eyes narrowing.

'What you want? We have blades of all shapes and lengths; we have axes, longbows, crossbows...'

'None of those,' she said, folding her arms and smiling. 'But it is long range, if you use it well.'

'Throwing stars?' Anahrik piped in, having resurfaced from the barrel with arms full of arrow points. He, too, was an Ittallan; though younger than the other trader by several years, and not nearly as stocky, with bright blue eyes, pale blond hair, and an even paler complexion. He had mastered the common tongue and spoke clearly, with no trace of the accent from his homeland. He flashed a wide smile and walked around the stall to Amarah's side.

Amarah laughed and shook her head, 'no, not those. I use a scythe. Do you have any?'

'Only the finest, we keep them off display as they're so popular, only on request do we show these, they're so beautiful...' Anahrik began, but Amarah had lost interest in his sales tactics already, her attention on the older Ittallan.

The larger trader turned to a heavy wooden trunk sat behind the stall, lifted the thick metal lid, and reached within. He carefully brought out a lengthy package, well wrapped in soft, red linen. 'This is the weapon we have for you,' he said, resting it on the counter of the stall. He unwrapped it slowly, showing off the dark ebony handle first, smoothed and carved to look like marble. The silver inlay wound around it like rope, and the blade at the head of the weapon was curved, serrated at the end, and glistened in the sun.

'Three florins,' Amarah said, after looking it over for a long moment.

'Three florins? An insult,' the trader spat. 'It is worth two crowns at least, but I can sell it for one crown, no less.'

'One crown would buy me all of your weapons,' Amarah replied, shifting her weight to her other hip. 'Three florins is my offer.'

'Three florins wouldn't cover the silver that went into that,' Anahrik jumped in again, leaning forward and picking up the scythe nimbly. He caressed the handle and ran his finger along the length of the blade. 'See the precision here, that's from Ittallan forges, as someone who knows weapons would realise,' he said, turning it over carefully, allowing the gleam of the low sun to run along the blade and catch the sparkle in the silver.

'Silver makes it weaker. Yes it looks very pretty, but I am no Goldstone, dazzled by something shiny but worthless. Do you want to sell the weapon or not? The day is getting on and trading will finish soon,' Amarah retaliated, pushing a loose strand of hair behind her ear. 'Scythes are not popular because they are uncommon. You could get rid of two dozen daggers as often as one scythe, and here I am, ready to take it off your hands.'

'Palom,' Anahrik growled, glancing at the larger trader.

'Three florins is not enough,' Palom retorted, shaking his head and folding his arms to mirror Amarah's stance. Neither was willing to budge.

Amarah exhaled, annoyed. She needed a good weapon, and this was by far the best she was going to find in Niversai at such short notice. Perhaps she could try and release Khanna without weaponry, win enough in the races, and buy the scythe with the winnings. She did not wish to risk stealing from Ittallan weapon smiths.

'If you can't afford it, stop wasting our time,' Anahrik muttered, handing the scythe back to Palom.

The backhand from Amarah came so swiftly and so suddenly that Anahrik was on the floor before he even realised he had been struck. 'Watch your mouth, you damned pig!'

Palom responded by laughing, the roar of his voice shaking the stall, 'he is young, I am sorry for any offence. But if you cannot buy the weapon, I cannot sell it to you.'

'I'm going to win so much gold in the races I'll come back and buy your entire damned shop,' Amarah continued, eyes locked on Anahrik.

'You race?' Palom asked, his eyebrows raised in interest.

Amarah turned to him with a scowl, 'I do.'

'I race, too,' Anahrik said, getting up, and grinning, one hand on his red cheek. 'But not in those bulky airships, they're far too slow.'

'You've never seen a real ship then,' Amarah replied, disliking Anahrik more with each passing moment.

'You have both hurt another's pride, why do you not instead race? If you win, you get the weapon for the three florins. If Anahrik wins-'

'Deal,' Amarah replied.

'I didn't finish,' Palom argued.

'Doesn't matter, I'll beat anything you could throw at me. I'm the fastest thing in the skies, even dragons can't keep up with my Khanna,' Amarah boasted, clenching and unclenching her fists.

Anahrik laughed at that. 'Ah yes, but how many Ittallan have you raced, in their true form? I chase airships for fun.' Lifting his arms from his sides, he leaped backwards, and in a flash of light, a grey falcon flew away from where a man had stood a moment before.

'Anahrik likes speed more than anyone I know, I have not known an airship to outfly him,' Palom grinned. 'You have agreed. When do you wish to race?'

Amarah took a step back, a little annoyed at jumping into the deal so soon. She was not one to back out, however, and slammed the three florins on his counter. 'The main arena, at sundown. Bring my weapon, and I promise not to slice that bird's head off.'

With that, she turned and headed off towards Rosecastle, the bellowing laughter of Palom following her every step of the way.

Chapter Three

By the time Morgen returned, empty-handed, to the castle, it was getting on for early evening. The taunts he received from the other officers were nothing short of pure torment, but he couldn't do anything about it. He had been so sure the escapees were hiding in a tent selling linens that he had to buy a new surcoat as an apology for wasting the seamstress' time and accusing her of harbouring criminals. While the coat was lovely, he was five florins down and no closer to apprehending Moroda or the woman who freed her. He had also lost Amarah and a Varkain convicted of goodness knows what, who were now roaming the streets unchecked. His punishment, several lashes no doubt, would come after the races were over and they could spare one of his captains to carry it out. Until then, he was to keep out of the way.

He sat on one of the large wooden trunks holding broken weapons, and gazed mournfully at the swords and crossbows adorning the walls of the armoury he had been relegated to keeping an eye on. Head in his hands, Morgen sighed—was this really what it was all about, in the Imperial army? Following orders you didn't agree with and being punished for every mistake? Not to mention constant jokes and jibes from colleagues and superiors both? Morgen had envisioned that a glittering career as a famous knight awaited him in Niversai; it was why he left his hometown, and he had no intention of returning to his small farm and working the land along with his brothers. He had left to prove his worth, and he'd be damned if he returned a failure.

The wage was marginally better than what he would earn back home—a small village called Kebbe—as were his lodgings, but other than that, he had little positive to say about his move to the capital almost a year on. He also felt for Moroda, for having the guts to speak out against the King's visitor that morning. He knew he did not agree with what the Arillian was saying either, but bound by duty, he was forbidden from reacting. It seemed at least one of the townsfolk had to say something, and he found it peculiar it was a Goldstone who finally spoke up. He had expected to escort her away from the castle grounds, maybe a small fine if she did not comply or continued to speak out. To sentence her to the dungeons and behead her? That was a punishment too far, and did not sit well with him. In truth, he was grateful she had managed to escape—if it came to carrying out the sentence, Morgen was unsure he would have the guts to go through with it. He wondered what his own punishment would have been for refusing an order.

The jewels from the Royal Vault had also disappeared some time that morning, and everyone had Amarah pegged. She was a thief known to most of the Imperial Guard, and had made off with thousands of crowns' worth of jewellery and trinkets in her career throughout Corhaven. So Morgen had been blamed for that, too— the king himself seemed hardly bothered, but locating the twelve coloured stones was priority number one just as soon as the races were finished.

All around him the castle felt silent; little sound carried through the thick stone walls, though he occasionally heard fading footsteps from the corridor outside. When he heard laughter, he frowned, fearing his peers were mocking him. It was his own fault, really, for leaving the keys unattended. Perhaps it was just as well he did nothing of any importance tonight. Or ever.

He exhaled again, crossed his legs and folded his arms, trying to get comfortable on the flat, wooden trunk. With weapons glistening around him, Morgen readied himself for a long, quiet night.

*

Elsewhere in the castle was also quiet—the majority of the guard were on duty patrolling the streets, or stationed at the city gates to monitor those entering or leaving Niversai.

Sapora had taken advantage of the fewer guards on patrol by skulking along the corridors of the castle, looking for a way out of Niversai, and preferably the country of Corhaven, too. He had tried to pay, barter and bribe various airship captains in the city, but none would permit a Varkain on board. The foolishness of these people sickened and frustrated him no end.

The thought of commandeering an airship crossed his mind, but as he had not the first idea how to fly one, the plan was procrastination at best. Perhaps he could stow away? Yes, that might be another option. He entered the inner dock of the castle which housed the Imperial fleet and other salvaged ships, and was his best chance of a way out of the country.

Making his way silently between the docked warships,

which boasted impressive defences, he thought it might be a safer option than something smaller. Looking one over carefully, Sapora thought it unlikely one would be sent out, nor did he like the idea of travelling with soldiers, particularly when he may be known to them. No, there had to be another way.

The Varkain ran a clawed hand along the smooth, varnished panels of the warships as he walked past, pupils wide in the low light, taking in every detail and trying to commit it to memory. Most had been painted in white, red and gold—Imperial colours—and their large sails, though folded while docked, were bright scarlet with gold highlights. His eyes narrowed at the colours—they reminded him of war, and left a bad taste in his mouth.

Deciding to look at non-Imperial ships, Sapora made his way across the dock when he heard approaching footsteps. They were light, yet hurried, and almost silent; if it weren't for his acute senses, he might have missed them altogether. They were not the loud clanking of guards in their armour, but the soft, well-worn shoes of one used to keeping quiet.

'Amarah, I did not think we would meet again so soon,' Sapora called into the shadows. He grinned as the footsteps halted and he felt her heart rate pick up.

'Nor did I wish to,' Amarah replied, several ships to his left. She continued moving soon after, short bursts in a straight line, then a pause, then another short burst in another direction.

'Your movements are not random. Are you searching for something my sky thief?'

'Khanna,' Amarah replied, further to his left than before. He barely detected her footsteps any more, but her heart and breathing were loud enough to keep track of her location in the large hangar.

'A quick escape? Are you running away from Corhaven?' Sapora asked, tracking her steps and trying to catch up to where she was searching.

'Yes, I've had enough of this fucking pit,' she spat, changing direction again and heading south, down a line of narrow scouting ships. 'I'm going to get some gold and get the hell out of here.'

'Sounds like an excellent idea,' Sapora replied, picking up speed to head her off at a crossroad.

Amarah was not the least bit surprised when the Varkain appeared in front of her, but she seemed mildly annoyed. 'What are you doing down here anyway?' she asked, sidestepping him to continue along the line of ships, glancing left and right with growing irritation.

'The same reason as you. I am done with the people here, and seek passage across the sea to Val Sharis,' Sapora replied, trailing Amarah several paces behind.

'Not on my fucking ship, you're not,' Amarah replied, glaring at him over her shoulder and picking up on his desire. 'Having you…things aboard will bring nothing but misery.'

'I am deeply offended. You're more a danger than I, pirate.'

He paused, mirroring Amarah, before glancing around. He could now hear the steel footsteps of a single member of the Imperial Guard entering the hangar from the other side. With so many docked ships between the soldier and the two criminals, they were not seen immediately, but it would only be a matter of time.

'Ah, here she is,' Amarah breathed, a smile growing on her face as she finally came upon her own airship—heavily varnished in black and grey, it was sleek and smooth, a fifth of the size of a warship, built for speed, not power. Clambering up the narrow steps carved on the side, Amarah got on board. She walked along the deck, checking her sails for rips or tears, and her propellers for signs of damage. Aside from a little scuff on the bow of her ship, Khanna was in the same condition as she had left it, and for that, she could have kissed Morgen.

Her joy was short-lived, however, as she, too, heard the footsteps of the patrolling guard growing closer. 'No, no, no, not now!' she said, racing to the side of the deck, trying to peer over the docked ships to where the guard was.

'Can you not fly away?' Sapora asked from the ground.

'Of course I can, I just need a minute to get her running,' Amarah replied, already away from the edge of the deck and heading down into the hold, where the ship's engines were located.

The Varkain grinned, baring all teeth. 'If I give you the time you need to start, you will take me across the sea?'

His proposition made Amarah pause. The idea of a Varkain on her ship made her retch, but without a few minutes to spare, she would be discovered, unarmed. Of course, if he wanted to cross the sea, he wouldn't attack until then at least…and she would have her scythe from the Ittallan traders. She would surely be able to hold her own against one Varkain in the place she was most at ease?

'I don't have time to waste, Amarah,' Sapora called,

readying himself to move against the guard, who drew closer every moment. His footsteps grew louder, echoing off the docked ships.

'Yes, yes, alright, alright. But don't kill him…I don't want to give them any more reason to follow us,' she conceded. Turning away from him, she raced below deck to give life to Khanna.

'Of course,' Sapora hissed, stepping back into the shadows of the airships to make his move on the approaching guard.

In the few minutes it took Amarah to start her engines and Khanna to rise slightly off the ground, Sapora was standing on the edge of the deck, a smear of blood at the corner of his lips and a smirk on his face. As Amarah resurfaced from the hold, she saw his eyes dance with dizzying pleasure, and she looked at him with disgust.

She strode to the wheel and grabbed hold with one hand. With her other, she pulled at one of the levers in the control panel, unfurling her sails and rising even higher. 'Before we cross the ocean, I have a race against an arrogant Ittallan to win. You've been at odds for centuries haven't you? I think you'd like to see me knock him down a peg or two.' She pushed the four engine throttles slowly forward to give her ship power, turned the wheel to the left, and faced Khanna towards the hangar entrance.

Sapora leaned on the side rail on deck, his smirk deepening. 'Yes, I would enjoy that spectacle very much indeed.'

'Let's get this done then,' Amarah said, engaging the throttles fully and powering along the hanger, past the docked ships, and out into the deep orange skies above the city of Niversai.

Chapter Four

Anahrik was bored of waiting. He had been ready at the front lines for the better part of an hour, watching the sun slowly begin its descent and the first moon rise. The second moon was soon to follow, and as the last rays of sunlight disappeared, the third moon's outline could just be made out among the stars.

'I don't think she's coming,' he scoffed, glancing at Palom, who sat at the bottom of the stone steps at the edge of the arena, oiling one of his broadswords with a heavy, blackened cloth.

'She will not have left three florins,' Palom replied without looking up. 'Light is still here. There is time. Are you worried about flying in darkness?'

Anahrik snorted in response, folding his arms and kicking at the loose stones on the edge of the dusty racing arena. Airships were already retiring for the evening—night races were not popular in Niversai, where most captains' poor vision warranted too many torches to be set up across the length of the arena, and audiences who would miss most of the action when the race turned even higher. In truth, Anahrik was far more comfortable in the day, but he would fly in low light, if it came to it. He couldn't bear the thought of losing to that arrogant woman, and was determined to show off his skills. He had a sneaking hope that an interested sponsor might be watching from somewhere within the waning crowd; that he and

Palom might receive a little coin for their trouble, but he knew it was doubtful.

'Ittallan! Ready to show me how slow you are against my ship?'

In the failing light, Anahrik had not seen or heard Khanna float gracefully up towards the arena, and it was only with Amarah's insult he noticed she had arrived at all.

Both he and Palom glanced skywards, finally spotting the small craft. It was not a long-haul vessel, and even without any engineering experience they could see the airship was built for speed. Her side sails were angled and half folded, like the wings of a dragon in full stoop. Others were tucked at the back and underside of the vessel, yet to be opened. The engines, one on either side, two at the back, were mounted low and looked nothing special, but were almost silent as they ran.

'Looks a good race, Anahrik,' Palom grinned, folding his cloth away and sheathing the sword. 'I will finish packing for the night, I shall meet you back here when you have finished.' He offered his colleague no more support or words of wisdom as he stood to leave the arena.

Anahrik nodded, glancing back to where Khanna hovered. It was now or never. Without bothering to respond to Amarah's taunts, he leapt into the air, transforming as he did, and climbed to meet her altitude.

There was enough fading sunlight to see the deck clearly, and Anahrik landed beside the captain before transforming back. 'You took your time, I thought you were going to forfeit,' he said angrily, glancing around the deck of the ship. When he spotted Sapora, Anahrik scowled before returning his attention to Amarah. 'Well, it's unofficial, but you and I will be the only judges. What course do you suggest? I'll leave it up to you so there can be no doubt of my superiority.' He folded his arms.

Amarah laughed, 'You're so easily riled. I'll have a lot of fun with this.' She turned and walked to the bow of her ship as it hovered in place, gazing out over the empty arena. The few remaining airships from the day's racing were already grounded or heading into secure hangars to be docked, ready for the morning. The usual course markers had all been removed, everything was empty. The sky was clear tonight, and ready for them.

'Let's make it very simple,' she said, after thinking about her options for a moment. 'We'll race from here straight out to the two league marker, circle Niversai once, returning to that marker as the finish. We can fly as close to or as far from Niversai as we please, as long as we do not fly over the outer wall of the city.'

'That's too far,' Anahrik replied immediately.

'Oh really? That's about the same length as a regular course—we'll just use the trees, valley and mountains surrounding Niversai as our circuit. Besides, I've got a big, bulky airship, remember,' Amarah said, one hand on her hip. She knew it would be hard work, particularly with her shoulder injury not yet healed, but she had no qualms about winning. With Khanna's colouring, she doubted Anahrik would easily be able to spot her, so she could cut a couple of corners without her opponent realising. 'I've circled the city a hundred times before, it'll take less than two minutes, flat out,' she added.

'Fine, let's get this sorted then.' Anahrik shifted back into his true form and landing on the side of her ship as Amarah manoeuvred to the starting position. She readied her sails, ensuring those she didn't need were properly tucked back, to keep Khanna as streamlined as possible for the flight.

Once at altitude, she took in a breath to ready herself. Glancing along the deck from her position behind the wheel and the control panel, she caught the falcon's eye and held up a clenched fist to signal her readiness. She mentally counted to three, then brought her arm down as Anahrik leapt from the deck, straight into a dive.

Lurching into motion, Amarah followed Anahrik's descent, tucking Khanna's sails tightly against the side of the ship as she started the race with an almost vertical nose-forward drop.

As Khanna began to build speed, Sapora gripped the sides of the ship, digging his claws into the wood to stop himself sliding towards the nose. 'Amarah, you will crash!' he called angrily.

Amarah disregarded Sapora's protests. She had dug her heels into the rough wooden floor and braced for the speed and angle of descent. Her eyes were solidly fixed on the grey falcon as he gained more and more speed in the dive, distancing himself from Khanna.

'Perhaps you are quicker in a dive, but there's more to go than that,' she growled to herself, pulling back on the wheel to lift the nose, fanning her side sails out and backwards to give the ship extra lift as her trajectory flattened out. She careened across the arena, over the city walls, and out into the darkening fields surrounding the city. She would reach the two league marker in a few moments, just behind Anahrik, but with enough of the course left, she felt confident she would be able to overtake and stretch out a lead in the twists and turns, where Khanna's speed was truly apparent.

*

Moroda and Eryn strolled down the emptying streets, enjoying the cool early evening air. Moroda had finally believed her sister's words that Morgen would not find them, and after spending most of the afternoon hidden in the tavern, it was wonderful to enjoy the outside again, particularly with the weather so fine.

'I thought the races were all over,' Eryn mused, glancing up as they saw a small airship descending with a speed the likes of which they had not seen before in the races.

Moroda narrowed her eyes as she watched the dark ship's flight. 'Hmm, doesn't that say Khanna on the side?' She watched, eager. 'Oh, dragons above, that's Amarah's ship!' she gasped, remembering where she recognised the name from.

'That woman you were in the cell with?' Eryn echoed, astounded. 'That's quite some ship, look at the speed of it! But…who is she racing? I don't see her opponent?'

Moroda shook her head. 'I don't know. Perhaps they're too far ahead to see. It's getting too dark…but I want to find out. Come on, this way, let's see if we can get a better view from the top of there.' She pointed to a marble fountain carved in the shape of a dragon at the top of a small hill at the end of the street, cold water spouting from its open jaws and the tip of its tail. 'Come on,' she said, sprinting over the cobblestones, past closed shops and stalls, trying to reach the vantage point quickly enough to watch the rest of the race.

*

Anahrik, too, had stopped his descent, and was now flying straight over the city walls, the marker in his sights. The world around him dimmed to almost black; only his goal was at the centre of his vision as it rushed towards him with every beat of his wings. He loved nothing more than speed, to outfly anything that tried to chase him, but Khanna was right on his tail, and he could not afford to turn his head to see how close she really was. It appeared that her boastfulness held some water, much to the Ittallan's annoyance.

'I don't see how…your ship can be faster than a falcon. An Ittallan falcon,' Sapora hissed, having slowly made his way along deck to where Amarah piloted the ship. The wind was chilling at these speeds, and he did not enjoy the coldness at all.

'Quiet, I'm bringing this pig's ego down a few notches. I might do the same to you, snake,' Amarah replied, her eyes only on the marker as she turned hard and deployed one of her side wing sails to make the turning angle more acute. Snapping back the power and opening the sails on the opposite side to hastily straighten out, Amarah pushed all four engines to full power. Swooping round the torch-lit marker, she levelled out Khanna and increased her speed as her circuit around the city began.

Her first, immediate obstacle was the great forest which surrounded Niversai. Huge conifers erupted from the canopy of younger trees, causing her to veer sharply left and right to avoid them, while still maintaining her slight left curve to follow the high stone wall marking Niversai's outer limits. Speed and manoeuvrability were her ship's strengths; the more twisty the course, the faster she could go.

In the darkness of the trees she lost sight of Anahrik, as the falcon avoided the branches, only glimpsing a flash of grey every so often as he appeared in the shadows. If he were alone, Amarah wouldn't think twice about shooting him down, but she didn't want to risk it with Palom somewhere close by.

But the violent turns shook Khanna to no end, and her arms ached from where she gripped the wheel so tightly.

It was not doing Sapora any favours either. 'It would be easier, would it not, to fly above the trees?' he suggested.

'No, it's further to travel—Khanna is agile enough to avoid them,' Amarah replied through gritted teeth, a bead of sweat running down her forehead despite the chill of the wind and the coldness of the evening.

In spite of her perseverance, Amarah could not get away from the falcon; both overtook one another countless times as they wound their way through the trees, and both were struggling. Through her peripheral vision, Amarah guessed they were halfway round the city, with neither appearing as the clear victor. She did not know what to do if the race resulted in a draw; she had simply assumed she would win, take her weapon and move on. She didn't want to hold back and lose, nor push Khanna too hard and end up damaging her, not if she wanted to win some coin in the remaining days of the races.

Clouds began to descend as the evening wore on, blocking out starlight and moonlight both, and the outer city was bathed in darkness. Inside the city's walls, small dots of light appeared as fires were lit; a sea of stars in their own right, and Amarah exhaled slowly, trying to focus in the poor light and calm herself down. If she got too worked up, there was no chance of winning the race. She would lose both face and the weapon, and the pirate didn't know which was worse.

The trees began to thin around the city's southern side, and Khanna was flanked only by the grey stone wall marking the city limits. Her speed increased as all sails were unfurled and her engines were each on full thrust. Anahrik soared past, inching ahead slowly, his own wings spread for maximum speed and lift. Both Anahrik and Amarah were concentrating on their course as they shot along the wall, and it was only at Sapora's sudden cry that they pulled away.

A plume of fire suddenly enveloped the ship and falcon from above. The ferocity and suddenness of the attack meant Amarah and Anahrik reacted instinctively, folding their wings and diving out of the way of the smoke and flame, back into the trees.

'What the—' Amarah glanced up, and her eyes grew wide as a dragon descended from the clouds. It roared in fury at missing its target, and swooped over the city wall in a wide arc as the dry trees below turned to flame. The beast turned after igniting the foliage and headed back over the wall for another pass.

'What in Linaria…' Amarah gasped; suddenly realising they were under attack. She focussed on pulling up and out of the trees, trying to get out of the thick, black smoke which rose from the burning branches.

'A dragon,' Sapora hissed, crouched down below the ship's controls, trying to shield himself from the heat of the flames. 'With no warning.'

Trying to look around and see where the beast was, Amarah spotted burning embers on her deck from where the wood had caught alight. 'Sapora, get those flames out now or we won't be in the air much longer!' She called, gaining height and leaving the smouldering treeline far below her. She searched desperately for the incoming threat as she flew into the clouds, all thoughts of Anahrik and the race forgotten. In the darkness, she could hardly see a thing, and fought to keep panic at bay.

Despite his fear of the flames, Sapora understood the sense in her order, and shuffled back along the deck. He covered his mouth and nose covered with his cloak, keeping the smoke away from his face.

A sudden roar caught his attention, and Sapora ducked as the dragon shot another plume of fire after the ship, tinting the clouds in dredges of red and orange heat. Keeping well below the side of the deck, Sapora hissed in anger, avoiding the scorching heat of fire overhead. The dragon's aim may have been true, but Khanna's agility kept them out of immediate incineration.

'You told me you can outfly a dragon, Amarah! Get away from this one!' Sapora cried, stamping out the flames building on the bow of the ship. 'Your hull may be alight. I am not going into the holds to look!'

Amarah glared at Sapora, but said nothing in response. If he had been one of her crew, she could order him however she wished. But he was a guest, and a Varkain to boot; she had no authority over him.

'I think flying away is a good idea, Amarah,' he snapped, fear and anger taking hold as the silhouette of the dragon passed over them again.

In the chaos and confusion, neither Amarah nor Sapora had noticed Anahrik crashing onto the deck in a heap of smoke and feathers. When he transformed back, Sapora flinched, angry with himself for not realising Anahrik's arrival.

The Ittallan had ash in his hair and had been scalded along the backs of his arms, but was otherwise in one piece, if a little out of breath. 'Where did that come from?!' he gasped, getting shakily to his feet. 'Who ever heard of a dragon attacking unprovoked like that?' he said, taking a step back and watched the dragon attempt another dive. 'Incoming!' he cried, diving to the deck floor and covering his head with his hands. He and Sapora felt Khanna balk under them as Amarah turned to avoid the next swathe of dragon fire, Khanna's mobility saving them from the core of the attack yet again.

'I think you're just annoying it now!' Anahrik called to Amarah. 'Head back to the city. That many people gathered might put it off attacking!'

With no better plan, and no way to counter the dragon's swift attacks, Amarah turned Khanna around and flew back towards Niversai, aiming for the thousand twinkling fire lights. Putting her engines back on full thrust now that tight turns and manoeuvres were no longer an option, Amarah charged back to the city, believing in Khanna's outright speed and hoping she would be able to keep ahead of the dragon's breath until she was too close to the city for it to attack again.

*

'Dragons above, she's leading it back to the city!' Eryn cried, tugging at her sister's sleeve in a desperate attempt to get her to run, as they watched the forest burn just outside the city's wall. The sisters had been enjoying Khanna's speed, what they could see of it, and were shocked at the sudden arrival and attack of the dragon.

Moroda, however, was transfixed—never before had she seen a dragon so close, nor seen its raw power. In days gone by, she had sat atop hillsides on warm summer afternoons and watched them circle many leagues above, lazily gliding on thermals and allowing the current of the wind to carry them far and wide. They had always seemed such gentle creatures, unafraid of people, and decidedly uninterested in their affairs. She had heard of dragon attacks, of course, but they were mostly in self-defence or in revenge when raiders and thieves tried to steal eggs. Attacks were never unwarranted, as it appeared in this instance. But it was the suddenness, more than the attack itself, which scared her.

'Why is it attacking?' she muttered, watching, fascinated, as Khanna tried to out-manoeuvre the beast and avoid its flames. 'I've never seen this before, what's going on?'

Eryn tugged at her sister's sleeve again, succeeding in

pulling her off their fountain viewpoint. 'If we stay any longer, we're going to go up in flames! Let's get out of here!'

'Eryn, she's in danger! We should help...and she has my florins!' Moroda replied, finally turning to look at her sister as she spoke. 'We need that money!'

'Didn't I tell you both to seek shelter?'

Moroda looked up at the question, and recognised the scarred traveller from the tavern that afternoon. 'It's you!'

'The dragon will be on the city in moments, and it won't stop.' His attention locked on Khanna and the approaching dragon, its bronze-red scales glowing from the raging fires below. 'These streets will go up in smoke and flame. Get away now, while you have the chance.'

'Someone we know is on that airship, we can't leave,' Moroda pleaded, unwilling to run and hide without seeing the result of the conflict, or speaking with Amarah again. She also held a fascination with the dragon, and needed to know why it was acting so aggressively.

With another deafening roar, Khanna and the dragon were upon them; the airship raced over the heart of the city and flew over Rosecastle, hoping to show all the strength of Niversai to scare off the beast. But it was to no avail. The dragon drew breath before unleashing another wave of fire upon the castle and surrounding streets, setting countless buildings alight and scorching everything stood in its path.

*

'Guess it's not afraid of the city,' Amarah breathed, allowed a momentary respite from the chase as the dragon turned its attention to burning Niversai. 'My ship is alight, I need to get away and I need water,' she said to Anahrik and Sapora. 'Jump off if you want, or knuckle down and stay with me.' She wiped the sweat off her forehead and cheeks. 'I'm not sticking around for that thing to attack me again.'

The makeshift bandage on her shoulder was slick with sweat and smoke, and was peeling away. With blood trickling down her arm and a stitch in her side, Amarah was almost overwhelmed with pain and exhaustion. Her hands shook as she held onto the wheel again and turned, pushing her engines forward and heading away from the burning city.

*

The traveller paused for a heartbeat, watching Niversai burn under the dragon before shaking his head. 'I am going to slay the dragon. Try and keep up if you can. I suggest getting out of the city now, before everything is locked down. The dragon will follow the airship.' He stepped away from the girls and took off running down the streets.

'Eryn, the city is going to burn. This is something I have to pursue,' Moroda said, determined to see her decision through.

Her sister opened her mouth to argue, but shook her head instead. 'I can't argue... Tell me what you want me to do to help,' she said, defeated.

'Just come with me, Ryn,' Moroda said, taking her sister's hands in her own for a moment. 'Trust me.'

It did not take long for the dragon to lose interest in the

newly burned streets, and it soon caught sight of the fleeing Khanna, already some leagues outside the city walls. It turned its head, narrowing its eyes to focus on the fleeing target. With another roar, it leapt off the castle turret it had been perched on, beat its wings, and began to trail the airship.

Eryn and Moroda watched it fly into the darkness, and Moroda knew her mind was made up. Both girls clambered down from the fountain and raced through the streets to the city gates, determined to follow the dragon and see the battle through to the end.

Chapter Five

Morgen was thrown awake by what sounded like a terrible thunder. The castle's stone walls shook, weapons secured to them falling to the floor with a clatter. He was on his feet in a heartbeat, sword drawn and raised, ready to face whatever threat had stirred him so violently from his slumber. Other than the shaking walls, there was nothing to be seen.

'What's going on...' he muttered, trying to shake the sleep from his eyes and focus on the sudden threat. He stepped forward to pick up one of the shields thrown from its holder to the floor, eager to have some protection.

As he knelt down, the castle succumbed to another huge tremor. Loose stones from the ceiling and walls fell to the floor, covering Morgen in a fine layer of dust. It was then that he felt the heat.

'We're under attack! Battle stations, soldiers! Get out there and get it under control! To the armoury!'

'Escort the king to the basement and seal the Royal chambers!'

Brushing dust out of his hair, Morgen heard the orders of his captains and the other officers stationed in the castle. He could hardly believe his ears—the castle was under attack by an unknown force, and everyone was reacting. Racing footsteps pounded down the corridors as his colleagues hurried to the armoury, and Morgen rushed to pick the weapons off the floor. As he stood up, weapons held in each hand, the few members of the Imperial Guard still stationed in Rosecastle burst into the armoury, frantic.

'Ten swords!'

'Six crossbows!'

'A dozen shields!'

Morgen handed out weapons as quickly as he could, worried what threat could cause such a response. 'What's happening? Who's attacking?' he asked, handing the last pair of shields to one of his captains.

'Dragon. Been years since one attacked. Grab a shield and get outside. We've got to get the townsfolk out of harm's way, then take it down. We tried to get on horseback, but the things all bolted when the stables went up in flames,' the captain replied, inspecting his shield for half a moment. 'We must bring it down. The safety of Niversai depends on it,' he said, before turning to follow the rest of his soldiers out of the castle and into the burning streets.

Morgen's eyes widened. In all his twenty-two years, he'd never heard of a dragon attacking a city as large and well-defended as Niversai. He knew they were creatures to be well-respected and feared; he had heard of the damage they had done to harbours and farms, particularly when they had young with them, but he'd not spied a dragon within fifty leagues of Niversai since he'd joined the Imperial Guard, and wondered what had caused the attack.

With time against him, Morgen grabbed two short daggers from the remaining weapons to arm himself: one for his waist, one hidden in his greaves; and gave his sword a final check over. Taking a breath to steady his nerves, and with adrenaline coursing through him, the young soldier charged out of the armoury and into the bright, fire-lit night air.

He had barely stepped into the chaos when he stopped, suddenly afraid. He could hear the roar of the beast from somewhere above him, but with the burning embers floating in the air and the thick smoke from the flames, Morgen could not see more than a hand's length in front of him. He coughed, covering his mouth with his forearm and walking slowly out onto the bridge connecting the castle to the town. Nothing in his training had prepared him for a dragon attack.

From somewhere to his right, he heard the whinnying of frightened horses, and headed in that direction. If there was at least one horse, he had a chance of getting a higher vantage point. His heart pounded in his chest, and his breathing was thick and laboured in the smoke, but he persevered. When the air finally cleared, he saw one of the Imperial horses still tied to her post at the edge of the stables. Her reins had become tangled in splintered wood from part of the collapsed stable wall, and she had been unable to flee.

'Easy, easy,' he said, edging towards the animal. Her eyes were white and rolling, nostrils flaring as she had the scent of dragon, fire, smoke and fear bombarding her. Taking one of his daggers, Morgen cut away at the wood, untangling the reins and freeing the horse. Once loose, he held her reins tight as she tried to bolt. When she had calmed enough, he clambered on and steered her over the bridge and into the city of Niversai.

Morgen crossed the bridge slowly, trying to calm the horse with each hesitant step, when a gust of wind cleared some of the smoke from above him, and, for a brief moment, he had an unblocked view of the clear night sky. In that moment, Khanna raced overhead, barely visible with her grey hull and dark sails, partially alight, and Morgen reined in the horse, causing her to rear in terror.

'Sshh,' he muttered, eyes locked on the ship overhead. From somewhere above him, on the castle's other side, the roar of the dragon echoed, and Morgen watched the great beast descend from the turret, open its vast bronze wings, and chase after the airship.

'So it is true,' he said aloud, shaking his head, and watching the dragon unleash another wave of flames onto the streets below as it followed the sky pirate's ship. Morgen's decision was made; he had to bring down the dragon.

*

'What? I cannot leave? My trading partner is on that airship! I must leave the city to help him!' Palom roared.

'You have too many weapons, it's forbidden,' the guard replied, coming up with a poor excuse to keep him within the city limits. Two other members of the guard stood side-by-side behind him, blocking the gate at the city's west entrance. All around them, townsfolk screamed, trying to flee the flames and get away from the danger from above. Ash and ember littered the streets, kicked up by the chaos of fleeing citizens.

'I am a trader, a weapon smith, it is my job!' Palom tried, barging his way past the first guard to be held up by the pair in front of the heavy iron gates.

'I don't make the rules. I can't let you leave so heavily armed,' the second guard replied, holding out his arm across Palom's chest, preventing him taking another step. 'The city is currently trying to deal with the dragon, I'm sure your colleague will be safe. Leave it to the Imperial Guard, Ittallan,' he added, widening his stance as a show of strength.

'Apologies, we're late,' Moroda gasped, skidding to a halt at Palom's side, Eryn only a few paces behind. 'We're travelling with him,' she added. 'The other weapons are for us, you see.'

'With all three of us, we're within the rules for those weapons. There's no trouble,' Eryn said, glancing at Palom with a wide smile. She tilted her head down ever so slightly; the faintest of nods.

'But now we're here, we need to go. We really should have left this afternoon, but we were held up with the races,' Moroda said, her voice clear and direct. She hoped in the darkness of the night and with so much smoke in the air, the guards would not recognise her from that morning. Her upbringing had made her used to giving orders, and her tone made the guards hesitate.

The three soldiers shared a look, flinching when the dragon roared from somewhere overhead. 'Look, we need to sort this dragon out, with three of them it's only a few weapons each,' the third muttered to the other two. They each shrugged, knowing the dragon threat was more pressing than their traveller controls and laws on held weapons.

'Alright. Just this one time,' the first guard turned back to

Palom and the girls. He shook his head but turned the chain winch to raise the gate for the three of them.

Without waiting for anything else to be said, Moroda and Eryn rushed through the open gate archway, with Palom following, a little bemused. They hurried down the wide walkway, until the trees just framed their path and they were well out of earshot of the guards.

Palom stopped, and held onto the girl's arms. 'Wait, you…are who? What…?'

Moroda shook her head, 'I'm sorry. We needed to get out of the city, and it looked like you did too. That was the quickest way we were going to get the guards to open the gates.'

'It is okay…I did not expect it,' Palom shrugged, but he was immeasurably grateful.

'We really do know someone on that ship,' Eryn added, worried she and Moroda would be seen to be liars in front of a trader.

'Yes, we need to try and catch up, but at the speed they're going, we may be too late.' Moroda shook her head, looking out into the path which wound its way through the forest.

Palom thought for a moment. He knew time was against them, and he did not like the idea of two young girls travelling through the night in rough territory. 'For helping me leave the city, I will help us all catch up with the ship and my trading partner,' he said, dropping his satchels of weapons on the ground with a heavy thud.

'I am faster in my true form than we all are,' he said, turning to the girls. 'If you will hold the weapons, I will track the airship and we will catch them before the dragon can do any more harm.'

Moroda and Eryn glanced at each other; both were suddenly nervous, and unsure of what they were getting themselves into. 'Father had some Ittallan trading partners, didn't he? In his trades from Val Sharis.' Eryn said, trying to convince herself as much as Moroda, almost reassuring her he would be no threat to them.

'We have no time to discuss; I will chase the airship. Will you come?' Palom asked, pushing them for an answer.

'Wait, we don't even know your name yet,' Moroda asked, trying to buy some time to think about the situation.

'My name is Palom; a trader and weapon smith. On the ship is my trading partner, Anahrik.' He was eager to be off—every moment delayed was a greater chance he would lose the ship and dragon.

'I'm Eryn, and this is my sister, Moroda,' Eryn said, before Moroda could shed more doubts on the arrangement. It was Moroda's idea, after all, and Eryn knew they couldn't back out now. 'We will come with you, Palom.'

'Good. Hold the weapons tightly, please,' the Ittallan nodded, before closing his eyes and lifting his face to the stars. In a flash of burning light, his features elongated and fur sprouted through his skin and clothes as he transformed.

The sisters took a step back, Moroda dropping to the floor to pick up one of the satchels, watching with a mixture of fascination and fear.

In hardly a moment, a man no longer stood before them, but

a tiger—eighteen feet long, nose to tail, with a broad chest and shoulders. Pressing his ears back, the tiger bared his canines and roared, before lowering his head and crouching down.

'Oh dragons above, he means us to ride on his back,' Moroda whispered.

'I'm with you, Ro,' Eryn reassured, rubbing her sister's arm to offer some support. 'Like you asked.' She knelt down to pick up the other satchel, and both girls clambered on to the massive cat's back, satchels of weapons and silver held securely between them.

Once the two no longer shuffled about, Palom stood to his full height, and glanced around to gather his bearings. Ear twitching, the tiger looked back at the western gate of Niversai, hearing hooves charging down the cobblestones.

'It's Morgen! He must be after us!' Moroda cried out, recognising the rider as he hurtled down the path towards them. 'Palom, we must go now, or we'll be caught!'

Hearing her words, Palom let out a low growl as he sprang forward, racing into the woods. Trees flashed by faster than either of the girls could blink, and tears came to their eyes almost instantly.

Moroda chanced a look back, but even the fastest of horses had no chance of keeping up with a tiger at full sprint, especially an Ittallan tiger. The relief she felt as she saw Morgen disappearing into the trees was palpable, and she found herself able to breathe easily once again.

'Ro, look! Up there!'

Moroda looked skywards at her sister's words. As Palom cleared the last of the trees, farmer's fields opened up wide in front of them, the horizon running as far as the eye could see. Up ahead, in the inky blackness of the night, Moroda could make out the silhouette of Khanna, illuminated every so often as the dragon flying close behind unleashed another plume of fire. But that was not what had caught her sister's attention—it was a figure far closer to them. He was following the airship and the dragon, that much was for certain, and he was closer to them than his quarry.

As the wind rippled through the air, the man's heavy travelling cloak whipped around, away from his body. In the moonlight, the scars on his face were clear, and Moroda saw his misshapen lip as clearly as if he were stood right in front of her.

'Ryn...that's...he's no Ittallan...' Moroda breathed, her voice small amid the rush of the wind as Palom ran over open ground, trying to keep Khanna and the dragon in his sights. 'He...'

The scarred traveller rose with the wind, his arms and legs limp under him as he raised his creamy-brown feathered wings from underneath the cloak. A strong, cold wind picked up around him, ruffling his hair and sending his cloak in all directions.

'That's a...he's an Arillian...'

With one powerful beat of his wings, the traveller flew after the airship and the dragon, intent on slaying it.

Chapter Six

'There's too much fire!' Anahrik screamed, his voice almost lost in the rushing wind. Khanna was descending slowly, and trees rose all around them as they cleared the farmlands and open fields surrounding Niversai and approached the nearby Burian Forest.

'Do what you can to keep it back, I'm gonna put her down somewhere or Khanna will be in shreds,' Amarah cried back, desperately trying to control her shaking airship. She'd lost half a sail from the back while another was currently alight; Khanna began to drop violently, the wooden hull creaking.

Sapora hunched low, arms protecting his face from the flames licking the deck, and shuffled over to Anahrik. 'I'd prepare yourself for a fight, Ittallan.'

Anahrik glared at him. 'Palom does most of the fighting, and I don't have any weapons.'

'If I can get one, clean strike, that may bring it down,' Sapora hissed, glaring at the dragon as it followed them through the darkness, and Anahrik narrowed his eyes at him. 'Of course it might be immune,' Sapora added.

'Brace yourselves!' Amarah called, as the airship lost its remaining lift and thundered to the ground, crashing into a large clearing, the surrounding trees bending in the shockwave. The lower leaves caught alight as sparks were sent forth from the hull as it splintered on impact.

All three passengers covered their heads and dropped to their knees, and Khanna let out a mighty groan as wood splintered off the bottom of the hull. Amarah cringed at the noise, but focussed on the dragon that followed them.

'You don't have any weapons at all?' Amarah shouted at Anahrik, who was still crouched and edging across to the side of the ship, waving away smoke from his face.

'I didn't pack them for our race, no,' he growled back, looking up at the night sky for signs of the dragon. Thick, dark smoke rose slowly from the airship's side and the surrounding foliage as they burned. The nettles which grew high and proud between the dew-covered trees were ignited from the explosion; they ringed the clearing and lit everything beneath the trees. The contrast made the night seem even darker, and none of them could see much over the tree line.

Amarah clambered overboard, hurrying down the steps carved into the ship's side. Sapora followed Khanna's captain off the ship, leaping over the side and landing heavily on the soft earth.

'The moss is still damp,' Amarah stated, glancing at her hand. 'Good thing it's not dry, or we'd all be up in damned smoke.'

'Where is the dragon?' Sapora asked, looking up. 'It was right behind us.'

A sudden flash of lightning lit up the sky, leaving it bright as day for a few long seconds. It was accompanied by a gust of icy wind as the dragon came soaring into view, a large tear in one of its wings.

'An Arillian?' Sapora gasped, crouching down, and backing away from the clearing into the shelter of Khanna. Anahrik, who had not yet disembarked, dropped to one knee, only his head poking over the side of the ship to watch.

They saw the dragon hurtle to the ground, a cloaked, scarred man holding onto its neck. Ignoring its roars, he managed to keep hold as they crashed into the clearing. Before the dragon could respond, the man raised his right hand to shoot another gust of freezing wind into the beast's other wing. As the moving air caught the thin, leathery skin, it tore through the membrane as easily as a dagger through flesh.

Roaring in pain, the dragon lashed out with its tail and thrashed its body, retaliating violently to the attack. As it brought its spiked tail round, the Arillian leapt into the air and opened his own wings. Avoiding the attack, he sent out another blast of freezing, razor sharp air, aiming for the dragon's eyes and nose.

'Should we help?' Anahrik called down to Sapora and Amarah. But both were transfixed, watching the dragon and the Arillian fight each other from the shelter of the airship.

The dragon was easily twenty-five feet long, not including its tail, which swung furiously at the Arillian. Its bronzed scales were blackened slightly from the flame and smoke it breathed, the spines along its back were brown, and darker close to the tail. For a creature so huge, it moved quickly; lunging and swiping with its tail, never still for a moment. With golden eyes tinged red, it watched the Arillian as he continued to avoid its lunges.

'Didn't think it'd be as much of a threat on the ground now,'

Anahrik said, though his words were again unacknowledged. He watched with the others and saw the dragon's long, serpentine neck and powerful spiked tail, and swallowed hard, realising it was just as much of a force to be reckoned with. The creature's spines along the length of its back and tail were vicious, the largest of them three feet long. And of course, it could still breathe fire.

All three spectators ducked periodically to avoid wayward flames, branches blown around in the wind, and other debris sent flying from the fight.

Despite the incredible weaponry and natural scale armour of the dragon, the Arillian did not seem at all fazed. He was fast enough to avoid teeth and claws, and had the ability to fly out of range of both flame and tail. Keeping up with his avoidance strategy, it did not take long before the fight began to tip in the Arillian's favour; a combination of torn wings and light wounds on the dragon's slightly softer underbelly began to weaken the beast. Its attacks soon came slower, without the fury from the start of the fight.

The dragon lunged suddenly, faster and farther than before, causing the Arillian to dive out of the way, its teeth snapping shut just above his back.

Cornered and unable to fly out of range, the Arillian flattened himself to the ground. Rolling onto his back, with the throat of the dragon just above him, he reached forward with both arms, gripped the hot scales, and sent forth all the strength he could muster.

The ice which formed on the neck of the dragon shone a

brilliant white-blue, freezing its chest and jaws. It grew slowly, encasing the hot scales and cooling them instantly, steam billowing from the contact.

On the other side of the clearing, Palom skidded to a halt, having sprinted the last few minutes, terrified Anahrik would not have survived the crash. He, Moroda and Eryn had watched the flaming ship's descent into the trees, and heard when it finally touched the ground. Moroda and Eryn clambered off the tiger, weapons still held safely between them, Palom letting out another roar to announce his arrival.

'Palom!' Anahrik cried, standing up to better see across the clearing.

The dragon was on its side unable to move, its entire chest encased in ice. 'It's over, now,' the Arillian sighed, standing beside the creature and shaking his head. The dragon attempted to lift its tail to attack, but did not have the strength to do so. The man raised his right hand and extended his fingers, summoning up another wave of ice and wind. A blade formed in his hand, made of solid ice and tapered to a sharp point. With one, swift strike, he sliced the dragon's throat, silencing the roars.

Trying to subdue his terrified horse, Morgen arrived behind Palom and the girls. He held on tightly as she reared up, but he was exhausted from the hard ride chasing the dragon; all strength in his fingers had left him, and he was unceremoniously thrown to the ground in her final act of fear and defiance.

Palom, now in human form, grabbed two swords from his satchel and stalked into the clearing, tense and ready to react.

'Palom, I didn't realise you'd followed us all the way out here,' Anahrik called, leaping over the side of the airship. Though he briefly glanced at the Arillian and the dead dragon, the young silversmith crossed the clearing confidently, making his way to Palom.

'You were too busy with that,' Palom said, looking at the dragon, now lying still after the final blow.

It was a sombre moment for Moroda; her skin was still flushed from the chill of the wind in the race to the forest, her heart still pounding from the adrenaline and sudden fear from the dragon attack.

Now that she looked at the dead beast, she felt nothing but sadness and pity for it. Never before had she seen a dragon act that way, even to egg thieves. Yes, they'd chase for a short while, then return to their lair. This one, though…this one had pursued them so doggedly, she had wondered whether they would ever catch up with the airship.

'I guess I should thank you,' Amarah said to the Arillian, stepping over to him with folded arms. Her skin was damp with sweat, blood and ash, but she ignored it all. 'If you hadn't come along, my ship might well be gone. I should be able to repair her after that heavy landing.' Khanna, still smoked in the night, but was no longer aflame; the Arillian's icy winds had seen to putting out most of the fires surrounding the crash site. Amarah would need to fix the damaged sails at the very least—until then, Khanna would not be winning any races.

Moroda approached the downed dragon, mesmerised. She

ran her hand over the dragon's rough scales, hard as stone, and over the ice still formed on its chest and front legs. 'Why did you act that way?' What did Niversai ever do to you, dragon?'

'You worry too much, girl,' the Arillian said, appearing next to her, not the least bit out of breath despite the intense battle. He still held his icy blade and was dusting off his long cloak with his free hand. 'Just stay away from them and you'll do fine.' He gripped his weapon tightly and plunged it deep into the dragon's chest.

Moroda jumped back, hands to her mouth, and watched him sink his arm in, all the way up to his elbow. When he drew his arm back, his fist was clenched around a small, brightly glowing rock.

'Is that its heart?' Sapora asked, slinking forward without making a sound.

'In a way,' he said, holding the stone close to his face and examining it closely. He ran his other hand over the edges, and Moroda could see it was not completely smooth. 'It is their strength and magic. The source of their fire, their power.'

'Dragon stones,' Amarah said, also watching the Arillian. 'I've seen ones just like them in Berel. Much, much bigger, though.'

'The power of Berel is from dragons?' Sapora asked.

'Sort of,' Amarah shrugged. 'Nothing like what is in the city of Berel still lives.' She turned her focus to the Arillian, and asked the question on everyone's minds. 'Who are you?'

Looking up, the Arillian pocketed the stone inside his cloak and brought his hat out. He spent a long moment picking at a fraying thread on the brim, then placed it on his head. 'My name is Kohl. I'm a dragon hunter. I was in Niversai during the attack and thought

I might help...The Imperial Guard didn't seem able.'

'Of course we weren't able! There are so few of us!' Morgen declared, also stepping forward. 'Your Arillian friend took most of our strength this morning, and there were hardly any soldiers left with the airship races going on! The priority was the safety of the people.'

'Hah, since when were you here, Morgen?' Amarah said, her eyes narrowing at the officer.

'Since the end of the fight,' Morgen said, raising his hands in defence but leaving his sword sheathed. 'I'm outside Niversai, I've no authority here. Just watching a bizarre occurrence is all. We're all permitted to do that.'

Palom and Anahrik approached the group. 'I've heard of the power of a dragon's stone,' Palom said, watching Kohl and Amarah carefully. 'You say there are more of these in Berel?'

'But much bigger,' Amarah replied. 'At least as tall as a man.'

As they discussed the fight, the dragons and their stones, the darkening clouds above finally let loose their bounty and the temperature dropped with it.

'We should be getting back, Ro,' Eryn whispered, pulling her sister off to one side.

'It'll take all night to get back to Niversai,' Moroda said, pulling her scarf tighter around herself. 'We're near that little town, Burian, aren't we? Perhaps we should stop off at one of their inns, instead?'

'Sounds like a good idea.' Morgen said. He stepped up to

the Arillian. 'I'd like to offer to pay for you, Kohl. On behalf of the Imperial Guard of Corhaven, and the city of Niversai, you have my thanks for ridding us of the threat. We are eternally grateful.'

'I am tired, and will need time to recover,' Kohl responded. 'I would like to see these other stones in Berel, it is not a place I have been before.'

Anahrik looked at Palom, having collected their satchels of weapons from the edge of the clearing. 'This is the power of the dragon stones you were looking for, Palom? The old legends? Sounds like something like 'em could be in this Berel city.'

'It sounds like it, yes. And whatever trade left in Niversai will be gone after the dragon's attack,' Palom said, folding his arms. 'Moving on sounds like a good idea. To Berel?' he nodded to Anahrik.

'If dragons are on the turn here, I'm happy to get going,' Anahrik said, brushing away soot from his clothes. 'Trade was crap in Niversai, anyway.'

'I'm done with Corhaven, the stupid country.' Amarah huffed, still watching Morgen. 'Arrested by you Imperials, having my ship locked up. No way of getting any coin back here. Damn it. If you're willing to pay, I'll take you to Berel. Palom, I'll ferry you across for my scythe. Passage out the country is worth more than three florins, isn't it?'

'How are you going to do that? The ship is half burned,' Sapora sneered.

'What do you know about flight, snake? She's recoverable. I'll sort her out, right now.' She said, before returning her attention to the Ittallan traders. 'Palom. My scythe.'

Anahrik looked at his colleague, hesitant to hand over the weapon without payment, but it seemed the tables had turned and they now owed her. The traders shared a glance, and they nodded.

'Done,' Palom said, though he looked away as Anahrik fished out her weapon.

Morgen shivered in the falling rain and brushed water from his hair. 'I will need to report to the town guard at Burian. They'll have seen the dragon's approach, and I can inform them of the attack in Niversai. They might need to prepare if this dragon attack isn't a one-off. Shall we get out of the rain? A hot meal will do us all good, I'm sure.' He checked his equipment, and once satisfied, made for the edge of the clearing and the forest path just beyond the trees.

'I'll move out just after dawn,' Amarah said, clambering back up onto her ship. 'If you're here, I'll grant you passage through Corhaven and into Ranski, all the way to Berel.'

'You're not resting tonight? What about… bandits or… forest creatures?' Moroda asked.

'I can defend myself, easily enough, little girl,' Amarah cackled, twirling her scythe, silver glinting in the darkness. 'Nighty night.'

Moroda shook her head, and ran to catch up with Eryn and the others. They hurried to get out of the rain and have something hot to eat. Talk focussed on the dragon, primarily, or on Niversai and the races. Moroda realised the dragon's attack held much greater relevance than she had initially thought. Of course, the timing was incredible—Niversai was full almost to capacity with the airship races, and she couldn't bear to think of how many people burned tonight. Coupled with the sudden appearance of the King's foreign visitor and the removal of a large portion of the Imperial Guard that morning, the dragon attack became much more significant. No-one could quite say why, or how, but it felt to Moroda like a signal. Her mind kept drifting back to the crystal Kohl retrieved from the chest of the beast, how it glowed softly blue, reflecting the dying flames.

The party were met at the gates of Burian, which were tall and carved of wood, rather than stone and iron as in Niversai, but well-manned and lit by a dozen burning torches. Morgen stepped forward to speak for the group, and a few words passed between the guards before the heavy gate was lifted by a steel crank and chains.

As the wooden gate rose, Moroda cast her eyes on the town of Burian. She and Eryn had been here once or twice before, when they were little more than babes in arms, but she had no recollection of the place or the people who lived in the small town. Despite the late hour, with the torches lighting the streets and hung off the sides of buildings, she felt the place was warm and inviting.

'Were you caught in the dragon's fire?' one of the guards asked Morgen, as he stood by the gate with a flaming torch held high for the group.

'No, luckily. Kohl was the one to bring it down,' Morgen replied, nodding to the scarred man, once again covered by his long, thick travelling cloak.

Kohl touched the brim of his hat to the guard in acknowledgement, but said nothing about the battle, instead returning his gaze to the ground.

'We were in a state of panic; thought the thing would come down on us. We've had a good harvest, but the boys are still bringing it in. If that dragon had attacked, we'd not likely survive the winter,' the guard said, his round face red and puffy in his too-small helmet. 'Any friend of Burian is welcome here, especially one of the Niversai guards. Stay at the lodge on the city's east side, and none of your party will go without. I'll make sure of that.'

Clapping one arm to their chests, Morgen and the guard parted, and Morgen rejoined the others. 'Looks like we're guests of honour at the Fourth Moon for bringing down the dragon.' He headed down the street and led them through the town.

'Fourth Moon? I thought there were only three?' Moroda muttered, glancing up. Palom gave her a look, but said nothing as the party followed Morgen. Moroda lowered her gaze and followed, keeping close to her sister. 'Do you think we're doing the right thing?'

'We're doing it. There isn't any point to worry now, I suppose. We can return to Niversai in the morning and see what damage there is,' Eryn said, stifling a yawn. 'You're the one who wanted to leave, I'm trying to keep us safe.'

'I didn't mean that.' Moroda shook her head 'Of course staying here tonight is the best thing to do. I meant...tomorrow...not going back to Niversai. Going to Berel with everyone.'

'Ro you cannot be serious! We don't know these people. That airship pilot is a murderer, you heard her yourself!'

Moroda sighed, doubting herself and her dreams. 'What if

they're right? What if this is…the start of something. Don't you want to know more? Else we'll end up stuck in Niversai for the rest of our lives…or until the next dragon or Arillian comes to burn us down.'

'Ro…'

'Maybe I'm tired. We'll have something to eat, and we'll go to sleep. We can work out what we're going to do in the morning.'

The creak of a metal hinge in the wind caused Moroda to glance up, a smile forming on her lips as she saw a dark green, weathered plaque with a pale grey moon depicted on it. Food and warmth. The top of the plaque was rusty, but the building it attached to was tall and made of stone and mortar, with a heavily thatched roof. As Morgen opened the low wooden door, a wave of warmth washed over her, and she heard the crackle of a fire over the raucous laughter from the patrons within.

'Ah, finally. Good food,' Palom roared, following Morgen inside, though he had to duck to fit through the narrow entranceway. Grateful for the warmth, Moroda and her sister followed, with Anahrik close behind and Kohl bringing up the rear.

Before entering the inn, Kohl paused, looking back into the quiet town, listening to the rain patter gently on the cobblestones. One or two of the townsfolk could be seen scurrying home, covering their heads with shawls or other garments. It was cold and quiet, save the noise of the rain. Stars glistened brightly where they could be seen between the heavy clouds, and Kohl caught just a glimpse of one of the three moons, before it vanished behind a cloud again. 'Fourth Moon indeed….'

His hand went to his pocket, where he grasped the cool stone he had claimed from the young dragon, his teeth gritting together. His free hand scratched at the old scar which tore his lip. Inhaling deeply, he turned and pushed open the inn door to follow the others.

Chapter Seven

Once Moroda was seated with the others at a large, circular table nestled in the warmth of the inn, she felt better. Though it wasn't a high class inn, the sort she had grown used to as a child, it was warm and comfortable, and the smell of food and fire instantly put her at ease. She found the fear and worry which had plagued her that morning through to the dragon attack had vanished, and she was eager to learn more about the dragon and the people with whom she and Eryn had found themselves.

Morgen had spoken with the innkeeper on their arrival, presenting him with the parchment from the town guard who had let them through the gate earlier, and secured food and lodgings for the entire group. It seemed the soldiers of this village were as good as their word, and Moroda relaxed in the knowledge they would be safe tonight.

Despite the circumstances under which Moroda had met Morgen, the man was more than likeable now he was out of his jurisdiction. He had expressed his remorse for her arrest and treatment that morning, and though Eryn was still suspicious of his apology, Moroda believed it to be genuine, and bore him no ill will. He was also a valuable source of information, having been stationed in Niversai while Aciel had stayed, and present when the orders from the king were received about many of the Imperial Guard leaving the town with the Arillian.

'What exactly does he want with them?' Anahrik asked, slurping from a bowl of steaming vegetable broth, his bright blue eyes focussed on Morgen. 'If he's putting an army together, we need to know for sure, and we'll need to be ready!'

'I couldn't say what he wanted them for. Our orders were vague,' Morgen sighed, poking at his own bowl with his spoon, cheek resting on his other hand. 'It was the most bizarre thing. Everyone was in full preparation for the start of the races, guards doubled at the city gates…But there was a weird atmosphere. Everyone seemed on edge, even the other soldiers at my level. Couldn't get a word out of any of the captains.' He played with his food as he paused.

'Then, one of the captains gathered us all up…This was yesterday morning, when we were just about to open the races for that day. We thought something had happened.' He paused and took another sip from his bowl. 'He said orders from the king had arrived. That's news in itself—the king leaves orders to the captains, he never commands us officers directly. But he said the king had made a direct order and we had to keep to it as we're under oath. There was a very important visitor coming. We thought maybe a Goldstone family, or a rich trader from Val Sharis, maybe even royalty. But then it turned out it was just some Arillian…except he had a hundred others with him.'

'One hundred Arillians? I did not see Arillians in Niversai,' Palom said, having drained his first bowl and already starting on his second. 'I would have known.'

'Yes, well, neither did we. We didn't even realise they were there,' Morgen admitted, finally finishing his bowl and reaching for a hunk of warm bread to mop up the remnants. 'They apparently were in some of the airships above the city. Never landed or anything, just floated above the castle, waiting for this man—Aciel, his name was—for his business to be finished.'

Palom and Anahrik glanced at each other, but did not interrupt.

'See, we're not allowed to question anything. Orders are orders. You get punished otherwise. But one of the others my level tried to ask the captain who he was and what one of those damned Arillians was doing here—no offence,' he hastily added, glancing to Kohl, who shook his head and gestured for him to continue.

'He got a real beating, so we just decided we didn't need to know. He stayed in Rosecastle with a couple of his men, kept real quiet. The next morning, Aciel went out to give that speech…and after Moroda's outburst, he carried on talking to the townsfolk and then took two hundred Imperials off in his ships.'

'Rubbish. I don't believe any Arillians were there at all,' Anahrik scoffed, folding his arms and looking away from the officer back to Palom. 'Everyone would have known! You know what they're like! All storms and devastation. There was hardly a breeze in Niversai.'

'We're not all like that,' Kohl said, his low voice quiet among the laughter and talking of the tavern around them. 'In the same way you Ittallan are not all savage beasts, or the Varkain soulless killers, hunting down people wherever they go.'

There was an uncomfortable silence at the table following his words, but Moroda was confused. 'I've never met an Arillian other than you, Kohl. What storms?'

Morgen glanced warily at Kohl, but said nothing, focussing on getting the last morsels from his bowl with his remaining piece of bread. The others behaved similarly, taking great interest in their empty bowls and mugs of drink.

'Anahrik means the war,' Kohl said at length, taking his hat off with a sigh and setting it on the table. 'I'd be interested to hear what sort of history you learned as children, Eryn, Moroda,' he chuckled, his scars in full view now he had removed his hat. 'I did not fight in it; we're not quite as long lived as that. But many of my forefathers did. The scars left on Linaria are worse than these of mine.' He smiled despite his words. 'We have three moons now. The scholars at the university in Berel would have you believe we caused one of Rhea's eyes to close to us, that our behaviour as a race caused all Linaria to lose favour with this supposed Goddess who created us. Parts of Linaria were left shattered and the fourth moon disappeared. This tavern is ironically named, but I suppose Arillians aren't seen much in this part of the world. I take no offence from it.'

Moroda hated to sound stupid, and she felt increasingly so since her life had changed so dramatically and she no longer socialised with her childhood friends. Her father had been incredibly successful trading in Val Sharis, a far off place somewhere across the ocean. He traded mostly with the Ittallan, in teas and coffees. His business trips kept him away from Niversai for months at a time, leaving his daughters to grow up independent, without a care in the world. Money was never a consideration for them, though they knew they were fortunate in that respect, and their family friends were much the same.

Their father had been returning from one such trip the previous winter and had been somewhere out to sea when his ship crashed. It had been incredibly sudden, for it was a journey he had made countless times before, and his navigators and captains were always experienced. Lives and bounty were both lost in the accident, yet word had spread through Niversai that the trading vessels had been beset upon by pirates who held no consideration for life. Moroda and Eryn were never told more than that, just that he would not be returning and his trade for that season had been lost.

In the weeks following his death, it became apparent their father owed a great deal of money to a great many people; his reputation as a Goldstone had shielded them from it. But that shield had disappeared along with his death. Too naïve to know otherwise, Moroda paid half a dozen people when they visited their home, demanding various sums of money. It did not take long before they ran out of coins to give away, and they began to trade their jewellery and trinkets.

The demands finally dwindled when the trinkets ran out, and she and Eryn could take stock of where they were. Moroda had been in the depths of grief, bombarded by important-looking people with famous family names, demanding the one thing from her which seemed to never run out: money. When it finally did, sometime near the beginning of summer, the weight of his loss finally hit her, and she struggled to come to terms with it.

Eryn had been invaluable, rationalising their loss and coming up with a plan to open up a stall to make money from their remaining valuables to try and keep some business going. Moroda felt abandoned and betrayed, terrified that whatever dreams she had would never come to fruition now she was considered little more than a peasant. Everything she had known, all her securities, had been taken, and she was left with the realisation of how little she knew and how incapable she felt. Joining a conversation with these common people highlighted that, as she struggled to think of what she had learned of the war as a child.

'I don't remember going into the histories in any depth,' she mumbled, thinking back to her schooling. 'Just that it happened a few hundred years ago. The Imperial Guard was formed then to fight back, and it's still around now...' She skipped over the violence, who fought whom, and over what. In truth, she didn't know much, and what she had been taught was biased, but she did not wish to draw attention to that fact, and left it there.

Kohl clearly felt at ease talking about the history of Linaria and his Arillian race, but Moroda was relieved when he chose to step away from the conversation.

'The past has passed,' Kohl said, closing his eyes. 'Grudges are a poison better ignored and forgotten.'

'How did you know the dragon was going to attack?' Eryn asked, holding her mug of rosemary tea with both hands and changing the subject back to the question lingering on everyone's minds. 'Back in Niversai, you warned us about it hours before it arrived.'

All eyes returned to Kohl with renewed intensity.

'There aren't many dragons in Corhaven. Val Sharis has more,' Palom added, his eyes still locked on the Arillian. 'They're common at my home. They live close to the Ittallan, but I've not once heard of an attack like that. You sure that woman didn't steal from it? An egg? Some treasure?'

Kohl shook his head, 'No. That was a young one. A drake. Too young to have eggs of its own, and I doubt it would have a territory, much less a hoard. No phoenixes either, did you realise?'

'Why then? Couldn't you have reported it to the guard so we would have been better prepared?' Morgen asked. 'Our defences were so small, we didn't stand a chance! Notice of a few hours would have helped ready weapons, clear townspeople, secured the stables!'

'I wouldn't have had that stupid race and gotten singed!' Anahrik added, pounding his fist on the table.

'I needed to bring the dragon down, not any of your Imperials or townspeople. They weren't my concern,' Kohl said, taking a sip of water from his mug. 'I think we'll find more answers about the dragons in Berel.'

'I want to see their dragon stones,' Palom nodded, his eyes dancing with enthusiasm. 'I've heard of weapons used through the ages, forged with dragon stone. The strongest. The most value. They won the war.'

Moroda cringed as talk again turned to the history of Linaria; it didn't affect her directly, but she felt uncomfortable given

Kohl's presence. As far as she could see, the only reason they were all still alive was because he had been able to slay the dragon. To then belittle his race and discuss the bad things they had done centuries before seemed in poor taste.

What also surprised her was the fact no-one seemed at all concerned about travelling across the country in the sky pirate's airship. She would have been far more comfortable in a regular chartered airship, though she didn't think the little village they were staying in had a dock. The nearest city was Niversai, and she couldn't recall seeing another town anywhere near Burian this side of the mountains. It seemed she and Eryn would have no choice but to accompany the group on Khanna, and hope they didn't get into trouble.

Less than a year ago, she and Eryn had had enough money to travel to the farthest corners of Linaria in the height of luxury. Now, she had barely a penny to her name and was effectively hitch-hiking across countries in the company of a thief. It had not taken long for her to realise she could no longer think like a Goldstone— that title of nobility had been taken the night her father died. To continue to believe you were something you were not was the quickest way to get into trouble, as she had found when friends she had grown up with suddenly turned their backs on her and Eryn. Had a title and money meant so much to so many people? That was all your worth was judged on? She had been sickened by the realisation, and Amarah's taunts in the cell that morning reinforced the fact that she was no longer worth very much. Perhaps it was fitting, then, that she and Eryn travelled with thieves and killers.

The chatter descended into several conversations, and Moroda felt herself losing track. The heat of the tavern and a full belly made her sleepy, and her eyelids drooped.

'What happened to the Varkain?' Anahrik asked, when a break in the conversation appeared.

'I saw him head into the forest,' Palom replied, his arms still folded as he leant back in his chair. 'He's not the type to stay at an inn. Not in Corhaven.'

'He disgusts me,' Eryn shuddered. 'He was in the dungeon with Ro! I would have left him there but she insisted on releasing him.'

'There are few who would do that for a Varkain,' Palom noted.

Moroda felt a flush on her face immediately. 'Well...I felt bad. I don't know what he'd done...he may have been wrongly accused...And...I couldn't just leave him there.'

'Ro, honestly, I don't know what's wrong with you sometimes,' Eryn shook her head. 'They're awful creatures. Frightening killers. They terrorise people for fun! If it was the other way around, he would have left you to rot, or worse.'

'Maybe. But I did what I thought was best,' Moroda said, suddenly feeling awful. Yes, it had been brave and she hadn't wanted to leave him behind, but she was more afraid of his wrath if she left and he had later escaped. Selfishness more than selflessness. She let the others talk over her, and decided not to mention the topic again.

'That was brave what you did before, though,' Morgen said.

'In front of the whole city, with the Arillian. I wouldn't have thought a Goldstone would speak out like that against a king's visitor!'

At the mention of her earlier actions, Moroda glanced up. She felt a sudden rage at the thought of Aciel, and shook her head. 'I can't remember his words or even the sound of his voice. Everyone seemed hooked on what he was saying. It was belittling and cruel and…and I hated the fact no-one was doing anything, just listening like obedient dogs.'

'Can't blame the Arillian for trying to get into everyone's good books,' Anahrik shrugged. 'Don't see why he had to make such a show of it. Could've just taken the soldiers and left and no-one would have known.'

'But that's just it—he wanted everyone to know,' Moroda said. 'He needed all of Niversai, the capital of Corhaven, to see him and the influence he had over our ruler. Don't you see? That's why I couldn't stand it. Talking down to us like that.'

Anahrik laughed, 'Don't be silly. He's just some crackpot Arillian. It won't be long before those soldiers see that and head back to Niversai. Especially after the dragon attack.'

'I'm not so sure,' Morgen disagreed. 'There wasn't any mention of when they'd come back.'

'So your captains and our King just let this Arillian walk off with over half his guard?' Moroda was shocked.

'No, no, there are more soldiers in Niversai. Of course there are. The ones he took were just the…Well, I guess the best trained.'

'Amarah would find that hilarious. The whole city burned,

and protected by few young soldiers who've never fought. Niversai is easy pickings. Shame she's too busy fixing her ship. Some great capital.' Palom snorted, unimpressed.

The words of her companions made it clear to Moroda that the place that had been her home all her life had quickly become dangerous, even without the dragon still around. The realisation dawned on her suddenly, and she wanted to get away from the others to think things through.

'Ryn, I'm going to bed now. Will you come?' Moroda said, getting up and rubbing her eyes. She still felt exhausted from everything that had happened, and half-hoped that when she woke, she would be back home, in her own bed with the events of the past day having been a nightmarish fantasy.

'Yes,' Eryn agreed. 'Thank you again, Morgen, Kohl…well, everyone.' She stood up beside her sister. 'See you in the morning.' Their companions nodded to them as they made their way to the back of the inn, picking through the gathered townsfolk, already thinning as the night wore on, and up the wooden staircase at the back of the tavern.

Thankfully the air was cooler and clearer as they climbed to the second floor. Morgen had arranged for the sisters to share a room at the end of the hallway, and Moroda was sure to lock the door behind them.

'Worried?' Eryn asked, as Moroda placed the key on the small cabinet next to the door. The room was small, but clean, with a large window opposite the door, a bed to the right, and a cabinet to the left. Above the cabinet, a large map was secured to the wall, faded with time, but still legible.

'A little. We're not at home after all. Better to be cautious and careful.' Moroda shrugged out of her thin, outer cloak and took her scarf off. 'I really think something has started here,' she said, as Eryn climbed into the bed, and drew the sheets about her to keep warm.

'Not this again,' Eryn yawned.

Moroda walked over to the window of the small room and opened it, allowing the night breeze to circulate. She could hear the rain still falling outside and took a moment just to listen to it. 'But it's true, don't you think? So much has happened. This Arillian, Aciel, taking so many soldiers, the dragon's attack…it's all so unusual. Kohl knows more, I'm sure of it.'

She got into the other side of the bed and lay flat on her back, staring up at the timber roof and playing with the ends of her hair as she spoke. 'I think we should go to Berel and learn what we can. You know I've always wanted to go there. The Samolen who live there, the university, the histories, the magic…Why not now?'

'What about home?'

'Home is probably gone, and even if it hasn't burned to the ground, Niversai is dangerous right now. You heard Palom?'

Eryn took a little more convincing. Moroda felt more comfortable with their companions than her sister, and Eryn's reluctance wasn't surprising, given she had always been the more sensible of the two.

'I want you to agree, to promise, that we get the first ship back to Niversai if anything goes wrong. Promise me?'

'Of course!' Moroda nodded. 'We'll return by ship or by train, if it comes to it. The train journey would be longer, but it'll be less expensive, better if we're keeping an eye on what coin we have left.'

Eryn remained quiet. Moroda took the opportunity to set out a plan. 'I know the train doesn't run too far into Ranski, but if we're only in Berel...' She got out of bed and walked over to the wall map, pointing to a city marked on the southern half of the western continent. 'All we'd need to do is get a ship up to the town of Zona.' Her finger moved further north to a small circle depicting the most northern town in Ranski, right by the Corhaven-Ranski border. 'I'm sure that's the end of the southern line; the train runs back into Corhaven from there. A couple of stops, lone inns, mines, straight back to Niversai.' Her finger followed the marked tracks north to the Corhaven capital, where she tapped it a few times.

'If only the train ran from here to Niversai,' Eryn sighed.

'Perhaps if it did, we wouldn't be going to Berel,' Moroda said, taking a step back to take in the map's details. Though the distance did not seem great on paper, she knew there were many days' travel between towns, and especially between countries.

Moroda felt better now she had a plan for the next few days; she now knew where she was going and where she had to get to, and was convinced Eryn would come around to her plan. Perhaps once they reached Berel, her sister would even enjoy the trip. That's all it was, a trip into Berel. She would decide then what would happen after.

'Can we sleep now?' Eryn asked, snuggling into the thick

linen.

'Yes, Ryn,' Moroda grinned, shaking her head and climbing back into bed. 'A lovely inn, good food, and nice, warm bedding. I don't think the airship will have such facilities, so we'd better enjoy this while we can.'

'Especially if we're up before dawn.'

'Goodnight, Ryn,' Moroda pulled the sheets over her as she curled up and got comfortable.

'Night, Ro,' Eryn snored, exhaustion taking over as they both entered a world of dreams.

Chapter Eight

Moroda was awake before dawn, unfamiliar birdsong breaking through her dreams and rousing her far earlier than normal. It took a few moments to realise where she was and remember events from the day before. It came back to her piece by piece: Aciel lecturing the townsfolk of Niversai; her arrest; the fear of the sky pirate and the Varkain in the cell; Eryn rescuing her; the dragon attack; the flames; the Ittallan; the Arillian; and the Fourth Moon Inn in the small town, Burian. It had all been real.

Through the open window, Moroda could not yet see the light of dawn, but knew it was not far off with the bird's commotion outside. She got out of bed and went to the basin to rinse her face and hair. She still couldn't quite believe where she was and the journey she was about to embark on. She wondered now whether they were making the right decision, despite having been certain the night before.

Eryn began to stir. 'Do we have to be up yet?' She yawned, both eyes still shut tightly.

Moroda smiled, 'Almost. I'm going into the town to get some supplies before we go.' She pulled on her boots and fastened the buckles.

'Mmm,' Eryn replied.

'Don't fall back asleep. Dawn is not far off. I'll meet you

back downstairs as soon as I can.' Moroda secured her small satchel over her shoulder and held it tight against her hip.

Unlocking the door, she exited the room. Torches burned low in brackets along the walls, providing a little light, and Moroda reached the end of the corridor easily enough. Carefully, she entered the familiar tavern room, seemingly larger now that it was empty of the night's patrons.

A serving girl was working her way around each table, wiping away spills with a thick rag and laying down fresh tablecloths. The innkeeper himself stood behind the bar, thumbing through some parchment with a deep frown.

Moroda spied Kohl sitting at one of the tables beside the bar, a flask in his hand as he read notices nailed to the wall opposite. He still wore his hat and thick travelling coat, which gathered at his feet.

'Good morning, Kohl,' she greeted, following his gaze to the notices. Many were old and faded, mostly requests for odd jobs. Moroda noticed a recent addition, a request to drive out or kill a dragon local to the area, and wondered whether it was the same one from last night or another.

'Moroda,' Kohl replied, without taking his eyes from the wall, engrossed in the notices.

'Are you the only one up?' she asked. She thought of Sapora hiding, and shuddered.

'Palom is awake, as is Morgen. I have not seen your sister or Anahrik.'

'Good, I have a little time, then. I'm going into the town

quickly to sort out something before the journey. Will you be leaving once everyone is here?'

'I believe so. I have flown into the forest already. Amarah is almost ready to travel.'

'I'll hurry back.' She nodded to the Arillian before turning to head out of the inn. She dreamt wistfully of having her own wings as she made her way into the town, its vendors already awake and getting ready for the day.

Moroda wanted some new, hardy travelling clothes for herself and Eryn. Trade started early during the tourist season, and many Linarians stayed in the cheaper towns and villages outside Niversai to save on coin. She was grateful to be in a small town as the prices would be less than a third than in Niversai.

By the time she returned to the Fourth Moon, Moroda's high spirits had dwindled. Dawn had arrived; a thin line of orange-red lighting the horizon as inky black sky gave way to deep navy blue. The sky was clearer here than above Niversai; fewer buildings and less smoke allowed the rich colours of the dawn to be seen more clearly. She had bought two thick travelling cloaks, influenced slightly by Kohl, two pairs of soft, fur-lined gloves and matching boots, and a small knife. Moroda counted her remaining money while she waited outside the inn—four pennies and a handful of shingles. It could buy a small sack of potatoes, or maybe a bushel of apples. Hardly anything.

She felt sick. She was still unsure whether or not Amarah would return her three florins, and even if she did, it was hardly anything. If the journey lasted more than a day or two, she and her sister would surely starve, or be forced to return home. They would be lucky to get one train ticket back, let alone two. And if they had to walk, they'd surely go hungry before they made it back. She considered the idea of just making their way home instead, to just give up on this silly dragon-chasing adventure and accept their fate in the bowels of Niversai.

Tears welled up at the futility of it, and she did not hear Palom's approach until he spoke.

'Why the tears, Moroda?' His voice was deep and rich with concern.

Blinking them away, Moroda took a step back and looked up at the Ittallan. 'Oh, nothing,' she stammered, annoyed with herself at being caught off guard.

'Doesn't look like nothing,' his eyes narrowed as he looked her over. 'Are you hurt?'

'No, no, nothing like that. I'm just…worried about the trip. Worried about what we might find, or how long it might take.' She sniffed.

'You're the daughter of a trader, aren't you?'

She nodded, wiping away the last of her tears and glancing skywards to try and stem the flow.

'What was the trade?'

'Erm, teas and coffees, mostly. Sometimes more exotic things. And the chests.'

'The Ittallan…we've traded with Corhaven for years. Relationships developed. Trust formed. We won the war together. We are allies. Anahrik and I will watch you, Moroda, and your sister. There can be no tears,' Palom said. 'You helped me out of Niversai last night. If not, I would not be here safe with Anahrik. We owe you.'

Too shocked to reply, Moroda remained silent.

'I smell bread inside. Come. The others are waiting.' Palom watched her for a long moment, before he gestured for her to enter the inn before him.

'There you are! You were gone ages!' Eryn squealed, hugging Moroda as she entered the inn. 'Are you okay? Have you been crying?'

'No, no...' She pushed Eryn off and looked around the room to see the remainder of their party were gathered, aside from Amarah and Sapora. Morgen had his back to the others and was talking to the innkeeper by the bar. Their voices were low, but Moroda picked up on the words, "Imperial," "dragon," and, "guard," frequently.

Once discussions were over, the innkeeper left, and Morgen turned to the group, 'It's settled. He will give us food and coin to see us through to Berel in thanks for bringing down the dragon, though he has several more bounties with larger rewards should you return, Kohl.'

'I may just do that, when we are done in Berel,' the Arillian replied.

'Is everyone ready to go?' Morgen asked. They all nodded their assurance, and Moroda and Eryn took a few moments to put on their new travelling cloaks to protect them from the worst of the wind. The deck of Amarah's ship was largely uncovered, and

Moroda was not sure how much room there would be in the hold. If they had several days' flight ahead, she did not want to freeze, not with autumn rolling by so quickly.

The innkeeper returned, carrying a large wicker hamper. Palom and Morgen stepped forward to have a look. Resting on the white linen on the lid of the hamper were eight bread rolls, still hot from the oven and dripping with butter. Morgen passed them out while Palom inspected the contents of the hamper—it was loaded with loaves of bread, cheese wheels, salted meat and fish, several large potatoes, a handful of green onions, two small sacks; one of rice, the other of beans, a clove of garlic, a wedge of butter laced with red berries, and springs of scented herbs wrapped with twine. There were also several glass bottles wrapped in leather and sealed with cork—filled with water or wine, perhaps, or cold tea. Finally, tucked in the very bottom, was a small leather bag full of florins and the odd half-crown; the full bounty for slaying a problem dragon.

Moroda realised knowing someone in the Imperial Guard obviously had its benefits when it came to doing business in towns and villages.

'See, he's trying to help us now.' Moroda said to her sister.

'What's to stop him trying to arrest us again when we're alone? Better to keep our distance.'

'Not to admit any distrust, but I will keep the coin, and no-one is to tell Amarah of it. We are relying on her for a safe journey, and we may need this should things turn sour,' Morgen suggested, putting the small pouch in the pocket of his surcoat.

The rain that had begun the previous night had not quite let up, though Kohl assured them it was warm above the clouds, and if the mist lifted, the day would be clear with excellent visibility.

Morgen once again spoke for the party at the village gates, and a few moments later, the group entered the forest beyond. In the early morning light, surrounded by birdsong, Moroda enjoyed the walk. Her eyes were not keen enough to spot the small, feathered creatures in the trees, but she heard them clearly enough, and managed to spot the occasional burst of colour as one songbird would flit from tree to tree.

Moroda and her sister followed along with renewed enthusiasm—perhaps the trip would not be so bad after all. She hadn't realised what a boon it would be to have a member of the Imperial Guard with them, not to mention a friendly Ittallan who knew how to fight. Moroda admired Kohl, too, despite his fierce appearance and blunt personality. He had also warned her and her sister about the dragon, so something had to be said for that.

'I can hardly believe Amarah stayed out here all night. How cold it must have been.' Eryn said to her sister, drawing her thick cloak tightly around herself.

'She looks like she knows how to handle herself.'

'You trust her?' Eryn asked, after a pointed pause.

Moroda said nothing in response, sharing her sister's uncertainty. She disliked needing help and protection, but this was not her world, and she did not have many options. Humility was a trait she had learned quickly, and so far it seemed to be serving her well enough.

Anahrik, Morgen, and Palom walked ahead of them, and she

watched and listened as their weapons clattered against each other where Anahrik carried the Ittallan pair's plethora of weaponry on his shoulders. He carried himself with a carefree confidence, running off on tangents in the conversation before being reeled back in by Palom. They were made for the world and all it had to offer. She and Eryn were stumbling along in the dark. She pondered their company as they walked along the forest path, orange and red leaves littering the edges having fallen from the branches above.

The pace slowed when they reached the clearing where Khanna had crashed the night before—the canopy was torn open, casting early morning light on the airship where she lay. Amarah had done an excellent job of clearing the space of broken branches, leaves and other debris. Moroda could see the remains of a small fire, still lightly smoking, not far from where the hastily repaired airship rested.

'Amarah?' Palom called into the clearing, his voice booming, vibrating the soft wooden panels along the side of the ship.

'Keep your voice down. Do you want to bring the entire forest on us?' Amarah replied from somewhere deep inside the airship, her voice muffled by the wood.

'Looks like she did survive the night,' Anahrik sighed, folding his arms and leaning on the side of the hamper.

'I heard that, you little punk,' Amarah called, stepping out onto the deck of the ship, cleaning grime and dirt from her hands with a grubby wash cloth. 'You can fly yourself the whole way there unless you keep your damned attitude in check.'

Ignoring her retort to his partner, Palom opened the lid of the hamper, 'Breakfast?'

'Sounds good. Ship is ready to go. Everyone who's coming, get on.' Amarah climbed down and took the buttered bread roll from the top of the hamper, now cool after their walk through the trees. 'Skinned a rabbit last night. Of course nothing beats fresh bread first thing in the morning,' she grinned, wiping away butter and grease from her chin with the same dirty rag.

Leaving Amarah to eat, Moroda and Eryn followed Morgen on board the airship. Moroda had never been on an airship so small. Her only experience of travel by air was on luxury airships: massive behemoths that lumbered lazily through the air at a snail's pace. She had been very young when she had last been aboard such a vessel, and her father had been very much alive.

Khanna was sparse, no doubt to keep weight down and allow for greater speed and agility. Jumping off the deck or clambering up the side steps seemed to be the route favoured by Amarah and Anahrik, but Moroda did not have the same gusto, and instead got on board through the small hatch on Khanna's side. The suspended metal stairs leading up to the deck were narrow and cramped, and Moroda saw the four engines which powered the ship nestled tightly in the hull. She marvelled at the sight as she climbed the stairs leading to the deck, noticing a floor and rooms above the engines.

'Sleeping quarters,' Anahrik said, running up behind Moroda and the others. 'Come on, come on, I want to get up on deck,' he pressed, hopping on one foot as Eryn and Morgen reached the top of the steps and came out of the hold onto the deck through a hatch.

Muttering a brief apology to Anahrik, Moroda followed, with the Ittallan bursting onto deck just after her. Looking over it for the first time, Moroda was again surprised at the simplicity. The ship's controls were set into a raised platform in the centre-rear of the deck. The deck itself was covered by a dark, thick fabric, some kind of leather, which stretched from the controls all the way to the back wall of the ship, providing cover from the worst of the wind or rain. Crates and boxes were littered behind the controls to suffice as seating. Palom clambered onto the deck with the hamper held behind him, and Moroda watched as he wedged it between two large crates that had been welded to the floor.

Anahrik, meanwhile, had raced along the main deck, past the main sail, and come to a stop at the pointed front of the ship, arms on the raised wooden sides as he peered over the edge. Moroda could still see the damage from the dragon attack; parts of the exposed deck were blackened and splintered from damage sustained during either the chase or the landing. Amarah claimed the ship was ready to fly.

Moroda rubbed Eryn's shoulder as they looked out to Burian Forest, now lightening as the sun rose far to the east.

'Kohl is with us,' Eryn said, watching the Arillian as he hovered a short way above the ship and the clearing, scouting the surroundings. On deck, Anahrik transformed and flew straight up to meet the Arillian in the sky. Unable to hover as Kohl could, Anahrik instead circled widely, rising and falling in altitude.

By the time the two landed back on deck, everyone was present and eager to get going now the light was upon them. 'Sapora not joining us?' Morgen asked Amarah, glancing around for the Varkain.

'He's below,' Amarah replied, rubbing sleep from her right eye. 'We'll head east, back towards Niversai, to the River Flynn. We'll follow that south into Ranski, and all the way to Berel. Khanna will fly, but she'll be no racer until we get her properly repaired. I've lost over half my power, and I don't want to push her. She still runs silent as stone, so that's something to be said for my engines. If the weather's good, we'll be in Berel within three days.'

Moroda smiled at Amarah's words. Three days to Berel, less than two days back on a ship in prime condition, surely? By that time, she didn't know what would have become of Niversai, or whether or not she and Eryn would be able to continue with their lives. Pushing it out of her mind, she felt her stomach dance with excitement as Amarah went below deck to get the engines going. A trip to Berel, that's all it was.

'I hope that Varkain sleeps for the whole journey. I don't like having one on board,' Anahrik said once Amarah had disappeared, folding his arms behind his head as he did so. 'Looks clear from up there. We shouldn't have anything to worry about. After that dragon attack, I doubt anything will be in the skies for a while, anyway.'

'We'll get weapons ready and ensure everyone is armed, even still,' Palom said. 'Dragons attacking is rare enough. We could come across anything. Best to be prepared for the worst.'

Moroda noted how concerned he was about their journey, and wondered whether Eryn was right to be cautious.

'Anahrik, sort through the weapons and get everything ready. Kohl has offered to scout ahead. When he tires, you will scout. Understood?' Palom asked his trading partner.

'Got it!' Anahrik replied with a wide grin, starting to go through the supplies the two Ittallan had brought with them. The engines below kicked into life with a violent shake as Anahrik untied the wrapped fabric protecting their weaponry. The sails to the side of the ship and along the mast fanned out, and the propellers began to turn with a low thrum.

'Moroda, Eryn,' Anahrik called from where he was crouched on deck, unfazed by the shaking ship as it slowly floated off the ground. 'What experience do you have with weapons?'

The sisters glanced at one another with unease. 'None, really,' Eryn admitted.

'You mean outside of schooling?' Anahrik asked, standing up straight with a short dagger in each hand.

'We weren't really taught that sort of thing,' Moroda said, embarrassed for the first time about her education. 'We learned to ride, to dance, to sew…History, geography. There were many books.'

Anahrik's eyes were wide. 'You've never learned to fight?' 'We have the Imperial Guard for that,' Eryn retorted, arms folded in defiance. 'We read about a few significant battles and the weapons used, but that was the extent of it.'

'Hmm…You may need to learn sooner rather than later,' he

said, looking at the blades in his hands. 'We didn't bring our full stock to Niversai, and we don't have any shields. Maybe we can get you a bit of armour and work on evasion and defence.' He scratched the stubble on his chin. 'The last thing we want is for someone to get hurt. Kohl, Palom and Amarah are fighters…Morgen obviously knows how to handle himself in combat too, so you shouldn't need to get involved.'

'We're fast learners; we don't want to be on the side-lines,' Moroda said, determined. 'We don't want to get in the way either.'

Anahrik grinned back, 'Maybe something long range, so you don't need to get up too close. The only threat we'll encounter will be dragons anyway, and Kohl can handle himself with those.'

The airship cleared the forest canopy and slowly turned to face the rising sun. Without the protection of the trees, the wind picked up, and Moroda shivered and adjusted her cloak, trying to focus on Anahrik.

Palom looked over at the girls, before glancing back to his stock. 'Longbows and shortbows need much time to train. Won't hurt dragons anyway. Crossbow, I think.' His accent became stronger the more he spoke, and Moroda smiled, watching as he reached into their sack of supplies and pulled out the metal weapon with one hand. 'Slow weapon but very strong. But as last resort. Leave any dragons to Kohl and I.' He offered the crossbow to them.

'We understand.' Moroda nodded and accepted the crossbow. She tried not to stare at the wicked lines of the weapon and kept her attention on the Ittallan.

'Leaving Burian forest,' Amarah called from her position at

the wheel, one hand steering the ship, her other on a lever to sort out one of her sails which had folded in on itself. 'Kohl, do you see anything?' she called up to the Arillian, who hovered a short way above the ship. He lifted his wings and caught the wind, gaining height until he was little more than a speck in the distance. As Khanna rose above the trees and morning mist, Moroda found that Kohl was indeed correct—the day was lovely and clear.

Kohl circled above at some distance, before continuing on a short way ahead of the ship.

'Guess it's all clear then,' Amarah muttered, keeping relatively low and steering her ship due east. 'So you know, my weapons bay below was badly burned,' she said, turning her attention to her passengers. 'We'll be flying low and slow, keeping out of the eyes of anyone around, seeing as we cannot fight. Kohl and Anahrik should give us warning enough to keep out of danger. I expect you all to pitch in where and when I say, and we'll get to Berel all the sooner. Everyone understood?'

'We understand,' Morgen said, joining the others under the deck cover. 'How long until we reach Niversai?'

Amarah shrugged, 'At this speed, an hour? Far cry from last night at full thrust, I'm afraid.'

Morgen nodded and sat down on the wooden crate. He lifted the hamper, pulled out one of the bottles provided by the inn, and took a deep swig. Readying himself for a long, slow flight through Corhaven, and south into Ranski, he watched Palom show Eryn and Moroda his weapons. He found it interesting that Goldstones were having to learn to fight for themselves now. It truly seemed Linaria was turning against them all.

Chapter Nine

Moroda held the Ittallan's weapon delicately—the crossbow was far heavier than she first realised. It was painted a sleek, dark purple with black detailing, and there was a little silver on the edges. Both sisters couldn't help but admire the craftsmanship that went into the building of such a fearsome weapon.

'That's my work there,' Anahrik said, hovering over the girls like an excited child. 'See the silver? Took me six days to get it just perfect. Custom order it was for some pompous Goldstone but he decided he wanted it in blue instead of black in the end.' He put his arms behind his head, and Moroda noted it was a stance he took up frequently when he boasted. 'Worked out in the end though, we got to keep it. He paid for both no problem, so then we had this one spare to show off the silver and show how it works. Had two more orders after last summer's trade back home.' He flashed a smile, and Moroda nodded, unsure of the reaction he was hoping for.

'You must get used to weight of crossbow, and to aim it, but most importantly, to reload. This is why it is a weapon for you both,' Palom advised, offering the bolts to Eryn and bringing their attention back to practicalities. 'How we have this weapon does not matter. Anahrik, we are not selling it.'

'I know, I know,' Anahrik waved his hands before putting them in his pocket and strutting over to the edge of the ship. Moroda wondered whether he was embarrassed or knew he wasn't needed any more.

Morgen watched as Palom explained how the weapon worked, pausing frequently while he thought how best to explain it to the inexperienced girls in a second tongue. Palom clearly understood the weapon, its strengths and weaknesses, but he was used to selling weapons, not training people to use them.

Finishing his drink, Morgen decided to assist. 'Simple as point and shoot,' he said, walking up to Moroda and taking the crossbow gently from her. 'The bolts are loaded here,' he pointed to the smooth recess, 'and then the string is pulled back slowly.' He nodded for Eryn to pull it back, 'then secured into place here, you see the clasp? Simply aim, and pull the trigger here, to fire.' He finished. 'Shall we fire it?'

Moroda looked to Palom for an answer, who nodded in response.

'Then let's aim off the edge of the ship, far into the distance,' Morgen guided Moroda, who took the loaded weapon back from the soldier. She stepped over to the side of the deck and looked out to the empty fields below. Palom, Eryn and Anahrik watched eagerly from the side, careful to keep their distance.

Moroda took a few breaths to steady her shaking, more to do with the weight of the weapon than nerves, then pulled the trigger and released the taut string with a sharp twang. The whole weapon recoiled and Moroda let go, pulling her hands back as a short, sharp pain tore through her fingers.

Morgen caught the crossbow before it crashed to the floor,

and Anahrik leaped overboard, transforming and folding his wings back immediately into a dive. He returned a minute later, the metal bolt held tightly in his talons.

Moroda and Eryn both watched him return to the ship with wide eyes, amazed at his swiftness and the speed of his reactions.

'You'll need to practice that a few times—learn the strength, learn how quickly you can reload and fire, learn how far you can carry it,' Morgen reassured the sisters, echoing Palom's earlier words.

'And just hope the Arillian kills any dragons we come across,' Sapora breathed, having watched silently from the edge of the covered deck.

'Sapora!' Eryn gasped, taking a step back.

'I doubt you'll need to use that before we get to Berel,' Sapora said, stepping away from the edge of the ship. He sat on the crate next to the hamper and watched the others, a small smile on his lips. 'I have no need of weapons to defend myself...or attack.'

'We don't all have your skills,' Morgen said with a frown, glancing back to Moroda and Eryn.

'I am most interested to see what we learn in the scholar's city. I've not visited Ranski before. I thought it was nothing more than a desert,' Sapora continued.

'It is nothing more than a desert,' Amarah agreed, turning away from the wheel to face them. 'Berel has an old and new town, with a lake surrounding most of the old. Hah. The old town is falling apart, and the new ain't much better. Bits of it have been rebuilt over time. They were trying to rebuild some of the real old buildings when I left.'

'When did you leave?' Moroda asked, grateful for the conversation change. She flexed her fingers to try and rid herself of the pain from firing the crossbow.

'Ages ago, I was ten or eleven.'

'You were born in Berel?' Eryn asked.

'Nearby.'

'It'll be an experience,' Palom said. 'I've always longed to travel there, to learn of the old legends, but there is no trade for my merchandise.'

Amarah shrugged, 'There's nothing duller in the whole of Linaria than Ranski. It's a whole country of nothing. Berel is the capital, but it's no Niversai. It's always preaching peace. But, I'll be able to get Khanna fixed, which is all I want.' There was venom in her voice as she spoke of the country she was born in.

'I've always wanted to visit Berel,' Moroda said, sitting down on another of the crates as she tried her best to ignore Sapora's piercing gaze, and allow the pain in her arm to subside. 'Their knowledge is incredible. I dreamt of being a scholar as a child.'

'Knowledge indeed,' Palom agreed, taking the bolt Anahrik had retrieved and checking it for damage. 'A nation to keep out of war, but with ferocious weapons. Agrio Machar. Legendary weapons. The dragons, I understand now, have lot to do with that, and I need to know more.'

'Legendary weapons?' Eryn asked, sitting beside her sister.

Palom nodded, his face splitting into a wide smile. 'Unlike

anything you've ever seen…As a boy, I grew up on stories of their power. It sparked a fire in me, a passion, deep, burning. The only way I felt release was by forging my own weapons.'

'Sounds like it's your destiny,' Eryn said.

'Something like that, perhaps. But they do exist. Or, they did. Whether they do any more, I do not know. I'm sure the Samolen of Berel will tell. They were critical in the war.'

'Does Anahrik have the same passion?' Eryn queried, glancing past Palom to the deck, where the other Ittallan stood at the side, watching the land below as they flew gently past.

'In a way,' Palom struggled a little for the words. 'But we are almost like brothers. One will go where his heart leads, and the other will follow. When I arrived in our trading city few years back, I had no…path. He helped me find it. If not for Anahrik, I would have been lost. We were competitors, first, but he had idea to work together for more profit. But for him it was always new idea, next thing to do, more, more, more. It was his idea to come to Niversai for the races. He says it is his instinct.'

'I feel like that's just what I'm doing,' Moroda said to Eryn. 'Following my instinct: my heart. I've always wanted to go to Berel, and now the opportunity is here, I just have to take it.' She was anxious about it too, but thought it a bad idea to mention that with Sapora lingering nearby. Her heart fluttered at the thought of his words to her the previous day, and she tried to push her sudden fear away.

'We call it meraki,' Palom said. 'It is your…essence, your soul, your heart, all together. Not unlike the destiny word you used,

Eryn. It is deep in Ittallan culture. It is our blood, our life. Meraki allows us to transform.'

'Can you tell me about that?' Morgen asked. 'The transforming?'

'There is not a lot to tell,' Palom answered with a shrug. 'Family history tells what form you will take, but your meraki tells the specific. It is innate…calling. Anahrik needed speed. It was part of his essence, his soul. When he came of age, his meraki, his true form, was a falcon. It was clear to everyone that's what it would be.'

'So he could have been another animal?' Moroda asked, leaning forward.

'If his family were not birds, yes. Maybe he would have been a deer or cheetah or something else for the speed. You are not completely free to choose. Your meraki comes from your family, from your blood.'

'Why did you choose a tiger?' Morgen asked.

'I needed strength and power…to protect and fight. That's what I chose. I could maybe have been a bear or a bull. But there are many…felines in my blood. My brother was a…leopard,' Palom explained, pausing every now and then to work out the right words to describe his heritage. The common tongue was a second language to him—one he had to learn to trade—and he often struggled with specific words, despite being relatively fluent, if a little formal, in his speech.

'Was?'

'He died twenty years ago.'

'I'm sorry, Palom,' Moroda apologised for Morgen, an

instinctive response, her eyes dropping in embarrassment.

'Things happen. It was my fault. I was young. I did not have the strength to save him at the time, and meraki permitted me to take the form of a tiger when I came of age. Too late to protect my brother, but I can look after Anahrik…and now these group of travellers from what the dragons and Arillians are doing.'

'Have the Ittallan always been able to transform?' Morgen asked.

'As far back as anyone knows. It is our nature.'

'Don't the Varkain transform as well? I'm sure I've heard that? What's the difference?' Eryn ventured, chancing her luck at talking about their decidedly unwelcome companion.

'The Varkain are fucking dirty creatures,' Amarah said, still eavesdropping on the conversation. 'Only snakes. That's all they change into. What does that tell you!?'

'Very rich coming from a thief. I've never stolen anything in my life,' Sapora retorted, riled once again, by the captain's comments. 'We are just as different from the Ittallan as they are to anything else,' Sapora turned his attention to the younger sister. 'Just as ancient, with our own customs, culture, languages. We are nothing alike.'

'Some would have us believe we were once the same, but the oldest Varkain split away centuries ago, cursing them to take the same form over and over,' Palom explained, shaking his head and watching Sapora carefully. 'A lost, sickened meraki.'

'Not true,' Sapora replied. 'Snakes, yes, but different types. We do not fly or prowl as Ittallan can; but we have just as much diversity, of more significance.'

'What… type are you?' Eryn asked.

Sapora blinked slowly, but did not entertain a response.

'We're coming up to Niversai now, if you want to have a look off port-side,' Amarah called to the party, distracting the group and bringing them back to the present.

Moroda got to her feet with the others, making her way past the controls and onto the uncovered deck beside Anahrik. With the clouds lifting, blazing sunshine filtered onto the charred wood, lighting it up along with Corhaven below. Niversai sat near the horizon, perhaps five leagues away. Even from such a distance, with the early morning sun, Moroda could see the rooftops were blackened from the dragon attack the night before.

Streams of people, carts, and horses were flooding out of the city. Moroda knew if she hadn't perished in the blaze, she and Eryn might well be among those now trying to escape Niversai and find safety and shelter in neighbouring towns and regions. There were a few members of the Imperial Guard among them, mounted on horseback and carrying flags and banners high to signal the way as they wound past farmer's fields and crops.

Surrounded by trees, Niversai's natural beauty was tarnished in the wake of the attack. Moroda could not distinguish people from this distance, but she could tell it was a large crowd. They seemed to be making their way to the station outside the city's walls, on the other side of the forest, perhaps hoping for a train to take them to a less ravaged part of Corhaven, perhaps seeing off relatives before heading back to the city to try and rebuild what was left.

She sighed and shook her head, watching as thousands carried their only belongings in search of security elsewhere. In the grass fields closer to where the ship flew, a large herd of aurochs grazed nonchalantly, and Moroda thought how simple a life they had in comparison. The aurochs were so enormous she wondered whether they ever felt afraid of anything.

Anahrik didn't stand still for long. He eagerly jumped off the side of the ship, transforming as he did so. The speed of the transformation was incredible; a blinding flash and half a heartbeat was all it took for the young man to become a falcon. Moroda watched him beat his wings several times, riding on the rising thermals to gain height more quickly.

Though her eyes were not as keen as Anahrik's, Moroda could still see the damaged outer stone wall, the castle towers, and the tops of tall buildings. The Imperial flags, which had once flown proudly in the sun, were now black, or gone completely. It was a sorry sight, and Moroda felt awful just by looking at it. 'We were there, Ryn,' she murmured, bumping her arm into her sister's. 'We could have been there, in the thick of it, if we had stayed.'

'Sshh, Ro. We're okay, we're not hurt. We're going to learn more about what happened and how, so we know what to do if it happens again.' Eryn nudged her sister back. 'That's even if it happens again. It was probably a once in a lifetime experience. A freak occurrence. Try not to worry, Ro.'

'Freak occurrence? You are more stupid than you look,' Sapora said, arms folded as he surveyed Niversai with narrowed eyes and a frown. 'This is the start of something great. I only hope I can understand it before all of Linaria is destroyed by dragon flame.'

'Palom?' Moroda asked the Ittallan, who so far had been the voice of reason and experience, and the only one other than Eryn whom she trusted.

'I agree with the Varkain. Linaria is disturbed, and the dragons are centre. Corhaven's King has fallen to this, I fear. Perhaps we should go to Val Sharis instead.'

'Khanna wouldn't make it across the sea in this condition' Amarah replied. 'I'm going as far as Berel, then you're on your own.'

Moroda looked back to the sky above, searching for Anahrik. She could barely make out the dark speck circling high above, but it was so far away, and the sun was so bright, that when she blinked, he disappeared from her vision. 'I wish I could do that,' she sighed. 'To go anywhere you like, whenever you like... How free that must feel.'

'He enjoys it far too much,' Eryn added, scowling as she tried to spot the bird. 'He should be far more humble with that gift. Such a show off.'

'Don't be jealous. I'm more free than him. More comfortable, too,' Amarah laughed from the wheel. 'I can carry food and water, coin and clothes, I can travel far longer than him, farther and faster, too. You need to get yourself an airship, girl, then you can be better than the birds.'

'But you have to pay for that,' Eryn said. 'Air taxes, too, and money to dock at port. Not to mention someone to maintain it.'

'Learn how to do it all yourself and you'll never be dependent. I don't believe in air tax, either,' Amarah looked away from the burned city and headed for the blue river glittering below, cutting through the land and ribboning slowly south.

'I suppose there are always compromises,' Eryn said, shaking her head at Amarah's outrageous words. 'How can you not believe in paying taxes?' She confided in Moroda, who simply laughed and shook her head.

'That'll be one reason she's a thief.'

Having turned away from Niversai, Moroda enjoyed the views below, of farmers in their fields, sheep and horses grazing, trees dotting the edges of one field to another. Even in the midst of chaos, work still had to continue. Wildflowers, though diminishing as it grew colder, still filled the green fields with spots of purple and yellow. The river below was a great landmark, and as the airship followed its gentle flow south, Moroda returned to the covered area.

Palom sat on the floor of the open deck, his back against the side, eyes skywards as he watched the other Ittallan dance on the wind, trying to coax Kohl into a race. Smirking, Palom shook his head and returned his attention to the others, for talk had come around again to dragons.

'I wonder what the stones in Berel are like,' Moroda yawned, leaning back on the crate and brushing dust out of her hair with her fingers. 'Amarah said they stood tall in the ground.'

'Yes, it'll be incredible to see. Most impressive. That's at least one positive to come out of the trip,' Eryn said.

'It's powerful, clearly, but I don't understand it. Is it the dragon's heart?' Morgen wondered, brow furrowed as he thought, trying to remember Kohl's words from the night before.

'Like… the dragon's meraki?' Moroda said, looking at Palom for confirmation.

'It is possible, I suppose.' He replied, after a long pause while he thought about the idea of it. 'When Kohl returns to the ship I will question him.'

Before Moroda had time to think over what lay ahead, Anahrik hurriedly landed on deck in a blaze of light and feathers as he hastily transformed. 'Arillians!' His breathing was ragged from panic and exertion. 'Arillian scouts ahead!'

'What!' Amarah shouted, angered at their sudden appearance. 'Great, caught out in the open and with Khanna damaged, too.' She folded in her side sails and tried to accelerate—her default response to a threat. The ship juddered and her engines whined, a far cry from their usual, silent flight. The speed increased a little, but it was hardly anything, and the dark smoke rose from her left engine.

'I can't outfly them like this!' she said, lowering her throttles and returning Khanna to quiet, slow flight.

Palom got to his feet and drew his broadsword, ready for any eventuality. 'You may need to try that crossbow sooner than we thought,' he said to Moroda, stepping to the edge of the deck and looking into the sky, trying to see for himself.

'Fantastic, I've not killed an Arillian in years,' Sapora cracked his knuckles as he stood up, eager for a fight.

Palom glared at the Varkain, 'We don't want to kill anyone.

With Aciel somewhere near…We don't want to turn his attention to us. We want to defend ourselves.'

Sapora scowled back at Palom, 'I'll do as I please, Ittallan. I defend myself in one way only.'

Palom raised his sword to Sapora, 'Not at the risk of this ship!'

'I'm not going to risk Khanna again. Another bad fight and she won't fly at all!' Amarah called back. 'Can we avoid them, Anahrik? How far are they?'

The young Ittallan held his thighs, leaning forward, trying to get his breath back.

'Doubt it, they're only a few fields away. I reckon if we can't escape, we're going to have to fight.'

'Oh perfect,' Amarah huffed, slowing her ship to a crawl and picking up her scythe, spinning it in her hands and readying herself. 'Looks like this might well be a short trip. Knew it would be too much to ask to get to Berel before being spotted by something.'

Kohl landed on deck a few moments later, arms raised in defensive peace. 'Hold it, put your weapons down. I will deal with my kin. It may not even be anything to do with Aciel.' He looked over his shoulder into the distance. 'Amarah. Get the ship low and out of sight. Land, if possible. They haven't seen you yet.' With that, he took to the wing again and flew rapidly in the opposite direction.

Amarah did not need telling twice, and immediately folded in her remaining sails, aiming downwards, where she landed on the edge of a field, using a line of conifers for cover. 'We wait here.'

'I'm going to follow him,' Anahrik panted, sharing a nod with Palom, before transforming again and flying after Kohl as quickly as he dared.

'You don't trust him?' Morgen asked Palom in a hushed voice, as the party huddled under the covered deck, trying to keep out of sight now hiding had appeared as a third option.

'Anahrik does not, but...I do not know.' Palom shook his head. 'But I want to find out. Morgen, come with me, let's see what we can learn from the ground if they are this close.'

The soldier nodded, and the two clambered down the side of the ship and ran off along the line of the field toward the Arillians.

'I'm not going anywhere until I see the all clear,' Amarah said to Sapora, Eryn and Moroda—the only remaining passengers. She stamped the bottom of her scythe on the deck floor. 'But I'd grab that crossbow if I were you, Moroda. Just in case...and prepare to actually use it.'

Chapter Ten

Kohl had hoped to approach the Arillians undetected, but it appeared they weren't scouts for nothing. The group also had a height advantage, and Kohl felt immediately foolish for trying to sneak up on them in the first place. As they turned to face him, Kohl lowered his altitude slowly, keeping his eyes on the group as they approached, before landing in the middle of a wheat field to await them. He was acutely aware Khanna was hidden nearby, with only two lines of conifers for cover, but was grateful he had approached from behind. There was still a good chance they'd not spotted the airship, and would be focussed on him now he was in the open.

He held his breath as they slowly descended, and felt the familiar, cool, rush of adrenaline as they drew close—a mixture of fear, anxiety, and anger. Shame was in there too, somewhere.

All six members of the scouting group surrounded him as they landed, and Kohl lowered his eyes after taking stock of who was present. Most of the grunts were practically faceless, there was nothing special about them, but the one who landed closest to Kohl was one of Aciel's generals, one he had to respect.

'Kohl, it's been a while. We did not expect to see you in Corhaven,' the general said, his voice soft despite the underlying anger in his tone.

'General Fogu,' Kohl replied, his eyes fixed on the ground.

He had briefly noted Fogu wore almost no armour—a little light metal guarding on his shins and and shoulders, but nothing that would provide any real protection. It seemed more ornamental than anything else. Was he that brazen? They were in a foreign land, where their kind were shunned at best and openly attacked at worst. Perhaps Aciel's visit to the Corhaven capital had resulted in a far stronger effect than Kohl had first thought. It was a worry.

'Well? Anything to report? How many dragons have you killed?'

'One, sir,' Kohl answered, though he immediately knew what he said would be unsatisfactory. The snickering from the scouting group surrounding him confirmed that.

'You've been gone three months and all you can show for yourself is one dragon?' Fogu snarled, his wings ruffling. 'Are you taking your orders seriously?'

'I've been tracking their movements, sir,' Kohl added, chancing his luck at raising his gaze slightly. The general was more interested in silencing the other Arillians, and Kohl breathed a sigh of relief. They all seemed to be young and relaxed, informal, even. They were lazy in their stance, fiddling with their own armour or glancing around, uninterested in the conversation between himself and Fogu. Distracted. Careless. These were not the ranks of fighters he knew Aciel and his generals to train. Had they all been influenced by their leader?

'I suppose it proves you're good for little else than exile.' Fogu sighed, shaking his head and returning his attention to the dragon hunter. 'We received a report of a small, dark ship seen heading in this direction. I don't suppose while tracking your elusive dragons, you happened to see anything?'

Kohl shook his head.

Fogu narrowed his eyes, 'You're very sure, Kohl?'

'Absolutely, sir.'

'Heh, too much wildlife around here.' One of the scouts commented, drawing the gaze of Kohl and Fogu. It was a young woman, with short brown wings and matching hair. She watched a spot in the sky and was fixated by a group of birds flying tightly together a short way above them. Raising her left hand, she drew her fingers into her palm for a moment, before releasing skywards and sending a bolt of lightning shooting up into the fray. The birds cried out and scattered, much to her delight.

'After that stupid dragon burnt half of Niversai down, there's been hardly anything in the sky. We wanna keep it that way.' She smirked at Kohl. 'It belongs to us. Not ships.'

'Looks like that's about as much excitement as we're going to have here anyway. Nothing but farming fields here.' Fogu mused, ignoring the outburst and turning back to Kohl. He mirrored the other woman's swift hand motion, and Kohl buckled in pain as the invisible blow struck his chest.

He sank to one knee and clenched his teeth to keep from crying out. The second blow was just as vicious as the first, but by the sixth, Kohl was almost numb to it. Bolts of lighting and cutting wind joined the fray as the other scouts released their pent up anger on him, and Kohl closed his eyes and held onto his tongue, waiting for the pain to pass. The thunder accompanying their attacks rolled around him and shook the ground beneath his feet, but he was able to wait it out.

He could not tell whether seconds or minutes elapsed until the end of his torment, but the group soon tired of their game and took to the skies, hovering just above where he hunched. Fogu remained standing above Kohl, delighting in his suffering.

'You're lucky you're a dragon slayer, Kohl. I'd kill you myself otherwise. Be grateful for your exile,' he said. Grinning, he took to the air after his scouts. 'We're heading deeper into Corhaven: takeover will be complete by winter, thanks to the wondrous Aciel. I wonder whether you'll even be allowed home when it's finished.'

Ignoring their laughter, Kohl dropped to the ground completely as his body tried to recover from the racking pain shooting through it.

By the time he had his breath back enough to open his eyes and stand up straight, the scouts were long gone, the thunder was a distant echo, and Kohl was by himself in the wheat field. He exhaled slowly and steadily, trying to calm his breathing and thoughts. His mind raced at Fogu's words and the Arillians' behaviour. Aciel taking over Corhaven by winter? Or was Fogu speaking of all Linaria? Regardless, he doubted the others he travelled with would last very long if real war was to break out. Some of them were fighters, yes, and all were clearly adaptable, but he did not think it would be enough to survive the takeover, even if they banded together.

As he stood in the field, thinking over his options, he felt eyes on him again. Turning around, Kohl tensed, ready to get off the ground and out of danger if he was attacked. When he saw Morgen and Palom step out of the crops, he relaxed. 'I'm touched you came to make sure I was alright.' He greeted, pleased to see a face not utterly full of contempt.

'Arillians…you can't be too careful,' Morgen said, his voice shaking after the run. 'I mean, erm, present company excluded. We heard the thunder. Definitely them, wasn't it?'

Kohl sighed and picked up his hat from the ground, dusting it off as he inspected it. Placing it securely back on his head, he laughed, 'Indeed it was. And I know exactly what you mean…I have to admit I agree.' Though his tone was humorous, Kohl did not smile, not truly. He knew his kind were not loved, no more than the Varkain, but to be shunned by your kin and never quite accepted by the remaining people of Linaria was something he struggled to accept. 'Is the ship okay?'

'Everyone is fine. The Arillians?' Palom asked, searching the skies.

'They're gone. Deeper into Corhaven from the sounds of it. They won't bother us if we make haste.' Kohl replied, brushing down his clothes and adjusting his heavy cloak. There was one thing to be said for Fogu's attacks—they very rarely left a mark. He was grateful the general was in a good mood—Kohl had seen Fogu's real power, and it was far above anything Aciel was capable of. Pushing the troubling thoughts to the back of his mind, he gratefully walked back with the other two across the fields, towards where Khanna lay hidden.

'You're not flying?' Morgen asked, watching the dragon hunter carefully.

'Saves energy by not. Besides, Anahrik keeps trying to push the pace. I'm quite tired after the first part of this morning's excursion.'

'The same reason I do not transform,' Palom added, beating Morgen with the answer to his question before the young soldier had even asked it.

'Sorry,' Morgen said, shaking his head as the trio made their way into the second wheat field. 'I come from a tiny village to the north-east of Corhaven. Niversai is the biggest place I've ever been, and I've only been in the Imperial Guard about a year. Just as soon as I feel I've got the hang of something, I'm thrown back to the bottom of the pile with loads more to learn.'

'You'll never learn until you experience new things, go to new places,' Palom said. 'Many Ittallan are travellers, you know. We rarely stay in our birth town. Is it the same with your people?' he looked to Kohl.

'Perhaps, once. Less so now. Unless you are Aciel or one of his followers.'

'Why is that?' Morgen asked, direct once again.

'I don't know,' Kohl said, unwilling to speak any more of his lineage.

Picking up on his reluctance, Morgen chose not to press the matter; though he promised himself he would discuss it later, when Kohl was a little more open.

Morgen found the walk back to Khanna more pleasant than

the rush into the fields. Though the day was still young, the sun was warm and the morning was mild. If he tried very hard, he might have been able to convince himself the dragon attack was little more than a dream, and the world would go on as normal. He knew it was foolish thinking, but the idea of change scared him. It had been such an incredible push to get to Niversai in the first place, let alone join the guard. The fact he had been promoted to the rank of officer within a year had turned some of his colleagues against him. Maybe everything had been leading up to the moment the dragon chose to attack? If not, he would still be a farmer's son half a world away, with no idea about the wider world, other people, their magic, or the power of the dragons.

'You've gone very quiet, Morgen,' Palom commented. 'Oh, yes. I'm just thinking about my report.' He lied. In fact he hadn't planned on returning to Niversai at all—the town of Burian was far more welcoming than the capital, and he was already a local hero, even though Kohl had done all the work in bringing down the dragon. 'I need to make sure I remember everything that happens, or my captains will have my hide!'

'I think this Amarah will have your hide if we keep her waiting. Let's make haste—the sooner we get to Berel, the better.'

'I'm not sure what's scarier, the thought of another dragon, or her wrath.'

'Keep your distance if you know what's good for you,' Kohl added, his voice low. 'She's nothing more than a thief and a pirate. She'll look for any opportunity to gain the upper hand.'

'Is that not what we all are doing?' Palom questioned.

'Not in such an illegal manner,' Kohl retorted, almost offended.

Palom grinned, parting the wheat before him as the three reached the edge of the next field and found Khanna berthed a short way along the line of trees. 'Let's go, quickly.'

Kohl crouched momentarily, before taking to the wing again, gaining height as he flew up the side of the airship and landed softly on deck. 'The threat has passed. Palom and Morgen are getting on board now. Amarah, may we leave?'

'Moving on now.' Amarah replied, stepping over to the wheel and unfurling her sails.

'No problems with your kin, I hope?' Sapora asked. 'I'd be most interested to hear your conversations.'

Kohl watched Sapora carefully. 'There isn't much to say. They were looking for the ship, I did not know its location, they moved on. We'll be safer in Berel.'

'That's a shame.'

Morgen and Palom climbed up on deck as Khanna rose gracefully out of the wheat field; loose straw falling from her underside where it had stuck to the splintered wood.

Amarah turned the airship slowly, keeping low to the ground, then powered east and south as she skimmed the tops of the field. As the river opened out below, she put on another burst of speed. 'We'll follow the river all the way to Berel. Kohl, keep a good eye out for us. Don't want to have any more damned surprises, alright?' Amarah said.

'I'm so glad that's passed,' Moroda breathed, happy once

again to walk out to the uncovered part of the deck, crossbow held at her side.

'I thought my heart was going to burst,' Eryn replied, shaking her head and watching as her sister looked over the sides of the ship.

'Shall we put our things in the crew quarters?' Moroda asked, turning back to the deck. 'Amarah said it'll be first come first served, and I haven't seen the others go downstairs yet.'

'Good idea. We can take stock of what we have. Plus it'll be warmer down there!' She glanced at the others before leaning close to Moroda, 'And away from him, too."

'We're heading below deck,' Moroda called to the captain, heading to the hatch and ladder below. Amarah replied with a grunt, her focus on the flight and little else, which suited Moroda just fine. Eryn was still quite wary of the woman, and was pleased with the opportunity to get away from being in such close proximity to her. Moroda could sense her sister's wariness, but there was little she could do—they were stuck on Khanna at least until Berel. Thankfully Amarah was busy enough to leave them alone, and Moroda hoped it would remain that way for the rest of the flight, for Eryn's sake.

Moroda tried to ignore Sapora's stare when she and Eryn crossed the deck to the hatch, and couldn't help but shiver a little as she followed her sister downstairs.

It was indeed warmer below, but it was noisier, too, and far more cramped. Eryn led the way, heading down the narrow metal steps and through the door which ran above the engines. A short hallway was on the other side, with three cabins leading off to the right and two to the left.

Amarah used one of the smaller left cabins as her pantry and armoury. The second was kept locked, and she had threatened them all with death if they so much as thought about breaking in.

Sapora had claimed the largest cabin on the right, and no-one was to argue with him. Palom and Anahrik were happy to sleep on deck with their weapons, as was Kohl. Amarah also slept on deck, which left Morgen one cabin, and the sisters the other.

Unwilling to sleep near Sapora, Eryn led Moroda into the first cabin on the right, the farthest they could be from the Varkain's chosen bed. It suited Moroda well enough—it was not luxury by any stretch, nor was it large or comfortable. But it was surprisingly clean, and she doubted they'd spend any more than two or three nights on the ship at any rate.

The fact that Khanna was a pirate ship had its advantages. There were vast amounts of storage and hidden holes, and between them they were able to stow away their valuables while the cabin itself still seemed unused.

A pair of bunk beds were built into the wooden wall opposite the door, Moroda suspected they may have started out life as shelves, and there was a washbasin on the right. The roof sloped at such an angle, there was only room for a small square trunk on the left, which served more as a seat than anything else.

Eryn sat on the lower bunk, pulling her own satchel off and resting it at her feet. Moroda put her bag on the floor next to her sister's, and sat on the crate, leaning forward so she did not hit her head on the sloped roof. 'Are you okay, Ryn? With everything that's going on? This won't be a straightforward trip.'

'With the threat of attack by dragon or Arillian looming?' Eryn raised an eyebrow.

'All the more reason to go on it. This sort of thing doesn't happen. The more we know, the more we can find out...well, I think the safer we'll be. I know it sounds silly.'

Eryn signed and rubbed her eyes. 'I don't know. I'm still tired from everything that's happened. Last night, this morning, all these people,' she trailed off, rubbing her forehead.

'There are oat biscuits wrapped up in my bag if you want some,' Moroda said, trying not to yawn in response to Eryn. 'From Burian. I picked them up this morning when I got our things.'

'Ah, sounds wonderful. A rare luxury,' Eryn pulled Moroda's bag over to her and rooted through it eagerly. She took out two biscuits, wrapped carefully in tissue, and handed one to her sister. 'This is really happening then,' Eryn said.

'Yes. But please, try not to worry. It's just a quick trip away, like when we were children,' Moroda answered as she wolfed down her biscuit. 'I just want to learn more about the dragons, really, and their stones. The Arillians, too. If change is coming, as Palom and the others think, we need to be ready. This is what we've been hoping for.'

'Hoping for change, yes, but not like this.' Eryn brushed crumbs off her lap. 'I know things have been hard. We're no good at running the stall. With winter on the way, all sales would have dried up. We were running it into the ground. It was stupid to think we could do it alone.' Tears gathered at the corners of her eyes.

'That's not true. It was one of your better ideas! We would have pulled through, we would have!' Moroda said, amazed at her sister's sudden pessimism. Moroda was usually the more reserved of the pair and Eryn far more open, and certainly far more positive. It was hard for Moroda to see her sister so worried. 'Whatever would have happened won't happen now. This trip is our opportunity. We need to learn everything we can to make it worthwhile.'

'How will we get back, though? If we have no coin?'

'Palom said he would look after us.'

'We can't possibly expect him to pay for us to get all the way back to Niversai.'

'Perhaps, perhaps not. He may accompany us—he was trading there throughout the airship races with Anahrik. He may have unfinished business and wish to return to the city,' Moroda suggested, trying to think of ways around the situation. 'Or, worst comes to the worst, we could fly back with Amarah? Offer to work for her, prepare her weaponry and armour, re-stock, clean, cook, if it came to it. We'll be fine, Eryn. Please, please try not to worry.'

Her sister sighed, busying herself by picking at a fraying thread on her cloak. 'I'm sure you're right.'

'That's settled then. You saved me from the dungeon. I'll make sure to get us both home safe and sound, and all the better for the knowledge this trip will bring.' Moroda knew her sister did not believe her, but couldn't face the argument. Given the unease in their companions, squabbling between themselves wouldn't help matters, and they had to remain united, now more than ever. She always took Eryn's guidance, always. But she had to stand firm, and Eryn knew it as much as she did.

She took out the last biscuit from her bag, and snapped it in two, offering Eryn the larger piece. 'We'll get through this together, Ryn. Promise.'

Chapter Eleven

Moroda was grateful the rest of their day remained trouble-free as far as attacks on the airship went. They had a clear path to their destination by following the river, and the skies were empty save Anahrik and Kohl. She found it comforting to look up into the beautiful blue and watch the falcon float on the wind, dive back towards the ship, and soar past with ease and grace. Amarah's words from that morning echoed in her mind—if she had a ship of her own, she'd be able to dance on the wind just as Anahrik did.

She mused it over, and even took the idea to her sister, who scoffed that they were about a year too late. Moroda had to laugh at their fate. Eryn was right of course (she was rarely wrong), but had she shown any interest in learning to fly a year or two ago, the purchase of a small ship wouldn't have been a problem. Leaving Eryn to nap in the cramped cabin, Moroda returned to the deck. She enjoyed keeping an eye on their journey and watching the country of Corhaven pass beneath them while Palom, Morgen and Sapora remained out at the front of the ship. Moroda could sense their unease with each other, but it was very decidedly Palom and Morgen against Sapora.

She had grown familiar enough with Amarah's presence that much of the fear she held for the woman was rapidly diminishing, and she felt brave enough to speak openly with her after they had been on the wing a few hours. 'When did you purchase this airship?'

'Seven years ago.'

'Wow, it looks so new. You must have maintained it very well.'

Amarah turned from the wheel to look at Moroda, suspicion evident in her narrowed eyes. 'You wanna buy it off me?'

'No, no, nothing like that. But I would be curious to have my own. A ship of this size would be perfect, I think.'

'You Goldstones are all the same. Throw coins at everything you like to claim for yourself.'

'I...I didn't mean any offence.' Moroda said, shaking her head and feeling flushed. 'I only meant to say...you're so lucky to have all this, and the freedom it grants you.'

'Nothing lucky about it! I didn't wake up one morning to find this ship sat outside! Damn hard work. That's how I got there. Have you ever done a day's work in your life, Goldstone?'

Moroda lowered her gaze; she hated when Amarah used the slang term for nobility to describe her or her sister. She wasn't considered a Goldstone any more, and hadn't been considered one since the death of her father. She and Eryn had worked incredibly hard in the weeks that followed, trying as best they could to keep afloat. As much as she wanted to tell Amarah she was wrong, she hated arguing, and the comments were so belittling that Moroda lost interest in proving the falsehood. Unfortunately, it appeared Amarah harboured resentment towards those with seemingly more than her. Moroda's initial bravery began to dwindle again at Amarah's blunt words.

'You even know how to clean anything properly? Or did your servants do all that for you while you learned to dance?' Amarah whirled round to focus on the wheel, and thrust the engines forward, jolting the ship. 'I paid for this in blood, sweat, and gold. A whole double-crown I paid for it. The only one I've ever seen, and I paid a seller for this ship. I could have lived off that money for half a year if I wanted to.'

Moroda decided not to respond lest she received another scathing reply. Amarah's words hit home again—the only double-crown she'd ever seen. They were the most valuable of all Linaria's currency, and yet she and Eryn regularly saw them when their father returned from his trips away. He had once brought back a tea box from somewhere deep in Ranski—it was ornately decorated with gold and silver, carved out of red wood and embellished with the jewels of the Samolen. It had been a gift for them, yet when their money began to dwindle, Moroda had traded it for six double-crowns at one of Niversai's auction houses. The money had lasted them four weeks.

'Cleaning the mansions of Goldstones was damn hard work, let me tell you. Glad I packed that in when I did,' Amarah continued, despite Moroda's silence. 'Awful people, really. No concept of value. Learning to fly was the best thing I ever did. Could leave whenever I wanted, go wherever I wanted. Never had to rely on anyone again.'

Moroda listened quietly, internalising everything the pirate said. Amarah's words echoed in her mind, and she felt more distant from the older woman than before. Amarah's strength was her self-reliance and unwillingness to compromise. She showed no fear, not even of Sapora, and had a prideful confidence in herself above all else. Moroda felt helpless in the best of situations. All she had known was a life of ease and luxury, where everything she needed was catered to. Her world had collapsed around her when her family's income disappeared, and she now found herself reliant upon this odd group of people to carry her to her next step in life. It was clear she didn't know how to cope, no matter what she said to convince herself or Eryn.

'I'm stopping here for a bit,' Amarah called out suddenly, bringing Moroda back to the present.

'What? Why? What's wrong?'

'Nothing's wrong. There's fishing here,' Amarah replied, pointing ahead.

'Fishing? But we have food?'

'Exactly. We know that food is safe. Better to eat new things when you can, while you know you've got a stash somewhere.'

Moroda was confused, but didn't want to ask more lest Amarah snapped at her. She looked up as Sapora and Palom approached, and shook her head slightly.

'Stopping for fish does not seem the best course of action when we are trying to get somewhere quickly,' Sapora said.

'My ship, my rules,' Amarah replied, keeping her eyes on the ground as she carefully manoeuvred Khanna to a flat patch of grass near a particularly wide section of the river. 'It's getting warm.

Fish'll dry out in the sun and we'll be on our way.'

Moroda tried to hide her smile at Amarah's words to Sapora, and looked over to the river where dozens of fish splashed about at the surface, turning it from blue to a foamy white. The thrum of the engines quietened before stopping altogether as the airship landed gently.

'What's happening?' Eryn asked, emerging from the hold and watching Amarah scramble overboard.

'Amarah's decided to go fishing,' Moroda answered with a sigh.

'Oh,' Eryn rubbed the sleep from her eyes. 'Should... should we go too, do you think?'

'Yes, why not? It'll be good to stretch our legs and get off the ship for a short while.'

The two girls clambered down the side, and the others were soon to follow. By the time they were off the ship, Amarah had already taken her boots off, rolled up her breeches, and had waded out into the river until the water was nearly waist high.

'She's very keen,' Morgen commented, standing next to the sisters. 'I'd have been testing the depth and making sure the current wasn't too strong before taking my boots off.'

'Just shows how reckless she is,' Sapora added, folding his arms and watching their captain fish. 'But she is the only way out of Corhaven....'

Moroda sat down on the grass by the riverbank. It was a lush, rich green, no doubt from the constant watering, and she splayed her hands wide, enjoying the feel of the blades between her fingers. She had no intention of getting in the water herself, and was perfectly content to watch Amarah.

Morgen and Eryn joined her, sitting down cross-legged and picking at the grass while watching. Though happy with their company, she found Sapora's lingering presence unnerving. She still hadn't seen him attack, or attempt to attack, anyone on board, but the fear she felt around him was instinctive—yet she wanted to give everyone the benefit of the doubt before judging them. With Sapora, though, she found it very hard.

A sudden splash distracted her from her thoughts, and she looked up just in time to see Amarah grab a silvery-blue fish from the water.

'Gotcha!' Amarah yelled, pleased with her catch: a large, fat catfish about a foot long. It thrashed around in her hands, trying to escape, but the pirate's grip was too strong, and it could not slip away. 'Goldstone! Catch!' she called, tossing the fish towards the shore.

Moroda half stood from her sitting position, caught off guard and with little time to think. She raised her hands, palms wide, and blinked. In the half-second it had taken, Sapora had darted in front of her and caught it by the tail, dangling it and watching as the fish continued to wriggle.

'What...where did...?' Moroda stammered. Sapora had been stood behind her. How had he managed to move so quickly, without her noticing? She stood up and stepped backwards, looking to Eryn and Morgen.

'Not a bad catch,' Sapora said, ignoring Moroda's

stammers. 'A few more like this and we'll be well fed.' He turned round and slunk back to the airship, taking the fish with him.

Eryn and Morgen were both on their feet, too, watching Sapora as he casually walked back to the grounded airship. 'Must he behave like that? He could have asked you to give it to him, Ro,' Eryn said, still watching Sapora as he got on board.

'I don't know,' Moroda said, shaking her head and looking back to Amarah, who was still busy in the middle of the river.

Morgen sat down once Sapora had disappeared inside. 'Don't worry about him. He just enjoys throwing his weight around and trying to unsettle us. I've met hundreds like him,' he reassured the girls. 'Try to forget him.'

'You're right,' Eryn agreed, sitting down again. 'Of course, Ro, if you hadn't freed him, he might have burned in the dragon's fire and none of us would have to deal with him in the first place.'

'Ryn!'

'It's the truth! You're far too forgiving, Ro. In fact, if I hadn't freed you, Morgen here would have killed you,' Eryn said, turning to the soldier with a scowl.

Morgen sighed and shook his head, looking from the grass to Amarah, but not at either of the sisters. 'I truly am sorry for how we met. I was following orders to arrest you,' he said. 'Everyone was acting strangely, maybe because of Aciel being in the castle, maybe not. I don't know.'

'No excuse,' Eryn said. Moroda knew her sister would take more convincing, and it appeared she still hadn't forgiven Morgen. 'You would have soon had an order to behead her. Would you have followed your orders then?'

'No!' Morgen replied, looking at Eryn as he spoke. 'I felt awful about Moroda being in the cell in the first place. Everything was…all so different to how it normally would have been. I thought I was escorting her away from the castle grounds…I'd maybe deliver a fine to her…but the King's orders couldn't be disobeyed. At least she was safe and out of harm's way in the cell.'

'Out of harm's way? You put her in a cell with a Varkain! I'm amazed she was alive when I found her!'

'There were so few of us in the castle, we had no choice,' Morgen said.

'Ryn, please, it's okay,' Moroda interrupted. 'I knew there was something different about the city that day. It might have been because of Aciel, it might not. I was sure nothing would happen,' she said, though she had barely convinced herself of that when she had been locked up.

'Really,' her sister scoffed, shaking her head. 'Morgen you're doing well enough to redeem yourself. Paying for lodging and food, and arranging for us to travel more securely. But don't think for one minute I trust you won't try and arrest us when we get back to Niversai.'

'Please, Ryn,' Moroda tried again.

'What promise do we have from you that you'll let us leave in peace?' Eryn continued, ignoring her sister.

'I'll give you my word? I can't do any more than that,' Morgen replied.

Eryn shook her head. 'Your word? The word of your captain

is stronger than that, what happens if he orders you otherwise?'

'Ryn…'

'Moroda, I'm trying to ensure our safety when we get home!' Eryn said, raising her voice for the first time since they had left. 'If we even get home. At this rate, we'd be better off walking to Berel and back.'

'I might not even return to Niversai,' Morgen admitted. 'I've not been happy there for a while. I was the one who arrested Moroda, not any of my captains. With everything that's gone on, I doubt they'd even recognise you by the time you went back.'

His answer seemed to pacify Eryn for the time being.

'Fish!' Amarah called, giving the three only a few seconds to catch another wide-finned catfish thrust in their direction. It was a welcome break from the argument, and Moroda was doubly pleased with herself for managing to catch it this time.

Grinning, she looked further downriver to see a tiger stood in the rushing waters, two fish clamped between his massive teeth. A pile of fish on the river bank showed his hunt was so far more successful than Amarah's, but Moroda supposed he had four legs in the water, better senses, and quicker reflexes. She was pleased their stop was not in vain and they would all eat well until they reached their destination. Although friendly, Palom and Anahrik kept to themselves. They were only allies in the loosest sense of the term, but perhaps it was a distrust of Amarah which fuelled it. She knew the pirate's manner and speech were uncouth, and she often came back with biting remarks to the most innocent of comments, but Moroda was sure she wasn't as bad as perhaps she wanted others to think.

Moroda watched the tiger wade through the water, whiskers bristling as he looked for movement below the surface, striking at just the right moment and often bringing up more than one fish at a time. Moroda marvelled at his efficiency and looked back to Amarah, who caught one fish for every three of Palom's.

'Looks like you have some competition, Amarah,' Moroda ventured.

The sky pirate glanced over her shoulder at Moroda's words, but shrugged and took a few steps along the river, knees bent slightly as she fought the current.

'Help me carry these fish onboard, Morgen,' Eryn said, standing up and pointing to Palom's pile of fish.

Whether it was the tone in Eryn's voice, or the fact Morgen was used to receiving orders, he stood up without question and followed her down to where Palom was fishing, leaving Moroda to catch anything Amarah threw haphazardly in her direction. Moroda was unwilling to speak with Eryn while she was in such a foul mood, so she remained quiet as they left.

She mulled over her sister's anger, regardless, and her gaze returned to the sky pirate. 'Amarah? Do you remember, back in the cell in Niversai, there was a loose stone slab on the floor?' Moroda asked, hoping she would be too busy to snap back at her.

'What about it?' Amarah asked, shifting in the water, her back to Moroda.

'Well, under the slab…were some florins,' she continued.

'Yep. Three. Some poor bugger left them there before they

died, I suppose.'

Moroda paused, wondering how to word her question. 'It was me.'

'What was you?'

'The poor bugger who left them there.' She laughed, nervous. 'I hid them, when I was arrested; it was all the coin I had left.'

Amarah paused and stood up straight, turning to look over her shoulder at her, 'Those three florins were your only money?'

Moroda wasn't sure she liked the fact she now had Amarah's full attention, but she was pleased she had finally spoken to her about it. At least Eryn wouldn't chide her for not asking for them back.

'All I had left, yes,' Moroda confirmed with a nod.

Amarah burst into hysterics, splashing the water about herself with her hands. 'A Goldstone with three florins? Really? What has Linaria come to? Maybe the world really is about to end!'

Moroda blinked and lowered her head. She was not used to being made a mockery of, and had no idea how to deal with such a response. 'So, you'll give them back?'

'Don't be stupid, girl. The florins are your payment for this trip, aren't they?'

Moroda stood up, shocked. 'What? But... Morgen paid you our travel fare? This morning? In the forest?'

'Travel fare? You Goldstones make me laugh. The florins are mine. You want money, you damn well better work for it. What's a florin to you, anyway? Pocket money? No, that's ridiculous, you probably got a couple of crowns in pocket money, didn't you?'

'But they're mine, you have to give them back?'

Amarah turned to face Moroda fully, the river water rushing about her. 'Come and make me, then.'

Moroda glanced around, but Eryn and Morgen were on the ship with Sapora, Palom was further downriver, and Anahrik and Kohl were not in sight.

'Well? I'm waiting,' Amarah called, no longer smiling.

'But I…But…But that's not fair,' Moroda mumbled. She had always hated conflict, and confrontation was something she actively avoided. She regretted mentioning the subject.

'Not fair? Then sit down and shut up about your florins. You were born never having to worry about food or clothes or money. I didn't have that luxury. How is that fair on me? It isn't! I had to work for every penny I ever had. I didn't expect anyone to pick me up every time I made a mistake, to get me through to tomorrow.'

'What about your parents?'

'Never had them,' Amarah snapped. She began wading through the river, back to the bank, where Moroda was stood.

'Everything I have is off my own back. Everything I've learned is from my own lessons. I don't have time to babysit entitled, lazy shits who can't take care of themselves,' she said, pulling herself out of the river, water dripping all over the grass.

Moroda saw her legs were bare, scars criss-crossing her shins, and she felt the heat of rage in her belly as Amarah insulted her yet again. 'I'm not lazy!'

'Really?'

'No, I'm not! I'm not sorry I was born into a family that had more than yours! That wasn't my fault! I didn't choose it! No more than you chose yours! You don't have to be so rude all the time or act like I'm ungrateful!' Moroda said, her voice shaking with emotion.

Amarah cackled again and shook her head, 'Alright, calm down Goldstone. I'm glad this is a wake-up call for you.'

'Losing my father was a wake-up call!' She felt the heat in her belly rise up to the back of her eyes, but she didn't want tears to spill, not in front of Amarah. 'Everything I've ever known has gone! It's just Eryn left, just Eryn and those three florins. Now there's an army being built! My city has burned down! Dragons are attacking people! I'm trying to adapt to this new life and I'm trying to take care of myself! You don't need to make all that even harder!'

Amarah said nothing, and Moroda was stunned by her own outburst, but her words continued, fuelled by emotion. 'What if you lost Khanna? What if you lost the ability to fly a ship? What if you lost everything you had and were put in a world where everything and everyone was against you all the time? I'm sorry I don't know how to deal with that as well as you want me to!'

Moroda could no longer keep her emotion back, and tears flowed down her cheeks. 'Keep my florins, then, if you think I don't deserve them! I'll find a way to make it work. I'll look after Eryn, too. We're friends just as much as sisters. I'll make sure we learn all the same lessons as you and know what to do.'

Amarah remained quiet as Moroda tried to steady her breathing. She felt vulnerable all of a sudden, when she realised the only thing she could hear was the rushing waters of the river in front of her.

'Alright. Glad to see you do actually have a bit of fight in you, girl,' the pirate finally spoke. 'I was waiting to see what you were made of. Keep thinking like that and you just might get through life without your family's money to look after you.'

Moroda angrily wiped away the tears from her face, grateful Amarah had spared her another insult. She didn't know how she felt about her. On the one hand, she admired her confidence and ability to fly an airship with such skill, but on the other, she detested how little she cared for anyone, or the feelings of anyone, around her.

'Looks like Palom has caught enough to keep us fed till next summer. Get back on board. We'll dry it all out and be leaving shortly,' Amarah said, having seen the Ittallan's generous catch.

Moroda remained stood where she was as Amarah picked up her boots and walked off, taking the time to sort her thoughts and ensure she did not cry again. Her lip trembled as she tried to steady her breathing. She had been so determined to do the right thing, to make sure everything would be fine, to stop the bad things happening, and yet all her attempts seemed futile. Was the decision to speak out publically against the King's visitor the start of it all? If she hadn't done that, she'd never have been arrested and met Amarah. Never have left Niversai. Never be on her way to Berel. Perhaps she should have burned that night instead. Perhaps Linaria would have been better off without a silly girl with no idea about the real world and how it worked.

Shaking her head, she took a deep breath, fighting back more tears. If she wasn't doing the right thing, then at least she was doing something. She would be swept along with the events of this bizarre group of travellers, just like the river's current. She wouldn't worry about what happened, she would just make sure Eryn got through it with her, and then got home. Somehow. Moroda had never before needed to question anything she had done, her life before had seemed relatively set. Working hard hadn't ever factored into it, and here she was, willing to do so, but it was being thrown in her face.

What else could she do but put on a brave front and continue? She felt incredibly small, and incredibly lost, and she didn't have the first idea how to fix that. She had to focus on what she knew—she had the love and support of Eryn, and it was as good a starting point as any. Yes, she would lean on Eryn as Eryn would lean on her, until they knew what was happening. Until then, she had to be open and willing to learn, now more than ever.

Feeling no better than before her argument with Amarah, but with some sort of plan in mind, Moroda finally headed back to the airship and climbed on board, as ready as she could be for the next leg of their journey.

Chapter Twelve

The short breaks Amarah permitted were few and far between, but Moroda enjoyed them when they happened. The captain could quite happily stay on her ship for days at a time, but Moroda loved the feeling of earth under her feet, particularly because it didn't shake quite as much as Khanna did. She had expected Amarah to tell them more of her home country as their journey continued, but the pirate had surprisingly little to say of Berel, of which none was positive.

Moroda knew hardly anything of the Samolen home country, Ranski, to the south of Corhaven. She knew of the great university, and knew the Samolen practiced magic there. She knew it was a good deal warmer than Niversai, and thanks to Amarah's comments, she had learned it was in fact mostly desert. Other than that, she was an open book, and felt butterflies in her belly at the thought of finally seeing such an esteemed city.

It seemed so bizarre after all these years she was finally going to Berel, to see it with her own eyes, and on a pirate's ship, no less! Her companions were a far cry from the sort of company she usually kept, and though the group was made up of people with vastly different personalities, they held a mutual tolerance—after all, their goals were the same. All but Sapora and Amarah, who outwardly showcased their distaste for one another. Moroda couldn't stand the tension their outbursts created; it would linger on board for hours, and made her uncomfortable.

She thought of Kohl and Anahrik, who could fly off if they chose and keep away from the spats, and wished she could do the same. Yet in the same breath, she looked to Palom and his calm voice of reason, and Morgen, who had a knack for defusing tension, and realised she could learn a lot from both of them, too.

Moroda listened to their arguments, trying to work out why they disagreed so much. Sapora seemed to loathe Amarah's vocation, and Amarah seemed simply to loathe Sapora's existence.

The arguing between Amarah and Sapora intensified as they left Corhaven and entered Ranski. Crossing the border into the neighbouring country was far less exciting than she had imagined. Amarah was following the course of the river south, and she pointed out several tall flags which signified the land had changed from Corhaven to Ranski. There were no Imperial soldiers, no walls, not even a hut by the side of the road to check travellers passing through. Moroda's heart sank—perhaps she was getting too worked up over the Arillians in Niversai. The whole of Linaria seemed oblivious to their movements.

The heat increased several hours after the border crossing, and Moroda assumed this had been the reason for Amarah and Sapora's increased arguing and digs at one another. Amarah had warned them Ranski was a desert, but Moroda hadn't quite been prepared for the sudden intensity of heat. The thick travelling cloaks she had bought in Berel did not help with the heat, but protected her skin from burning under the harsh sun. Amarah had not been lucky with the sun; after only a few hours, her arms were red and her bare shoulders sported blisters.

Kohl's wide-brimmed hat came into use when he was on deck, and when he flew, he kept below the ship to remain in Khanna's shadow. Palom, already deeply tanned from years of work outdoors, did not mind the heat as much as the others, much the same as Morgen, but Sapora disliked it most of all. Moroda found him terrifying at the best of times, but a Varkain with a temper was definitely one to avoid, and she and Eryn made a point of keeping to the opposite side of the ship as he.

Corhaven, to her, was beautiful—full of hills and forests, fields and flowers, all swathed in rich green grass. Ranski had plains, yes, but of brown, brittle grass which soon gave way to a barren, sandy landscape. The wind strengthened, too, and on the vast, flat plains, it picked up loose dust, pushing it into huge clouds which bombarded the airship every time it flew too low or too quickly.

The further they travelled, the more intense the dust storms became, and the harder it was for Amarah to avoid them. The ship's sails bore the brunt of the dust storms, and Moroda worried they would rip off completely off if their journey lasted much longer.

As the view turned from green to brown, much of Moroda's initial wonder left her. The sky and land merged into one, shapeless colour, the hours seemed to drag on, and she felt herself wondering once more whether she had in fact made the right choice by leaving Niversai.

'Kohl, what is that?' Amarah called out sharply. Moroda stood up, cloak covering her shoulders, and walked to the edge of the ship. Wiping away the sweat on her forehead, she squinted in the sunlight and looked for the Arillian.

Against the bland skyline, she could not easily spot their scouts, but Kohl came back into view at Amarah's call—by far the most obedient aboard Khanna, and the only one to listen to Amarah's every instruction. He held his hat low as he reached the ship, keeping it safely on his head against the rush of cool wind that accompanied his landing. 'Phoenixes, Amarah. A pair of them half a league ahead,' he said, looking off the edge of the ship toward a faint orange glow in the sky.

'Phoenixes?' Moroda echoed, struggling to see the scaled birds.

Amarah shook her head and altered their course slightly. 'Great warning, Kohl. There'll be dragons about then.'

'None for a few days' travel, Amarah. Your ship will be safe. Phoenixes are everywhere in Ranski, I understand. They don't all follow dragons here.'

'Phoenixes won't hurt you anyway.' Morgen added. 'Ranski is the safest place in all Linaria. Don't worry.'

'I'm not worried!' Amarah replied. 'But Khanna isn't fireproof, whether phoenixes intend to harm me or not!'

Eryn hugged Moroda's arm; she was exhausted from the heat and their rations were swiftly dwindling. Talk of more fire and danger put her on edge, and Moroda could sense her sister's anxiety.

'Lucky for us the ship has a good pilot,' Morgen said, flattering Amarah to lessen the tension on deck. Amarah snorted in response, but Moroda could see a small grin playing on the captain's lips.

Moroda glanced towards the open part of the deck, where Palom and Sapora stood opposite one another. Amarah could often be appeased by a calm word or a hint of flattery, but Sapora was more unpredictable, and Palom seemed to have taken it upon himself to keep a close eye on the Varkain. Their dislike for one another seemed to run deeper than Amarah's, and Moroda was perfectly happy for them to stay on the other side of the ship for as long as they wished.

'The Ittallan and Varkain are more closely linked than they'd like to admit.' Morgen had explained when they watched Palom stalk away from Sapora. 'Kind of like disowning a parent or sibling, you know? You're trying to strike off on your own, but you keep being reminded that you're related.'

It was close to evening on the sixth day of their journey when Amarah announced Berel was in her sights. On form, Anahrik raced ahead to see for himself, though Kohl chose to remain on deck with the others. Moroda, Eryn, and Morgen looked over the edge of the ship to see the city sprawling beneath them.

'We're coming up on the old town now,' Amarah said, as she slowed the ship's approach. 'The university's down here, on the lake.'

Moroda's eyes widened. The lake was enormous, sprawling in all directions for several leagues, an oasis in the dry landscape. Torches shimmered across the waters' surface, and the current was visible even in the low light. Great stone pillars arose in a circle from the centre of the water, with a high plinth atop them. It gave off a strong force, not unlike wind, preventing Khanna from flying too near. 'Samolen magic,' Amarah muttered, turning to avoid the pillars and take a slightly more roundabout route into the city.

Beside the pillars was the island of the old town. It was connected to the land by a thin bridge, but bright lights lit it beautifully. Moroda leaned over the side, trying to get a better look, before being jolted back as Khanna turned under her.

'Docks are in the new town,' she explained, bypassing the old town and its University, and approaching land once they flew over the expanse of water. The new town was larger and more advanced than the old, and much more built up. It did not take long before Moroda could make out individual streets and buildings as the ship slowly descended. Their timing could not have been better—Amarah's port sails had suffered terribly in the dust storms, and one was ripped almost in two; she thought it a wonder the ship could still fly at all, but she supposed Amarah was used to the odds being against her.

'Looks like the docks are pretty empty. See, no-one visits this bastard desert,' Amarah said, steering towards a large overhang jutting out from a hillside. The fabric canopy overhanging the dock entrance was thick and red, richly embroidered with jewels, which shone more brightly the darker it became. Using their light as a guide, Amarah carefully steered Khanna into the hangar, and docked her near the entrance.

Now darkness had descended fully, the day's heat vanished, replaced by a welcome chill. Killing her engines, Amarah breathed a sigh of relief. 'We're here, finally.' She yawned, stretching her arms above her and cracking her joints. 'Dragons above, I ache.'

Eryn rubbed her eyes as she made her way across the deck to her sister, 'Me as well. I'll be so glad to be off this ship. I think I've decided I don't like flying on airships quite so small and cramped.'

'Or with a touchy Varkain aboard,' Moroda whispered back, once she had checked the offending person wasn't within earshot.

'Whose ship is this?' a male voice called up to the passengers.

'Captain Amarah—this is Khanna, a racing ship that had a tangle with a dragon outside Niversai,' Amarah called back, clambering down the steps on the side of her ship. 'I would have thought you'd recognise this old girl, Topeko.' She winked at the approaching Samolen as she stepped onto the stone floor and brushed herself down.

'Amarah? I can't believe it!' the man replied. He wore ornately jewelled red robes matching the canopy above the entrance to the hangar. His bright eyes sparkled green against his dark skin, and the three thumbnail-sized jewels embedded under his eyes shone vividly in the darkness.

He embraced the dirty, burnt sky pirate and wrapped his arms completely around her, spreading warmth into the cool air all around. 'It has been far too long, I feared you would never see me again! We heard of the dragon attacking Niversai; it is a wonder your ship survived its flame.'

He released Amarah and took a step back to greet the others who were disembarking. 'These are your…friends? You always had quite eclectic tastes, didn't you? Not only do you have those from Corhaven, but Ittallan, an Arillian, and a Varkain, too? Who would have thought one small airship would bring peoples from all of Linaria together!' Topeko exclaimed, the purple jewels under his eyes bursting with light and colour as he became happier and more animated.

The sounds of drums beating and flutes playing from somewhere beyond the hangar enticed the party forward, along with the warmth emanating from the Samolen. 'Goodness me! A prince of the Varkain, no less! My word, Amarah, whatever have you been doing these past few years?'

Sapora froze mid-step, glaring at the Samolen and refuting the warmth he gave off.

'Prince?' Amarah echoed, caught completely off guard as she stared at Sapora.

'Sapora's a prince?' Moroda gasped, one hand raised to cover her mouth. She couldn't believe the Samolen's words, and thought back to all the times she had been less than courteous to Sapora, or when Amarah had outright insulted him. She had no idea they had royalty on board, and all she had wished for the entire journey was he would leave them in peace. Moroda had been so wrapped up in Amarah calling her Goldstone every chance she had, she didn't think anyone else would be as…important. She felt awful at the realisation.

'You did not know?' Topeko asked, raising a hand to his heart as he realised his mistake. 'My prince, I apologise if I affronted you,' he bowed, a little of the sparkle from his jewels disappearing.

The Varkain blinked slowly and looked away, poorly concealing his annoyance. 'I'm sure someone would have figured it out soon enough,' he muttered. 'I am too tired to be angered now. Shall we rest?' Sapora suggested.

'Of course, of course,' Topeko nodded, straightening up and turning back to Amarah. 'I'll have your Khanna repaired in no time. I presume that's why you came to me and not another city? Shall we return to my quarters for the evening? Of course, your friends are guests just as much as you. They are more than welcome to stay with me during their time in Berel.'

'Thank you very much, sir,' Moroda said, stepping forward and returning his bow. 'Are you one of the scholars here?'

'Indeed, I am a teacher,' he replied, pointing to the right jewel under his eye. 'Purple is the colour of the teacher. There are many colours to mark the speciality of the Samolen,' he explained. 'Come, come, there is plenty of time to learn. You must be thirsty, and hungry, too? I will have something prepared to mark the end of your journey,' he said, and once again became animated, his jewels dazzling as they pulsed with ever brighter light. 'Please, come, it is not far.' He beckoned, turning around in a flourish of red and purple as he led Amarah and the others through the hangar and into the new town of Berel.

Moroda nodded, finding herself immediately calmed by his words, and she hugged Eryn as they followed him. Kohl remained indifferent to both Sapora's status and the fact Topeko had realised he was an Arillian despite hiding his wings under his travelling cloak. Moroda realised both Palom and Anahrik looked to be in some discomfort, but she had no time to speak to either of them about it as they were hurried along.

The flutes and drums grew louder with every step, until Moroda felt the walls themselves were alive with the sound of music, and she felt her steps changing slightly to match the beat. She'd never experienced anything like it—she felt the music as heat, not unlike the warmth generated from Topeko—it was fire, flickering and dancing, rising and falling, and immersing itself into the very earth below her feet. Her eyes shone with it, and she felt the aches and pains of her journey slowly drift away. She felt the pain moving from her limbs down through her legs, into her feet and into the ground below.

'Eryn, can you feel that?' Moroda called to her sister.

'It's incredible! I hardly ache anymore!' Eryn said, grinning broadly. 'This is the Samolen magic indeed!'

Topeko laughed from somewhere ahead, 'Of course it is! We start and end every day with our music. In the morning to refresh and energise us, and in the evening to remove the stresses and pains of the day. There is no truer way to be at peace.'

Though Moroda did not quite understand his words, she understood the idea behind it. She knew of the Samolen magic from her childhood, Palom spoke of their legendary weapons winning the war, Amarah spoke of their huge dragon stones powering the city, and she was now more eager than ever to learn. She knew the Samolen were great scholars and could use magic—yet she had never known how powerful it could be.

As they followed Topeko through the streets of Berel, Moroda tried to take in everything, but her eyes were beginning to droop as the aches of the journey left her. She tried to look for the instruments or the musicians themselves, but could see none; the large, wide streets, paved with sandy coloured brick, no doubt taken from the desert surrounding Berel, were empty.

Archways and bridges floated overhead, covered with lush green vines rimmed with gold. Lanterns hung from the archways at regular intervals, burning brightly and lighting the streets as they walked along. Square, flat-roofed buildings dotted their path, and she noticed every doorway had a lantern burning above it— some with the yellow flames she was familiar with, others with purple flames matching Topeko's jewels, some green, some blue, some fierce red, while still others were silver. Too tired to ask, Moroda decided she would speak to the scholar in the morning, when she had more of her wits about her.

With the chill of the descending night cooling her skin, and her aches and pains removed, tiredness began to creep in, and Moroda felt overwhelmed, almost dizzy with exhaustion. The anxiety she felt at Sapora's title being revealed had disappeared, too, and she thanked Rhea herself when Topeko stopped at a large, domed building only a few minutes' walk from the hangar.

The building was elaborately draped with looping sashes of thick, purple fabric over the entrance and walls. 'Here we will stay,' Topeko said, pausing to ensure all of the party had followed him, before leading them inside. 'My home is your home, Amarah. It is also home to her friends.' He waved his hand to the others.

Sapora had also followed the group (Moroda thought he might have gone off to hide, as he had in Burian Forest), but she could see he looked angrier than she had seen him before, even during one of his arguments with Amarah. She thought he actually enjoyed riling the sky pirate, but this was a reveal not on his terms. Perhaps that was why he seemed so bitter about it.

She noticed once again Anahrik and Palom seemed particularly unhappy about the revelation. They kept close to her and Eryn, casting Sapora glances every so often, as if looking at him would answer the questions they thought internally. Moroda knew she should feel nervous, but the power of the Samolen magic was too much, and she had no energy left to worry.

'Andel, please.' Topeko called into the dark room once the party had entered. Barely a moment later, a child appeared; he couldn't have been much older than eleven or twelve, and wore the same robes as Topeko. He had the brightest blue eyes Moroda had ever seen, with a shock of dark hair in contrast. Andel bore one small blue jewel under his right eye, and smiled broadly at the party. With a wave of his hands, the torches fastened to the walls burst into flame, lighting the large, circular room and providing warmth against the night chill.

'Andel, please ensure each room is stocked. Amarah has returned, and she is with company.' Topeko instructed. The child bowed to the scholar, before disappearing down the hallway he had emerged from. Moroda noticed his feet were bare under his flowing robes, but said nothing of it.

'Thank you for your hospitality,' Anahrik said, lowering his head in not quite a full bow—an imitation of the motion he had seen Topeko and Andel perform. 'But to tell you the truth, I'm not happy with any of this. All this secrecy.' His eyes rested on Kohl and Sapora as he spoke, before flicking over to Amarah.

'About you, Kohl, and the dragons, what you're not telling us…and you, Amarah—how in all of Linaria do you, a low-class sky thief, know a scholar of Ranski?' He then rounded on Sapora, not in the least bit intimidated by the Varkain. 'And how did we have a prince among us without realising?!'

'You're too ignorant to realise, Anahrik.' Sapora responded coldly.

'Too ignorant? You do nothing but criticise us and skulk about, throwing out your sly comments,' he replied. 'I'm keeping busy, scouting ahead and making myself useful. You and your kind bring nothing but fear and misery to Linaria. Even if you are a prince.'

Sapora narrowed his eyes at the Ittallan's words. 'I'd be very careful what you say, Anahrik.' He unfolded his arms, letting his hands drop to his sides.

'Hold your tongue, Sapora,' Palom interjected, drawing his sword and pointing it at the Varkain. 'You delight in causing conflict and misery. This is the second time I am stopping you from doing this.'

'Ah, of course, Anahrik's back-up from the great tiger,' Sapora said, lowering his voice once again to a cool rasp. 'Drawing your blade in a show of strength will do nothing to stop me from doing exactly as I wish, Palom. You won't always be around to protect Anahrik. One day that young Ittallan will mouth off too much and I won't be in such a forgiving mood.'

'Please, this is a place of peace and rest,' Topeko said, stepping between the Ittallan and the Varkain with raised hands. 'Do not squabble. Your rooms are prepared. You will find food and drink there, and comfortable beds. There are no airships flying out this evening, and the desert is too dangerous to travel on foot at night. Do stay, there will be much to discuss, I think, in the morning.'

'Thank you, sir,' Morgen bowed, more deeply than Anahrik's attempt, as he tried to calm the mood, turning to follow the young boy, Andel, as instructed.

'Make sure you lock your door, Anahrik,' Sapora grinned, flashing all his teeth in a pointed smile.

'Don't you dare,' Palom growled, shaking as rage began to build.

'I have the strength of my crown behind me, yet I have little need for it against an arrogant Ittallan like you,' Sapora continued. 'You rely too much on Palom's strength to get you out of trouble.'

'Sapora!' Palom lunged forward with his sword, no longer caring the Varkain was royalty.

Topeko had been ready to jump in between them when the fight broke out, but Sapora had already dodged the blow, and was stood behind Anahrik in half a heartbeat.

'Get away from me you damned snake!' Anahrik shouted, drawing a short dagger sheathed at his side and slashing at Sapora as quickly as he could. He hadn't even seen him move.

'There. Now you feel the fear, as you should. You are nothing but prey... Entertainment for me.' Sapora hissed, pupils dilated.

Topeko raised his hand, and a breath of wind filled the room. It was cool and calming, and almost sent Moroda to sleep then and there. 'I have once requested you cease. I will not do it again. Please, retire for the evening. My home is yours, as my honoured guests. Accept it and do not insult my offer.'

Amarah cackled and shook her head. 'Look what I've had to put up with, Topeko. I must be learning your patient ways to have not killed any of them so far.'

'Oh, Amarah, you need not be so violent,' Topeko shook his head, though he smiled. 'Do follow Andel, he will show you to your rooms,' he gestured to the hallway, where the child stood silently, patiently awaiting the others, unfazed by the aggression. 'I will bring your things.'

Moroda sleepily followed the child's steps, with Eryn close behind, stifling a yawn every second step. Andel stopped at a door varnished in pale blue, and gestured to the gold-ringed handle while looking at Moroda.

She reached forward and turned the handle, pushing the door open and revealing the room within. 'For us?' she asked the boy, who nodded in reply and bowed to her once again.

Moroda attempted to repeat the gesture as best she could, which seemed to permit Andel to leave—he skipped off down the corridor without so much as a hello or goodbye.

'Eryn, look at this,' Moroda called to her sister as the two entered the room. It had a low ceiling, lined with thick beams of wood to hold the fabric canopy above. Despite the fabric, the room was cool, with a washbasin and mirror and two large beds opposite. A large steel bathtub was in the far left corner, and a small wooden table sat in the centre of the room completed the furniture.

'I really thought blood was about to be spilled.' Eryn confessed, shaking her head.

Moroda nodded, and knew the Samolen magic had somehow calmed their tempers. She couldn't bear the thought of what might have happened without it. She hadn't realised how deeply the dislike between Ittallan and Varkain ran, and with Sapora a prince, no less. 'I can't thank Topeko enough for preventing that. I don't know whether Sapora was just teasing, or if he was going to attack Anahrik.'

'If he had, Palom would have killed him.'

'I'm not so sure. I don't think Palom would have caught him. He missed him just now.' Moroda shuddered at the speed Sapora could move when he chose. None of them would stand a chance of escaping if he wanted to attack. She closed her eyes and tried to push the thought out of her head.

Eryn took off her cloak and boots, shaking her head all the while. 'Well, we're here now. This is what you wanted, isn't it, Ro? To go to Berel? The sooner we get away from these people, the better. I knew this was going to be a bad idea.'

Their high, plush beds were fitted with white sheets trimmed with the same red fabric that seemed to fill the city, and Eryn wriggled into it.

Moroda was exhausted from both the trip and the Samolen magic. She had been scared when they were first warned of the Arillian scouts way back in Corhaven, and she had been uncomfortable on a number of occasions during their trip, but it was only then, stood in the entrance to Topeko's home, that she realised how dangerous these people were, and wondered whether it would be worth it. Her sister's words echoed in her mind, and she blamed herself for being naïve.

The troubling thoughts stayed with her as she got into the bed beside her sister. Sinking her head into the deep pillow and pulling the soft, warm duvet over her, she was asleep before she heard Eryn whisper goodnight.

Chapter Thirteen

When Moroda woke, she immediately wanted to return to sleep. Being awake meant she had to face Sapora and the others; sleeping allowed her to remain in the soft cosiness of the bed.

She could feel the heat of the room growing around her, and though the heavy fabric curtains blocked most of the desert sun, it emanated too much warmth to ignore. Moroda glanced at the other bed and found it empty, the sheets already made up. Confused, she sat up and found a handwritten note on the pillow.

Ro,

I woke earlier than you. Andel brought me down to breakfast. Come down when you're ready, but I think he has a knack of knowing, so don't be surprised if he's already at the door.

Still haven't got him to say anything.

Ryn

Smiling, Moroda dressed quickly, trying to push her fear of Sapora aside. Her mind swirled with memories of the confrontation between her companions the previous night, and she felt a flutter of icy panic in her chest as she remembered the fear she had felt last night. She closed her eyes and exhaled slowly. She was certain it wouldn't have come to blows, but she could not ignore the anger and nervousness Palom and Anahrik showed towards Sapora. Especially now they knew he was a prince.

She dressed quickly, breakfast on her mind, and left the room in search of her sister and food. When she reached the main room, she saw a long wooden table had been laid out with benches either side. Her travelling companions sat, eating and talking, with Topeko wandering among them, serving food and drink.

'Finally, you're up!' Eryn grinned, shimmying over on the bench to make room for her sister. 'I thought for a moment we'd have to come and wake you! It's almost midday.'

'I slept that long?' Moroda replied, looking along the table for Sapora.

'None of us have been up very long, really. Something about their magic really takes it out of you,' Morgen added, drinking deeply from his glass.

Black rice, bitter greens, and sweet, yellow tomatoes were piled high on her plate. The bowl beside her plate held grain with currants and mixed berries scattered in. Flat breads filled with dried fruits and covered with spices and oil sat next to every plate, and tall bottles of coloured glass stood between the dishes, the liquid within clear and sparkling.

'Please, Moroda, help yourself. I have offered to show your company around our city today, as you have asked to learn more of Berel. It is hot and there is much walking, so you should eat.' Topeko said, gesturing to her plate.

After struggling with rations on Khanna, the large meal was most welcome, and Moroda eagerly tucked in to her breakfast. She was sat between Eryn and Morgen, who both seemed perfectly at home, and there was no sign of Sapora, so she relaxed. Eating quickly, she watched her other companions; Palom and Anahrik were on the other side of the table, deep in conversation with Amarah; Kohl, however, was stood at the edge of the room, looking up at the full bookshelves which lined the walls.

She paused her breakfast to watch the Arillian who had, for the first time, removed both his cloak and hat. His wings sprouted from his shoulders, reaching almost to the floor, and the brown feathers grew in length and darkened closer to the tips.

Kohl ran his hand along the front of the bookshelf, his fingers barely touching the volumes stood before him. His fingertips left a light dusting of frost where they brushed the spines, and he withdrew his hand immediately.

'Do not worry, my friend,' Topeko said, remarking on Kohl's reaction. 'Those old tomes have been around for hundreds of years, enduring heat and dust and being moved around. They can withstand a little cold, too.'

The Arillian looked at him for a long moment, before nodding and stepping away, ruffling his wings slightly. Moroda tried not to stare—Kohl had kept his wings covered for their entire trip. Even when he flew, he wore his cloak. They all knew he was an Arillian, yet he kept himself covered. Moroda hadn't understood that—Palom and Anahrik changed form on a whim. Why couldn't Kohl be more open with who, and what, he was? She thought his wings were beautiful, and was jealous of the ability they gave him.

'You carry a dragon's stone. May I see it?'

Moroda glanced up as the scholar spoke again, still watching Kohl.

'You may,' Kohl nodded after considering Topeko's request another moment. He walked along the length of the table, past where Moroda sat, to where his cloak was folded, his hat resting on top. Reaching into the cloak pocket, Kohl withdrew the small jewel he had claimed from the dragon in Corhaven.

'Ah yes, it was a young one,' Topeko said, taking the stone from Kohl with both hands. He held it gently, brushing his fingers along the top of it. 'Yes, very young, and not, I think, in complete control of its actions.'

'I've never been chased by a dragon before,' Amarah said, watching Topeko and Kohl with narrowed eyes. 'I've shared the skies with them for years.'

Topeko shook his head, attention still on the stone. 'No, I wouldn't have thought so. No, this is that Arillian's doing.'

'What Arillian? Kohl didn't attack my ship.'

'No, no, of course not,' Topeko replied. 'Another... a more powerful Arillian who was in Corhaven at the time. He leads a growing army. I feel the power of the dragons move across Linaria with him.'

Moroda's half-finished plate was long forgotten, all her attention on the Samolen as he mentioned dragons.

Unprompted, Topeko continued, 'He has the power of compulsion. A rare gift, not seen for many generations. Hypnotism, they used to call it. A way of coercing others to your way of thinking without violence. Aciel has skill with it. Skill enhanced with every dragon's jewel he takes. This is a rare magic, and it is why his strength grows so quickly.'

'That's how he managed to take so many of the Imperial Guard at Niversai,' Morgen said. 'They'll all be under his compulsion, too?'

'Very likely. There are those who can fight it, of course. But when you are surrounded by warriors, I imagine you'd go along with your orders. Why risk your life otherwise? As you see, even dragons can succumb to it.' He held the jewel up to the light.

'Now you mention it, there were several small jewels in Rosecastle which disappeared during Aciel's visit,' Morgen said, looking skywards as he thought. 'I always thought they were just jewels, nothing special about them. I was blamed for allowing their theft! They're tiny, like smaller versions of the one Kohl has. If they were dragon stones... was that how he was able to control so many people that morning? The morning you stood up to him, Moroda? They enhanced his power?'

Moroda felt her skin redden, and cast her eyes to the floor, unwilling to add her part to the conversation. A feeling of dread began to well in the pit of her stomach. Aciel's words sickened her and yet no-one else seemed bothered. Were they succumbing to his compulsion? Was she able to fight it without realising?

Topeko sighed and turned to face the others. 'If one dragon burned Niversai to the ground in a single night, think how Linaria would fare if a hundred dragons laid siege to our world? This is a fate more deadly than the Arillian you fear. You told me you wished to understand the history of Berel and more of these dragon stones, so please, do come with me.'

Topeko's warning could not be ignored, and Moroda worried about the destruction the dragons could bring to the world if they had mind to. She certainly wanted to learn more—as much as she could.

Topeko opened the door to the city. 'Shall we?'

Amarah followed the scholar closely, still chewing on her flat bread, oil dripping down her hand. Intrigued, Moroda followed her lead, with Eryn and the others close behind. As she exited the building, she turned back to look at the table, and saw Sapora skulking out of the dark hallway to follow them. She held the door open as he approached, dropping her gaze on reflex. When she looked up, he was in line with the others, though she hadn't heard or felt him speed up.

If Moroda had thought Berel beautiful at night, it was staggering in the day. The cloudless sky above was a bright, rich blue, and the streets were a sandy yellow, soft in sunlight. The archways and bridges were brought to life by the same rich, green vines she had seen the previous evening, but the torch brackets were now empty.

Moroda had many questions she desperately wanted to ask, but unwilling to be seen as too forward or naïve, she remained quiet, relying on Topeko to answer her questions naturally as he spoke. She kept beside Eryn and Kohl, and found herself looking at Kohl's reaction to the scenery more than the scenery itself. He looked pained as he reached to touch the desert ivy which grew up many of the sandy buildings, never quite touching anything but longing to understand something he seemed afraid to ask.

'You may know Berel is divided into two halves—the old and new towns.' Topeko said, leading them through the streets and grabbing Moroda's attention again. Other Samolen going about their business took little notice of the group, and those who did were nothing but friendly. One or two inclined their heads slightly in a shallow bow, which Moroda was sure to return. They seemed used to visitors touring their old city, and she wondered how many thousands of people had walked these same streets and learned what they could of Linaria's past.

The scents of lavender and cinnamon ran through the streets, but no music played. She was a little disappointed—she had been looking forward to seeing and hearing more of their magic, but was careful not to let her disappointment show. Her mind wandered to Aciel and his compulsion, to the other dragons and their powers being taken, and what it meant for Linaria. With Niversai burned, she was certainly in no rush to return.

'We are in the new town,' Topeko continued, waving his arms to showcase their surroundings. 'Built over 600 years ago, it has been slowly expanding ever since we laid the first stone down. Each archway signifies a new section—you'll notice the further we walk, the older they appear, with cracked and faded brickwork, as we go towards the old town.

The old town is the very centre of Berel, in the middle of the lake, with the new town built around it as it expanded. The two are connected by one narrow bridge, as you can see,' he explained.

Moroda stopped and inspected the architecture around her.

Running her hands over the wall of one archway, she felt how coarse the material was—roughly hewn slabs of sandy brick carved straight from the desert. It had a sort of beauty to it, with its uneven edges and lack of symmetry.

'The old town houses the university, the altar where the dragon stones sit, and is surrounded by the lake, as well as our pillar defences... everything Berel is known for. It is our job to protect the wisdom of Linaria here, to teach it to our children and those who wish to learn, but above all, it is the job of the Samolen to maintain peace.' Topeko came to a stop at the bridge. It was marked by a huge archway and flanked by wide pillars on either side. Moroda looked up at the pillars and archway both, taking in the details of stone dragons carved into them, their wings half-folded, tails wrapping around the pillars before coming to rest on the ground.

She saw Amarah peering past where they stood, trying to look at the enormous stones embedded in the ground on the other side of the bridge—the island of the old town. Moroda recalled what the sky pirate had said of the size of the stones back in Corhaven, and she felt her heart flutter with sudden excitement.

'They say in ancient times, when Rhea created Linaria, she drew the first dragons from the sands Berel was built on, and then she drew the people.' Topeko said. 'They nested here, side-by-side, and the people grew in numbers very rapidly in this beautiful, fertile place. Soon, all of Linaria was covered with people, who spread across the land and sea, outnumbering dragons a hundred thousand to one. The country of Ranski was overwhelmed; we farmed and fished and hunted the land until nothing remained. We claimed dominion over the land and slaughtered those who got in our way. This angered the dragons, who had brought them life, and they turned furiously on Linaria, burning the earth with their breath and turning everything to dust, thusly destroying the first people.

Once Ranski was bereft of life, they stopped, their rage over. In time, the Samolen nomads returned to this sacred, yet violent place, and made it the centre of peace and prosperity, settling here, by the very source of all magic—the lake—and building Berel. Legends read the dragons will one day reduce all of Linaria to ash and sand; from dragon-flame begun, from dragon-flame undone.'

'Why would they? We've not done anything to hurt Linaria, have we?' Eryn asked.

'That is for the dragons to decide,' Topeko sighed. 'There is more to see in the old town. Perhaps more of your questions will be answered there,' his cheek jewels pulsed with colour as he led them across.

'The lake is below us,' he said, as the party grouped to the edge of the stone bridge to look into the blue depths below. 'It carries no life, no fish or plants, but it is immeasurably important to Linaria, and the Samolen. It is the root of... the deepest of our magic, its very essence.

I have shown many people my beautiful city over the years, but I am always overwhelmed when I reach this point. Words... cannot describe,' he shook his head. 'It is Rhea's breath, it is the source of all Linaria's energy and life, and it is the very blood of our world.'

'Very fascinating, Topeko,' Amarah huffed. 'Let's get to the actual source of power—those huge dragon stones!'

The scholar ignored Amarah's outburst and remained still and silent, looking to the lake as though seeing it for the very first time.

Moroda looked down on the blue waters with fascination and awe—her eyes grew wide and goose bumps rose along her arms at his words. She glanced up at the scholar and watched as his cheek jewels shone in the sunlight. 'Topeko? The jewels you have, is that... are those from this water too?' she asked.

'You are most perceptive, Moroda,' he smiled. 'Yes, the water is the source of all magic in Linaria, and we Samolen have condensed it into small jewels of power which we can call upon as we need,' he said, raising one hand to his jewels. 'It is as much a part of every Samolen as one's hands or feet.'

'How do you do that?' Eryn asked, also studying the jewels in Topeko's face.

'Who cares about your damned face! I want to know about these dragons and how to avoid going up in smoke when the next one turns on my ship!' Amarah demanded, folding her arms and walking ahead of the others.

Moroda shook her head, embarrassed by Amarah's brusque approach, 'I'm sorry about her.'

'I know Amarah and her ways quite well, I take no offense,' Topeko reassured them. 'It is a sore subject for her, I think.'

'A sore subject?' Palom interjected, having been listening quietly up until Amarah's outburst. 'How?'

'I do not think it my place to speak for her—but you wished

to know more of our jewels. Come. I will show you in the old town,' the Samolen chuckled, continuing along the bridge after Amarah.

Moroda's eyes lit up as she looked through the archway to the five dragon stones stood on a raised altar. They were almost eight feet tall and shone in the bright sunlight.

'You do know the real treasure when you see it.' Topeko smiled.

Moroda felt her cheeks flush a little, but continued through the archway and into the old town, joining Amarah who stood beneath the stones with a scowl on her face.

Kohl took to the wing as they arrived, sending out a chill breeze and raising dust from the ground. He perched on the archway by the bridge and crouched down, feathers rustling as he admired the stones from above.

Moroda couldn't help but smile, though Eryn scowled at the sudden behaviour.

'This is the university's central courtyard—in fact most of the old town is part of the university—and these stones are from very old, very powerful dragons, willingly sacrificed,' Topeko explained, looking up at the stones as he spoke. 'They were given to those who would not use their immeasurable power for destruction. It is why the Samolen do not partake in war and do not take sides in conflict. We are above all political involvement and we are all bound to this pledge.'

'Not to be used for destruction?' Sapora asked. 'What about your ability to create fire? Seems pretty destructive to me.'

Topeko shook his head, 'We are capable of creating fire,

water, weapons, yes, but not for war. Though permitted, our magic is strictly regulated.' The Samolen returned his attention to the huge stones, 'The last ancient dragon, a rare type called Sevastos, died and gave its stone long before the war, around 500 years ago. No Sevastos have been seen since, so they are thought by most to be gone. We only have the younger dragons now—ones as old as these haven't been seen in our lifetime.' He touched the stone nearest him with his palm and looked up at it. 'Throughout the world's history, only five Sevastos have willingly sacrificed themselves to Linarians, and we hold their stones here.'

'So these stones are the source of your magic?' Eryn asked, echoing what Topeko had mentioned earlier.

'Not the source—that's the lake—but they do enhance it immeasurably,' Topeko replied. 'These stones power our city, and strengthen our own magic, which comes directly from the lake.' With a wave of his hand, the torch mounted at the top of the archway burst into flame. A matching wave later, and a new flame appeared on the torch set to the left of the first.

'How do you do that?' Moroda asked, stunned at seeing the magic so close up.

'It's just energy,' Topeko replied. 'It is the simplest of all magic, our children learn this technique. I am moving the energy from here,' he gestured, 'to here. No more. Anyone can learn to do this, not just the Samolen. Everyone has innate magic. We are all of Rhea's creation.'

Amarah snorted in response.

'There are very few who do not,' Topeko coughed.

'Arillians, for example. They have another type of magic in them, a far more destructive one, giving them power and flight. But the source of all magic, all power in Linaria, is the dragons, and that comes from the lake here.'

'How so?' Morgen asked, curiosity piqued now talk had turned to dragons, the very thing which had triggered their journey to Berel.

'The heart-stone, the dragon's jewel, the soul, the crystal... it has a thousand names. It is the source of their fire, first and foremost.'

'I thought they were just beasts?' Palom questioned, his eyes resting on the tall stones set into the ground.

'Oh, they are. In the same way we are. But as descendants of Rhea's children, as gods in Linaria, their stone is their heart and soul and strength. It is this which gives them fire. Here in Berel, we have no need of engines for power, we use our own stones.' He gestured to his cheeks, where his three small gems protruded. 'But we have to take the water from the lake and condense it into our jewels to harness this strength. The dragons are born with this power already within them. It is innate. This is why many people have come to revere them as Gods, and Rhea, the oldest and most powerful of all dragons, the strongest Sevastos to have ever lived, as the Goddess, the creator of Linaria.'

Topeko closed his eyes and took several deep breaths before continuing. 'This Arillian, whose strength grows every day... I cannot see how his plan will work. Collecting the stones of drakes and dragons is all well and good, but he will turn them against his forces and bring their wrath to Linaria. This will not be so much a war of Aciel and his followers against the people of Linaria, I fear. It will be Arillians against the dragons… and, perhaps, the dragons will cast their flames on the remaining people and burn them all, reducing Linaria to nothing. If Aciel continues, this will surely be Linaria's fate.'

'Is that truly the source of Aciel's strength?' Palom questioned, 'slaying dragons and seizing their power?'

'I believe so,' Topeko nodded. 'As a scholar, it is my duty to learn all I can of this world, and all those who inhabit it. While I cannot claim to understand everything, I understand balance, and I understand dragons. Aciel has ruined the balance in favour of selfishly boosting his own power. It cannot continue.'

'But, how do we stop him?' Anahrik asked. 'His followers grow every day.'

Topeko sighed and shook his head, a little sparkle leaving his jewels. 'I wish I knew. Many of his followers are under his compulsion—perhaps if there was some way to lessen his power, his hold on his army would weaken and they'd break away? I don't know if there is a way. He seeks revenge for how Arillians were treated, for their losses in the war, their suffering. Perhaps it is time Linaria was cleansed of all the hate that has grown in its people.'

'The war is past. Arillians know they cannot stand against us a second time, we will crush them again, before the dragons even think about turning on Linaria,' Palom growled.

'But Palom, they're already turning! Look what happened to Niversai!' Morgen replied.

'No, it was under compulsion and did not act on its own,' Topeko countered. 'There is still time, yes, but how much is hard to say. But this Arillian…His people have been mistreated for generations, and he seeks to right the wrongs inflicted by the rest of the world.'

Amarah scoffed again and shook her head. 'Plenty of people have been mistreated—you see them building an army and trying to burn down half the world? Damn coward. I bet he'd lose in single combat, that's why he's hiding behind all these people who don't even want to follow him!'

'Amarah…' Topeko sighed.

'No. I've had enough of being pushed around. I do what I want. Always have done. Yes, I might help myself to some pickings, but I don't kill for fun like that snake does,' she glared at Sapora. 'If anything, you should get your subjects to take this Arillian on. Destroy each other. That'd do a world of good and rid Linaria of both you vermin.'

'Watch your tongue, thief.' Sapora said, stepping towards her.

'Ro, what are we going to do?' Eryn asked, shaking her head.

'Well, what can we do?' Morgen replied to her question. 'We need to stop this Arillian. And avoid any dragons, too,' he added.

'This Arillian… He may be weak alone. What Amarah says may be true,' Palom added.

'Exactly.' The sky pirate agreed.

'You're not going to fight him alone, Palom?' Anahrik asked, incredulous. 'I thought you just wanted to get back to Val Sharis.'

Palom nodded. 'Yes, I do. But there may be no Val Sharis left if he continues his rampage. Our cities can fall as easily as Niversai.'

'So there's no way of stopping his takeover?' Moroda asked, defeated.

'I do not know,' Topeko shook his head. 'Perhaps you should seek wisdom and enlist the help of an old dragon, one who may become Sevastos in years to come. Reach it before Aciel. His power greatens with each passing moment, and it will not be long before Linaria will truly be at war. But with key figureheads under compulsion, or left with small armies, it may be a short takeover.'

'An old dragon?' Moroda asked.

'There are many dragons in Val Sharis. Aciel has not yet touched my homeland, I would know, if he had,' Palom growled. 'If these old dragons, or even Sevastos, still live, there is where we will find them.'

'I agree,' Sapora said. 'The time of my birth approaches, and with winter, I shall ascend the throne of my own people. Returning across the Sea of Nami is the best next step.'

Topeko nodded, 'Then it is decided. Amarah, I will ensure your ship is repaired as swiftly as possible. In the meantime, you should rest and resupply before your journey across the ocean.'

'What if I don't want to fly you all there?' she folded her arms. 'Why should I risk Khanna or myself again hunting for these bloody beasts? You saw what the last one did to my ship, and apparently that was a young one!'

'Where else would you go?' Topeko asked gently. 'You told me you wished to cross the ocean and find a new crew. Why not take this group with you? Surely they can be of use on the ship?'

'A clean ship does not clothe, feed or arm me.'

'Then I shall pay on arrival to Taban Yul,' Sapora hissed. 'My sister, the princess, will have enough crowns for even your thirst, I think.'

Amarah glared at the Varkain. 'Food will be needed also, and weapons, and travelling gear.'

'All will be taken care of. Amarah, you are like a daughter to me. Do not spoil your chance to help something far greater than yourself because of selfishness.' Topeko hushed, one hand raised.

'Selfish indeed. You won't even save your own skin unless you profit,' Sapora replied. 'Shame you can't earn gold fairly—you could have wowed the crowds in Corhaven with a few of your Samolen magic tricks, but even that was beyond you.'

'What did you say, snake?'

Sapora's grin grew wider, exposing a few of his teeth. 'Just because you were incapable of learning magic does not mean you need to insult me every time I'm in your presence. I am a prince, and do not take kindly to threats.'

'How dare you!'

'It's very obvious. I now see where you developed that chip on your shoulder. You're a worthless magician. I did wonder how a low-class peasant knew one of the esteemed scholars in Berel.'

Amarah drew a small blade from her pocket and brandished it towards Sapora. 'One more word and I'll slit your throat!'

'Amarah, calm yourself,' Palom said, standing beside her. 'Ignore his words.'

Amarah's hand shook where she held the blade, and Moroda stepped towards her sister, her heart racing as she watched. The sky pirate's face was flushed, and she widened her stance, ready to attack.

'Looks like I've hit a nerve, thief. It explains that little scar on your cheek, too.' Sapora added.

Amarah lunged at the Varkain's next jibe, but was held firm by Palom's swift action. 'Let me GO!' Unable to wriggle out of Palom's grasp, she threw the blade at Sapora, who easily stepped aside as the weapon clattered to the floor. Moroda saw tears well up in Amarah's eyes, and she felt a swell of pity for their captain.

'Amarah…' Moroda said.

'I don't need your fucking pity. Get your hands OFF me, Palom!' Amarah yelled, still attempting to wriggle out of his hold and resorting to scratching the Ittallan before he relented. 'Fuck the lot of you!' she snapped, picking up the blade and storming off.

Moroda watched her race back across the bridge. She saw the smugness in Sapora's grin, and felt sickened. She was embarrassed for Amarah's inability to use magic, and hated Sapora for insulting her so very publicly. It was shameful. She felt a knot in her stomach and wanted to follow Amarah to make sure she was alright—but knew the pirate's pride would probably be injured even more if she did so. That, and she wasn't even sure she would be able to comfort her. She risked another glance at Sapora, wondering why he felt the need to attack her so much. The two had picked at each other constantly, but Sapora seemed to enjoy feeling superior.

Topeko seemed unflustered by their outburst, and was crouched in front of the nearest stone, set a little ways above him, on the altar. Moroda looked up at the stones as they glistened in the sunlight.

If they provided so much power, why couldn't Amarah use it? She hadn't even realised the pirate was a Samolen, but it made sense for her to be, it must have been why Topeko referred to her as a daughter.

She thought of the dragons they came from, and what an awesome sight they must have been alive. Moroda reached out to touch the side of the stone nearest her. She was amazed at how rough the edges were, almost sharp, and withdrew her hand swiftly as a tiny shard splintered off. 'Oh, sorry!' she gasped.

'Haha, its good luck from Rhea. Keep it. Perhaps it'll bring you good fortune,' Topeko smiled, getting back to his feet and brushing his robes down.

Moroda smiled and studied the thin shard for a moment, before pocketing it. As she looked up, she felt the atmosphere had shifted following Amarah's exit, and she suddenly felt uncomfortable—wanting to return to Topeko's house, where it was calm and safe.

'Will there be anything else?' Topeko asked.

'Weapons,' Palom said, raising his head. 'I would like to see the ones you hold which have been made from your dragon stones.

Are these real, or just stories?'

'Using dragon stone as an ore in weapons is very real. Several of these exist, still, and some are on display within the university. If you would like to see them, return to my home and I shall have some brought there. I feel a lot of frustration and emotion with this group, and perhaps a rest would be best.'

'Let's go, Anahrik,' Palom replied as his trading partner stepped up beside him.

Moroda felt relief at the words, and she looked to Eryn, who shared in her happiness, and the two linked arms. 'We'll stick close to Topeko while we're here. At least Sapora isn't interested in us while Amarah is such an easy target,' Eryn whispered as they made their way back across the bridge.

Moroda felt a lump in her throat but nodded—she didn't want anyone to be singled out, but she was quickly coming to realise that she could not control her world anymore, and all she needed to do was keep her promise to Eryn.

Chapter Fourteen

Moroda enjoyed the scholar's home; it was warm and comfortable, vast yet cosy. Andel catered to their every need without so much as a whisper, and she and Eryn had talked at length about his "silent service." Andel didn't seem at all put out by it, but Moroda knew it made Eryn a little uncomfortable. They had grown used to doing things for themselves, and it was a little unnerving to have a servant cater to them again. But she was not here on a leisure trip.

Her mind buzzed with questions—about compulsion, the dragons and their stones, and how to find them. The tour that morning, though brief, had opened her eyes and mind to the wonders of Linaria, and she yearned to understand more.

When she and Eryn returned to Topeko's home, she had found Amarah pacing the room, muttering and grunting to herself. She held a large tome in her arms and flicked impatiently through the pages, dust flying to the floor at her rough treatment. When Moroda and Eryn entered, Amarah slammed the book shut and threw it carelessly onto the table before storming off. Moroda found herself less and less shocked by the pirate's abrupt behaviour, and paid it no mind as she and Eryn sat at the table.

Kohl stood where he had been that morning, with his back to the room and his hands raised to the volumes lining the shelves. One was missing: the one Amarah had taken, but otherwise the scene was a mirror of earlier. She wondered why he was so interested in the books, what he hoped to find, but was not so bold as to ask outright.

Palom and Anahrik had been chatting non-stop on the walk back, blind and deaf to all but the intricacies of their conversation, each getting more animated the longer it went on. Palom had mentioned weapons after the battle with the dragon back in Burian Forest, and in the knowledge he would see one of them, he could not contain his excitement.

'Good to see him smiling again,' Eryn said, watching the Ittallan. 'Ever since they found out about Sapora, they've been so dark and angry.'

'I know exactly what you mean. At least Sapora is back to picking on Amarah instead of Anahrik. I don't think Palom liked that at all,' Moroda replied.

Morgen sat opposite them and leaned forward. 'He doesn't like Kohl either,' he whispered, glancing around the room. 'Best keep a close eye on him, too.'

'Kohl? Why?' Moroda raised her eyebrows. Kohl had given her and Eryn a warning when they'd been in Niversa, and for that, she trusted him.

'Well… you know,' he replied, scratching the back of his neck.

'No, we don't know. Why isn't he to be trusted? Has he said something?' Eryn asked, her voice assuming a disdainful tone.

'He's an Arillian, isn't he? Can't trust 'em.'

'Morgen! If it weren't for him—' Moroda began, but

Morgen shook his head.

'I know, I know. Just saying what Palom said is all.'

Topeko entered the room before Morgen had a chance to elaborate, clutching two longswords by their bejewelled hilts. His arrival hushed the room, and even Amarah stopped pacing to look up.

Palom stepped forward to greet the scholar, his eyes on the swords, Anahrik at his side. 'I…cannot thank you enough, Topeko,' Palom said, his voice cracking with emotion.

Topeko nodded, allowing the Ittallan to take the weapons off him. He reached into a pocket within his robes and withdrew a small book about the size of his hand; it was burnt around the edges and there was a large hole through the cover. 'This belonged to the last of the smiths who were able to imbue the weapons with such power. Treat it with care, please.'

Anahrik reached forward to claim the book with both hands, immediately studying it and turning it slowly, while Palom stood holding the weapons as gently as though they were newborn children.

Topeko wrung his hands and stepped away from the enraptured Ittallan, and caught Moroda's eye as he looked up. 'How are you feeling, child?' he crossed the room to where she stood to meet him, embracing her in a warm hug and enveloping her in his robes, before doing the same to Eryn. 'Are you both well? Are you hungry?'

'We're fine, thank you,' Moroda nodded, straightening her own clothes and sitting down.

'You're a delightful host, none of us have wanted for anything while we've been here. We're indebted to you,' Eryn said with a broad smile.

Moroda shivered as the air cooled around them at Kohl's approach.

'I wondered whether there was any way to break the compulsion Aciel holds on his... followers. There don't seem to be any books on it,' the Arillian admitted. Moroda was pleased to see him speaking freely among the others, he remained quiet for so long, though Morgen's words troubled her.

'If there was some way to break that, his forces would halve, or more! They might even turn on him. Do the job for us.' Amarah said, tapping her toe against the stone floor, arms folded.

'We're not out to kill him!' Moroda replied. 'These people will be confused, hurt, angry. Do they have any memory of their actions or is it more like going to sleep? It's such a cruel thing. They're... losing part of themselves. He's taking it from them. Time. Their hopes and dreams, memories and hearts.'

'You should be a poet,' Amarah smirked.

'But no, there is no way.' Kohl stated.

'Not as far as we know,' Topeko agreed, shaking his head. 'Those who can resist it seem to have the luck of the Goddess on their side, but there have been so few with compulsion and even fewer who can resist, it's not something there's a great deal of study on.'

'So your advice is, what, to avoid him?' Mogen asked.

'I think it would be for the best if you do.'

Morgen looked at Moroda and Eryn, before looking back at the scholar. 'But if he finds us? If one of his generals attacks and Anahrik misses their approach... How are we to defend ourselves?'

Topeko closed his eyes at the mention of an attack. Moroda had noticed every time talk turned to anything resembling aggression or combat, the scholar would turn away or pretend not to hear. Even now, his back was to Palom and Anahrik—no, his back was to the swords they held.

Topeko's shoulders sagged and he shook his head, 'Running and avoidance can only work for so long, if Linaria has come to war.'

Moroda wondered why he was deliberating all of a sudden. She stole a glance at her sister before looking back to Topeko.

'All magic comes from the lake, that's the essence of our power. Our stones are formed from its water, which enhances our own power. But it can be greatened further through the stones of the dragons. They are both made of the same essence. We call it Rhea's breath, the blood of Linaria, from which life itself derives. The Goddess is Rhea, the dragon mother and creator of our world. Our magic comes from her, and it has two forms; Ra and He, one to create, and one to destroy.

'Ra is for new life, it's why the traditional families add that as a prefix to their names when they have a child. It is also why the suffix He is used for a death or loss, or to signify mourning. We cannot use He, we only have access to Ra—the raw life and strength. It is this which gives us power,' Topeko said. 'Perhaps, before you leave, I can teach you a little of this power, to protect yourselves… should it come to a violent encounter.'

Moroda grinned in spite of herself, Topkeo's tone contained no joy or excitement, it was a necessary lesson, but one Moroda would be more than happy to learn. 'It would be an honour, Topeko,' she bowed her head.

'Of course, non-Samolen students at the university study a minimum of two years to learn as much as we are able to teach, and those of Samolen descent study far longer as their capabilities reach greater depths. Khanna will be repaired in a matter of days, so I will give you books of theory to study on your way. I shall teach the practical side of things as best I can in the little time we have.'

'I definitely want to learn,' Moroda said.

'And me,' Eryn agreed, taking her sister's hand and nodding to Topeko.

'Good. Morgen?'

'I can fight already. But I'll learn whatever I can from you, too.' Morgen said.

'Anyone else?' Topeko turned to the others.

'We'll listen to anything you have to say on these weapons,' Anahrik said, still clutching the book with both hands. 'To put the power of a dragon stone into a weapon… to make it stronger, awaken it, almost. It could be used against Aciel, couldn't it? Wouldn't that be our best attack?'

Topeko's cheek jewels pulsed again, and he smiled thinly at the Ittallan. 'The real legends are not imbuing this raw magic into weapons and armour, but harnessing the power of the stones themselves. That was the turning point in the war. The power you seek is not within your grasp, I'm afraid.'

Moroda saw Anahrik shrink away at his words, and understood then why Topeko, a man of peace, was so willing to give the bloodthirsty men the weapons they sought. It was not something they would be able to replicate. She thought to his words on using the stones themselves to turn the tide of war, and tilted her head to one side as she mulled it over. The stone itself, surely would do no greater damage than throwing a rock. But the powers within the stone… that was something quite different.

'Can the dragon's stones provide power not just to a weapon, but to a person, also? Like your stones from the lake do?' Moroda asked, wondering whether she was thinking along the right lines.

'Yes, they can,' Topeko nodded.

'Kohl took the power of a dragon.'

'Yes, the death of a dragon, even in self-defence, is always saddening. But, Kohl has not stolen any power for himself. Please, rest a while. I will be back momentarily.'

The Arillian nodded, but had drifted back to his silent ways following Topeko's confirmation of his thoughts on compulsion, and Moroda wished to steer the attention away from him lest he was uncomfortable. She didn't know what else to say on adding a dragon's stone to your own power; perhaps it was something she could learn from one of Topeko's books, and instead decided to think of more practical matters.

'We need to think of a way of finding one of these old dragons you spoke of earlier. There must be a way to find one.

Something that old and that powerful can't live unnoticed, surely?'

'We need to do what Palom said and go to Val Sharis,' Anahrik said, irritated. 'As soon as the ship is good to go, we need to cross the sea.'

Andel entered the room from the hallway as they sat down, bringing a large jug of iced water and a small wooden bowl full of fruit and cheeses, and Moroda was pleased with the distraction, when she was struck with a thought.

'I wonder, do you have any books I can read on the history of dragons? Or about the Sevastos?' Moroda asked the young apprentice. 'I should like to read them, if you do. Finding one is most important.'

With another bow, Andel turned and left the room.

'Have you ever been to Val Sharis?' Eryn asked Morgen, turning their attention to the trip looming ahead. 'You must have travelled a lot, in the Imperial Guard?'

Morgen shook his head, 'Actually, no. Up till now, I'd never even left Corhaven. I was born in a little village in the north of the country before I made the move to the capital. The king rarely leaves, and if he ever did, I'm probably too low in rank to go along as part of the escort. If they need more members of the guard on a warship or the like, I'd probably be called up.' He shrugged, finishing his drink and making a start on the cherries.

'Same as us, this is the furthest we've been from home,' Eryn admitted.

'Moroda. Eryn. Morgen,' Topeko called, entering his home and summoning them to the far side of the room. He held a large gold-covered chest, rubies set in the lid.

Moroda was on her feet at once. Was it another gift? Eryn touched her hand as she got up, and Moroda squeezed it gently.

Topeko placed it on the edge of the table and lifted the lid of the chest as the three approached, taking out a small vial of silvery-blue clear liquid. He held it up to the window and Moroda watched the refracted light dance around the walls of the room. Turning back to the chest, Topeko produced a small ring of dark silver, at which Anahrik hurried over, suddenly intrigued.

'I had a feeling you might want to see this,' Topeko smiled, as Palom, too, joined them. Amarah and Kohl remained in their corners of the room, and Sapora, whom up until that point Moroda hadn't even seen, seemed more interested in the food and drink Andel had produced. Moroda turned back to Topeko, and watched as he tipped a few drops of liquid into the small recess at the top of the ring. He then handed it to her, holding it flat so as not to spill any.

'Hold your thumb over the top, Moroda,' Topeko instructed, as he took out a second ring and repeated the process, handing it to Eryn when he was done. Eryn did as she was told, holding her thumb over the top to keep in the liquid, as Topeko took out a third and final ring, and gave it to Morgen once he was done.

Moroda's hand shook as she held her thumb over the small ring. She knew it was nerves more than anything else, and held her breath to calm her shakes.

Topeko flicked his wrists to drop his long robes down his arms, and reached out with both hands, taking Moroda's outstretched hand in his own. He crossed his thumbs over hers and closed his eyes, whispering something under his breath, an incantation too faint for Moroda to hear or understand. She felt the warmth from Topeko's hands spreading through her own; it grew hotter and hotter until she could hardly bear it, and when he finally released his hands, flames licked at her skin.

'Topeko!' she gasped, but the flames died in an instant, leaving the ring cool with the liquid solidified into a small, blue crystal, about half the size of the Samolen cheek jewels.

Moroda held the ring flat in her palm, a few wisps of smoke floating from it. 'This... is...?'

'Let me see,' Anahrik demanded, holding his hand open for her to give him the ring. Moroda handed it to him without question, and the young Ittallan inspected it closely, picking at the crystal and turning it in his hands.

'Put it on, Moroda. It will help,' Topeko said as he carried out the process on Eryn's ring, and then Morgen's.

'Is just a plain silver ring?' Palom asked, peering into Anahrik's hands, unimpressed with what he saw. 'With your stone in it.'

Once Anahrik and Palom were satisfied, Moroda took it back and slipped it on the index finger of her left hand. She caressed it with the thumb on her other hand, and felt quite out of place all of a sudden.

'I said earlier that we are all Rhea's creation. We all have access to the power she has given us, the energy, the same magic of the dragons. Ra,' Topeko said. 'The crystals in these rings will harness your inner power, and bring it forth to protect you when you call upon it. You will have little time to practice, so you must listen carefully, and do as I tell you, to be able to access it. The crystal is a conduit of your own abilities. Do not forget this. The stone does not hold the power. You do. The stone simply helps enhance it in useful ways. Do you understand?'

'Yes.' Eryn said, echoing Moroda's thoughts. 'Linaria is full of life. Of energy. Every living being is connected to it. So we can move flames, we can warm up or cool down, we can take the energy we have moved or drawn and shield ourselves from harm. It saps your own energy while you are learning, and you will have no time to build up your reserves, so you will find it draining very quickly. But, it will keep you safe, if you have no other options.'

He waved his arms, and caused all the torches around the room to ignite simultaneously, save one, right in front of where they stood. 'Raise your ring hand to one of the lit torches,' he instructed. 'Feel the heat, feel the vibration on the palm of your hand, allow your eyes to blur and see yourself and the flame as one stream of energy, of light.'

Moroda did as she was told, and although she could feel the heat from the fire, she struggled to see herself and it as one.

'Relax your arm, allow your elbow to bend. Your stone will identify your energy and the fire's energy when you do. When you have this knowledge, this connection, you can see it can be moved easily from one place to another, like tipping water from the jug into a cup.'

The three of them stood beside Topeko, arms outstretched. Moroda found her arm trembling with the effort to keep it held up, and Topeko's advice to relax was not helping. Amarah snorted again, eating the fruit and watching, but giving no encouragement.

Moroda could feel Sapora's eyes on her, and her stomach quivered at the sensation. Her body trembled, and she felt a chill along her back, though his gaze pierced right through her. It made her uneasy, and she shook her head, trying to regain focus. But the cold sensation on her back was hard to ignore, and she whipped around to see whether he was actually looking at her or imagining things.

It was a mistake.

The flame from her torch burst from the bracket and followed her hand movement, whirling around the room as it flew towards where Sapora sat. Moroda's eyes grew wide as she realised what was happening, and Sapora, reflexes on form, bolted out of the way as the chair he sat on burst into flame.

'Watch what you're doing, Moroda!'

Moroda blinked and jumped back—Sapora was stood right beside her, and he did not look pleased.

'I... I... I don't...'

'She is a student, Sapora. No harm was done,' Topeko said, extinguishing the flames with another wave.

'She is careless and stupid,' Sapora replied, glaring at Moroda, his nose almost touching hers. 'In my country you can be killed for attempting to harm royalty.'

'Then it is good thing we are not in your country,' Palom

said, brandishing one of Topeko's swords at the Varkain. 'It was accident. She is clever enough for being able to do this magic trick.'

'Sapora, I'm so sorry, I... I didn't mean,' Moroda said, overcome with fatigue and fear. 'I was trying to do as Topeko said, I...'

'All is well,' Topeko said, earning another scowl from Sapora. 'An excellent first attempt. It's a natural ability, but it isn't easy to harness. Eat, all of you. Then try again.'

'Without using me as a target.' Sapora added, skulking off to the other corner of the room, away from where they would be practicing.

Moroda and Eryn shared a look, and Moroda saw Morgen's concerned face, though the three of them were tired from their first attempt. The last thing she wanted to do was incite a battle, especially with Sapora, but she couldn't help but feel elated that she had used Samolen magic and hardly realised she had done so.

She sat down and gratefully took some of the fruit, her mind spinning with possibilities.

Andel returned carrying two large tomes, dusty from their time in storage, and a small parcel wrapped in soft leather. He bowed to Moroda, placing them on the table in front of her.

'Thank you,' Moroda said, immediately opening the cover of the first, and thumbing through the thick, dry pages. The small parcel rolled off the books and onto the table, the leather unravelling as it came to rest.

'What's this?' She picked up a small glass sphere—a red-brown feather curled up within. 'Andel?'

'I've never seen something like that before.' Morgen said, leaning close to the item as Moroda held it up. It was divided into two halves by a thin sliver of gold, and the feather within floated as she turned it in her hand.

'Isn't that an ereven sphere?' Eryn said. 'Andel—you've brought an ornament, too? Andel? We only need the books?'

Moroda looked around the room, but the young apprentice had disappeared, leaving them to study the tomes and the ereven sphere. 'Is it a gift for us, do you think? They're worth a lot of money. Could help finance the rest of the trip?'

'I don't know. Be careful, looks like it's delicate. You don't want to break it.' Morgen said, taking the small, glass ornament from Moroda and inspecting it closely.

'You definitely want to fly across the sea?' Eryn asked her sister, watching as Moroda turned back to one of the tomes, scanning the scrawling text and faint illustrations on the pages.

'Ro?' Eryn pressed again, causing her sister to glance up from the pages.

'You want to go home?'

Eryn remained quiet, dropping her gaze to the bowl of food on the table.

'We couldn't possibly return to Niversai now, not after what we've learned from Topeko,' Moroda said. 'You're not returning, Morgen, are you?'

The soldier shook his head, placing the ereven sphere on the table. 'Not yet. The guard is stretched thin, but one man won't make much difference. Besides, I can learn more on this trip, and hopefully come back with information that'll help. If war is coming, as Topeko predicts, I need to know all I can of Aciel, of the dragons, of anything that might be a threat to Corhaven, or Linaria itself.'

Moroda looked back to her sister. 'As he said. We may not be in the guard, but this is bigger than all of us. If we are to survive, we need to know more. Palom and Anahrik are doing that, and so are the others. Look at what we've just learned! We're here now, it's an opportunity, and we would be foolish not to take it, Ryn,' Moroda said. 'I'm scared to go back… to go back to the dark of not knowing, not being aware. With Aciel coming to Niversai, using his compulsion on the King, on the guard, on the townspeople… it scares me. The trip ahead of us scares me too… but less.'

Eryn sighed and shook her head.

'We're here for each other,' Moroda smiled, reaching her hand across the table to clutch Eryn's. 'Morgen is looking out for the group, so is Palom, and Anahrik…even Kohl, in his own way. Plus, Khanna will be fixed before we leave, so the journey will not be long at all.'

'If you want to learn more, why don't we just stay here and read?' Eryn suggested, pointing to the two heavy books on the table.

'These are histories. The real thing is out there. We need to find a dragon, an old one. Sapora will notify the armies of Val Sharis through his sister, their princess, when we arrive, so they'll be ready. Remember he told Amarah he'd pay?'

'Wow, you've really thought all of this through, haven't you?' Eryn asked, raising her eyebrows.

'I wouldn't trust Sapora,' Morgen added. 'Especially after

your close call just now. Best thing you can do is stick together. That's how the last war was won. We stood side by side with the Ittallan against the Arillian threat,' he explained. 'The majority of the battles took place in Val Sharis, the Ittallan homeland,' he continued. 'The Arillians were wild with power, and couldn't be controlled. So the King of Corhaven met with the Council of Val Sharis, and the Imperial Guard was formed of a collection of personal guard, mercenaries, and those who wanted to earn a bit of coin. It made all the difference, when it came to it.'

'They all banded together to fight a common enemy,' Moroda added. 'We're doing that too.' She stood up, raised her hand again, and practiced.

Chapter Fifteen

By the time Khanna was repaired and ready to fly, Topeko had filled the ship to bursting with food, drink, clothes, accessories, and books; more books than Moroda could ever read in a lifetime, and she was in awe at his generosity. She vowed to take the greatest care with them, especially as she would need them to practice her magic and further understand what she had learned in Berel.

The scholar had provided them with an intense lesson on their innate magic the evening before they set sail—using their rings as a tool to help harness and direct it, and both sisters were giddy with joy when they learned how to confidently move a flame from one side of the room to the other.

Moroda took to magic more naturally than her sister, but was humble enough not to point it out or boast. Morgen felt more comfortable with steel in his hand, and Moroda could understand that; after all, he'd been training with sword and shield for the past few years. Magic, that intangible power, felt unnatural in comparison.

Amarah had found the whole thing ludicrous, and if there were any unexpected fires on her ship, she'd hold the pair personally responsible and wouldn't hesitate to throw them overboard into the sea.

Moroda felt close to the scholar, and gave him a warm hug

in farewell before boarding Amarah's ship. She wanted nothing more than peace in Linaria, and she felt Topeko was the only one in their company who shared her views. He also had a lifetime's worth of knowledge and access to vast resources; he wasn't just guessing, he knew what he was talking about. He had opened her eyes to other cultures and to the rich history of Linaria and its people, as well as that of the dragons and their crystals, and of course, magic. It was an incredible gift, and Moroda felt doubly fortunate and very grateful for the experience.

'I feel more at home in Berel than Niversai, especially now.' She confided in Eryn before they left.

'I can see that! You're certainly in your element here, Ro. It's quaint. Pretty. There's a lot to learn… but it's too hot and dry, and nothing really goes on. It's too quiet.'

'Ah, but I love how simple it is. There's too much going on in the city. I feel overwhelmed there.'

'We'll come back.'

'We have to! I have so many of Topeko's books, I'll need to return them! I'm sure we can get an airship back here, even if it isn't with Amarah,' Moroda said, making her mind up. 'But first, we need to sort out the finding an old dragon… and Aciel.'

Anahrik flew out ahead, as had become his routine—he preferred knowing all that was around him, and with his incredible swiftness, could report back to alert the others before a threat had any chance of becoming a real danger.

Moroda enjoyed sitting up on deck and reading through Topeko's library of books while talking with Amarah. The sky pirate had not been keen on the idea at first, but when it came to discussing Khanna; how she worked, how fast she could fly, what scrapes she had managed to escape from, Amarah became much more animated and open to discussion. Moroda saw it as another opportunity to learn. It was wonderful to see which levers did what, how the sails and wings worked, and feel the wind through your fingers.

Their journey to the sea was short due to Khanna running at full speed, as Amarah was sure to remind them. Moroda was pleased with what they'd learned in Berel, and her own magic, though nothing like Topeko could do, did not fail to amaze her every time she tried something and found it worked. Her fears of Aciel and his growing army seemed to fade now she had unlocked secrets within herself she hadn't even known were there. The threat of dragon attacks, of Arillian scouts, of bandits, of Imperial soldiers... everything paled in comparison to her wonder she had at her fingertips.

Topeko had taught her how to move energy from one place to another, and she had gotten the hang of moving fire or igniting sticks of wood fairly quickly. He had also tried to teach her to create a shield, a field of energy that was barely visible, to protect herself from any attack. But that was taking a little more practice. Moving energy was one thing. Conjuring and holding it still and strong while under attack... that was something quite different.

Eryn had warned her about not letting the newfound power go to her head, and she tried, really, she did—but it felt she had been asleep her whole life and only now had opened her eyes. She knew this magic was not some toy to be played with, but a very real connection with Linaria, with Rhea, with everything living. How she wished she could simply be left to explore the depth of her powers and see what she could really do, given time to study at the university—or perhaps under Topeko himself, if he would have her.

Moroda skipped along the deck of the ship on the third day of their flight, fingers tracing the sides, feeling the warmth and strength of the engines below which kept them afloat. She had practiced moving power from one engine to another, much to Amarah's amazement, but after a few minutes she was told to leave Khanna out of her sorcery lest she did irreparable damage.

'Have to admit, I'm impressed with how fast you picked up Topeko's tricks,' Amarah said, though she did not look at Moroda when she spoke. Moroda glanced up from the page she was reading, but remained quiet. She could sense Amarah wanted to talk, but interrupting her would remove any chance of hearing what it was she had to say. 'Never had the knack for it myself. Sapora made that clear enough, didn't he? Bastard.'

'It's alright,' Moroda soothed.

Amarah snorted again and looked off to the side of her ship. 'Even those damn books didn't help. Letters all jump about on the page. Gave me a headache trying to hold them still, never mind read what they said!'

Moroda looked back at the page of the book she was reading. It was a book on compulsion, some wider reading to give her a break from the intense studying of magic.

"Beware sweet-speakers who say only words you wish to

hear. For this is the charming, venomous tongue of Apii Asi, the Heart-Eater, who lives an existence only for his selfish desires. As much as his words tell you he has your best interests at heart, they are spoken only to trick and fool you. He will use you, swallow your soul and leave you a poisoned husk without a second thought. While you provide some use to this creature, his seemingly nice nature will endure. As soon as he has no use for you, you will feel his true nature and be cast aside when he is done. You will be used as it suits the Heart-Eater."

'Of course everyone said I was stupid back then 'cause I couldn't read it, and 'cause I couldn't do the magic, either,' Amarah continued, laughing at herself. 'Even had that damn crystal in my cheek and it did fuck all.'

Moroda looked up again and remembered Sapora's jibe about the scar on Amarah's face. She marked her page and closed the book, giving Amarah her full attention.

'Cut it out myself when I left. Family didn't want anything to do with me if I couldn't do it. Why would they? I was worthless. Well, I was some half breed mixed blood piece of shit anyway. No better than the gutters I crawled to after I left.'

In spite of learning what she had about the sky pirate, Amarah seemed to bear her no ill will—her disdain seemed to last only for the other Samolen, and Sapora, which Moroda was grateful for. She understood what it was like to lose those you called friend, to have those you had always been there for turn their back on you the moment you needed help of your own. While her life had not been changed as dramatically as Amarah's, the feelings of broken trust and sorrow were there. Perhaps rage, too, buried somewhere deep. To be something you're not, having been told one thing your whole life for it all to change in a heartbeat... that was something Moroda could relate to.

'I'm self-taught of course,' Amarah admitted. The Sea of Nami had opened out before them through the night, and the small ship was surrounded by deep blue in all directions. The speed and smoothness of their flight out of Berel was far better than their flight into it, and they ate up the leagues effortlessly.

'When I made it to Corhaven, hah, I got there mostly stowing away on airships. My cabin was just the engine room. Loved the noise. Was amazed to see what all the machinery did, and what happened when I messed around with it.'

'You did what?' Moroda gasped.

'Nothing that bad,' Amarah waved her hand dismissively. 'Just opened up the casings, pulled at some of the pipes, you know. These were massive cruisers. They had five engines for each wing! Nothing like my little Khanna, here! Even if I completely wrecked one of the engines, it'd never fall out of the sky. More indestructible than warships, I tell you,' she cackled. 'But I got to know them. I got to know the different types of engines, the ones that purred, the ones that roared, the ones that just rattled,' she said. 'There's not a lot of variety.' She adjusted one of her sails slightly. 'So you have to customise. Build your own out of the best bits of others. That way the Imperial scum don't know what you can do, how fast you can go... You can always, always outrun them.'

'Why would they chase you? It isn't against the law to have

your own airship, surely?' Moroda questioned.

Amarah shook her head, 'No… but in owning one and flying one you have to pay for the thing, you have to get it maintained, especially if you take on passengers. You have to pay air tax. The Imperial Guard take it pretty seriously. A few petty thefts on your record and they shoot at you as soon as they spot you in the sky.'

Moroda had nothing to say in response, but her stomach turned at the thought of the ship coming under fire from the Imperial fleet.

'But, Khanna's plenty fast enough to get out of trouble. So don't you feel bad about me.' Amarah grinned.

'Dragons,' Palom called out from further along the deck. Moroda got to her feet and hurried over to him, looking skywards all the while. Raising one hand to shield her eyes from the sun, Moroda soon spotted several dark shapes circling several leagues above them.

The sight brought a smile to her face, not the grimace found upon her companions. It was nostalgia more than anything—the sight of dragons circling high above, lazily drifting on the wind was a common sight to Niversai, or at least it used to be when she was a child. Bar the dragon that had attacked Niversai, she'd not seen one for a few years. From everything Palom and Anahrik had said, they were still common in the Ittallan homeland.

These dragons were too far away to make out their features, but when the sun caught their scales, Moroda caught glimpses of rusty red-orange, pale yellowish-gold and mottled brown. As her gaze broadened, trying to count them, more and more seemed to appear: their wings spread wide, catching the warm thermals to keep their vast forms aloft. She had counted twenty seven before the wind gently pushed them away, towards the east.

'Probably going to Val Sharis,' Palom said, his arms folded and eyes narrowed as he scowled up at the sky. 'Better there than on us. This ship struggled with one dragon, what in Rhea's name would we do against whole tribe?'

'Khanna would be fine, stop complaining.' Amarah said, watching as the dragons allowed the wind to carry them away from the ship.

'I don't think all dragons are like that young drake,' Moroda said, still trying to keep the dragons in sight as they drifted farther and farther away. 'I've seen hundreds of dragons over the years—that was the only one to have behaved in that way. Even Topeko said he was under compulsion. The Arillians must not have crossed the sea yet. We're safe.'

Palom did not respond, and instead kept his gaze fixed on the sky above. Clouds were beginning to drift closer together and thicken. 'Best get under cover,' he said, eyeing the rolling clouds as the wind picked up.

Moroda nodded and made her way back to the covered area by Amarah. They had encountered rains and wind on their journey so far, but thanks to the scouting eyes of Anahrik and Kohl, along with Amarah's knowledge of the skies, they had never been caught in a storm.

Moroda picked up her book again, and continued to read.

Perhaps there was something in understanding compulsion that could be used to fight against it, or free those trapped within it. There was little else she could do of use during their flight other than read and practice, and practicing sapped her strength and left her exhausted after only a few minutes.

"If you escape the Heart-Eater, he will be angry. He will call you names. He will lash out at you. He will attempt to hurt you overtly, now his cover is blown. In the same breath, he will seduce his next victim with lies, with deceit, with pretend pain. He will not speak of the terrors he inflicted on you. He will not tell anyone of the ugly truth of what he is because his reputation is built on portraying himself as the victim, drawing in his quarry closer, until they cannot escape, and he can feast."

Moroda sighed, shivering a little in the cool air, heart heavy at the words on the page. 'You've lost your light-step," Palom commented. "Not the right word, I think... but... you look now like you carry the pain of the world in your heart. This should not be the case, Moroda.'

Moroda laughed at his jest. She knew he was concerned, and felt embarrassed. 'Don't be silly, Palom,' she brushed it off. 'I'm tired studying Topeko's books, that's all. They're quite draining!'

'I know. You have spent whole flight reading and practicing. You should rest—even I cannot spend more than a few hours in my true form, and that is most natural of all things to me.'

'You're right, I've been working too hard, I'll—'

'Moroda?'

She had been hit by a wave of something not unlike water, but not quite as tangible. Goosebumps rose on her arms and legs as she faced the source, peering out into the cloudy sky and the sea which raged below. Thunder rolled out low and slow in the distance. 'A storm?'

'Something more than that,' Morgen said, joining the two of them. Eryn trailed behind him, her eyes wide. 'It's too much too quick. Arillians again, I'll wager.'

Moroda shivered as she felt the wave of energy pulse again, the air thick around her as it touched her skin. 'Better tell Amarah,' she murmured, staring into the distance. 'Is it him…?'

It did not take long for the rain to fall, and when it came, it was relentless. The wind, which had been nothing more than a calm, cool breeze for most of the day, turned vicious, picking up and buffeting those on deck. It caught the rain and threw it into their faces like a thousand tiny needles as thunder echoed off the waves in the distance.

'What the hell is going on,' Amarah said, angrily wiping rainwater off her face and trying to peer into the darkening sky. 'Whoever heard of rain rolling round that fast and that heavy?'

Khanna trembled in the wind, and the low lighting in the cabin and out on deck was snuffed out in an instant, plunging the airship and her crew into darkness.

Moroda wrapped her thick travelling cloak around herself, trying to keep the biting wind out as she stood up. 'It's daytime. Why is it so dark? Are the Arillian storms that strong? Is this what Anahrik meant when he spoke of them before?'

'This is not right. This is definitely not right,' Amarah said, opening her sails and wings fully, her right hand hovering over Khanna's weapons. Her eyes darted all around, looking for the hidden enemy.

Morgen drew his sword and looked at the skies above, his grip tight despite his sweaty palms. 'Palom, what do you think?'

'Arillians,' the Ittallan muttered, all warmth gone from his tone. 'Kohl is coming in, look above.'

Rain continued to fall as Kohl landed, and another roll of thunder echoed from afar, louder than before. 'It's another scouting party, on an airship,' he said, holding his hat down in the wind as it picked up around him. 'Amarah, if we change course, they won't see us. It's too dark and the storms they've brought with them have reduced visibility. No need to get involved.'

'But they're crossing the sea, too, aren't they?' Moroda asked. 'We'll just run into them again when we reach Val Sharis...even if we get there before them, it won't be long before they start attacking the cities! Doing what they did in Niversai?'

'Amarah, this ship has weapons, does it not?' Palom turned to their captain.

'How many Arillians are there? If it's one or two, maybe we can pick them off in a sneak attack,' Amarah replied, raising the altitude of Khanna.

'I'm not afraid to fight them,' Palom replied.

'Good, go and fight them, then. I'm not risking my ship a second time. Kohl, is it a warship they're on?'

'It... may be.'

'There you are. Khanna has no chance. I'd rather fly away and avoid any chance of a fight, to be honest.'

'Kohl, what do you know about this?' Palom asked, turning to him.

The Arillian walked out onto deck, where he was besieged by the full assault of wind and water. 'Flight may be preferable to fighting in this instance. Everyone should get below deck while Amarah steers the ship away.'

The words caused Palom to growl. Moroda knew he had been distrustful of the Arillian as Morgen had told her and Eryn. It seemed Palom he did not approve of the knowledge Kohl held of the enemy—knowledge he seldom shared with the group.

'I'm not going below,' Palom replied, defiant. 'I do not run from a threat, not these damned Arillians. I want to see what I'm up against.'

Kohl looked at the Ittallan and shook his head. 'The weather will only get worse as we get closer. Visibility, whatever we have of it, will be reduced to almost nothing.'

'Amarah can't go below deck. I can be her eyes at the front. And I want to see what your colleagues are up to.'

'Colleagues?'

'You're all family aren't you? You know a great deal about them. I need to see for myself what you're up to—you're not going below, are you?'

'What exactly are you accusing me of? If it weren't for me, you'd all have been captured by those scouts back in Corhaven!'

'Palom, Kohl, please!' Moroda cried, rushing over to them,

one arm pressed against her cheeks to keep the worst of the wind and rain from her eyes.

Palom's hands were beginning to ball into fists at the prospect of a fight, and Kohl responded by flexing the lower feathers on his wings.

'We may have a very real fight on our hands, please don't fight one other,' Moroda tried, pulling at Palom's arm, but she had no chance to say anything else to quell the fighting; a flash of lightning ripped through the darkening sky, bringing with it a shockwave that shook Khanna and brought everyone on deck to their knees.

The wind picked up again and slammed into Khanna, dropping the ship's altitude and throwing it towards the sea.

'Good thing we can fly! I would not want to be a sea vessel in those waters,' Morgen said, holding onto the side of the ship tightly as he peered over the edge. Moroda knew he did not wish to break up a scuffle between Palom and Kohl, and silently thanked him for his distraction.

Amarah scoffed. She knew better than to fly too low and risk her lower propellers or sails getting waterlogged. But if she flew any higher, she risked losing all her sails to the vicious winds.

The wind continued to buffet Khanna, the sea writhed under its influence, and Kohl watched as maelstrom began to form off the port side. 'Amarah—get a little higher! We might be pulled in!'

Palom, too, had seen the developing vortex, and watched as it grew larger, its downdraft strong. 'Another one!' he said, as a second vortex began to form on the ship's other side.

'It's Jato,' Kohl spat, watching the first maelstrom grow in both size and power. 'She's the only one able to create a storm like this.'

'Jato?' Palom asked.

'Aciel's second-in-command,' Kohl said, stepping away from the sides of Khanna and shaking his head. 'It means Aciel himself is likely to be with her.'

Palom followed the Arillian's movements, but it did not detract from the anger he felt. 'When this is over, you're going to tell us everything you know about Aciel and his followers. If we had known he had this person to create this storm, we'd not have come this way!' Fangs began to grow in his mouth as Palom's fury took over, his body transforming involuntarily.

'Don't you dare attack me, Ittallan,' Kohl retorted, trying to keep one eye on the sky and one eye on the tiger beginning to appear in front of him.

Palom's response was inaudible as he completed his transformation, fur bristling and fangs bared towards Kohl.

'Kohl, do they even know we're here? Or are they just creating this weather for a damned laugh?' Amarah called to the Arillian, ignoring the tiger taking up most of her deck.

'It… is not completely foolhardy to suggest Jato is causing this for the pleasure of it. I suspect a storm as large as this would be seen from the coast of Val Sharis—it would be just like her to announce her arrival on the new continent with such a display of strength. Or perhaps there are other trading ships crossing the sea, and they're her intended target; Khanna is simply caught up in the size of her attack. It seems a lot of trouble to go to for just one, lone ship, especially one as small as Khanna,' Kohl said. 'Whether it's a direct attack on us or not, Jato's storm is not something to be caught in. I can't say for certain whether Khanna will come out completely unscathed, but there's a good chance she will, if we are not her target.'

Thunder continued to rumble, drowning out Palom's roars, and yet Kohl had not seen anything in the sky since the pack of dragons from earlier. Still, he was on edge, kept in an anxious state of fight or flight.

'Well? Kohl?' Amarah asked again, forcing Khanna to stay under her control as she was buffeted about by the winds.

Kohl relaxed his stance, and to his delight, Palom relaxed also. 'You may be right, Amarah. We should lie low. Wait it out.'

'Hah. Stealth is my specialty,' she replied. 'Palom snap out of it. Need you alert without Anahrik's eyes. Dragons above, where has that falcon gone?'

Though Palom was unable to speak in his true form, Moroda knew he could understand others well enough. He prowled the deck of the ship, peering intensely over the side into the darkness with his more sensitive vision. He remained there for a long moment before relenting.

When he transformed again, he remained on one knee, shaking slightly from having exerted so much energy for no good reason. 'I could see them, in the distance,' he said, once he had his breath back. 'An Arillian with black wings, stood on big merchant ship. Few leagues ahead of us. She...the Arillian had raised her hands. I saw two water cyclones in the sea, moving at her will. There were others stood with her.'

'It seems she wants to make an entrance to Val Sharis. If she's focussing on that, she'll be too busy to notice us,' Kohl explained. 'But we came close.'

Moroda felt a sudden chill as Sapora slunk into view, having emerged from his cabin below deck. Eryn grabbed her hand when she noticed his arrival, and Moroda squeezed her sister's fingers in response.

'I think you are missing a most valuable opportunity, my sky thief,' he said, joining the rest of the party. 'An opportunity to obtain something most valuable and precious.'

Amarah huffed and shook her head.

'I thought you pirates were always on the lookout for treasure?'

'Sapora, what are you on about?'

'The Arillians are hunting dragons, no? To steal their power for themselves? Their power has grown quickly. They have a way to track down the dragons. A way that we could use…'

'An ereven sphere?' Moroda asked, catching on. She reached into her pocket and took out the sphere Andel had given her in Berel. Everything clicked into place at once—she had been too fascinated by magic to realise he had fulfilled her exact request of finding a dragon.

'Very astute,' Sapora grinned, baring his pointed teeth.

'But…this one…is an ornament?' Moroda breathed.

Amarah glanced up. 'Stole a bagful of those when I left

Ranski. The Goldstones in Corhaven love them. Sold them four crowns a piece.'

Moroda looked up as Amarah spoke, then back to the sphere. It was an ornament, true, and a valuable one. But it was an imitation of the real thing. A real way of tracking down a dragon using the tail feather of a phoenix; creatures which nested near dragon lairs and followed dragons through their territory, keen for flame and ash. Her heart raced as it sunk in.

'They will be crossing the sea, looking for more powerful dragons. We've discovered their method of hunting them down. Stealing the real sphere from them would have two benefits—they would no longer be able to find the dragons, and we would have the means to,' Sapora said. 'Now. If only we knew someone who was good at stealing valuables…'

To her side, Palom growled, but said nothing, and Moroda felt he was right to be hesitant.

'I don't steal from people who usually fight back,' Amarah laughed, dismissing the idea at once.

'Well, they won't fight back if I come along, too,' Sapora continued, his smile broadening.

'I don't want you to kill anyone!' Moroda said, her throat tightening that the thought. She had been halfway to thinking his plan was a good one, considering they had no other options, but his delight in causing death and destruction made her reconsider.

Amarah narrowed her eyes and mulled over the idea for a few, long moments. 'If they found us, they'd kill us, you know that, don't you?'

Moroda lowered her gaze, half-distracted by the wave of power emanating from the Arillian's ship. The thunder did not relent, and with every roll, she felt herself getting dizzier.

'Stealing the sphere will make Aciel lose his edge—he certainly won't be able to add to his power—but it'll turn his attention onto Khanna,' Amarah continued, one hand on her hip. 'But we've got the cover of darkness, of the brewing storm, and Khanna at full speed.'

Moroda could tell Amarah was convinced already. Anything else she said was an act to save face in agreeing with Sapora. 'I'll ensure their attention is not on Khanna,' Sapora pressed.

'Amarah, I do not think this idea is good...there will be other ereven spheres in Val Sharis, I am sure. We can buy one there,' Palom said, stepping forward.

'Yes, buying... that'll cost a few crowns though, a real one will. Or there's this one right here,' Amarah replied. 'And it takes away the enemy's eyes.'

Sapora's grin grew until Moroda was sure his face would split in two, and she shivered, shaking her head and looking away from him. She knew what Amarah's decision was, and she didn't know what game Sapora was playing, but his happiness made her uncomfortable.

'Let me come with you,' she said, blurting out a spontaneous idea without any thought. Immediately, the group's focus was on her. 'I just... I don't want anything to happen, bad to happen... and... I... I want to go and make sure everything is alright. I can help, too, if you need me… The magic, I mean.'

'Ro, what are you thinking? You want to go on the Arillian ship with those two?' Eryn gasped.

'Fine by me. Darkness is upon us, we should move, now,' Sapora said, turning to walk down to the front of the deck.

'Hold on a minute,' Amarah barked. 'I haven't got a plan yet!'

'I will go on first and ensure you are not met with resistance. You will locate and take the sphere, and then return to this ship. We'll continue our journey, with the Arillians none-the-wiser.'

'That's not what I meant…Palom, Kohl, how many Arillians are there? Could either of you see? Morgen, you'll have to hold onto Khanna for me while I'm off ship. You do remember what I told you about flying? You and Eryn are always hanging about while I tell Moroda what's what.'

Morgen shuffled forward at mention of his name, his face pink. Kohl straightened out his cloak and hat and followed Sapora onto the deck, with Amarah and the others close behind.

'I could not see, but I should think the ship carries Imperial soldiers,' Kohl replied. 'Arillians have no need of airships. But Aciel has a large following now, who cannot fly.'

'Hmm, didn't wanna hear that. Those ships can hold a hundred soldiers,' Amarah said, both hands on her hips. 'But I don't see as we have a choice. This is an opportunity, as our friend pointed out. It's too good to pass up. Plus it gives our snake a chance to make himself useful for once.'

Moroda swallowed, nervous about whether she was making a foolhardy choice, but she couldn't let those two alone on the ship, she just couldn't. As Khanna approached the ship, she exhaled, readying herself to join Amarah's ranks of thieves.

Chapter Sixteen

'Alright. My heist, my rules,' Amarah said, keeping the airship low as she approached Jato's ship. 'I'll get as close as I can to the ship, and keep behind and above them. Morgen will hold Khanna while Sapora gets on the rear deck of the ship. We'll use the steps on Khanna's side to get down. Me and Moroda wait while Sapora deals with any guards. Once the coast is clear, we join him, get the sphere, and get back onto Khanna. Kohl will be our eyes, and Anahrik, too, in case we have to get off sharpish. Everyone clear?'

Eryn shook her head, the only one in a crowd of agreement, but Amarah ignored her and continued on course. 'Ro, I don't like this at all. This is far too much. This is above anything we were going to do.'

'Please try to understand, Ryn,' Moroda said, giving Eryn a hug in a feeble attempt to reassure her. 'Without this sphere we've no chance of finding a powerful dragon in Val Sharis. Without the dragon, we've no chance of stopping Aciel.'

'I do understand! But I don't know why it must be you who goes. I don't know why anyone of us here needs to get involved. Can't we just go home?' Tears formed in the corners of her eyes as she pleaded. 'You're going onto an enemy ship, Aciel himself could be on board! You'll have a pirate and a Varkain at your side!'

'I've got the Samolen magic, don't forget. I can look after

myself.'

Eryn shook her head, words choking in her throat.

Moroda took her gently by the hand and led her to where Morgen stood by Amarah and the wheel of Khanna. 'Please, Ryn, I'm scared enough as it is.'

'Then don't go! Stay on the ship with me!'

Moroda could feel tears threatening at her sister's pleas, but she had to remain firm. 'Morgen, please may you look after her? Ryn, I promise I'll stay safe, I promise it'll be worth it.'

'Ro!'

Moroda remained with Eryn, hugging her and soothing her as best she could. Amarah manoeuvred the ship into position, and stepped away from the wheel, leaving Morgen in charge.

Eryn's sniffles were muffled as she cried into Moroda's shoulder, and slowly grew quiet.

'Ro, I'm so scared,' Eryn said, not lifting her head from Moroda's shoulder.

'I am too. But… I'm less scared when I do something. I have the power to do something. You do, too. We've never had that before. It'll be alright.'

'Moroda! We're going. Now!' Amarah called from the front of the deck.

'Ryn, you're safe here,' Morgen interjected. 'For all their flaws, Amarah and Sapora can handle themselves if Moroda needs back up.'

'See? I'll be just fine.' Moroda smiled, stepping back when Eryn lifted her head. Her heart ached at seeing her sister so distraught, but she understood why. 'We won't be long,' she said, holding Eryn's hands and bringing them up to her lips in a kiss of reassurance.

Unable to stall any longer, Moroda turned and hurried along the deck, forcing her way through the torrential rain before clambering onto the steps carved into Khanna's side. Amarah was halfway down already, scythe in hand, and held her position. Jato's warship flew below them, just a short drop beneath the edge of the steps. Moroda could hear the waves far below, but it was too dark to see the water, and Jato's ship took up too much room. The rushing wind drowned out all noise, and Moroda's ears rang. She shook her head and focussed on her footing.

'Sapora's on board. We wait here,' Amarah shouted above the wind.

Moroda shifted her weight and braced herself against the force of the wind, flexing her fingers. She could feel the now familiar warmth through her hand from the crystal, and it calmed her. In truth, she was almost as scared as Eryn, but she knew what had to be done. She was sick of being bullied and pushed around, of reacting to every threat. This was something proactive. This was a decision she had made to try and regain some control over her life. She took a deep breath and looked down at the warship, wondering if it was indeed the right course of action to regain control. But it was too late to have a change of heart.

Sapora stepped into view, eyes and teeth glinting in the darkness. 'He's back,' Moroda said. 'Do we go?'

'We go.' Amarah nodded, grabbing Moroda's hand as they

shuffled down the last few steps. Moroda had no time to ready herself when Amarah leapt, the pair of them dropping onto the deck below like stones. Moroda felt the wind knocked out of her as they landed; she did not have the grace of Sapora or the skill of Amarah, but she had Amarah to brace against, which helped a little. She let out a muffled squeak as she landed, but Amarah did not reprimand her for the noise.

'Follow me. Keep up. Keep quiet.' The pirate let go of Moroda's hand and darted after Sapora as he disappeared below deck.

Moroda ignored the stinging pain in her feet and shins, and hobbled after Amarah as quickly as she could. Her breathing was laboured, and she worried half the ship would hear her pounding heart as she scurried along the wide corridors.

While she'd been aboard luxury cruiseships before, it was the first time she'd been on a warship. It dwarfed Khanna, and after a minute of darting down corridors and glancing into empty rooms, she felt the whole place was a maze. The warship had several decks, with others towering above the rear one they had landed on, and could have easily held a thousand people. For a ship of this size, it was eerily deserted, and Moroda began to tap into her crystal to feel whether anyone was close by. People gave off a warm buzz the closer she got to their energy, and her crystal remained largely quiet.

She and Amarah followed Sapora once he had scouted ahead and checked rooms and corridors were clear for them. Outside, the storm continued to rage, so even Moroda's less-than stealthy footsteps wouldn't be heard above the raging wind. It gave her a little comfort.

After checking everything on the rear half of the ship's floor and finding nothing, they followed Sapora up a flight of stairs. Light flickered at the top of the stairway, and Moroda felt the heat from her crystal signifying life. 'Amarah, there are people up there.' She said, slowing down. The two dropped back as Sapora raced ahead. He came back a moment later and nodded, before continuing.

When Moroda reached the top of the stairs, she saw three members of the Imperial Guard lying on the floor in various states of undress, no doubt due to the late hour. She could see a little blood on the arm of one of the men, but as she walked closer, she gasped. At first glance they seemed unharmed, but on closer inspection, it was clear they no longer lived.

She shuddered and stopped where she was, bile rising in the back of her throat. Her crystal had cooled once again, confirming the result of Sapora's swift attack. 'Please, as few casualties as possible.'

'Hah, Sapora chooses to kill them, you know. His venom can paralyse as well as kill. Depends on the strength of the bite.' Amarah crouched by the bodies and rummaged through their pockets.

'No…That's not true? A bite always means death,' Moroda replied, watching as Amarah callously moved to the next body. 'Why would he choose to kill them if he didn't have to? I know you don't like Sapora, but surely…' She tried not to look at the bodies, half-fooling herself they were in a deep sleep and ignoring the truth from her crystal. She felt dizzy and sick and wanted to run away.

Amarah paused and looked at her, rolling up the bottom of her breeches to expose her left calf. 'These scars? A Varkain attack.' She traced a finger along her discoloured skin, thin white scars ribboning her leg. 'I'll tell you about that another time, if it makes you feel better.' She stood up, pocketed the florins and crowns she had stolen, and made for the door Sapora had slipped through. 'Keep up, Moroda. You wanted to come.'

Moroda swallowed and took another breath, Eryn's words echoing in her mind. She reminded herself why she was on board, that getting the sphere was the most important thing. That everything else could be looked past, even senseless killing. With a shudder, she followed Amarah through the door and onto the corridor.

'Dammit, he's disappeared,' Amarah said, glancing up and down. The corridor stretched out to their left and right, with doors on both sides. 'Which way, which way,' she muttered, before choosing to go left and heading off. 'This way.'

Amarah opened the nearest door and entered one of the ship's cabins.

'Who're you?' A man bellowed, whirling around at their entrance. He was fully armed and armoured in Imperial livery.

Amarah raised her scythe and he lunged at her with his drawn sword.

She ducked out of the way and countered with her own weapon, bringing up the scythe to his helm. The guard reacted instinctively, blocking her attack with a round, metal shield attached to his vambrace, and the clang of steel-on-steel rippled through the air.

'Amarah!' Moroda raised her hand and felt the energy in the guard's swing, the heat in his blade. She held it there a moment, unable to move it as she would a flame, but the moment was all Amarah needed to retaliate.

Bringing her scythe across his face, Amarah knocked him to the ground. Spinning the weapon in her hand, she lunged again, but Moroda sapped the strength from her attack, and Amarah sank to her knees, her scythe falling from her grasp. 'What do you think you're doing?!'

'No more casualties. Sapora will kill too many. I don't want that number added to!' Moroda replied, defiant.

'You're far too forgiving. It'll get you killed if you don't change!'

Moroda lowered her head and said nothing. She didn't understand why she had to change, why she seemed to be so wrong for who she was. She was doing her best, wasn't it enough?

'We're getting close if there are guards here.' Amarah said, ignoring the guard as he bled on the floor. His body shook, but he was alive. She got to her feet and picked up her scythe, giving Moroda a long look as her strength returned, before exiting the cabin.

'I think we need to carry on this way,' Moroda said, one hand on her ring. She could feel the heat surge every time she faced a certain direction. 'Something is definitely along here. More people could mean the sphere?' She took over the lead and hurried along as quickly as she dared.

Her heart continued to pound as the heat began to rise, and they hurried up another flight of stairs. She did not know how many decks the warship had, but she felt what they sought was on the top deck, as high as they could go. The crystal really did tap into her own abilities; she likened it to having her own intuition intensified and enhanced a hundred-fold. She could hear and feel the murmur of chatter behind closed doors as they passed rooms and private cabins, and everything grew louder and busier the closer they got.

She followed the crystal, trusting in its power as much as she had trusted Topeko, even though it was still unfamiliar. As they reached a crossroads, Amarah grabbed her by the shoulder and pulled her down behind a large barrel of supplies. 'Ssh, people coming.' She crouched down beside her.

Moroda frowned, turning her ring this way and that, but she couldn't feel anything. She was about to argue when she heard footsteps approaching, and ducked back down, peeking round the barrel when they passed. Two Arillians wandered past, and Moroda's heart sank. Topeko had said something about Arillians having their own branch of magic, not unlike the Ittallan, so they could not use the Samolen crystals. Was that why she was unable to tell when they were near? She could only pick up on others like herself? Those from Corhaven?

As she mulled it over, the Arillians stopped a short way down the corridor, laughing and joking with one another. She and Amarah watched them closely, but remained hidden, waiting for an opportunity to get past them without being seen.

'Won't be long before we're in Val Sharis and the fun

begins.' One said; he was tall, like Kohl, but far surer of himself in the way he stood, and more strongly built.

'Tell me about it. Glad we finally cleaned up the last of those damned merchant ships,' his companion replied, rolling his shoulders and yawning. 'Took over a year to pick them all off! How many times do they need to be told? The sky belongs to us!'

Moroda felt a cold, numb sensation in the pit of her stomach. Her brain struggled to keep up with what he was saying, much less try to understand it.

'Aciel's got everything under control. Won't be long before the land is ours again, too,' the tall one said, smiling. 'Now the last of them Goldstones are gone.'

Moroda trembled. Her body was cold, the sensation in her stomach spreading to her limbs and snuffing out the heat in her hand from the crystal. Amarah said something to her, she thought, but she couldn't quite hear what it was. The Arillian's words rang. Those damned merchant ships. Were they…? Could they have been the ones responsible for her father's death? For the lack of information she and Eryn had? For the black flag hung above their home while they were in mourning? For the loss of her friends, her lifestyle, her value?

Moroda blinked and went numb. She was dimly aware her cheeks were wet, but she did nothing about it. Both hands were raised, fingers tingling, as a surge of emotion welled up within her, and fire rippled across the barrel she stood behind, along the walls, ceiling, and floor—to where the Arillians stood.

'Moroda!'

She whirled round to see Amarah screaming, flames burning all around where they crouched.

'Amarah... I...' she stammered, her body returning to normal after her outburst, and her vision clearing.

'Go, go, go! Up the stairs!'

Moroda shook her head and ran after the pirate, her flames distracting the Arillians while they ascended to the next deck. 'Amarah, I don't know what came over me,' she said, following the pirate onto the next floor. She put her hand to her chest. The cold sensation had passed, but she felt shaky.

'Perfect diversion, Moroda. Don't be silly,' Amarah replied, tapping the blade of her scythe against the floor as she continued. 'Could have done with a bit less fire, though. That'll spread quickly. Most of the ship is wood. Won't be long before it hits an engine or two.'

Moroda inhaled and shook her head. She had hardly realised her actions. She just felt rage flowing through her body at the realisation of what she heard. Her father had not been killed in an unfortunate accident. He had been targeted because he was a merchant, because he was in what they thought were their skies. She was sickened. She sniffed, trying to refocus. She felt the heat from her crystal and the heat from the flames below, and tried to blink away the tears rolling down her face.

As they rounded another corner, the ship lurched underneath them, and Moroda steadied herself against the wall.

'Let's hope that's one of the auxiliary engines,' Amarah said, glancing back.

A moment later, the ship juddered again, and the power went out, plunging them into darkness. 'Hope ain't on our side, then,' Amarah sighed.

'Will the ship crash?' Moroda asked, her eyes wide. 'I'm so sorry!'

'Nah, big old lump like this'll drop a bit. Worst case it'll still float in water. Arillians on board, don't forget. If they wanna, they'll keep something in the air.'

Moroda felt a wave of panic wash over her. Amarah headed off again, and she followed, stumbling along in the semi-darkness, the orange glow of the flames partially lighting things from below. Moroda squinted as she followed Amarah, the low, flickering light making it harder to focus than if they'd been in pure darkness.

'Watch your step,' Amarah said, just as Moroda tripped over a thick coil of rope. Moroda braced with her hands as she slammed into the floor, adding to the pain in her legs from her earlier rough landing.

'I said watch your step,' Amarah said, scowling at her.

'Sorry.' Moroda kicked the rope out of the way as she clambered to her feet. 'Stupid thing.' As she shoved it away, the light caught it, and she realised it was not a length of rope at all. It was snakeskin. 'A...Amarah!'

The skin moved, and Moroda jumped back.

'It's Sapora,' Amarah said, tutting. 'Harder to see a snake in darkness.'

The snakeskin was very dark grey, almost black, and about two foot wide, but the light was too low for Moroda to make out any details. She watched him move, silent, and shuddered at the thought of how many he had killed that night, and how many he would go on to kill.

'Moroda. The top deck is here. It's the captain's cabin! Reckon our treasure is locked away in there. No sign of this Jato yet. Dragons above, we've been lucky,' Amarah said, clambering up the final set of stairs and stepping out into the open.

Moroda followed, and the wind buffeted her at once, but she was grateful for the fresh air and open space. She pulled the hood of her cloak up against the bite of the wind, and felt the familiar waves of energy as Arillians flew wildly above. Flames licked at one end of the deck, and she felt the ship slowly dropping from the sky. They didn't have much time.

She saw Amarah a short way ahead, crouched by a door to the captain's quarters. The sphere was there. She knew it. The crystal knew it. She nodded, and Amarah picked the lock, breaking in just as Moroda caught up. She clenched her fists, ready to take on whatever danger was inside. She knew she was capable, the flames from the corridor were proof of that, she just needed to have faith in herself, and control it.

The door swung open quietly, odd, amidst the chaos outside, and as Moroda stepped into the large cabin, she immediately saw him. The Arillian sat in the corner of the well-furnished cabin, eyes closed, arms folded, hunched forward slightly, a staff of ebony laid on his lap. The sphere was mounted on a stand behind the wheel of the ship, completely unassuming for those who did not know what it was: a pale orb nestled among rich mahogany. Moroda's crystal burned so hot she could barely stand it. She held her breath again, unsure whether to speak, watching as Amarah approached.

Amarah took a few steps, then paused, before daring another few paces, watching Aciel all the while. Moroda could hear nothing but her blood pumping in her ears and the wind rushing outside, and Aciel seemed completely unaware of their sudden intrusion.

She clasped her hands together as Amarah grew closer to the sphere, praying they wouldn't be seen.

'Amarah.'

Moroda gasped as Aciel opened his eyes and looked at the sky pirate. Amarah froze and looked back at him, tightening her grip on her scythe, ready if it came to blows.

'What are you doing?'

Moroda glanced fervently between the two, almost hopping from one foot to the other. Where was Sapora when you needed him?

'The sphere,' Amarah said.

'Is not yours to take, is it?' Aciel replied.

'No.'

'Then leave it and go back where you came from.'

'Amarah!' Moroda called, rushing forward to Amarah's side. 'Don't listen! We need the sphere!'

'You.' The cool voice was now speaking to her. Moroda ignored the chill and grabbed Amarah, shaking her, trying to get her away.

'Moroda.'

His words filled her, drowning out the wind, fear and panic.

He didn't speak another word, but her mind rang with his voice, his whispers, and the intense, biting cold that came with it. She held her head in her hands, trying to drown out his words. 'No!'

Anger filled her once again, and with it, the heat from her crystal. She forced back his coldness, his voice, and pushed forward with her own fire. An explosion rang out, blinding her for a moment, and when she could see again, the captain's cabin was alight, rain pouring in from the gaping hole in the roof.

'Moroda! Grab it and run!' Amarah called, bringing her back to the present. She had her scythe held across Aciel as she fought to hold him down. His skin and hair were pale, almost translucent white, and he wore similarly light robes, even white gloves, but his wings were deep black. His eyes, though, almost glowed silver-white, and she could not see his pupils.

But her fire had broken the compulsion he pushed onto her and Amarah, and Moroda didn't need telling twice. She darted forward and grabbed the ereven sphere with both hands. Immediately, she felt the power and energy of the dragons she sought, and those Aciel had claimed for himself. Sickness replaced the heat and cold, and she now realised the difference between the imitation ornament Andel had provided her, and the real thing. She took several deep breaths, trying to will the overwhelming nausea away, then lowered her head and raced out of the cabin. She heard a clatter behind her followed by a shriek, and Amarah bolted out behind her.

'I've got it! Where's Khanna?' Moroda called, running out onto the open deck. The few Arillians and guards that Sapora had yet to deal with were out on deck, panicking and trying to douse the flames which ripped through the wooden hull. There was another shockwave as another engine took to flame, and the ship let out a mighty groan. In the smoke, wind, rain, and darkness, Moroda could not spy Amarah's ship, and she fought to keep her rising panic at bay.

'Moroda.'

Aciel's voice somehow penetrated her mind in spite of the noise around her. She held the sphere to her chest and ran to the front of the deck, hoping to get away from him. Scared of what he might make her do. Sweat loosened her grip on the sphere, and it took all her efforts to hold it safe.

She knew Palom had seen Jato on the deck somewhere, but so far there'd been no signs of Arillians save those in the air, and they were preoccupied with stopping the flames.

'Where are you going? Stop running. There's nowhere to run. You cannot run.'

Moroda halted, unwilling to continue running. She felt her body cool at his words, and the nausea swelled again.

'Turn around.'

'I don't want to,' she whimpered, turning around.

'That's okay. Hold out your hand.'

She could see him walking towards her, his feathered wings in contrast to his hair, his staff held in his left hand. He did not hurry, he did not seem to mind the raging fires surrounding him—he simply allowed his energy to extinguish the flames. A few gusts of strong wind pushed them away, and another reduced them to little more than embers. As he grew closer, she could see a large jewel mounted to the top of his cane. She tried to think what it might be, but her mind was hazy, filled only with the thought of not running.

Moroda could hear Aciel's thoughts, could just touch on them, as he instructed her. She shivered where she stood, and held out her hand, the sphere held tightly.

'Step forward.'

Moroda shook her head, but her body obeyed, and she took a step toward him. 'Please don't.'

'Hush. It's okay.'

She watched as he fluttered his wings, loose black feathers floating to the burnt deck underfoot. She saw each step, felt every wave of energy, and couldn't move. She knew he was looking at her, but refused to meet his gaze, forcing her eyes shut. Her crystal still buzzed on her hand, a tiny speck of warmth in the coldness she felt.

Moroda tried to focus on the heat of the crystal and drown out Aciel's whispers. She wouldn't give up the sphere. Not after everything they went through. Not after she promised Eryn she'd come back safe. 'It's not okay!'

'Yes it is. Step forward. Give me back what you stole. You're above stealing, aren't you? Why are you travelling with thieves and criminals, Goldstone?'

His words stung, but all Moroda could feel was sickness and shame.

'You cannot get away without being punished. What would be a suitable punishment for you? Murderers are beheaded, aren't they?'

'I'm not a murderer.'

'You are a murderer. You're killing my followers.'

Tears streamed down her face. He was so close to her now.

'Give me back what you stole, murderer.'

She trembled and flattened her hand, the sphere rocking slightly in her palm. Her hood had fallen back in the wind, and the rain soaked through her hair and clothes. She forced her eyes to stay shut, and knew he was standing right in front of her. She felt him take the sphere from her hand, and could do nothing about it.

'Murderers don't deserve to live. Turn around and walk. If the fall does not kill you, you will drown.'

Unable to resist any longer, Moroda opened her eyes and looked into his. Now he was at arm's length, she saw his eyes were the softest green, not silver, and were utterly devoid of emotion. A new wave of fear washed over her, and she turned around.

'Walk.'

The command struck her like a hammer. Her knees shook in defiance, but he had control of her body. She took a few steps, and the instruction lingered in her mind. She tried to think of her companions, of Amarah and Sapora, but her thoughts were dim, like ghosts in her mind, and disappeared before she could make them concrete. She took a few more steps.

Eryn flashed in her mind; her sweet, strong, loving sister, who was far cleverer than she, more positive, too, and who had said from the start the journey was a mistake. Moroda closed her eyes and stepped off the side of the warship.

Chapter Seventeen

Moroda tried to scream, but her breath caught in her throat. The wind rushed as she fell, the dark, angry sea rose to meet her, and towers of swirling water raged closeby. Aciel had let go of the mental hold on her body the moment she stepped off the ship, so her mind was once again clear, but fear gripped her as she plummeted.

Half a second later, she felt cold hands gripping her waist, feathers all around her as she stopped falling and began to rise. 'Kohl?'

She closed her eyes, dizzy, and only when she was laid down on solid ground did she open her eyes. But she was not safe on Khanna. Fires burned around her. She struggled to breathe and coughed, shaking her head as she tried to get her bearings. When she looked up at the Arillian who had caught her, Moroda realised it was not Kohl.

'You... you're Jato?!'

'Pleased to meet you, my dear.' Jato flexed her wings, a cruel smile on her lips as she leered at Moroda. She had dark blonde hair and grey eyes, and her wings were dark brown. She wore a little armour and had a small, oblong shield fixed to her right arm.

'But... Aciel said...'

Jato laughed, a hollow noise without true mirth. 'Aciel lets me play games.' She raised her hand and spread her palm wide;

blue-white light flickered from her skin, and she struck Moroda with a ball of lightning. The force of the strike sent Moroda flying, and she rolled over when she landed. Her hood covered her head, and her skin smoked from the intense heat of Jato's attack. Moroda cried, tears streaming down her cheeks as her body convulsed.

Moroda heard Jato's laugh and attempted to push herself onto her hands and knees, to get away, but was struck by the next ball of lightning before she managed it.

'Pathetic. No fight in you. Not so fun, anymore, is it? Where's your fire now? You killed my followers. Destroyed my airship! Perhaps I should have let Aciel make you kill yourself.'

Moroda coughed again, her hands burning as her entire body stung. She rolled over and lay flat on her back, and her breathing quickened as panic took over. She was exhausted from using magic, Aciel's compulsion, and the intense fear, and she was unable to get up or defend herself. She screamed as Jato attacked her with balls and bolts of lightning. The corners of her vision dimmed as the pain took hold of her, her body spasming under the intensity.

'Oh I wonder whether you'll cook first? Or ignite? You like the fire, don't you?' Jato taunted, sending forth another strike.

Moroda shivered as she was buffeted about, her cloak singed. 'Please…'

Jato laughed, taking to the air and diving back down, striking Moroda with lightning bolts with renwered intensity. 'Aciel has already won. You've thrown your life away by coming here. So silly.'

Another strike.

'Looks like you're almost done, now!'

Another. Another.

'Get up, Moroda.'

Moroda opened her eyes, only half-conscious. 'Sapora…?'

'Best you stay alive,' he said, no longer in his snake form. The Varkain's back was to her, his focus on Jato.

Moroda tried to respond, but she had no voice left. She shuddered, weak from the attacks.

'Hmph. A Varkain? Dirty worm. Shouldn't you be buried in the ground somewhere?' Jato said, while Moroda feebly attempted to get to her feet. 'You're a disease on Linaria. Disgusting creature. Aciel plans to get rid of your kind after the Ittallan are gone. Maybe we'll strike the holes to your underground cities and burn you in your tunnels while you sleep. Just you wait.'

Sapora didn't reply, but Moroda watched as he drew two scimitars from his sleeves and widened his stance. She fought to get onto her hands and knees, and shuffled backwards, trying to get her breath back, eyes locked on Sapora and Jato as they squared up to one another. She was in too much pain to register anything other than the attacks had stopped, and she needed to get away.

After several long breaths, she managed to get to her feet, but stumbled over her cloak. It was bunched up around her boots and she was sent sprawling again. Laying where she was, Moroda tried to will away the pain that stung her arms and face, and looked around her. The warship was chaos; fire and smoke mixed in with the heavy clouds above, torrential rain, and rolls of thunder. She tried to work out the best way to escape, but could not see Khanna in the darkness.

She was dizzy, exhausted, and her body shivered as it recovered from the lightning strikes. She heard the clang of weapon against shield, and turned to look over her shoulder. Sapora danced around Jato, his movements too quick for her to register at first, while the Arillian took to the wing and countered with her electrical attacks. Moroda felt the waves of energy pulse around her, and couldn't get to her feet. Turning away, she crawled along the deck of the warship, avoiding smoking debris, no plan in mind other than to get as far away from the fighting as she could.

'Moroda.'

She winced, closing her eyes as she heard his voice. How had he spotted her in the utter confusion? She continued to crawl. It was painfully slow, but she had no strength to get to her feet.

'Stop, Moroda. You're too tired.'

She paused where she was, unsure whether she was giving in to her own exhaustion, or his compulsion again. Behind her, explosions sounded and she felt, more than heard, the crack of thunder from Jato's lightning. She opened her eyes and looked at Aciel from where she lay, waiting for the inevitable command. He was some thirty paces away, stable and calm amidst the turmoil, almost a halo of light surrounding him as he fended off the rain and fires with his own energy. Aciel was scarier than Sapora, Moroda realised. He was evil. Whatever his reasons for starting this war, whatever his justifications, they fell flat. He was a true horror she had never known existed.

Tears streamed down her cheeks and mixed with blood,

rain, and soot. She shivered as he grew closer. Twenty paces. Ten. Five.

A shadow passed overhead, dimming Aciel's light for a heartbeat. Moroda sniffed and shook her head, still trembling. In her peripheral vision, she saw the glint of silver, but didn't understand what it meant until the white of Aciel turned crimson as Amarah's scythe bit deep into his arm.

Everything happened all at once. Aciel's hold on her disappeared, filling her with sudden warmth and clarity, blood gushed from the open wound on his forearm as Amarah's weapon sliced through to bone, and she pulled her scythe back, yanking him to the ground, and Jato's scream somewhere behind her drowned out all else.

Amarah fell onto Aciel as he hit the ground, her blade still pressed deep into him. Blood pooled beneath them. Moroda shivered, pushing herself up onto her hands and knees, too afraid and too shocked to do anything else. She saw the sky pirate wrestle with the Arillian leader—despite his grievous wound, he could fight back. He sent off waves of electrical energy through the air, the thunder deafening at such close range, but Amarah's gaze was steely. She endured his attacks and held his good arm with one boot, her other knee in his back, pushing him to the ground; one hand held her weapon while the other grasped at his neck and chest.

Jato's attacks joined the fray, and Moroda saw her swoop towards the two. Sapora was faster, though, and he slashed at her with his weapons, seeing she did not reach Aciel and Amarah. Blood continued to spill and the chaos shifted into panic.

Moroda hyperventilated, panic gripping her as well as her surroundings. The waves of Aciel and Jato's attacks threatened to shove her backwards, and she couldn't understand how Amarah and Sapora could fight them. Movement from above caught her eye as a falcon dived towards Aciel. She knew it must have been Anahrik, but couldn't speak or move to acknowledge him or signal that she needed help.

Anahrik's talons slashed at Aciel, but he and Amarah were both thrown off as the Arillian screamed and lightning blazed in all directions from his body. The shockwave shook the ship, and Moroda, Amarah, Anahrik, and Sapora were hurled backwards.

Shuddering, Moroda's head span from the impact of her landing, and she felt a wave of familiar cool wind as another Arillian descended. Even in the midst of panic, she recognised the hat and cloak of Kohl, and watched as he grabbed Amarah from the deck and flew off with her. Moroda struggled to her feet, her confidence renewed at the sight of Kohl.

She was shaky on her feet, and backed away as Jato rushed to Aciel's side. Even in the darkness and confusion, Moroda could see the river of crimson growing. Where once she would have pitied him, she had a flash of a dark thought: perhaps he deserved it.

Jato looked up as Moroda stood there, and raised her hand to her once again. Moroda ducked, but the lightning strike did not come; Sapora had darted to Jato's side, his claws holding the Arillian still as he bit into her shoulder. She shivered, watching as Jato went limp at once, and as the warship finally crashed into the sea, she dropped to her knees.

Moroda lay flat on her back, unable to muster any more strength. She was overwhelmed by the smell of sea salt, blood, and burning, and saw a familiar wide-brimmed brown hat as her world went dark.

*

Moroda felt a weight on her chest and muffled voices all around her. She struggled to listen, unable to make any sense of what she heard, and when she opened her eyes, she found she was wrapped up in Palom's large cloak. Amarah was stood some way in front of her, by the wheel of Khanna, and further ahead, Kohl stood out on deck, Sapora beside him. She looked to her right, and saw Palom sat on a crate, his arms folded. To her left, Eryn and Morgen sat beside her; everyone seemed lost in their own thoughts.

Kohl walked towards the covered area, and Moroda took a deep breath, trying to control her shivering. 'I fear Aciel's power may have increased more than can be stopped.' He sat down beside Palom. Moroda didn't move, and closed her eyes again, listening. 'I feel this is perhaps a fruitless quest. Jato's power has grown since I last saw her. Aciel is also stronger, despite Amarah's attack. We've no chance. Once we arrive in Val Sharis, how long before he decides to wipe out all non-Arillians?'

'Kohl don't be foolish,' Sapora hissed. 'When the snows start, I'll succeed my father as King. I'm not giving up my birth-right for a rogue Arillian who wants to play war. Princess Isa will have more information for us when we reach the capital.'

'We're in this too deep,' Amarah said, from a little way ahead. 'Give up now after everything we've been through? Don't be stupid. Besides, after that stunt, they'll be after us. Arillians seem to do revenge well. Hold grudges a long while! At least Aciel and Jato will be out of action for a bit. Buy us some time. We got the sphere though. Excellent bit of thievery if I do say so myself.'

Moroda's heart pounded at Amarah's words.

'Indeed, if you say so.' Kohl said.

'Shame I didn't kill her, too,' Sapora said. 'I'm out of practice, it seems.'

'Sapora, if it weren't for you, they'd be after us right now. You were merciful to Jato, intentional or not. It's a good thing.'

'Kohl you are talking rubbish,' Palom said. 'Whole lot of them deserve to burn.'

Moroda couldn't feign sleep any longer. 'No they don't. They're not in control of their actions. It's Aciel who's to blame.'

'Moroda!' Eryn gasped, jumping to her feet and leaning forward to hug her sister.

Kohl nodded to Moroda and walked away, his shoulders sagging. She watched the Arillian take to the sky from the relative warmth of the covered deck. The nausea she felt on the warship had not completely passed, and she regretted her decision to go on the ship. But she had learned invaluable information and Amarah had succeeded in stealing the sphere. For all his terror, Aciel's edge would be lost. 'Eryn, I'm so sorry.'

'Oh Ro, its okay! I'm so glad you're back with us now. We were so worried.'

'I've not... been asleep long, have I?'

'Not even an hour,' Morgen said, standing up. 'Dragons

above, I can't imagine what you went through on there.' 'But...the ereven sphere? We have it? It was worth it?' 'We have it, Ro,' Eryn said, still hugging her. 'We so nearly lost you, though. What were you thinking, going on that ship?'

'Ryn, I'm sorry for scaring you.'

Eryn finally let go and kneeled beside where Moroda lay. Her eyes were red, but there were no fresh tears. Moroda smiled at her and wriggled her hands free of the cloak to hold her cheek for a moment. She took Eryn's hands in hers and kissed them. 'I promise I'll never do anything again without you agreeing. It was selfish of me.'

'How do you feel, Moroda?' Palom asked from her other side.

She shook her head. 'I'm okay. A bit sick, but no pain.' It was a white lie, but nothing she felt now was comparable to Jato's attacks. She'd never been stabbed, but imagined the hot, blinding pain to be similar. 'Is Amarah okay? And you, Sapora? Thank you for what you did there. You saved me.'

'Both fine,' Sapora replied. Moroda met his gaze and nodded, no longer feeling a chill when she looked at him. One of the Varkain, the supposed cruellest creatures to walk Linaria, had stepped in to defend her against Jato. She saw him in a new light, especially after being under Aciel's control.

'I'm pleased to hear that. What about Anahrik?' 'Everyone is okay, Moroda. Anahrik is scouting as always, but skies are clear to Val Sharis now,' Palom answered.

'You sure you're okay, Ro? It's okay if you aren't! I

mean… Aciel… He…' Eryn said, looking away as she trailed off. 'I don't know how anyone can fight that. He… his voice… it's inside you,' Moroda said, shaking her head. 'I don't know how Amarah managed to attack him!' She suddenly remembered the blood. 'Amarah, you cut his arm off!'

The sky pirate cackled. 'Good weapons of yours, Palom. Not quite. But I made sure he knew not to mess with me. Don't think that Jato took too kindly to it, though.'

'And… now we have the ereven sphere, his way of finding dragons… he's weaker now?' Moroda asked.

'Damned good heist. Not had a bloody one in years. Sign us up for round two.'

'Pay her no mind,' Eryn whispered, leaning close. 'She was just as worried about you as I was when Kohl brought you on board. She had a go at him for bringing her back first instead of you.'

'Amarah…' Moroda breathed, smiling. She shuffled where she lay, sitting upright, her nausea beginning to fade. She exhaled slowly, trying to soothe her stomach and ignore the fresh, painful memories of her experience on the ship. It was no easy matter, and she was so tired that she risked drifting off to sleep.

'I should have gone,' Palom said, rousing her.

'Palom?'

'I said I would look after you. If I was there then maybe you would not… you should not have been hurt, Moroda.'

'It's okay. Perhaps I shouldn't have gone myself,' Moroda replied.

'No. You were doing what you had to do. This I understand.

But to see you hurting…'

'Thank you, Palom. I'm okay,' she said. 'If one of the Arillians had spotted Khanna and attacked, you'd have been here to look after Eryn.'

Palom gave her a pained look, but nodded.

'Amarah keeps saying how she's the best pirate in the skies,' Eryn continued, keeping her voice low. 'Stole the most valuable treasure from the most dangerous ship, and walked away unscathed.'

'She is good,' Moroda said.

'What?'

'Defended herself and me against the guards we found, took Aciel on one-on-one, and I have to say she came out better. I couldn't even stand against him.'

'Ro…'

'You are not as weak as you think,' Sapora said. Moroda and Eryn both looked up. 'You do not need Palom's protection, nor anyone's. You spoke out against Aciel in Niversai. You freed a Varkain from prison. You willingly entered the enemy's warship, and did not give up against that freak Arillian. Perhaps if you stopped whinging, you'd see that.'

Moroda swallowed, her cheeks flushed. She could not deny Sapora's words, even if the bite in his voice embarrassed her. Everything he said had been true, though not all of her intentions were noble. She had given in to Aciel's compulsion, but it was true she had not given up, if there was a difference. She had tried to fight, tried to get away, however futile a fight it was.

'Gotta agree with him,' Morgen said. 'For someone with no battle experience, who never even held a weapon until a few days ago, you're not bad off.'

'I must be dreaming,' Moroda said, shaking her head. 'You know I want to look for a ship home as soon as we get to Taban Yul, though? Eryn said, bringing Moroda back to reality.

'As soon as you get the smallest taste of the real world, you wanna scurry back home?' Amarah laughed. 'Didn't you hear a word the Varkain said, Eryn?'

'I know you do,' Moroda said to her sister, feeling subdued. All her confidence built from the Samolen magic had faded. She still wore her crystal, but understood now it could not be relied upon to get her out of all scrapes or keep her invulnerable. Topeko had said it was a last resort, something to use in defence if fighting could not be avoided. It was her overconfidence that had led her to the ludicrous decision to accompany Amarah and Sapora on the heist. A hastily made decision, one she felt had been necessary at the time, but thanks to her companions, she wasn't too much the worse for wear.

She thought back to Aciel, his clothes, his eyes, his voice. How he had so very nearly sent her to her death. Running head first into the heart of the Arillian war was something she never wished to do again. 'Ryn, I promise I'll work with you more instead of being stubborn. Next time, I might not be so lucky. I don't want to put you through that again.'

'Ro...'

'You best get some rest,' Morgen chimed in. 'Still a little

ways to go to Taban Yul. You, too, Eryn. You look exhausted with worry.'

'I'm fine, thanks Morgen,' Eryn said, not looking away from Moroda.

'Sure, Ryn?' Moroda asked, her body itching to rest.

'I'm sure. You rest. We're all here. You're safe.'

Moroda smiled and let herself drift into sleep, hoping she would not endure any nightmares of Aciel and Jato.

Chapter Eighteen

As the sun began to set, a wash of blues and purples streaked across the sky. Bright bursts of orange interlaced between the clouds, burning like distant fires. The sight was so simple, so beautiful, that Moroda spent several minutes gazing overboard at the sight, lost in thought and memory.

She remembered her father had spoken fondly of the bustling city of Taban Yul, capital of the Ittallan homeland, Val Sharis. It housed more people than Niversai, but was over twice the size, and so never felt crowded or overwhelming. Taban Yul was said to be the largest and richest city in all of Linaria; that the streets were paved with gold. The majority of Linaria's coins—crowns, florins, pennies, and all their variants—were minted deep within the city's financial district, and the Imperial Army had been formed within the palace walls several hundred years ago. Moroda imagined a lively, warm place, full of the jewels of Berel and the peoples similar to those of Niversai.

In her mind's eye, it felt like a second home. The same market stalls and traders, taverns and nobility. The same members of the Imperial Guard patrolling the streets and airships floating overhead.

'If it's getting too much for you, we can always get a ship back to Niversai once we land.' Eryn suggested, breaking Moroda from her thoughts.

'No, no.' Moroda shook her head, pulling Palom's cloak more tighly around her shoulders. 'We can rest properly when we get there, and decide what to do after. How long until we reach Taban Yul?'

'We're already across the Sea of Nami,' Morgen said, glancing ahead. 'Amarah reckons we'll be there before dark.'

'Sapora has informed us there'll be quite a party when we land.' Anahrik said, a bite in his tone. He approached the three and sat beside them, folding his arms and looking ahead towards Sapora during one of his rare rests.

Moroda nodded at him. 'Not a party for us, surely?'

Anahrik shook his head, eyes still focussed the edge of the deck where the Varkain stood. 'No, it's an Ittallan ceremony to mark the beginning of winter. It's normally in a few weeks' time, but given he's royalty, they'll bring it forward for us. Looks like we timed this just perfectly. Could be a great boon to business, eh, Palom? Make a few crowns, if we're lucky?'

Palom laughed at his colleague's words, and made his way to join the other Ittallan. 'I would like to formally welcome you to Val Sharis, the birthplace of my people.' He extended his arms as though in a wide hug. 'Taban Yul is our capital. It is most beautiful city in all Linaria, no question. But, yes, business is business and we need to go back to our workshop. There is not much time before trade finishes for the season.'

Moroda raised her eyebrows. Were Palom and Anahrik really leaving? She had thought the group would remain together when they reached the city, and frowned, realising her naïvety.

'Is it true the city's streets are lined with gold?' Eryn asked.

'Some are. Around the palace.' Palom smiled again. 'But the city is large, and there are much other sights to see, too.' 'The harbour is always worth a look. Great from the sky,' Anahrik chimed in. 'Food and fishing and it's great to watch boats and airships come in over the sea. Trader's Alley is where we're based, and you've also got the Food Quarter, The Three Bells, The Upper Rails—finance and money there—Maitload Corner, Little Yomal—that's where I stay if I'm not at the workshop—then, what else… East Cross, you can get anything you need there, it's great for tourists! And as for views on foot, all of South Galeo is worth the trip. From there you can see the harbour and the beach as it stretches south.'

'Wow, sounds incredible!' Moroda said. From his hurried description, she thought the place more exciting than Niversai. Her city's districts paled to the Ittallan's description of Taban Yul.

'Lived in the city all my life. Was born there.' Anahrik grinned, on his feet again and pacing. He glanced skywards again, as though itching to be airborne. 'Taught Palom what was what and where things were when he arrived. Can't wait to be home. Before Aciel and the others get there. At least the city'll be better prepared than Niversai was.' He glanced at Morgen, smirking.

'Other than Jato, there has been no sign of more Arillians,' Palom said. 'This is good thing.'

'The city is fine, Palom. You'll see,' Anahrik said.

Moroda could sense the tension and worry the Ittallan felt,

but agreed with Anahrik. Even if there were Arillians here, they'd stolen Aciel's eyes. He wouldn't be able to increase his power unless he was lucky enough to find a powerful dragon or two. It wasn't to say he'd not already amassed enough followers to attack the city, but as they hadn't come charging after them following their escape, Moroda believed them to be weakened.

'I'm really looking forward to it—father always told us wonderful stories of Taban Yul, of the people and of the wealth of the city,' Eryn said.

'The whole city isn't all like that. There are parts you should avoid, but that's the same anywhere.' Anahrik pulled a short dagger from the holder on his thigh and inspected the handle. 'But me an' Palom need to get back to our workshop. Got some things to repair, some things to make. When the snows really hit, tourists disappear and work slows. Dunno if we'll have time to go to the palace for this celebration.'

'I am sure we will see you again if you stay in the city a while,' Palom said. 'But our work is our value and it has been too long.'

Moroda smiled. She could feel the passion Anahrik and Palom held for their hometown, though she noted Anahrik loved the city and Palom loved the country. She, too, loved Niversai, but she didn't care for it in the way the Ittallan did. She looked at the jewel in her ring, the most valuable thing she owned now, and signed. She knew more now than she ever had before, thanks to Topeko's teachings, books, and her experience with Amarah and the crew. She had to embrace what she had learned and tackle every opportunity thrown her way.

She sighed and scratched her head. She'd read a little more of Topeko's books since getting back on Khanna, but needed a good night's sleep to focus again after Jato's attack. Thankfully, when she had drifted off, her world had been dark and pain free. She and Eryn were safe, and they had the sphere. She had touched it a few more times, and slowly grew used to the heat in her fingers. The book Andel had originally given her had explained more about the ereven spheres—that they worked using the natural magic of phoenixes and dragons. Inside the sphere was the feather of a phoenix, a real one, not an ornamental red feather, covered with droplets of clear water, she presumed from the lake in Berel. Moroda had to hold it up close to her face to see the detail, and as she turned the sphere in her hand, the droplets moved along the feather's barbs, focussing on one direction, like a compass always pointing north.

Where the droplets gathered, the heat of the sphere intensified and hummed gently. 'This is how we find a dragon,' Moroda breathed. 'A stronger response for a stronger dragon?' She thumbed through Andel's tome, but the writing was small, written in an old style she had to work to make sense of. It was too much for her right now, but she understood the gist of how it worked. At least she could read it tonight, or in the morning after sleeping.

'That little thing is worth a lot of money, Moroda,' Amarah said, breaking her from her thoughts. 'Even if it doesn't work, I can sell it.'

Moroda smiled, shaking her head. 'It works. Don't worry.' 'I'm not worried.'

Moroda placed the sphere on her lap and looked up at Amarah, thinking about Eryn's words of the sky pirate's concern for her. 'Were you going to tell me about the scars on your leg?'

Eryn frowned and looked at Morgen, then Moroda, and back to the sky pirate.

Amarah cackled and turned back to the wheel, slowing their speed as they approached Taban Yul. 'Came to Val Sharis a few times as a kid. After I left home. It's all Ittallan and Varkain over there. Aside from tourists. Wandered out of a tourist spot one night and ran into a group of Varkain.'

Moroda glanced up as Sapora appeared at the mention of his kin, but he remained silent.

'Guess they thought I'd make good sport,' Amarah continued. 'Managed to get in a few blows but they outnumbered me, and they're so damned fast. Most of the scars from their blades healed, aside from a couple of deep stabs on my back. But my leg never got better. They wanted to keep me from fighting back so they could enjoy themselves. One of them bit me as I kicked out. It's awful, when you can feel everything but your body can't move to scream, when your chest can't rise when you breathe, so you take short breaths. It's crushing. It's cold.' Moroda saw her shiver.

'Dragon's above, Amarah,' Morgen said. 'How did you get away? Surely they'd have killed you or left you for dead?'

'Fellow pirate. Not at the time he wasn't, but we became allies after. Since then, I've never go anywhere unarmed. Well, not if I could help it.'

'A lucky fate. They'd have taken you back to Sereth, no

doubt,' Sapora said. 'Children are most prized, but anyone who gets into a scrap will do.'

'Why...?' Moroda asked, hesitant.

Sapora looked at her with another smile, his fangs bared. 'If you were in Val Sharis when it happened. Why didn't you report it to the Guard? They'd have helped you! They'd have arrested those who hurt you!' Morgen said.

'Morgen, Morgen, Morgen.' Amarah shook her head. 'You don't know much about Val Sharis, do you?'

'I know what acceptable behaviour is and what its not!'

'In Corhaven, perhaps.'

'Is Val Sharis so different? I thought our countries were allied?' Eryn asked.

'Yes, but the Ittallan and Varkain live throughout Val Sharis and Sereth. They're pretty damned different to us. Behaviours change and cultures change. What's illegal here is legal there. I learned what the Varkain really were that night.' Amarah said, bitterness evident in her tone.

Moroda lapsed into silence, thinking about what happened to Amarah, and wondering what happened in Sereth. It was something awful, but no-one would tell her. She shivered, and wondered whether that was perhaps for the best.

A flurry of cold wind washed over the ship as Kohl landed on deck. Moroda looked up, worried he'd seen more Arillians, but a smile played on his misshapen lip when he caught her eye. 'Moroda. You remember in the Fourth Moon Inn? Burian? I told you about the scars the war left on Linaria?'

She nodded, the ereven sphere still clutched tightly.

'You might want to have a look down now.'

She got to her feet and rushed to the side of the deck. The sea was a thin, blue line on the horizon, and ahead, a wide valley splayed out before her. Great jagged cliffs jutted out from the land where they shouldn't, breaking up the sweeping plains, and she followed their lines as the land was carved up and split over several, grassy steppes. Further inland, as the mountains grew and the steppes turned into forests, buildings dotted the landscape. Ahead, just barely in sight, a city emerged, and beyond the city, far in the distance, dragons and phoenixes flew.

Moroda absorbed the sight before her, the wind blowing her hair as they continued inland. Despite her wonder at the view, Sapora's words worried her. What was it the Varkain did? She looked at Sapora, the prince of his people, and was curious and afraid of him in the same breath. Her nerve gave out, and she decided she didn't want to ask him.

'You okay, Ro?' Eryn rubbed her sister's arm. 'Quite the view, isn't it? I'm afraid Niversai looks rather drab in comparison.'

'Built in a different time. Different purpose,' Morgen said, standing next to Eryn and leaning over the side. 'Val Sharis is a land of gold, if ever there was one.'

'You do know a lot about these cities,' Moroda commented.

Morgen laughed and shook his head. 'All part of the training. You need to understand the basic geography of the world! I don't know everything about every town. Just the important ones.' He grinned, but Moroda looked away, more interested in watching

Taban Yul growing as they approached. As the sun reached the horizon, the sky above them began to darken. It was going to be a cold night.

Her mind raced. Aciel and Jato following them. Anahrik and Palom leaving. A party in the palace. The ereven sphere and finding a dragon. The Varkain and what exactly they did to non-Varkain. She was still tired from her encounter with Jato, and was very much looking forward to a soft, plush bed as been promised to her and Eryn by Sapora.

'The palace is ahead,' Amarah called. 'Straight east.'

'I see the city,' Morgen said, walking past the wheel and out onto deck.

Moroda shrugged out of the large cloak, but kept her own on. She and Eryn joined Morgen near the front, and she inhaled sharply. Taban Yul stood tall, a mighty city surrounded by two high, gleaming walls. They shone bright white in the low sunlight, and as they drew nearer, Moroda saw they were made from what appeared to be solid marble. It was mostly a creamy white, with ribbons of pale grey and blue running through it. They were unlike any city walls Moroda had ever seen before. The inner wall stood an extra five or six feet taller than the outer, but was not quite as thick, with a thirty foot gap between them.

Other airships lingered in the air; most were more than twice the size of Khanna, and far more heavily armed. Moroda saw them the same time Amarah did.

'Royal Guard,' Palom explained. 'Those are warships—they keep an eye on ships coming into the city.'

The skies were full of trading ships, too; most of them were large, triple decked vessels, with wide sails of many bright colours. The city below came into view as Khanna flew slowly over the outer walls. Moroda was slightly disappointed to see there were no golden streets, though there was more white marble.

'Well, Palom, seeing as this is your town, where am I docking?' Amarah asked the Ittallan.

'The palace,' Sapora said, stepping up to Amarah. 'You are all travelling with me and will be permitted. I will speak with Princess Isa on the situation, and seek wisdom from the Council of Val Sharis.'

'I can't believe I'm actually flying right into the guard's hands.' Amarah said, shaking her head, and altering her course slightly towards the palace. 'They best leave Khanna alone!'

'Don't be so pessimistic, Amarah.' Sapora grinned at her, his pointed teeth glistening. 'You've benefitted the travel of a royal. I'm sure you'll be well rewarded for your inconveniences.'

The palace became clearer as they approached, and Moroda was stunned at how pretty it was. It loomed ahead, set atop a hill, the highest point in the city, and entirely clad in gleaming marble, with dark blue, almost purple veins snaking across walls and pillars for visual contrast. The palace must have been four times the size of Rosecastle, and twice as high. Tall, slender turrets rose up around it, connected by equally tall bridges. It almost looked like the palace floated in the sky.

Gold statues of animals adorned with cut gemstones topped the many pillars surrounding the palace, spaced at regular intervals.

There were tigers and lions, elephants and bears, bulls a stork, and several birds of prey she couldn't identify. Looking up from the gold statues, she saw the city of Taban Yul was set before the incredible backdrop of the distant Feor mountains; the border of Val Sharis and Sereth.

'Unquestionably the finest city in Linaria,' Palom said. Moroda couldn't help but nod in agreement.

'The docks are to the east,' Sapora said, directing Amarah. When it was clear they were heading for the palace, one of the airships that had been floating, dormant near one of the turrets, began to move towards Khanna, and Moroda suddenly felt apprehensive.

'Can't just fly up to the palace unannounced, eh?' Amarah asked. Though her words were light, Moroda could hear the nerves in her tone. Being so close to her on Jato's ship had made her see another side of her.

'Here's the envoy,' Anahrik said, watching as a raven flew the short distance from the airship to Khanna. It flew above the small ship, circling as it looked down.

'Tismat. I am Prince Sapora, returning to Taban Yul for the winter ceremony. I shall see Princess Isa and the Council at once.'

The raven circled twice more, before flying back to the airship. Two Ittallan, in their form as huge brown eagles, formed the front of the escort, and the raven made its way behind them, getting lost behind the larger birds of prey.

'Great welcoming committee. They better keep away from Khanna. Don't want any scratches down the side from those damned

talons!' Amarah said, glaring at the birds as they followed behind.
'For someone who makes their living thriving on opportunities, you have an incredibly pessimistic view of the world.' Sapora said. 'Your precious ship will not be damaged. Stop whinging about it.'

'Money just so happens to be a worry of mine. I know you don't have the same concerns, prince.'

'Do stop arguing, Amarah. You will be paid once we arrive, Princess Isa will see to it. I've given you my word, so try to relax and enjoy being in the palace. It's likely the only chance you'll see it out of bars, anyway.'

They followed the escort into the palace docks while there was still light outside. As Khanna gently flew along lines of already docked ships, their escorts slowed the pace, eventually hovering in mid-air. 'Looks like this is where we'll be docking today.' Amarah said, grabbing the wheel and pulling levers to bring in her sails. Khanna gently manoeuvred into position, wings tucked in and sails folded down, before resting on the wooden plinth extending from the marble palace wall. There were lines of ships docked beneath them, and one or two above them, but the extensive hangar was, in fact, mostly empty.

'After you, Varkain.' Amarah said, waiting for Sapora to take the lead.

'Prince Sapora.' The guard dropped to one knee to greet the group as they disembarked. 'We were not expecting you. Apologies for the brusque security; things have been in uproar for the past few days with that damned Arillian charging about in Corhaven.'

'Rise.' Sapora said, looking at the three Ittallan, who had landed and transformed back, joining the guard on his knee.

'Prince Sapora, please, will you follow me? I'm sure Isa will be glad to see you.' The shortest of the three, the raven said, stepping forward. He was balding, with wrinkles deep in his skin, and wore ill-fitting robes, with his sleeves bundled up about his wrists.

'Princess Isa.' Sapora corrected, his eyes narrowed.

'Yes of course, Princess Isa will be most pleased to see you.' The raven echoed, dropping to one knee again and bowing his head low.

Moroda and Eryn were the last to disembark and shared a worried look at hearing the exchange between Sapora and the raven. Eryn opened her mouth to speak, but Moroda hushed her. 'We'll find out.'

'What of the rest of your party, my prince?' The raven asked, head still bowed.

Sapora turned to them all and calculated his response for several long moments. Moroda held her breath, afraid suddenly.

'I expect they will have free reign of the city and palace alike. Have rooms prepared for them all, and invitations extended to tonight, should they wish to attend. Everything will be at the expense of the crown.'

'Your father's crown, Prince Sapora? Are you sure-'

'I would not presume to correct me again, raven.' Sapora interjected, pupils contracting into slits, the only expression of his rage. 'Once more and you'll regret it.'

'Please follow me, my prince.' One of the other guards stepped forward, his arm in front of the raven, saving him from the edge of Sapora's tongue. 'We will have food prepared immediately for you and your guests, and preparations are already underway for the banquet this evening. Please, do follow me. I shall show your honoured guests to their quarters.' He turned to lead the party into the palace.

The raven remained on one knee until they had all passed, before standing up and joining the remaining Ittallan at the back of the escort. Moroda trailed behind with Eryn, and glanced at him as he whispered. 'I wish we had known the prince was coming. I do not like how things are going.'

Chapter Nineteen

The palace of Taban Yul was unlike anything Moroda could envisage in her wildest dreams. She had thought Berel was beautiful, and in a rural, ancient, way it was. Taban Yul, on the other hand, was vibrant where Berel was drab, busy where Berel was peaceful, and covered in glittering gemstones where Berel had sandy bricks. The armour worn by the Royal Guard inside the palace was polished to a mirror-sheen, making Morgen's look incredibly dull in comparison. They all wore the same gold and red livery of the Imperial Guard, but their helms boasted three long spikes protruding from the top, matching shoulder pads, and even a short metal spike on their boots. The Ittallan trademark fabric sash crossed their back and breast, and was tied at their sides with a triple bow. Morgen explained the colour of the material denoted rank; blue was for lower-ranking officers, green were senior officers—his own rank—and red sashes were for captains. It was different in Corhaven, where they only had a different coloured helm rather than the sashes in Val Sharis. The raven, however, wore no armour, only soft robes, bejewelled slippers, and a black sash. Morgen didn't know what it signified, and Moroda did not wish to ask in case she caused offence.

The royal guard bustled around the corridors in twos and threes, a far cry from the thinly stretched guard in Niversai, and despite how hurriedly everyone seemed to be racing around, Moroda felt quite at ease—the rushing around was not centred on her or Eryn. Every other word was 'prince,' and Moroda was simply part of the entourage.

'We part here.' Palom said, stretching his arms out in front of him with a yawn. 'My forge is here in the city. Anahrik and I will go to be working there now.'

Anahrik shuffled up to his side and yawned, too, rolling his shoulders. 'We'll be smack in the centre of Trader's Alley. Enjoy your party tonight. With everyone rushing around so much, looks like it's gonna be a busy one.'

'The city will be quiet, I think. Many people will go to the palace tonight.'

'Taban Yul? Quiet?' Anahrik laughed. 'Palom, you've been away from home too long. Goldstones won't be about, but everyone else will. Not that we'll see much of them locked away in the workshop! Just need to get these little projects finished!'

Moroda looked up as the two joked and nudged Eryn's arm.

'Thank you for allowing Anahrik and I on your ship. We will meet again soon, Amarah, to give your parting gift.' Palom nodded to the sky pirate.

'Parting gift? How kind. But lucky for you, Sapora's sister has enough coin for a hundred trips, apparently.' Amarah laughed.

'Is money all you care about?' Sapora asked, and Amarah turned away.

'Enjoy your first taste of Ittallan culture tonight,' Anahrik said to the others, ignoring Sapora's jab at Amarah. 'If you fancy a tour of Taban Yul, I'm sure I can sneak away from Palom for a couple of hours tomorrow. I know all the best spots!' He tilted his head to the group and headed off.

Palom waved and followed his partner.

'Farewell...' Moroda said, her lip quivering a little as she watched the two Ittallan turn down a corridor. They were deep in talk, Anahrik gesticulating wildly, as was his nature, more engrossed in their work than in long goodbyes. Even though Sapora was royalty, they'd barely glanced at him. She thought to their first meeting, seeing the tiger appear outside the gates of Niversai as her city blazed under the dragon's attack. Palom had offered her and Eryn his protection, and had kept Anahrik safe from Sapora. She still remembered their confrontation in Topeko's home. Palom and Anahrik hadn't trusted Kohl, but both had warmed to him a little after he had rescued her from Jato's airship.

Her ring warmed her finger, but it did not buzz here. The meraki of the Ittallan was clearly too strong for her to feel anything in the palace.

'You okay, Ro?'

'All okay, Ryn.' She looped her arm through her sisters' and followed Sapora as he led them across one of the many covered palace bridges.

On entering the palace proper, they had immediately been offered refreshments. When Moroda declined their offering, the servants wished to take a request so as to provide what she wanted. Laughing, she had asked for some roasted peanuts, and within a few minutes, she had been provided with a bowl of them. Amazed at the service, Moroda shared them with Eryn, Morgen, and Amarah, and relaxed into being waited on.

'I bet it's like you're a Goldstone again.' Amarah sneered, taking another handful of the sweet and salty snack.

'It is. It's lovely.' Eryn nodded with a smile.

Moroda, however, had not missed the accusation, but chose to remain silent, turning instead to Morgen, who was more interested in the Royal Guards.

'Just look at them all!' He eyed the armour of another trio of guards as they jogged past, their armour clinking together in harmony. 'They even run together…' He shook his head and returned his attention to his own armour, picking at a small spot of rust on one of his shoulder pads and flicking it away in disdain.

'It's a different place, different regimes, different armour.' Moroda said, trying to ignore the other soldiers and focus her attention on Morgen. 'Besides, there are so many other things you can look at instead of them.'

Magnificent tapestries adorned the walls along the length of the corridor. They were meticulously woven artworks of famous people, former kings and queens, battle scenes, landmarks, and all were laced with gemstones sewn into the fabric itself.

Moroda noticed the top half of the tapestries bore resemblance of a king or queen of old, and the bottom half flipped the image, like a playing card, depicting their true form. There was a great black bear, a swan, a stallion, two lions, an eagle, and the one furthest along the hall was a huge brown cobra. 'My father.' Sapora said, having watched Moroda's gaze.

'I thought… but… aren't the Varkain snakes?' She asked, pausing before the tapestry.

'Yes.'

'Then why on the Ittallan tapestry? In their palace?' Moroda asked, keeping her eyes on the cobra and not on Sapora.

'My father, Vasil, is the King in Sereth, my homeland, a country which borders Val Sharis. He has been re-forging the bond between Ittallan and Varkain.' He looked up at the tapestry and narrowed his eyes. 'He… conquered Val Shris and married an Ittallan woman of high rank. As his wife, she became a queen in Sereth. He became the King of Val Sharis through his takeover. He has power in both countries, but resides in Sereth. The tapestry was made shortly after. An Ittallan tradition. I am their child.'

'And the princess?' Moroda asked, looking down the hall at the other tapestries hung along it.

'My father's daughter with an Ittallan noble woman some months after my birth. You would call her a Goldstone.' He returned his gaze to Moroda. 'Vasil returned to Sereth with me when I was old enough to transform. He left governing Val Sharis to the Council and Ittallan nobility, though he still exerts power over them.' He smiled as Eryn and Morgen leaned in closer.

'I was raised here, in the palace, until I could transform. Among the Varkain it is common to take several wives or husbands. The woman who gave my father his daughter remained here in Val Sharis, until her death. An unfortunate accident, I believe. But my sister… she is no snake. When she was old enough to transform, she could not come to Sereth under the law of our ancestors and so has remained here. Vasil took a third wife in Sereth, and they have a son, Tacio.

Varkain strength and customs are a fading shadow in Linaria, and our influence dwindles even in Val Sharis. We'll need all the strength and resources we can get if Aciel is as serious a threat as he seems. You know firsthand how formidable he is.'

Moroda nodded, thinking back to the fear she had felt aboard the warship. Jato was strong, that much was clear. But she didn't like Jato in the same way she didn't like street thugs. Aciel was something else. She looked to Eryn and back to Sapora. 'I feel for your sister. No mother and not being able to see your father.'

'Ancestral laws ought to be changed.' He said, folding his arms.

'Ancestral laws should indeed be changed.' Kohl added, having listened in on part of their conversation.

Sapora turned and smiled a little at the Arillian. 'You'd make a fine Varkain, Kohl.'

'I'm sure you'd make a fine Arillian also.' Kohl replied. 'When you have to sneak up on dragons, or at least trail them undetected, you learn a few things. I hear there is to be a ball tonight—the palace servants are asking your orders?'

Sapora glanced behind the Arillian to see the raven wringing his hands and pacing the floor. The smile fell from Sapora's lips. 'Koraki. I really should have him removed from service. Go. Enjoy the palace and city. Rest while you can. The ball will begin in a few hours. I will have more information regarding the Arillian by morning.' He swept past Kohl and Moroda to the raven.

'I can't believe we didn't realise he was a prince for so long.' Moroda said, watching Sapora order the raven about.

'He fits the role as well as he does skulking around in the shadows scaring people,' Amarah said, twirling her scythe.

Another pair of the Royal Guard marched past. 'Sure, they look busy. But are they actually doing anything?' Morgen scowled. 'They're just prancing about!'

'Envious?' Eryn asked, an eyebrow raised.

'Not at all.'

'Let's get some rest. I'm quite looking forward to a proper meal and the ball,' Moroda said, turning the conversation away from Morgen's insecurities. 'Coming Morgen, Kohl, Amarah?'

'I shall accompany you to rest, but I shan't partake in the ball. With Linaria in this state, I do not think the presence of an Arillian would be much accepted.' Kohl said.

'But Sapora said—' Eryn began.

'Sapora is one person. He does not speak for everyone in the palace, nor the city.'

'Can I help you?'

Moroda looked up as another Ittallan approached. He wore loose robes and a black sash, but was older than the raven and portly, with brown eyes, a thick brown beard and several wide, gold chains around his broad neck. He carried several leaves of parchment under his arm and furrowed his brow as he looked down at them.

'Elafion. You received the message?' Sapora called, walking back to the group.

'Hmph. I hoped Topeko had arrived, but it's you, prince. I understand you've decided to call a meeting of the Council? At this hour?' The man replied. Moroda saw him look down his nose at Sapora, decidedly unimpressed. He carried himself with an air of righteous self-importance. Moroda's stomach twinged as she recalled similar behaviour from other Goldstones in Niversai. His words about Topeko gave her pause, though. Was it the scholar he spoke of?

'Correct. Once Princess Isa returns, we shall begin.' Sapora said.

Elafion sighed, an exaggerated action that reminded Moroda of a petulant child denied a sweet. 'Many of us have just had supper and we now have a ball to get together last minute. If we'd notice of your arrival, perhaps we could have done something.'

'We begin when the princess returns,' Sapora repeated, his voice cold.

'Sapora, we can't just drop everything when you decide to show up unannounced.'

'Must I remind you to whom your allegiance lies? Do not forget yourself, fodder, else you'll lose your head, not just your tongue.'

Elafion stiffened, but didn't say anything.

'I expect the others to be ready. While we're waiting, why don't you show my honoured guests to the east wing where their rooms are prepared.'

'Sapora! I am the head of the Council of Val Sharis! I have—'

'You have been ordered by your prince. I will see you in the Council Tower shortly.' Sapora turned to Moroda and the others. 'Elafion shall take you to the guest suites.'

'And my payment?' Amarah turned to Sapora, ignoring Elafion and the others.

'Yes, yes. Come. I will have your thirst satiated.' Elafion trembled where he stood, heaving and reshuffling his papers as Sapora and Amarah continued down the corridor. 'Well come on, come on, then. The prince has spoken.' He snorted, turning around, his robes billowing as he marched back down the corridor.

Moroda wondered why he did not hide his distaste of Sapora, but had little time to worry—she had to jog to keep up with Elafion's wide strides. They turned a corner to a large entranceway. Stairs led down and up, and Moroda glanced both ways, trying to get her bearings in the unfamiliar surroundings, but Elafion led them up the wide, curved stairway. Oak and marble interlaced, and the floor was covered by thick, red carpet, jewels lining the edges.

'You spoke of Topeko? Do you mean the scholar from Berel?' Moroda asked, but Elafion did not reply, too intent on charging down the corridors.

She and Eryn glanced at each other, and Moroda shook her head. Clearly she was too low class for the Ittallan to bother speaking with.

'I trust you're attending tonight's entertainment?' Elafion huffed as they passed through a large foyer. 'The ballroom is here, if you are. Don't be late.' He hurried up the wide steps, giving none of them time to even glance through the door.

Moroda looked to her left and right; Eryn hurried along as quickly as she could, but Morgen lagged behind. Kohl moved quickly, though she suspected he used his wings to take longer strides when they weren't looking.

Elafion stopped abruptly at another wide corridor. 'Well I don't know what rooms you've been given but the guest suites are all along here, right up to the far balcony at the end.' He waved his hand vaguely. 'Use the bells if you need anything and the servants will help. Now if you'll excuse me, I've a meeting to attend.' He snorted again and whirled around, gold chains jingling as he stomped back down the stairs and out of sight.

'He seems most vexed,' Eryn said, one arm on the wall as she tried to catch her breath. 'We might as well have run the whole way!'

'From the looks of things, I don't think anyone expected Sapora's return,' Kohl said, cool and calm as ever. 'The reactions seem either to be fear or irritation.'

'I'm not surprised. Sapora ordered someone on the Val Sharis Council to guide us to our rooms. That's a real kick to his pride,' Moroda said. 'Plenty of guards about, he could've asked one of them…'

'Sapora likes to throw his weight around. He always has! Look at how he is with Amarah, or Anahrik. Especially when he's insulted!' Eryn replied. 'But enough of him, let's go and sit down. We wanted to rest?'

'I cannot say I blame him,' Kohl said, as they entered a

large sitting room. Gold once again lined the ceiling and windows, and the dark wood furniture was ornately gilded with the precious metal. A small silver bell sat on a small table beside the door, as Elafion had said, and a lit fireplace dominated the wall to their left. Morgen went over to the large arched window and peered out, while Moroda and Eryn sat by the fire, looking at Kohl.

'He is a mixed blood, and the Ittallan are a proud race, almost as proud as the Varkain. I imagine he has a lot to prove. His knowledge. His strength. His competence. The best way he knows how is with poorly veiled threats and actual attacks.' Kohl said.

'I'd never thought that before,' Moroda said.

'But he's their prince? Surely it wouldn't matter?' Eryn asked.

Kohl shook his head. 'It shouldn't, but it does. Sapora will have a hard rule ahead of him. In the middle of an Arillian war, with his own people mistrusting him. I do feel for the prince.'

'Orders are orders. Doesn't matter if you agree with them or not, or who gave them.' Morgen said, still peering out of the window. The last traces of sunlight disappeared, blanketing the city in darkness.

'Maybe in Corhaven. The Ittallan and especially the Varkain do things differently. They are two races connected by ancient history, and the Ittallan try to distance themselves more with each season. Sapora will continue his father's work of trying to undo that to strengthen himself.'

'How can you be so sure?' Eryn asked.

'Sapora keeps talking about taking his throne. And now,

instead of being respectful of the Ittallan, he's immediately trying to put his mark down. Although he helped you when we crossed the sea, Moroda, you should still be wary of him. There's a reason non-Varkain do not travel to Sereth. I do not think we ought to stay in the palace too long. We ought to look for the dragon now, while we have a head start over Aciel.'

Morgen turned from the window to look at her, and Moroda suddenly became aware of all eyes on her. Sapora had saved her life on the airship. Amarah, had, too. There was little love for the Varkain among the people of Linaria, but she was sure it was misplaced. For all the atrocities she'd known Sapora to commit, he'd never harmed her. But Kohl's words on finding a dragon sooner rather than later held truth. She looked at her sister, and remembered her promise. It was an easy decision. 'I need to read more about the sphere. I need rest, too. We know Taban Yul is safe for the moment. Let's stay here for tonight, at least. Is that okay, Ryn?'

Eryn's smile told her she was happy with her decision. 'The ball will be a welcome relief from flying and eating rations! I can't remember the last time we were able to relax and have a proper meal.'

'Best keep watch, then. Just in case.' Kohl said, frowning.

'You both deserve a break and to enjoy yourselves. I can get some new armour while I'm here, too,' Morgen said. 'Kohl and I will keep watch tonight.'

'Thank you, Morgen,' Eryn said.

'We'll see if Sapora is true to his word about having more

information in the morning,' Moroda said, yawning. 'For now, let's try to enjoy the evening. Dragon's above, it's been a long time since we enjoyed anything.'

*

Once his business with the raven was finished, Sapora exited the palace through a grand set of double-doors at the end of the hall, trailed by Amarah. They stood at the top of an enormous flight of solid white marble stairs which led down to wide, golden gates, and the city beyond. Stationary guards stood posted at either side of the doors, halfway up the stairs and six of them were stood by the gate. The city beyond expanded as a mirage of colour, sound and movement, even as the darkness of the evening took hold.

'My prince, refreshments will be ready for you in the West Hall when you are ready.' The raven shuffled over, still wringing his hands.

'Good. That will be all.' Sapora said, dismissing him while keeping his attention on Amarah. He did not bother to offer the Ittallan even a cursory glance, and Amarah tilted her head as she watched the servant slink off.

A roaring hiss drew their attention. Glancing upwards, they spied a large, red-gold cat crouched on the wide marble wall which framed the top of the palace doors. Bright amber eyes glinted in the darkness, and it bared its sharp, white fangs at them. The fur of the cat was short and wiry, with dark brown, almost black markings dotted about its ears, back, tail and hindquarters. Crouching, it hissed again, then leapt almost ten feet vertically into the air and descended with claws drawn.

Amarah instinctively leaped back to avoid a collision with the feline, but Sapora held his ground, his knees slightly bent. Cursing her luck, Amarah clutched her scythe in preparation, but before she could act, a flash of light emanated from the cat as it transformed before her.

'Princess Isa, I have missed you.' Sapora said, his lips turned slightly upwards as he embraced a young woman. She had the same amber eyes as the cat, and wore her brunette hair tied high in four thick braids. Jewelled drop earrings shimmered from her ears, and bracelets and anklets chimed as she moved.

'Sapora! I'm so glad you're here! I knew you'd come back before your coronation!' Isa gasped, clutching him in a tight hug.

'You have grown so much since I saw you last.' Sapora said, letting go and taking a step back. 'I apologise for not keeping in contact for so long. I have been on errantry.'

Isa nodded. 'I know. Well travelled?' She paused and looked back to see Amarah stood there, slightly bewildered. 'Who is this?'

'Ah yes,' Sapora said, retuning his attention to the sky pirate. 'Sister, this is Amarah. She is captain of the airship I have been travelling on. We owe her some coin for the trip.'

Isa blinked, suspicion gone. 'Thank you, Amarah. I'll see to it you're paid well for helping my brother. Will you be joining us at the ball tonight?'

'Not my kind of thing,' Amarah said, chewing on her lip as she leant on her scythe.

'Oh please. Do come along, you'll be my special guest,' Isa

said, stepping forward and grabbing Amarah's hands. 'If you've not packed for the occasion, you're welcome to anything from my wardrobe—or a servant can go into the city for you.' Isa released Amarah's hands and paced around, never still.

'Well, if you put it like that… how many people will be there?' Amarah asked. Sapora narrowed his eyes, he could see her mind working out how to turn it to her advantage.

'The ballroom will be full. The whole Council will be there, too, and half the Ittallan nobility, I should think.' Isa nodded, dancing around on her tiptoes. 'Please, take this.' She reached into her pocket and withdrew a small round onyx stone. The crest of her family was etched into the surface, and she handed it to Amarah. 'With this, everything will be paid for by the crown. You'll have no problems in the city getting whatever you need for tonight. There's not much time.'

'You are too kind,' Amarah said as sweetly as possible. She licked her lips and looked at Sapora with a smirk. 'Sapora, Isa, I shall see you this evening.' She bowed her head, reminiscent of the Samolen, before sauntering down the stairs and into Val Sharis.

'One must hope she does not bleed us completely dry. I should have told you she's a thief. Was that wise, dear sister?'

'Of course not. We've more pressing issues than one woman's greed. I know what is going on in Linaria. Aciel causing trouble and gaining followers,' Isa said. She stopped her pacing for half a heartbeat. 'I was hoping you'd get here before he started to do any real damage. I heard you were in Corhaven. I don't suppose you came across him?'

Sapora shook his head. 'The takeover is real. Morgen, the young man I arrived with, is in the Imperial Guard, stationed in Niversai. It seems Aciel swooped in, helped himself to their King's crystals, brainwashed half the army and left with near two hundred soldiers in a single afternoon.'

'No!'

'Indeed. It is not just Arillians we need to be concerned about—it is any person weak enough to succumb to his compulsion.'

'Compulsion?'

'He has the ability to brainwash, control, hypnotise. Moroda succumbed to it on the trip, but fought through it a little. He is slaying dragons and stealing their power to boost his own, through their crystals. It is how this has come about so quickly. I fear he will make his move before any of us are ready, sister.' Sapora said. His pupils narrowed again. 'I will not have my power stolen.'

'We must convene the Council at once.' Isa said. 'I detest every one of them, but they have influence and they have contacts. We can prepare the city immediately.'

'I have already requested it. I'll do away with it when I am in power. Don't worry about that.' He turned away from Taban Yul and walked back into the palace, Isa in tow. 'Who do we have on the Council now?'

'Keros and Elafion still lead. There's a peacock and a swan, too. The old vixen. The raven.' Isa counted them on her fingers. They turned a corner and made their way up a flight of stairs.

'Fodder.'

Isa nodded as the two continued down the elaborate hallway, both floor and ceiling heavily gilded. 'The peacock is relatively new. Only been on the Council half a year or so. He replaced Sierra.'

'The lynx?'

'Yeah. I miss Sierra, she was one of the few who didn't hate me.'

'Well I can imagine why that was,' Sapora said. 'Honestly, this Ittallan thought process must be done away with. I don't understand it at all. Palom and Anahrik seem to get along well enough; one is a tiger, the other a falcon.'

'Really? Surely they'd have nothing to say to each other?'

'They are trading partners. Palom is a weaponsmith, Anahrik works in silver. They combined their talent for more profit. A little brain but too much brawn.'

'It was quite the menagerie you were roaming with.' Isa giggled, flicking her hair.

'I should have known you'd be watching.' Sapora hissed. 'I hardly believe it myself... travelling with such riff-raff. From Corhaven, too.'

Isa paused in front of a lone member of the Royal Guard stood to attention in front of a heavy oak door. 'The Council shall convene now.'

'Yes, Isa.' He nodded and darted away from his position.

'I do not like how they refer to you as Isa, like you are some common cat.' Sapora said, watching the soldier disappear as they entered the door to the library.

'I'm bastard-born. If it weren't for the threat of you visiting, I'm sure I would be out on the streets like a common cat.'

'I shall put a stop to it at once. You will be their queen before winter is over, it's about time they learned some respect.'

'I cannot wait, brother.'

Sapora shook his head, following Isa as she led them up the narrow stairwell at the back of the library, and through doors towards the Council Tower.

'That one, Moroda you called her? Smells more Samolen than anything else. That crystal of hers stinks. Mind yourself with her.'

'I did not know that… but my sense of smell is not quite as keen as yours.'

'Or sight,' she teased, poking out her tongue. 'Or hearing, or speed, for that matter.'

'Speed I'll have you on.'

'Perhaps for a strike. Not in general. Stealth, I think is your only advantage, and even then, there's not much in it.' She flicked her hair, earrings jingling.

'This is why you'd make a fine queen, Isa.'

Isa grinned broadly and pushed open the door to the Council's meeting room. It was round, located at the top of one of the tallest towers of the palace. The floor was marble, like the rest of the palace, and adorned with rich, plush rugs. Tapestries lined the walls, surrounding a long, wooden table already set with empty wine glasses and silver cutlery. The windows were holes set into the walls, allowing wind to blow through and cool or warm the room as the seasons dictated. They also allowed those who could fly to enter or leave without traipsing up the stairs.

Three members were already sat, talking in hushed, fervent whispers. Keros, with his shaggy black hair and broad frame, Koraki, the raven, and Tring, the old vixen. Despite seeing Elafion only a few minutes prior, the stag was not present. They stopped talking immediately as Isa and Sapora entered the room, and got to their feet. 'Prince Sapora.' They greeted, dropping to one knee. 'Your princess is present also, where is her address?' Sapora said.

'Princess Isa, we are in honour of your presence.' They mumbled, and Keros and Koraki, who had stood, dropped to one knee again.

'It seems things have fallen lax in my absence. I had expected, as my father expects, the Council to run Val Sharis while we attend to business elsewhere. But I hear Aciel has been sighted in our land and rumours haunt the streets. Does anyone of this ruling Council have information on the Arillian upstart?'

None of the Councillors answered.

'Really? The Council is half present, and yet not one of you has any information about Aciel?' He hissed. 'I suppose you all have your preparations for the ball sorted, though, don't you? Your outfits are cleaned and pressed and guest lists have been organised? Perhaps if you bothered to spend a little more time running the country and less time preening each other, this meeting would be more conducive.'

He allowed the silence to linger, and the power of his words to sting their pride a little longer.

'This meeting is dismissed.' Sapora finished. 'Finished?

But, my prince… others have yet to arrive…'
Koraki stuttered.

'And so they shall be punished. I expect you all to be at the ball tonight, and I expect information by then. It begins in a few hours, so you had best get to it.'

As the silence prevailed, Sapora stepped back and opened the door to allow the few Council members gathered a chance to leave.

Isa remained still, watching as the three walked past and exited. 'Sapora, I've never spoken to them like that.'

'They are in the Val Sharis Council. The highest ranking citizens of Taban Yul. Of all Val Sharis. They live in the palace. They should have known I had arrived in the city the moment Khanna docked. Their disregard for you and inability to provide information proves to me that they are worthless. I have learned much during my travels, and more still in these last few days. It will all be to our advantage, sister. You've waited nineteen years, wait one more season.'

Chapter Twenty

'Look, Anahrik. Still here, exactly as we left it.' Palom smiled as he entered their old workshop, hauling the large satchel of weaponry over his shoulder. A thick layer of dust had accumulated in the two seasons they'd been away, but he preferred it like that. If everything was clean, it would mean trespassers, or possibly thieves, had broken in and disturbed his work.

'I still think you should have paid a cleaner to keep this place in order.' Anahrik said, cringing at the dust and grime which had accumulated on the surface of everything. 'This is disgusting!' He shoved his hands in his pockets and leaned away from the benches and work surfaces, his nose crinkled. 'Five florins a week, that's all it would have been!'

'Dust won't hurt you.' Palom dumped the weapons on one of the large benches to his left, and made his way to the back of the workshop, where his coal-fired forge sat, dormant. The hearth was stone, blackened from years of use, with a heavy-duty cast iron fire pot bolted to the centre. All around him, half-finished weapons leaned against walls and benches—swords and shields, spears and axes, all dull under the dust. 'I am too excited about this project to worry about a little dirt on floor.' He pulled his thick, leather apron from the racking behind the forge and threw it on.

'A little dirt on the floor?' Anahrik gasped. 'Are you blind?

It's on every surface, it's in the air it's, ugh...' He covered his mouth with his hands and shook his head violently to emphasise his point.

'Do not cry, you are not child. Open the back door.'

'First thing in the morning, I'm going down to East Cross to get someone to sort this mess out.'

Palom tutted, but did not respond. He had lit his forge and was powering the bellows to feed the flames. He had never dreamed of attempting what he was about to, but he had patience enough to work through the entire night if he had to. 'This is more important than cleaning, Anahrik. This is the future. You are the one who read the text in Topeko's book. The Samolen did not think it was possible.'

'You're too optimistic. There's no guarantee it'll work here as it did for the Samolen.' Anahrik said, sitting down on a chair, having carefully dusted it first.

'No guarantee... but there is a chance. A chance is all I need.' Even Anahrik's discomfort did nothing to quell his excitement and anticipation at finally forging a new weapon—the one he had been dreaming of since he was a boy.

'I only know what I read and what I understood from Topeko and the crystals he gave to the others,' Anahrik crossed his legs as he thought. Waves of heat rolled around the room, but with the back door open, it did not become a furnace. 'If it weren't for that little lesson Topeko taught, we'd still have been none the wiser.'

Palom continued to press the bellows, watching as the

flames roared and took shape. They were short on details, with no temperatures or times given. He just had to trust in the crystal, and hope. 'Brave one, that Moroda. She should not have gone on the Arillian's airship.'

'No, but she did well.'

'Barely. Kohl had to save her.'

'And Amarah and Sapora, too. Heh. Prince Sapora. He's no prince of mine. Snake.'

'No. But he will be your king in few days time.'

Anahrik went silent for a while, and Palom continued to work, wiping his brow as sweat dripped down his face.

'You want to leave the city?'

'Was it that obvious?' Anahrik chuckled, shaking his head. 'Maybe I do. Maybe we should head back up north for a while. I've got a few cousins that'd have room for us, if we needed.'

'And the weapons?' Palom looked up from the forge, his face already beginning to darken with smoke.

'Bring 'em with us. Wait out until next season. At least we can defend ourselves if it comes to it. The idea of another Arillian war… Just hearing the thunder from Jato's ship made me wanna get out the sky.'

'Anahrik…'

'I know, I know.' He bit his lip and looked away, his foot twitching. 'This Aciel. There's nothing like him. I don't trust Sapora to keep the Ittallan safe, even in Taban Yul. You know the Ittallan. And he's a half-breed. He doesn't make many of us confident.'

'What about the tour you have promised the others?' Palom

laughed, one foot still pressing onto the bellows, sending up wave after wave of air and heat, allowing the flame to burn hotter with each press.

'We'll tell them to leave with us. There's nothing in Corhaven, but Val Sharis is bigger, safer. We keep on the move. Stick to the ground, away from them.'

Palom thought about leaving. The idea was ridiculous, they had only just returned to the city, and now they had to leave? 'You led me down the right path all those years ago when I first came to the city. I would be dead if it weren't for that. Maybe you are right again about this.'

Anahrik looked up. 'Moroda faced Jato because she was silly. She didn't know better, and none of us stood up to stop her. But we know better now. I think we high-tail it out of Taban Yul as soon as we're done tonight. Go up to the palace and grab the others. Then head off. Sapora can stay and try and do what he can, if he wants. I trust my own eyes and talons first.'

'Done, then. Give me a shard.' Palom said.

Anahrik reached into his bag and pulled out several small shards of crystal, barely the length of his thumb, taken from Berel. They were wrapped in thick leaves to keep them from damage and moisture, though sand from the desert country spilled from his fingers as he unwrapped the leaves. 'If this works, Palom…'

Palom rubbed the sweat from his palms onto his apron sides, readying himself to handle such a delicate and potent substance. They looked no different from other cut gemstones, but Topeko had shared with then a book containing the secret to their power, perhaps unwillingly. 'You have learned the way, Anahrik. You have learned how to harness the dragon's power in a weapon. We are forging new legends, you and I.' He took one shard and held it delicately in his huge hands.

'Potentially.' Anahrik licked his lips.

'This may be long night, if not done correctly. The book did not say exact timings of the forging, so we will wait and see how it goes.'

Anahrik nodded, rapt with awe.

'My broadsword.'

Anahrik turned to the workbench behind them, where Palom had slung the weapons they arrived with. Unhooking the satchel lid, he pulled out the enormous sword with both hands. Cast in dark steel, it had barely been used during their time out of Val Sharis, but the blade would be the fist thing to test their technique. Hands trembling, Anahrik carried it to the forge, and held it out to Palom, handle first.

'Get ready to retreat. We do not know what may happen...' Palom clasped the handle of the weapon with his other hand, and drew it to the flame. He took a breath, not daring to glance at Anahrik, and dropped the shard into the heart of the forge while holding the blade over the top of the flames.

The resulting explosion was so sudden and so violent, it knocked the breath out of the two of them. Palom's stance was strong, and he withstood the blast, but the explosion was so bright that neither Ittallan could see for several seconds after. When his vision returned, Palom gasped—the fire burned purple. It was furious—raging and thrashing in the forge like a caged beast. 'Looks like things are going well. Let's get these weapons made.'

Outside, clouds gathered as the temperature dropped. Thick snowflakes drifted down silently from the heavens, at first melting on contact with the ground, but as it accumulated, it settled, coating the rooftops of the city in a fine, white fuzz.

Palom and Anahrik continued working into the night, seeing through the teachings from Topeko's books, arrogant in their dismissal of his words that the power they sought would not be theirs. But attempting to create dragon-forged weapons was not only a boyhood dream of Palom's, it was something to give Anahrik and himself incredible advantage in battle, and a way to secure a successful business for the remainder of his days. If it came to it, he would join Moroda, Eryn and the others in their fight against Aciel. His distaste for lies and deception ran deep, and he would not tolerate Aciel's attempt to dominate those in Linaria through these means.

Even if he and Anahrik did not join the fight, they would be on the move to avoid the violence Aciel brought with him to their home.

*

In the rushed preparations for the ball, Amarah slipped back into the palace, scythe and all. The city had been a hub of activity, even at the dusk hour, and she'd been pushed and jostled by the large crowds. By the time she returned, her pockets were considerably fatter, and, thanks to the Ittallan's lack of modesty, she'd overheard the wealthiest of the ball guests would be staying in the palace. Amarah planned on making herself very rich indeed that evening.

As she sauntered through the palace, imagining how it must be to be a real Goldstone, she spied the raven muttering to himself under his breath as he shuffled along. Narrowing her eyes, she trailed him, keeping a safe distance in case he turned around to look.

It soon became apparent she did not need to practice any form of stealth, as he was too engrossed in his mutterings to pay any attention to anything bar where he was going. His black sash, too long for him, dragged along the floor, picking up dust and dirt where he walked, and Amarah followed as he entered a drawing room.

'...that damned filthy snake. Bastards, the both of them. How dare they stroll in here? Ordering us about like servants. And the ball tonight. No right to be doing this to us. I won't stand for it! I won't! I'll get together with—'

'I do hope you're not speaking badly of Sapora.' Amarah said, slamming the bottom of her weapon on his sash, pinning it to the ground. The raven whirled around, eyes wide. 'He's a very dear friend of mine, I'll have you know.' She grasped the handle of her scythe and leant the blade close to his chin. 'Considering I've not seen any other Varkain in the city since turning up, I'll have to assume you were talking about your prince? Badly of him, too? Tut, tut, tut.'

'Y—you!'

'Something going on that I should know about?' She twisted the blade so the edge poked at the loose skin on his jaw.

'If... if you're a friend of Prince Sapora then there's no

problem!' He raised his hands defensively, cowering at her blade.

'I'm not so sure about that. Sounded like you were plotting something.'

'You've no right to order me about!'

Amarah pushed the edge of the scythe into his skin, drawing blood. 'I think you'll find I have every right to know. Tell me what's going on, and I'll let you leave with your head.'

*

Upstairs, Moroda picked at a speck of dust on her silk ball gown, looking at herself in one of the mirrors of the dressing room. Palace servants had brought them a selection of outfits for the evening, and she and Eryn had delighted in changing out of their travelling clothes and into something comfortable and clean. Eryn had opted for green, while Moroda had worn midnight blue to complement her ring. Being guests in the royal palace certainly had its benefits; she had been able to bathe in a tub of hot water and scrub away dirt and dried blood. As she admired her reflection, she wondered whether it was a step too close to being a Goldstone again.

Wrinkling her nose, she wondered what Amarah would think to see her dressed this way. She dwelled on the thought as she left the room and made her way downstairs to where the others waited in the foyer. She saw Eryn in conversation with Morgen—dressed for the occasion in a red and gold doublet, sword still at his hip—with Kohl stood off to the side, looking pensive.

'Kohl?'

'Moroda. You're looking lovely, too.' Kohl said, glancing

down at her when she broke him from his thoughts. 'You have the sphere safe?'

She reached into the pocket of her outer skirts and withdrew it to show him. 'I'll keep it with me the whole night.'

Kohl nodded, and glanced up, tapping his hat to the pair of royal guards who approached at Moroda's arrival. 'Ladies, Sirs. The prince and princess await.'

'Thank you,' Moroda inclined her head. 'Are you sure you don't want to join, Kohl?'

'I'm sure you will have plenty of fun for me. I wish to keep watch.'

'Look how many of the Imperial and Royal Guard are here,' Morgen said. 'Nothing will happen. Aciel is still out to sea, I'm sure.'

'All the same. Enjoy the evening,' he tapped his hat to them and walked downstairs to the palace entrance.

Moroda watched as he left, but knew she could not change his mind.

'Don't worry, Ro. As he said, let's enjoy the night. Dragons above it's been too long since we had any fun,' Eryn said.

'Ryn? Ro? Shall we?' Morgen stepped up, holding out his arms. The sisters smiled at each other, looped their arms through his, and followed the two members of the guard into the ballroom.

The grand doors were opened for them, and Moroda's breath caught in her throat. It seemed the ballroom was the jewel in the palace's crown of opulence thus far. The floor was solid marble, and ten pillars lined the room, each carved in the likeness of a different animal, and all were draped in gemstones and gold. The ceiling was over thirty feet high, and three six-tier crystal chandeliers hung from it, filling the vast room in shimmering, gold light.

Tables were laid at the edges and top of the room, leaving a wide, empty square in the middle. Musicians stood on a small, raised stage to the edge of the hall, and strings and wind instruments gently accompanied the murmur of conversation as the seated guests spoke among themselves. Moroda tried to count the tables as they followed the guards across the room, but her head span. The room must have held two or three hundred people at her best estimate. She looked to Eryn and saw childlike wonder on her face as she marvelled at what she saw, her eyes locked on the chandeliers above.

'Happy, Ryn?' Moroda asked.

'You have no idea, Ro. This is amazing! What a palace!'

They paused as they approached a wide table at the head of the room: the royal table. She recognised Elafion sat looking rather uncomfortable as he drank heavily from a goblet of wine. Other Ittallan sat beside him, Council members, she assumed, though she did not recognise their faces. Sapora sat in the middle of the table. He was listening to a Council member speak to him, but Moroda could tell his focus was elsewhere. She shivered a little as their escort announced their arrival.

Sapora lifted his gaze to meet Moroda's, and he blinked slowly. 'Sister, this is Morgen, of the Imperial Guard, and Eryn and Moroda—Goldstones.' He did not wait for a response, and instead resumed conversation with the woman beside him. They were immediately directed to four empty spaces several seats to Sapora's right, and the three of them sat down together. Wine was poured immediately into their waiting goblets, and they were then left alone to enjoy the hubbub of noise and activity.

'Not much of an introduction from the prince!' Morgen huffed. 'After all we've been through!'

'He's playing the part well,' Moroda said. 'Was that Isa beside him?'

'I don't know, I haven't seen the princess before,' Eryn replied. 'Must've been, though. He said "sister," didn't he?'

Moroda sighed and leaned back in her chair, happy to be warm and comfortable. They saw Ittallan guests and servants alike bustle around, drinking wine and water, and speak freely. News they were being joined by Prince Sapora had spread throughout the palace, and Moroda could see everyone was on their best behaviour.

'You'd think they were all trying to impress him.' Eryn giggled, as the fifth pair of Ittallan approached the royal table to greet Sapora.

'Can't think why they'd want to be in his good books.' Morgen tutted.

As the music changed to something softer, the food was served. It was exquisite, as befitting a royal banquet, and the hall came alive with the music of the piano and strings, drums and singers. It was nothing like the incredible magical essence of the Berel music, Moroda had to admit, but it was pleasant to the ears and went well with the food.

'Ro, this is amazing.' Eryn said, resting her fork on the side of her dish. They had eaten well in their youth, but the richness of the meats, variety of vegetables, and depth of flavour in the sauces was beyond anything either of them had tasted. Moroda and Eryn both cleared their plates, though Morgen picked at his food, claiming an upset stomach.

'Morgen, it's okay to say if you don't like it,' Eryn said, leaning forward past Moroda.

'Huh?'

'Really. You're not here to prove anything to anyone.'

'Oh, right. Yeah.' Morgen reached forward for a slice of bread with a thick crust, and chewed on it.

Eryn smiled at Moroda, but didn't press him.

The second, third, and fourth courses passed by in similar fashion, and it was only at dessert—a soft sponge filled with sweet cream and berries—that Morgen's enthusiasm returned, wolfing down his own plate and finishing Eryn and Moroda's too.

'I suppose something is better than nothing.' Moroda giggled. She had kept half an eye on Sapora for most of the night, and when she spied the raven entering the ballroom shortly after dessert, she tugged on her sister's sleeve.

*

'My prince, are you ready?'

Sapora glanced up and saw the raven was back, hovering in front of the table, almost whimpering as he waited for a response. He turned to his left, where Isa was sat. She wore a grey-blue dress adorned with topaz and amber to match the bright yellow of her eyes. 'Sister?'

Isa looked up from her half-eaten plate, eyes darting to the raven then back to Sapora. 'It is time already?'

'If you are ready, then yes, indeed.' The raven nodded. Isa glanced down the length of their table; she saw nothing but swans and peacocks pruning, showing off and boasting to one another. Sapora's invited guests stood out like a sore thumb. 'I am ready,' she said.

'I shall inform the musicians.' The raven said, shuffling back across the floor to the orchestra on the other side of the great ballroom.

Isa stood from her chair and walked around the table. She stepped out onto the golden-marble floor—so well-cleaned it held an almost mirror-like quality—her silks skimming the ground with each step. A thin length of fabric draped from each wrist and connected to the back of her dress, billowing out behind her. Conversation quietened around the room as she crossed the expanse of the floor, her shoes making the quietest of taps as she took each step.

Moroda watched Sapora, garbed in a dark blue coat and tails, as he stood by the edge of the floor, waiting for Isa to take position. She swallowed the last of her wine and placed the empty goblet on the table.

Sapora stepped into the open space, paused, and then took another few steps. He was silent as he slowly and pointedly made his way across, every eye in the hall watching as he moved. Moroda shivered, a little of her fear of him returning. Though this was an evening of entertainment, she couldn't help but think Sapora looked like he was stalking his prey as he approached Isa.

The princess raised a gloved hand as he drew close, watching him, determined. She ignored the many Ittallan looking up at her from the surrounding tables, and watched nothing but him. Sapora placed one hand on the small of her back and the other in her left hand, and they held their position for a long moment. The pianist began to play, and the two began to dance.

Moroda watched, fascinated, as they hardly touched one another, Isa's skirts wheeling with her motion as though she had a pair of wings. The strings joined the piano, and Sapora and Isa waltzed across the marble floor in exaggerated movements, slightly facing away from one another. Their steps were quick and light, almost completely silent. Practiced and precise. Two hunters dancing around one another rather than with one another.

To her left and right, Ittallan rose from their tables and stepped onto the ballroom floor, joining the dance. Silks and tails span as the dancers moved, jewels sparkled as the light of the chandeliers dimmed and the music rose.

'Shall we dance, too?' Eryn asked.

'Dance?' Morgen spluttered. 'I... I don't know...'

'Why not? We're dressed for it. We're invited guests.'

Tables emptied around them as half the hall joined the waltz. People changed partners as the music shifted, men danced with men and women with women. Moroda longed to join them. It had been years since she had last danced, and she very much doubted the opportunity would come up again. It was another taste of her old life, another reminder of how things were, how they could have been, if it weren't for Aciel.

'Ro?'

Moroda looked at her sister. Eryn wanted to. She had denied what Eryn wanted for the whole trip. Joining in with the dancing at a ball they had been invited to wasn't wrong. It certainly wasn't as reckless as sneaking aboard Jato's airship.

'Ryn.' Moroda smiled, standing up and holding out a hand for her sister.

The two joined the other Ittallan, fitting into step smoothly. Moroda watched as Eryn's smile broadened, and then her sister giggled. They twirled with the music, and partners changed again.

Her new partner was a man, taller than she by almost two feet, but his steps were incredibly light. He carried her with an easy strength, and Moroda felt she was hardly dancing at all. Out of the corner of her eye, she saw Eryn partnered with a woman in red, feathers billowing from her dress and shoes. Eryn continued to smile.

Moroda was hardly aware of the change in music as partners changed again, and again, and again. Eryn laughed and smiled whenever she caught glimpses of her, and she found herself smiling, too. She was hardly aware of the time, either—had she been dancing for two minutes or twenty?

She watched as Morgen stepped in, grinning as he timed his joining to partner with Eryn. His face was red in the heat of the room—or embarrassment, perhaps—as he held Eryn's arm and back stiffly, trying to keep up with the music while she whirled around him.

Partners changed again, and she found herself with Isa. Her breath caught as she realised who held her arms. They span and stepped together, then away, and Moroda was very aware of how heavy her steps were in comparison to the princess's.

Isa leaned forward as they span, almost kissing her ear. 'I'd leave now if I were you, little Ro.'

Moroda's eyes widened. Despite the glass of wine, she knew her senses had not dulled enough to have misheard Isa's warning.

Partners changed again, and she found herself back with Eryn. 'The princess says we should leave.'

'Why?' Eryn leaned in, then twirled away from her as the strings grew louder. 'It's not finished yet!'

'I don't know.' Moroda's pulse increased, and she suddenly became aware of the sweat at her temples. 'Something's going to happen.' She looked around the ballroom, and saw Sapora and Isa were again dancing together, turning faster and faster. She looked for Morgen, but in the crowd of colours and fabrics, she could not see him. The music continued to rise, and she stopped, holding Eryn still. 'Ryn...'

As the song reached a crescendo, light engulfed the prince and princess as they both transformed. Moroda's jaw dropped as she saw the Varkain transform for the first time, and a ripple of similar shock and fear cascaded through the guests gathered in the hall. A grey-green cobra, more than thirty feet in length and with fangs almost as long as a sword, sat coiled on the floor, hood fanned out and green eyes gleaming. Flicking out his black forked tongue, Sapora raised himself from his coil to look about the room, his pupils little more than slits in the bright light.

Isa joined Sapora's hiss with her own, and bared her teeth, her tail lashing.

The music and dancers had stopped, and Moroda saw the raven hurry away, hiding to the side of the musicians' stage. She held Eryn's hand tightly.

'None can call him anything other than a true Varkain.'

'For a half-breed, he's certainly formidable.'

'What's this damned Varkain doing back in our court? He should go and rule those filthy tunnels of his and leave Val Sharis to the Ittallan. Hmph. Showing up here unannounced and trying to throw his weight around.' Moroda gulped and looked to where the voice came from, and saw it was an Ittallan who was still seated: Elafion, the one who lead the Council of Val Sharis. She knew he did not think highly of Sapora, but the wine had clearly loosened his tongue. In the silent all, his voice was not missed.

Sapora turned his head, his gaze locked onto him, and flicked out his tongue. Moroda took a step back, pulling Eryn with her. 'Ryn...'

In the next moment, Sapora had struck, his fangs so large they pierced through the Ittallan's chest. Blood cascaded to the floor.

'Ro...' Eryn whimpered.

'Don't look, don't look! We're going now!' Moroda said, turning away as panicked Ittallan screamed all around her. 'Run!'

'Ryn! Ro!' Morgen called from the far side of the hall, catching Moroda's attention. She darted forward, pulling Eryn along with her as they tried to navigate through and around the frightened Ittallan. In her peripheral vision, she saw the enormous snake strike again, and again, and again. By the time the three of them escaped the room, she'd counted seven strikes.

'I want to get away from here!' Eryn cried. 'I want to go home!'

'Hush, Ryn,' Moroda said, frantically looking for a way to the doors. The two members of the Royal Guard stood at attention outside didn't move at the cacophony of noise from within the ballroom. Moroda fought back tears as she looked up at them and their stoic expressions. 'We can't stay here. We have to go.'

'But where? How? I don't know where Amarah is!' Morgen said.

'Anywhere! Anywhere but here! I want to go!' Eryn cried. 'Please! I can't stand this killing!'

Moroda squeezed Eryn's shoulders. 'Let's get out of the palace.'

Morgen winced at Eryn's tears, but nodded. 'Alright, follow me. Let's find Kohl and get out of here, now.'

*

'Please, settle everyone, settle. The floor will be open again momentarily.' The raven called, signalling the musicians to start once again as brother and sister returned to their alternate forms. The corpses had been removed and servants worked to clean the blood spilled on the floor and walls, hunkering down to keep out of sight. Sapora paid close attention to those who hadn't screamed, run, or tried drawing a weapon in defence against his fangs. He knew who would remain loyal to him, or at least stay fearful enough to not threaten his authority. His act of brutal strength had shown the many doubters he was not only serious about his throne, but ready and willing to squash any rumours about his perceived mixed-blood weakness.

By the time he and Isa had returned to the royal table, the ballroom was three quarters full. He smirked as several pairs returned to the floor in a display of loyalty, continuing the dance and resuming the evening as though nothing had happened. He knew their fear of the Varkain had been refreshed, and would keep them in check so long as he remained in Val Sharis.

'Not long to go now. The snows have started,' Sapora said, lifting his glass to his lips as he spoke.

'As long as Aciel doesn't get to us first,' Isa sighed. 'The fodder might be cowering before you, but you can't scare him with your transformation.'

'I will not rule a ruin, sister. You will be fine with your fleet and the Royal Guard if he is foolhardy enough to attack. I've not let you down before. I do not intend to start.'

Chapter Twenty-One

The air was crisp and snow silently fell as Moroda, Eryn, and Morgen hurried through the wilds of Val Sharis on horseback. They'd left Taban Yul at Eryn's behest, and Morgen had secured them three strong horses from his colleagues in the guard. He'd been promised they knew the terrain well and wouldn't lead them astray. Moroda had not wanted to leave in such haste, but Eryn had panicked and wanted to get away from Sapora's sudden savagery. Moroda couldn't blame her, and she kept thinking to Princess Isa's words. The nickname she called her by seemed taunting, but the warning was real enough. Had she wanted to spare them from Sapora's wrath? Had he chosen to attack them, they wouldn't have stood a chance. Or was she trying to protect them from the gruesome sight, perhaps? Moroda couldn't be sure.

Kohl kept ahead, staying on the wing. The Arillian's emotions seemed mixed, and he was quieter than ever, but Moroda's priority was Eryn's safety and security. She could deal with whatever mood he was in later.

Eryn wanted to get as far away from the palace as possible, and when that brought them to the city outskirts, she had charged on. Evening gowns were not the most practical of clothes to wear in the snow on the back of a horse, but they'd had no time to change. Thankfully the royal guard had offered them some thick blankets to wrap around themselves as they rode, but Moroda was more than a little uncomfortable after half an hour of forced pace.

Eryn pushed the horses to canter as often as possible, and Moroda had asked her to slow down several times—especially where the path narrowed as they travelled through the forest surrounding Taban Yul—but it was only when a small brook crossed their path did Eryn finally stop.

'Ryn,' Moroda called, reining up and sliding off her horse so it could drink. She hurried over to her sister. 'There, there, it's okay. We're far away now. You can't even see the city anymore.'

'Ro...'

Moroda stepped forward and took Eryn's hand, helping her down from her horse and embracing her in a hug, blanket and all. 'It's okay. Don't worry. I know you wanted to get away. Sapora isn't here.'

The cold around them intensified with Kohl's presence. Every step or turn he made sent a breath of cold air in every direction, and Moroda shivered. They were stood on a well-used path, which followed the natural hollow of the trees. The brook was only three or four paces wide, shallow and fast flowing. She could no longer hear or see the vast city of Taban Yul, and the trees thinned as they continued along the pathway. She still had the ereven sphere, and took it from her pocket to warm her hands.

'You okay, Ryn?' Morgen asked, stepping forward and clambering off his own horse. 'I know it was horrible for you back there. Goes to show you can't trust a Varkain! Don't know what he was thinking. The Royal Guard all kept quiet and didn't do a thing!

A planned massacre!'

Eryn sniffled and buried her face in her blanket for a moment.

Moroda rubbed her shoulders, wondering how to lift her sister's spirits, and thought back to the dancing. Eryn was happy, then. Happier than she'd been in ages. Moroda could hardly remember the last time she laughed so much. But none of them had known the night was to end in a blood bath. She didn't understand Sapora—what he wanted or why he behaved as he did. Kohl had gone some way to explaining his actions, but his senseless killing sickened her. Did he have to show his strength over the Ittallan so violently? And Isa, the princess, she hadn't joined in, had she? They had left before they could see the entire macabre act. In the little she had gleaned of the princess, she and Sapora shared many similarities, and Moroda knew she was one to be wary of, too. Moroda touched the ring on her finger, a habit she had developed, and frowned.

'I'm sorry, Ro.' Eryn sniffed, lifting the blanket from her face. Her eyes were red and cheeks puffy.

'Don't be sorry, Ryn! Please! You've done nothing wrong. I wanted to get away, too.'

Eryn sniffed again and nodded, bundling her hands up in the blanket around her. 'Where are we?'

'North of Taban Yul,' Kohl said. 'If we keep on this course, we'll be heading for the Feor Mountains. I don't know the lie of the land past that. There may be villages on the way.'

'We should keep going then,' Moroda said.

'You don't mean that? It's the middle of the night. It's snowing.'

'And we have the ereven sphere. We might as well keep going. The Feor Mountains will be the best place to start looking for a dragon, anyway.'

'The mountains? What makes you think that's a good place to start?'

'Topeko's books—the older the dragon, the higher it will be. Sevastos wandered the skies of Linaria endlessly. So an old dragon, one that is powerful or might become a Sevastos, will be found at the tops of mountains or flying above clouds. Younger dragons are the common sight. They're too young to fight an old dragon for territory, so they rarely venture too high. Not what we're after.'

'Smart girl.' Kohl conceded, tipping his hat to her once again. 'It would probably be wise if you three returned to the city. I can fly further and faster than any horse can run. I could be in the mountains before dawn.'

'Trying to get rid of us that quickly, are you?' Moroda laughed, brushing down the mane of the mare she had ridden with her fingers. 'We're in this together, remember. It means as much to the three of us as it does to you. If it takes an extra day, it takes an extra day.'

'What about our stuff? Supplies? Proper clothes?' Morgen asked.

'We have clothes on our back, don't we? If there are any villages, I'm sure we could trade some of these palace jewels for coin or food?'

Kohl shook his head and ruffled his wings. 'Time is of the essence, or did you misunderstand that?'

'There's no need to be rude,' Eryn said. 'You wanted to look after us and make sure we were all okay. Now we're here, there's no need to race off and leave us behind.'

Kohl sighed and shook his head again. 'I don't want to leave you behind. But I know the true danger of Aciel and his generals. Not to mention the danger of the creatures we seek. It makes more sense if I continue alone. The pace I wish to set would not be fair on any of you. Go back to Taban Yul. Find an inn, if not the palace, and get some rest.'

'I don't think you're going to change our minds, Kohl,' Moroda said. 'We may not be able to fly as you can, but we started this together and that's how we should finish it. Eryn doesn't want to go back to the city, and if I'm honest, neither do I. I've spent the whole trip ignoring what she wanted, and look what happened!'

'There's not much for us in the city, anyway,' Morgen said. 'Sapora is off to be King, Amarah said she'd only ever take us as far as here. Palom and Anahrik will carry on their business now they're home. Our party has broken up, so all the more reason for us to stick together considering the dangers.'

Kohl twitched his nose and scratched at his scarred lip. He looked up to the falling snow and sighed. 'I suppose you are on horseback. It's not as if you're as slow as on foot. But the snow is getting heavier by the minute.'

'We'll keep going until we can find some shelter to wait out the worst of the snow and get some rest in.' Morgen suggested, looking at the path ahead. 'We can use the time to work out how to approach a powerful dragon without getting burnt to a crisp!'

Moroda clambered on to her horse, her brow furrowed. She had been so preoccupied with how to find a dragon, she'd not stopped to think what to do once they found one. An old dragon would be more powerful than the drake that attacked Niversai. How would it be approached, let alone interacted with, distracted, or even, if it came to it, subdued?

She held the sphere in her hand, struggling a little with her blanket to keep covered from the falling snow. It worked in a similar way to her ring, but she had to pay close attention to the liquid inside to know the best course of action. As she predicted, it pointed straight towards the mountains. 'Let's go.'

'Maybe we should look for something to feed it.' Eryn said, once they were underway. 'You know, how sometimes you approach an angry dog with a bit of meat? Makes it more likely to trust you?'

'That's not a bad idea.' Morgen nodded. 'But I don't think it'll be too impressed if you compare it to a dog!'

'That's not what I meant!'

'The books mention dragons and their intelligence. Sevastos, and a dragon of the age we seek will understand our tongue.' Moroda said. 'We'll just need to talk to it, be polite and respectful. It's a hundred year old creature.'

'I never heard of a dragon that could talk.' Morgen said as his horse crossed the brook.

'I suppose Val Sharis seems to be the home of the old dragons.'

'Still... I wonder how would it know not to eat us?'

'Do not concern yourself with that, Morgen,' Kohl said. 'The dragons are not your gods for nothing.'

'Your gods? Don't you mean "our" gods?' Eryn asked, turning her head to look back at Kohl.

'No, I don't. Arillians don't hold with such nonsense.'

'Nonsense!' Moroda said, almost stopping her horse in its tracks. 'Arillians...?'

'We follow quite a different lore. Rhea and her dragons are stories we speak of, but nothing more.' He ruffled his wings and half leapt, half flew across a stretch of path.

Moroda's teeth chattered as the icy breeze kissed her exposed skin.

'Sorry, Moroda.' Kohl landed a short distance from them. 'Hardly realise I'm doing that, sometimes.'

'But everyone in Linaria... even the Varkain—' Morgen began.

'I know everyone seems to be repulsed by the Varkain, but they are just as much of Linaria as you or the Samolen, or the Ittallan. We Arillians don't even live on Linaria, we are above it. Our homes float. We are shielded by our powers. And all of the world has exiled us to the farthest reaches that we might never be seen or come into contact.'

'Kohl, that's so awful.' Moroda shook her head. 'I didn't realise.'

'I understand Aciel. He is doing what he thinks is right. Why should an entire race be wiped out because of what our forefathers did? The world is against us. So he has decided to take the world back. He and Sapora have much in common.'

Moroda saw Eryn flinch at Sapora's name, and her lip quivered. Eryn had been so strong. Always so strong. Quick-witted and clever, incredibly optimistic. To see her so anxious tore at her heart. She knew she was responsible for the change in her sister. So far she had kept her promise of doing as she asked, but she needed a long-term plan. What was she to do after they found the dragon? Even if Aciel was stopped, how could she find peace when Linaria was so ravaged?

'What did you mean when you said your homes float?' Eryn asked, breaking Moroda from her thoughts.

Kohl looked back and sighed. 'Arillians live on scattered islands far to the north. Those of us who are left. The islands are suspended, held aloft with our storms.'

'Goodness. I should love to see that one day.' 'Ryn...' Moroda said.

'Perhaps if peace ever comes to Linaria you will. As it stands, no-one visits our homeland in the same way non-Varkain do not enter Sereth.'

Moroda could feel the sadness in his voice. She could sense frustration, too, but he did not become angry. She pondered on his life before they met as the trees surrounding their path fell away a few leagues short of the base of the mountains. In the cold, crisp night, perfectly untouched snowy fields lay before the small party.

'So beautiful.' Moroda said, taking in the view. 'See Eryn, we'd never see anything like this if we had stayed back in Niversai.'

Eryn nodded. 'I know… I'm glad I came, Ro… but it hasn't been easy.'

'Hardest part is still to come.' Moroda smiled. Despite Eryn's earlier tears, it seemed she was finding her confidence again.

'The sooner we find our dragon, the sooner we can bring an end to Aciel's terror.' Morgen said, taking point as he spurred his horse to the front of the group. 'There's got to be a village nearby where we can sleep for the night, before the snow gets too bad. We can leave first thing tomorrow.'

Eryn followed behind him, and Moroda took in the view for another minute before nudging her horse forward. Kohl, horseless, drifted above the group, exerting little energy to stay airborne as they crossed the snowy fields.

'Do you want to fly ahead, Kohl? See if you can find anywhere we might rest?' Morgen asked.

The quiet was shattered an instant later as a bolt of lightning ripped through the black of the night and crashed into the centre of the field. Morgen's horse reared in fright, and he was thrown off, landing with a thud on the freshly fallen snow.

Moroda and Eryn's horses were also spooked, but were further back and had not reared. 'Morgen!' Eryn called, clambering down and running over to where he lay in the snow. 'Are you alright?' She crouched down and pulled him up by his elbow.

'Y—yeah. Just dazed. Snow cushioned the fall, I think.' He said, sitting up, one hand on his head. 'What happened?'

Kohl landed at once, his eyes locked on the Arillian hovering in the night sky just above them.

'Well, well, well, what do we have here?' Jato said from above, her dark wings almost invisible in the night. 'What a find, what a find!' She descended to the snowy field and landed softly; several other Arillians landed at her side, all in full battle armour.

Kohl stepped back and helped Morgen get to his feet, his feathers bristling.

'Oh no, not again!' Moroda clambered down from her horse and stood beside her sister, grabbing on to her arm.

From the looks of it, Jato had been preparing to come to Val Sharis—the armour she wore was lined with gold, delicately etched in winding patterns across the silver-grey surface. Like the other Arillians, she carried no weapon, and she folded her arms as she took in the sight before her.

'Killing you three will be an excellent way to start the night.' Jato said, her eyes glinting in the darkness. 'I'm sure Aciel would be pleased.'

'General, why kill them? They've done nothing to you.' Kohl said, stepping forward.

'Orders are orders, Kohl. Or have you been away so long you've forgotten how things work?'

Moroda gulped, holding onto her sister and taking a step back. Her horse stood nearby, whickering and pawing at the snow. 'Eryn… we should run…' She tried not to move her lips. She was grateful Jato's attention was on Kohl.

'We'd never outrun them.' Morgen whispered back. 'A

whole scouting party... we'd never make it back to Taban Yul before they caught us. But they won't be expecting us to stand and fight, I don't think.'

'Of course I haven't forgotten.' Kohl said, looking at the other Arillians. There were six in all.

Jato grinned and closed her eyes. 'Good. Your first order is to eliminate those three.'

Kohl froze.

'Aciel has now made his move, hadn't you heard? After your attack... where is that woman with the scythe? She damned near sliced Aciel's arm off! She'll pay for that. You'll all learn that Aciel is not to be crossed. We're to kill anyone we come up against. Those three should be easy for you, shouldn't they, great dragon slayer?'

'Jato... Aciel is mistaken. You cannot—'

'Don't question your superiors! Or shall I add you to my list of people to eliminate?' Jato snapped. 'My loyalty is to Aciel, it always has been, and nothing will change that! Now I don't have all night. Kill them now, or I will—and you afterwards.'

'Kohl?' Moroda took a step back, her heart thundering. She watched as he turned to face her, his hands shaking as he raised them. Moroda caught his eye, and looked away immediately.

'I cannot... I...' He spread his wings and slowly drifted into the air. 'I am... sorry...' His voice shook. Kohl called upon his own powers and unleashed a wave of frost in all directions. The few surrounding trees collapsed under the sudden freeze, and sent up thick, dusty white smoke as they crashed into the snow.

When the dust settled, Kohl had vanished.

Jato and the other Arillians coughed as the dust surrounded them. 'Traitor!' She glared into the sky then turned to one of her Elites. 'Follow him. Bring him back to me alive. He'll pay for that. I don't care who he is!'

'Yes, Jato.' He took off in a flurry of wind and feathers, charging after Kohl.

'As for those three...' Jato turned to glare down. 'I need to report to Aciel. Finish them off, quickly. We'll regroup after.' She took to the air as soon as her order was given, and flew off in the opposite direction to Kohl, back towards Taban Yul.

Moroda knew there was no escaping this confrontation. They were left with five Arillians, all of whom had been ordered to kill her, Eryn, and Morgen. There was no time to think or plan, no time to size up the situation. She gripped Eryn's hand as Morgen rushed forward, sword drawn, and swung it up at the closest Arillian. He glanced at Morgen, avoided the strike by flying out of range, and replied with a short bolt of electricity. It connected with Morgen's wrist and sent his sword careening from his grasp.

Morgen dove for his weapon and grabbed it as two of the other Elites flew overhead, their attentions on the sisters. The remaining horses had fled—they had little bottle in them at the best of time, and their frightened whinnies carried well through the crisp, cold air.

Moroda clenched her hands into fists, and felt the ring on her finger. To be used when a fight couldn't be avoided. She stepped in front of Eryn and raised her hand; summoning all the strength she could muster to form a shield in front of her and her sister. She had nothing to draw energy from except her own body, and she was already tired from the events of the night and the ride outside the city. But the shield worked, repelling the Arillian's vicious wind and electrical attacks, which singed away the snow to leave the scorched earth barren and blackened underneath.

Again and again they came, flying at her and shooting balls and bolts of lightning, their wind attacks blasting Moroda and Eryn where they stood, but the shield held through pure desperation. Morgen sliced at the enemy as best he could, but the Arillian's flight advantage stopped his attacks from connecting, and he found himself battered by their energy.

Thunder rolled around them, and sweat ran down Moroda's forehead, her arm straining to keep her shield of energy up. But the strength came from her body, and it was running on empty.

'Ro...' Eryn stood beside her, her own arms raised as she fed Moroda's shield with her own energy. It was a meagre effort, and Moroda could feel the shield weakening and she and Eryn tired.

Another bolt of lightning, and the shield halved. 'Hold it, Ryn! We can... keep them away!' Moroda had practiced the magic taught to her by Topeko and his books, but the strength of the Arillian's attacks and fear threatened to overwhelm her. Three Arillians spiralled down from above, and Moroda tried to strengthen the shield, lifting her other hand to move more energy to it. Eryn trembled beside her. She felt the breath of the Arillian's wind attacks and the sting of their electricity, and then snow crashed all around her again, filling the air with a white, whirling storm.

Moroda remembered little else from the battle. The Arillians attacked without hesitation and showed no mercy. The snow underfoot was swept away by the fury of their assault; already bare trees ripped up by their roots and cast about as vicious winds whipped around in a hurricane. Thunder roared through the air and the ground trembled. Moroda was knocked off her feet more than once by flailing branches, and it did not take long before blood and bruises littered her skin.

She had barely enough time to take in what was approaching her, much less keep on her feet or mount any sort of defence. The reduced visibility did not help, and her panic froze her feet in place. Where anyone else was, she had no clue—Eryn, Morgen, or the Arillians; they were little more than grey shadows lost in the swirling winds.

Every so often, Moroda would feel a jolt of intense heat as she was struck by an electrical blast. Whether they were direct hits or offshoots, she did not know, but the pain was cripplingly intense, and left her more stunned than when she was struck by one of the trees. Doubled over, Moroda sank to her knees, exhaustion taking hold. The biting cold from the snow left her legs and hands numb, and the pain in her head and stomach from multiple attacks drowned out everything else.

The wind was deafening, and she covered her ears, trying to keep low to the ground, hoping simply to survive the onslaught. It was only when a sudden splash of orange appeared among the dull greys and whites did she realise she was no longer alone.

Forcing herself up from her knees, Moroda stumbled back,

her skirts snagging on an uprooted tree. She wrenched the cloth free, sending tiny jewels flying, and fell over to her side once again. As she looked up, she realised the roar was not from the whirling wind, but from the fangs of an enormous tiger that had joined the fray.

'Moroda! Run!' Morgen screamed, clutching his bloody arm as he limped over to her. Despite the cold, his hair was stuck to his forehead, sweat dripping down his cheeks.

'Morgen!' Moroda called, getting back to her feet, her eyes wide as she saw the extent of his injuries. 'You're hurt! Badly!'

'Get away! Get back to the city!' He spun around to dive out of the way of another bolt of lightning, the heat stinging Moroda's cheeks as it passed. Morgen broke his fall with his good hand and immediately rolled away, narrowly avoiding the follow up attack.

Anahrik leapt to his defence, appearing in a flash and blocking the Arillian's electricity with a short sword—it was little more than a dagger. Moroda watched in amazement as the blade glowed bright blue, reflecting light from the snow around them.

Anahrik took in a breath before pushing the Arillian back, his blade continuing to glow. The Arillian intensified his attacks, slivers of electricity bouncing off Anahrik's blade, but nothing connected. Anahrik forced himself closer, deflecting the electricity, taking slow, determined steps until he was close enough to attack— in one, quick movement; he drew a second blade from the holder on his thigh and sliced clean through the Arillian's hands.

He shrieked, blood gushing from his wrists, staining the ground a deep crimson, and he staggered backwards. Anahrik did not relent, and forced him further and further back as he slashed with the blades. The Arillian could not call upon his magic and could not defend against Anahrik's flurry of attacks.

Moroda looked away as Anahrik ended the scuffle, and rushed over to where Morgen tried to catch his breath.

'I told you to run!' Morgen clutched his left arm.

'I won't leave anyone!' Moroda said, shaking her head. 'Where's Eryn? Thank the dragons Palom and Anahrik came when they did!'

Morgen shook his head. 'Can't see her. Damn that Kohl! Bastard!'

The wind buffeted them, picking up snow and debris and flinging it around as the field turned into a snowstorm. The whiteness masked her visibility, and Moroda couldn't see anything aside from occasional bursts of orange, or if an Arillian flew close to her.

She needed to find her sister and get back to the city. Get back to safety. She needed to warn them that Jato and maybe even Aciel himself were in Val Sharis, and war was on their doorstep. How could the Arillians have been so close to the city?

'Incoming!' Anahrik yelled, racing up to where the pair huddled, his attention on the sky as a pair of Arillians dive bombed them.

Before Morgen or Moroda could react to his warning, the sheer force of the Arillian's wind attacks slammed into them. Squeezing her eyes shut from the violent storm, Moroda heard the crack of thunder as Anahrik leapt into the air to meet the tag-team attack and defend against it.

Though his left arm was weak, Morgen clutched his sword—his fingers dipping with blood. 'Please run, Moroda. You don't want to see the end of this!' He rushed into the midst of battle to join Palom.

The tiger's roar drowned out all else, and Moroda could see the thick of the fighting was now in one location—on the ground, thankfully. She knew the Arillians would not have an advantage if Palom and the others could keep them on the ground, but she was still terrified.

She wanted to run away; with every fibre of her being, she wanted to cry, to get away, to hide and never face the situation again. But she couldn't leave without Eryn.

Seconds passed, or minutes. She couldn't tell. Time stopped while all the world around her span. The pain from her wounds slowly made themselves known; an itch, at first, then a dull throb, and then the hot pain as she realised her dress had been shredded around her legs and torso. Blood trickled down her arms and face. Her head ached; the snow and sky were too bright a white to even discern shapes.

Moroda became dimly aware of moving. Her world was still blurry, wind and snow rushing all around her. She was cold and sore, and pain wracked her body as she was blasted again by another ball of electricity. The intense shock of the heat and energy sent her flying to the ground, and her sight turned black.

Chapter Twenty-Two

When Moroda awoke, she was bathed in sunlight. She blinked several times, her mind very much alert, as she adjusted to the brightness. Where was she? What happened in the battle? Her mind raced and yet her body was sluggish. She knew she was lying down, and could feel the weight of her body absorbed by something soft. A bed. A small voice in the far reaches of her mind begged for a few more minutes' rest, but Moroda shook it off. She had to concentrate.

Twitching her fingers, she tapped each one against the soft fabric it was laid on. All digits were accounted for, and her ring was still on her finger. Her body began to respond, slowly, but when she finally managed to sit up, the strain of moving left her exhausted. Her mind was furious—why was she being so slow? Why couldn't she just get up and see Eryn? See her friends? It was infuriating.

As she sat, catching her breath, she took in her surroundings. Looking to her left and right, she saw empty beds lined against the wall, and bright sunlight streamed in from windows behind each bed. It was daytime. How long had she been asleep? There was a large tapestry hanging above the door on the wall opposite her, surrounding by gold detailing. She deduced she had awoken in the palace, no doubt in its infirmary.

Glad she still had her mind, even if her body was slow to wake up, she glanced down at herself, and found she wore a plain, white gown, and bandages covered her arms. The searing pain she had felt during the battle had dulled to a throb, and as Moroda readied herself to stand up, the door opened.

Never had she been so grateful to see Palom; the huge Ittallan filled the door with his broad frame, but his eyes were red. He had a few wounds of his own, minor, in comparison to Moroda's bandages, but appeared otherwise unscathed. He stepped through the door and closed it behind him. 'Moroda.'

'Palom.' Moroda was grateful her voice still worked, even though it was quiet.

'Morgen… is bringing the others, now.' He glanced back at the door. His voice was unsteady, breaking as he spoke. His whole body shook, and Moroda could see him fight to keep from transforming. Was it sadness? Rage?

'Palom…?'

'I swear… by all the dragons… by my blood… I will kill Kohl for what he has done.'

Moroda struggled to think, closing her eyes to cast her mind back. Kohl had fled from their side before the battle had begun. A twinge of pain raced through her as she thought of Jato and her elite fighters, and of the snowstorm that caused chaos and confusion.

'Anahrik is gone.' He closed his eyes, and Moroda saw tears in the corners. 'Eryn is gone. Both killed… those damned Arilliams!' He wavered where he stood, threatening to topple over. 'Kohl is traitor and coward. I will chase him to the ends of Linaria to make him pay.'

Moroda sat in stunned silence for a long moment as Palom

shook, only his ragged breathing breaking the quiet. 'Eryn…? But… I can't… but she… I didn't see her… I didn't say…'

The door behind Palom flew open as Amarah charged in, trailed by Morgen, Sapora and Isa. 'Palom! How in Rhea's name could you let this happen?' Amarah screamed at the Ittallan, her eyes full of rage. 'A few Arillians and people die? What kind of fighter do you call yourself?'

'Do not blame me you thief!' Palom roared, turning on the sky pirate. 'Kohl's betrayal took those lives! He fled when Jato appeared!'

'Kohl? He left you?'

'That's right. Soon as they were there, he took off.' Morgen confirmed. 'Palom and… Palom didn't get there until it was almost finished.'

'I just want to go home.' Moroda said, tears spilling down her cheeks. 'Everything happened so quickly… I didn't get to speak to her before it all happened… Eryn… I can't… say goodbye…'

Her words did little to soften Amarah's harshness, and the sky pirate turned to Sapora and Isa. 'I want a warship. Nothing with Imperial colours on it. I'm gonna track down Aciel and kill every one of his followers.'

Sapora blinked slowly. 'Well, we've no shortage of those. Linaria is officially at war. This attack is one of many Aciel carried out simultaneously. We received word at dawn that Arillians attacked Niversai in the night, and the castle has now fallen. It's a ruin, and the city is under siege. He is beginning his decimation of Corhaven, beginning with the capital. Val Sharis will follow. Taban

~ 315 ~

Yul is going to be a nice, fat target for him.'

Moroda looked up, her eyes wet. 'Niversai, too...?' 'I'm afraid so,' Isa said, her voice low. 'We are amassing counter armies, but Taban Yul is likely to be next on his list. We are the nearest city that would be able to send reinforcements across the sea. Trade, too. With no fresh supplies or troops, Niversai is unlikely to recover any time soon. All Corhaven is going to be in turmoil. We must prepare to defend ourselves.'

Moroda shook her head, her mind a cacophony of confusing thoughts and raw emotions. The thought of going through another battle terrified her, but with Niversai under siege, would it even be possible to return home? Moroda clutched the bedsheets. All the world was crumbling around her, again, and she was lost in it— unable to do anything. First her father, and now Eryn and Niversai. She trembled and sobbed.

Morgen limped over to Moroda and sat beside her, leaning against her shoulder with his good arm as her emotion flooded out. His eyes watered, but he held back tears, the pain of his own wounds a welcome distraction from Moroda's intense grief. Amarah continued to talk with Sapora, Isa, and Palom, but he didn't hear their words, nor did he care to. The war Topeko had warned them of was no longer nipping at their heels; it had overtaken them. As part of the Imperial Guard, he'd be expected to fight. He'd be expected to defend what was left of Niversai, or join the ranks of his colleagues here, in Val Sharis. They'd been lucky on Jato's warship.

The more time he spent with the "crew" of Khanna, the more he'd realised he no longer wished to be part of the Imperial

Guard. Joining was an easy decision, but the reality had been very different. He knew he wanted to leave. Cowardly? Perhaps. But he didn't belong in the ranks of the Imperial Guard. That much, he knew.

He felt Moroda shudder beside him, her sobs quiet. He'd lost a cousin once, many years ago. She was only a baby, and though she hadn't lived for more than a few weeks, the pain was just as acute as if she'd grown to twenty before being snatched by death. He had only been a boy, but he understood the sorrow which tore through his family and through Moroda and Palom now.

His mind flickered to Kohl. If he had stood and fought with them… Anahrik and Eryn would probably still be here. But he hadn't. He'd fled with his tail between his legs and left them all to die. He must have known Moroda and Eryn wouldn't be able to fight, that they were outnumbered by the Arillians, that his departure sealed their fate! Palom's words of chasing Kohl down sparked a fire in him. He wanted to get revenge, too. Perhaps he should leave the Imperial Guard and join Palom on his hunt. If they survived Aciel's war.

Moroda felt the immense weight of loss wash over her as she sat on the edge of the bed, crying until she felt her eyes would bleed. Loss of her father. Loss of her sister. Loss of her friends. Loss of her home. She realised she hadn't grieved before, not truly. She hadn't been allowed to—she'd had to carry on for Eryn's sake and for her own. But now she'd lost Eryn, her quick-witted, sharp-tongued, resourceful, rational, remarkable sister… Now there was no Eryn, she could weep.

Emotion flooded her body. Anger, white hot and fluttering, coursed through her veins in her moments of respite, sapping her of what little energy remained, pushing her once again into fits of sobbing. She leaned against Morgen's arm and gave in to it.

'Palom. You once said I looked... like I was carrying the pain of the world in my heart. I am now... I can hardly breathe because of it. It's burning me, my lungs, my heart, my eyes... my skin crawls with it. It's my fault she's gone.'

Palom looked up her and shook his head. 'No. Do not say this.'

'We can't sit here waiting for Aciel to attack!' Amarah said. 'I'm not going to wait to be picked off! Moroda. That dragon you were looking for in the mountains. That'll be our only hope.'

'I'm not going to mountains. I'm going after Kohl.' Palom said.

'Kohl can wait, war cannot. It will not,' Amarah said. 'I don't have time for you to go charging off. We need to do whatever we can to survive what's coming. If that means fighting, I sure as hell want a dragon on my side.'

'Very well.' Sapora nodded. 'I shall return to Sereth to ready the Varkain. Isa, you will prepare one warship for Amarah. Double the guard and do not let any patrol alone. They must be in threes or greater. I do not wish to return to Taban Yul to find anything has fallen.'

'Of course,' Isa said.

'Amarah, you will fly us into the Feor Mountains. I will dismount near the base—it's quicker for me to get to Sereth underground than you flying over the mountains. Plus, you'll need all the time you can get to find that dragon. I hope you're ready if you encounter any more Arillians out there.'

'Good. Finally we're getting somewhere,' Amarah said. 'Don't worry about me, Sapora. My blade will hit its mark, like always. Palom, Morgen, I want you both with me. If I'm coming up against a dragon, I'll need people who can fight.'

'I will go with you too, Amarah.' Moroda said. Her voice cracked as she spoke, waves of emotion coursing through her. 'There may be nothing for me in Niversai... but I wish to do whatever I can to protect those who are left.'

'Better than sitting around moping.' Amarah said.

'I, too, will come along.'

The group looked up as the door opened—the twinkling gemstones gave Topeko away as he entered the infirmary.

'Topeko?' Amarah gasped. 'What in Rhea's name are you doing here?'

He smiled, though his cheeks did not sparkle as they usually did. 'I was invited by the Council when Arillians were first spotted in Val Sharis. I left only the day after you did.' He bowed to them, his robes fanning out to his sides. 'Prince Sapora, I would like to visit Sereth once we have seen the dragon you all seek, if it is not too much trouble?'

Sapora narrowed his eyes slightly. 'I will not wait for you, but I do not see why I cannot permit it. The Samolen have little to offer or take from us.' He handed Topeko a small onyx stone, etched with his family crest, the same as Isa's. 'You'll need this to get past the Cerastes.'

'I thank you. Although it appears that those who invited me have befallen an unfortunate accident. None in the palace seem to know anything about that.' Topeko said.

'You've very welcome to Taban Yul nonetheless,' Isa interjected. 'The Samolen are held in the highest regard among the Ittallan.'

'Princess Isa.' Topeko bowed again to her.

'We can't wait any longer,' Amarah snapped, folding her arms. 'Let's get on with it and find this damned dragon.'

'Let's pray the city is still standing on our return,' Palom said.

'Praying is for the weak. Our actions will ensure the city stays safe.' Amarah countered. 'On your feet, Moroda. It's tough but we must be stronger than them.'

Moroda nodded and heaved herself off the bed, onto her feet. 'Thank you, Morgen.' She smiled weakly, straining against her inner turmoil. Her tears had ceased, and she felt numb.

'You don't have to come, Moroda. You could stay in the palace and rest,' Morgen said.

'I want to do something.'

'Still? After all that's happened?'

'Still. I'd be a wreck if I stay here with my own thoughts.'

Morgen nodded and followed her out the door.

'Little Ro,' Isa called. Moroda stopped in her tracks and looked across to the princess. 'Might want to change your clothes before you leave. It's cold out there.'

'Yes, thank you.' Moroda shuffled over to her, and felt as though she was being swept away. It was a familiar feeling, and unwanted. It was as though she were floating down a river whose current was too much for her to fight against. She barely registered changing, or walking down the palace hallways, or into the airship hanger, or even getting onto Khanna. She was dimly aware of her companions; Amarah, Palom, Morgen, Sapora, and Topeko, but couldn't focus on anything they said or did. She was in a daze.

*

It was half an hour or so into the flight, when she noticed the cold wind rushing across her face and she woke up properly. She was sat on deck, her cloak wrapped round her shoulders, the dark mountain range in the distance growing larger every moment.

'Sapora was right. We were not the only ones attacked last night.' Palom said. Moroda glanced over the edge of the deck at his words and saw smoke rising from fires yet to be extinguished. Corpses littered the snow beneath them, and the predominant colour was now a dirty red.

'Arillian scum.' Amarah said.

Even in her state of shock, Moroda could feel the tension on the airship. The mood was low, and the storms they saw writhing in the distance did little to help. Even the dragons that had been seen in the skies on their arrival to the country were fewer. She felt sick at the prospect of more conflict, of more war, of more pain, death, and destruction.

'I should never have joined the guard.' Morgen shuddered, shaking his head and rocking slowly where he sat.

Moroda looked over to him and watched as he berated himself, sometimes mumbling aloud. His left arm was still heavily bandaged, and she felt a pang of pity and guilt. 'Morgen.' She got up to sit closer to him, an echo of his earlier actions. 'You cannot blame yourself, how were you to know this war was coming? No-one knew.'

'I couldn't stop them,' he continued, seemingly oblivious to Moroda's reassurances. 'I couldn't protect her. I couldn't...'

'Morgen, stop it, please.' Moroda said, holding back a fresh wave of tears at the mention of her sister. 'Aciel is the one responsible, not you. You couldn't have done any more than you did. You didn't flee.' Her mind wandered to Kohl. The Arillian had first warned Eryn and her about the dragon attack in Niversai. How long ago that seemed. She had always trusted him because of that first action, and found the betrayal especially bitter.

Morgen stopped mumbling at her words and lifted his head from his hands, as if noticing she was sat there for the first time. 'I thought he was with us.'

'As did I. But he didn't attack us... that's got to count for something, right?'

Morgen shook his head again, his eyes still red raw from emotion. 'You always have to see the best in people, don't you? He abandoned us and you can only think that's better than being attacked?'

Moroda said nothing for a moment. She knew he was right, and had always thought it was a nice trait to have—to see the best in people. Aciel was changing her mind of that, and now perhaps Kohl was, too. She knew Amarah and Palom were keen to lump all blame on Kohl, but she couldn't make a solid opinion of his actions, and wanted an explanation more than anything else. 'Is that so bad? We don't know anything about him, really. He never said much, but he always helped us, always. I'm not excusing it. But if he were to explain it...? I'm hurting so much... losing... losing Ryn... and Anahrik... I don't want to think badly of anyone else, anymore. I don't want to wallow.'

'I know you don't want to wallow. If you did, you'd have stayed in Taban Yul. For someone who's not a fighter, you have some strength.' Morgen said.

They grew quiet, listening to the low hum of Khanna's engines as they drifted further away from Taban Yul, and snow began to fall.

'Amarah, land by that village.' Sapora instructed, once the great mountain range loomed above, their tops veiled by thick clouds.

'Feoras Sol,' Palom said. 'My hometown.'

'Alright. Hurry up about it. Snow's falling and I don't wanna be caught grounded by any damned Arillians.' Amarah said, bringing Khanna down a short way from the village. 'Topeko, you best be right about finding an old dragon to help against Aciel. We're going to be in a whole heap of shit if not.' She folded in her sails but kept her engines running as Khanna touched the snowy ground.

'We part here.' Sapora said, crossing the deck. 'When next we meet, I shall be a king.'

Moroda glanced up. She had been so wrapped up in the loss of Eryn and Anahrik, she had forgotten Sapora would be leaving their party. 'Sapora...'

'I would suggest non-Varkain avoid Sereth.' Sapora warned. 'Topeko, I await your visit.' He nodded to the Samolen then clambered down the stairs without as much as a goodbye to the others.

'All the gold in Linaria wouldn't be enough to get me into that hell hole!' Amarah said, cackling. She leaned on the steering wheel as Sapora departed. 'I say good riddance to that damned snake, especially after everything that happened in the palace!'

'You were there?' Moroda asked.

'Yup. Upstairs though.' She cackled again, and Moroda doubted she was upstairs sleeping. 'No commotion outside that ballroom, but saw a load of servants carrying bodies away. Sapora and his sister seem to be changing things. That raven is terrified of him.'

'Is this the unfortunate accident which befell Elafion?' Topeko asked.

'The same. What are you going to Sereth for, anyway? Dirty bloody hole in the ground.'

'A few answers. I wish to pay my respect to the changing of kings, too.'

'Palom... How did you know where to find us?' Moroda asked, suddenly wondering about his arrival the night before.

The Ittallan was stood by the edge of the deck, frowning as he looked to the village. 'We had gone back to palace. One of the

Royal Guard told us you from Corhaven had left earlier in the night. We tracked you.'

Moroda felt him pause.

'I want to find the dragon and end this nightmare.'

'Avenge Anahrik?'

'Eryn, too. I want to track down Kohl.'

'I understand how you feel, but please don't let it cloud your judgement,' Topeko said, resting a hand on Palom's shoulder.

'We're all in this together, we're all on the same side,' Morgen added.

Palom nodded. 'Yes. We will act with clear heads.'

Once Sapora was safely off Khanna, Amarah increased power to her engines and got them airborne again. Moroda could see nothing on the surface which showed Amarah had been affected by anything, but she could see emotions taking their toll on Palom, and she vowed to be of more use in any fighting to come. Given Topeko's presence, surely there would be no better opportunity to hone what little skill she had picked up from her time in Berel.

'You are more worried now, Moroda?' Topeko asked, as Khanna began to climb steadily.

'We were completely unprepared to fight. I was completely unprepared. I couldn't do anything.'

'You are not a fighter, Moroda. You've been thrown into a situation where coming out alive is a huge success. I can't imagine how frightening it must have been for you.'

'I do not want it to happen again.'

'The way things are going, it will happen again. When it

does, the stakes will be higher than just your life. It'll be the lives of everyone in Taban Yul. Perhaps the lives of everyone in Linaria.' He hunched his shoulders, the gems on his cheeks dull.

'I don't want to fight. I just want everyone to be safe. I've lost my father, my sister, and now my home. I don't want it to carry on. I just want peace.'

'Aciel has lost all that and more, too. Look how he reacted.'

'It's so wrong.'

'Is it? His kind have been persecuted for centuries. He has lost friends and family. Everything of importance has been taken away from him and all the Arillians he knows. He has nothing more to lose. He wants to destroy those who hurt his people.'

'But for what reason? To be left with those who adore him? I don't see that as fulfilling.'

'Maybe not, but there are thousands who would.'

'Look at Palom,' Morgen said. 'He wants to kill Kohl for what he did. It's no different. Live and let live is a kind notion, but it's not always possible.'

Topeko gave Morgen a long look. 'The Samolen have practiced peace since the beginning. We dedicate our lives to study, to love, to kindness and compassion. We are all the stronger for it. The blood lust that seems to lie within every Linarian cannot always be suppressed, it seems.'

'Defending yourself isn't blood lust. Revenge isn't blood lust. It's righting a wrong!'

'How is killing another "right"?'

Moroda looked at Morgen as the young man thought about

Topeko's question. She could see him rolling his tongue and wondered whether he was annoyed.

'It just is. People who do bad things should pay for it.'

'But who says it's bad? Aciel would say the war was bad, that we should all be punished for it.'

'I don't know! I just do what I'm told.' He threw his hands up, exasperated.

Moroda looked up at Topeko and said, 'That's what most of Aciel's army is doing, too. But not of their own choice. Let's not bicker, please, not when we're all hurting so much.'

'There's darkness in everyone. Good and bad is never set in stone, nor is it clear cut,' Topeko said.

Morgen walked away at his words, and Moroda reflected on them. The snow thickened around them as the ship approached the mountains. She wondered whether the dragon would see them as a threat, or food, and incinerate what was left of their party. Kohl, the only dragon hunter among them, was no longer there. Then again, she supposed not having a dragon slayer in the presence of a dragon you didn't want to hurt would not be considered a bad thing.

She thought of her remaining companions; Amarah, as she carefully navigated the terrain in the poor weather, stubborn, confident, and proud as always, and fearless to boot; Palom, sombre and silent in his grief, waves of anger pulsing from him; Morgen, a trained soldier, but with more emotion than any of them, it seemed; and Topeko, a worldly scholar with an aversion to fighting and destruction, who was perhaps the only one who would keep the group alive in their next encounter.

Then, of course, there was the final member of the party. A former Goldstone of Niversai, able to clean and cook and dance, with a thirst for knowledge, but lacking in wit, confidence and decisiveness, a hunger for peace, but now alone in the world. What would it matter if they were killed by the dragon, she wondered. Would Linaria even mourn their passing?

Chapter Twenty-Three

Falling snow masked the way ahead, and the wind picked up at their altitude, buffeting Khanna with strong surges. 'The storm is getting too much!' Amarah said, holding her engine throttles as steady as she could. 'I'm going to have to land soon or risk damaging Khanna! Not to mention I can't see a damned thing ahead!'

'Land there.' Palom called, pointing ahead.

Moroda held onto the side tightly and looked down at a large cliff overhanging a flat plateau. She supposed it would provide a little cover for the ship while it was grounded. When she was not crying, she was overwhelmed with emptiness, and held onto her ring for comfort. Topeko had taken the ereven sphere from her and used it to navigate the small group closer to where the dragon was located. She was grateful to have one less responsibility, for she didn't feel able to even dress herself at present, and held on tightly as Amarah navigated Khanna into the little hollow.

'This feels like an Arillian storm.' Topeko said as they dismounted.

'Oh, please, no, don't let it be...' Moroda whispered.

'This is too far out for an Arillian.' Palom said, growling. 'If there is one, I will tear him apart.' With one deep breath, the Ittallan trembled again, and Moroda stood back as he transformed into his true form.

'We should follow Palom.' Amarah said, the last to dismount. She gripped her scythe tightly and looked back at her ship. 'He can pick out a path up the mountain. Weapons ready. Eyes up. Any sudden movement could be an attack.'

Moroda shivered despite her cloak as they followed the tiger up the trail. She had pulled her hood up, the fur warming her face, but there was a cold, deep fear in the pit of her stomach that her cloak was unable to warm. She felt now, more than ever, she was being swept along in events, with no say in what was to happen. Deep down, her fear kept her from truly wanting any further part in their 'grand' adventure. She wanted to go home, even though she had no home to go to.

When she and Eryn had first left Niversai, all that time ago, she had thought it a great idea to leave the city and see what the world had to offer. Times were changing and she was able to glimpse into the world outside Niversai, into something that was bigger than herself. She had wanted desperately to know more, to learn of Linaria and the people in it, to learn of the dragons and magic, and everything it had to offer.

Eryn had been against the idea from the start, but gone along with it anyway, trusting in her sister to see them through safely. Eryn was five years her junior and often gave in to what Moroda wanted, but Moroda had never thought it'd go this far. Now Eryn was gone, Moroda blamed herself more than the Arillian who killed her. Her idea had been to tag along for a bit, to see Berel and the university, and then make their way back to Niversai. But Moroda had continued on to do what she'd wanted, with no clear plan on how they were going to get back in one piece. She'd learned the dragons were more than the stunning creatures she used to watch lazily circling high above Niversai. They were beasts of unrivalled strength and power, and Aciel, that awful creature, had harnessed so much of it for himself. Now she was caught in the middle of his war, and more than that, trying to influence it.

Moroda kept her eyes on her feet, focussing on each step. The ground underfoot was frozen solid and covered in a thick layer of snow, and she did not want to stumble or trip. She thought Palom was forging his own path, suitable for huge paws, and she worried he planned to leave them all in the snow while he hunted down any Arillians on the mountain.

Moroda glanced up occasionally, ensuring she followed Morgen's steps, and Topeko did not fall behind. But the Samolen kept up easily enough, and the four of them managed to follow Palom through the blizzard.

'You doing alright, Ro?' Morgen asked, looking over his shoulder.

'Yes, thank you.'

'Do you want to break? We can rest for a minute if you need—'

'I'm fine, Morgen, really. It's easier to keep moving.'

'Alright, just wanted to make sure…' He stopped where he was, the steep path widening a little, and waited for Moroda to pass by. 'Hopefully not long to go now. Dragons above, this is a hard walk!'

Moroda smiled at him as she trudged past, grateful he was

trying to lighten the mood, but unable to humour him with laughter. The snow fell thick and heavy, and the strong wind threatened to push them over at any moment. Her feet grew colder with each step until they were numb.

'Don't suppose you can warm us up with your magic, Topeko?' Morgen asked as the Samolen passed him, his red robes vivid on the white mountain.

'I am not so skilled in the art of healing and conjuring, I am afraid, Morgen.' Topeko said. 'If there is any warmth to be had when we rest, I can enhance it.'

'Any shelter would be great.' Morgen limped after Topeko, now bringing up the rear. His sword hung heavy at his hip, slowing his progress up the trail. The wounds he'd sustained in the battle against Jato's Arillians had yet to heal properly, and a deep gash to his left leg made walking especially hard. He could still remember the searing heat of their electrical attacks; it was no wonder they didn't use steel when they could strike you down with lightning. He hobbled along, keeping Topeko's bright robes in sight at all times. Jato had no right to do what she did. But neither did Kohl. 'Damned traitor.' He muttered aloud. 'He'll pay. He'll pay. He'll pay...'

'There's a break in the storm.' Amarah called back from where she led. Moroda stopped where she was and looked ahead. Indeed the sky pirate was right—the wind died down enough for their visibility to clear. Moroda couldn't have been more grateful— the cold was sapping her strength and she thought she'd freeze if they were out in the elements any longer.

Moroda saw Palom charge forward towards a cave opening

half-hidden on the side of the mountain, and she hurried after him as quickly as they could.

There was an unexpected wall of intense heat as they entered the cave, and Moroda blinked back the tears which suddenly formed in her eyes. Throwing her hood down, she rubbed one eye while waiting for the other to adjust to the darkness of the cave—a harsh contrast from the bright white of outside.

The tiger's roar was sudden, reverberating in the confined space, and Moroda covered her ears, dropping to one knee. She squinted in the darkness and gasped as she saw a battered and bloodied Arillian slumped against the cave wall, his feathers in disarray. The hat he wore was unmistakable. 'Kohl?'

Palom lunged towards him, claws extended and fangs bared, little more than a flash of orange in the darkness. Before he could pounce, he was knocked off his feet by something huge and dark, nigh invisible in the cave.

Amarah raised her scythe to attack. 'Keep back!'

'No. You will keep back. I will fight to my last breath.' The voice echoed around them, low and grating.

Palom scrambled to his feet and snarled, fur bristling as he readied to lunge again.

'Palom, look! It's the dragon!' Moroda gasped, still on her knee. Her eyes adjusted and she could see the silhouette of a dragon huddled in the darkness. She could not see the roof of the cave and could not see exactly how large the creature was, but it dwarfed the one that had attacked Niversai.

Topeko lowered his hood at the realisation and also dropped

to his knees, his cheek jewels twinkling in the darkness. 'Archon, I am honoured and humbled to be in your presence.' He lowered his head in bow, exposing the back of his neck as his nose touched the ground.

Morgen sank to his knees and Amarah lowered her scythe slightly, both pairs of eyes trained on the dragon while Palom transformed back.

'Dragon! Why are you protecting the traitor?' Palom bellowed. 'I swore to kill him!' His rage was palpable, but Moroda could see he was torn between attacking Kohl and his wariness of the dragon they faced.

The dragon moved in the darkness, and Moroda felt the shifting strength and heat, more than seeing its dark grey body move in the shadows. 'Ittallan, you do not harm this one.'

'I've been... trying to heal her... to help her.' Kohl whispered from the other side of the cave. 'Trying to keep her safe... with the blizzard outside.' He staggered to the dragon's side, his wounds still fresh and bleeding. 'I made it to the cave... after Jato's elite fighter attacked me... She defended herself and inflicted these wounds. When I was... no longer a threat, I spoke with her... Promised to help her. Promised to heal her... But she is... she is the one... Aciel found... the source of his power.'

'That cannot be, she would be dead.' Topeko said, getting to his feet. 'If her stone is gone—'

'My power was stolen from me!' The dragon hissed, steam bellowing from her nostrils and heating the air. 'I was tricked by an Arillian's eyes...'

'But… how can you be alive?' Topeko asked, daring to step closer to her for a better look.

'I was stronger than he thought. I am… very weak. I have prolonged my death for countless days.' She breathed, a hissing growl filling the air at the motion. 'Hibernation has helped, but I cannot heal from this wound. It kills me slowly. But I do not wish to die.'

Moroda felt the cave walls and floor rumble, and she was very aware of the enormous strength the dragon possessed. She clutched her ring and found it burning hot. She looked to Topeko—for all his wisdom and books, he looked like he'd seen a ghost.

'The thought of a dragon surviving without its stone is simply unheard of!' Topeko said, a hand to his mouth. 'Aciel took your stone and left you to die, and yet you still live?'

'Yes.' She moved closer so they could see the deep wound on her chest. It was black with dried blood. 'My residual power would move to the despicable Arillian when I die. I do not wish to give him this joy…'

'This is astonishing. Kohl, I commend you for your bravery.'

'Commend him? For killing Anahrik and Eryn?' Palom said, stepping towards the Samolen. 'Kohl! You left them! You left them!'

Kohl shuddered, leaning against the dragon as the strength went in his legs. 'I do not deserve to live.'

'Then I shall kill you!'

'Do not touch this one.' The dragon snarled, heat rising

from her nostrils.

'I have done such terrible things...' Kohl wept. 'I should have... stayed and fought with you. But I could not fight. I could not...'

'Because you fight for Aciel!' Palom snarled.

'No! No! I'd never fight for him.' Kohl shook his head, his wings fluttering from underneath his long cloak, loose feathers falling onto the cave floor. 'I am in exile... because of him.'

'I don't believe you.' Palom straightened up. 'If you do not fight for Aciel there is no reason for you to leave Anahrik and Eryn to die!'

Moroda could do nothing to diffuse the tension. Palom demanded the same answers she desperately needed, and she waited as Kohl gathered the strength to speak.

'I do not... I did not...' Kohl stammered, heaving as blood continued to trickle from the gashes on his arms. 'Killing one's own kin... is a shameful... abhorrent act. We Arillians are so few... But Aciel has permitted such deplorable behaviour. Those who disagreed, he has controlled... so they agree with him. But it is against our laws, against... our beliefs.'

The dragon's ragged breathing filled the cave between Kohl's words, and Moroda listened carefully.

'His compulsion has... changed our kind. For better or worse. Most are under his control. I am immune to his sorcery... But some... like Jato... believe in him and his words. Truly. I had hoped... I had prayed... that she was under his compulsion, too. But... But... I know now that she loves him...'

'Kohl...?' Moroda asked, holding her ring tightly.

'For all... the terrible things... she has done. I cannot harm her. I cannot defend myself against her. She... she is my daughter. If she had been... under his spell, perhaps I could have... I could have done something. Found some way... to break his compulsion. To free her. But she is... she is...' He sobbed, unable to speak any more.

Moroda saw a broken soul who had realised the extent of his loss and failures. If she had been told to attack Eryn, she too, would have fled. It was not something she could imagine facing. She remembered Kohl had looked through the tomes of books on compulsion at Topeko's home, remembered his insistence they flee Jato's warship and avoid coming into contact with her. Her heart pounded as she understood his unwillingness to speak of his past, and of his unwillingness to fight. Had Jato spoken for him? Asked Aciel to exile him instead of execute him? Kohl was immune to Aciel's compulsion, he couldn't be forced to bow to him. Were the scars on his face from Aciel, too? Or his generals? She felt tears welling at the realisation. 'Please, Palom... Forgive Kohl... What would you do if you were told to kill Anahrik?'

Palom growled, but said nothing.

'I escaped the battle... barely.' Kohl continued. 'I sheltered here and found this dragon. I... I used my strength to create the blizzard... So Aciel and the others wouldn't find her... I do not think he... realises she still lives. If you found her, you could help her... It matters not what... happens to me. You can... take back... Aciel's stolen power.'

'I do not forgive you for what you have done.' Palom said, turning away from Kohl. 'You do not turn on your friends. No matter the enemy. You are a coward. A traitor.'

'Palom.' Moroda whispered again.

'Leave him.' Morgen said. 'We need to carry on with our task. We need the dragon's help, don't we?'

Amarah swung her scythe, allowing the blade to clatter loudly on the cold stone floor. 'Enough babble. This dragon is alive, yet Aciel has her power. What do we do about that? If we could somehow return the dragon's power, would that not weaken Aciel?'

Moroda kept her gaze on Palom for a moment longer, but his silence told her he was no longer going to act on his impulse. She was shocked over Kohl's confession, but knew they did not have time to dwell on his words. Their priority was Aciel.

She cautiously approached the dragon, and looked over her scales and the deep wound she bore. 'Aciel has her stone. Remember his cane, Amarah? The jewel on top? That must be this dragon's stone, where her power is held...' She thought aloud. 'What if...? No, I don't think it...'

'What are you thinking, child?' Topeko asked, gently resting a hand on her shoulder.

'Her power is energy, isn't it...? That's what you said? What if... what if we just moved her energy back? The way you do with candles and flames?'

Topeko thought for a moment, before exhaling through his nose. 'Goodness. That is a fair distance to move energy, Moroda. I... I don't know if it could be done.'

'But it is the same thing as the candle, isn't it? Just moving energy? From Aciel's stone back to this dragon here?'

The Samolen nodded, though his brow was furrowed. 'Well, yes... it sounds no different. But we would need something to move the energy to—I've never moved energy to a living thing before, much less a dragon. I do not know how to do this.'

'But we do have something to move the energy to. Kohl, don't you still carry the stone from the drake? The one who attacked Niversai?'

Kohl put his hand in his cloak pocket and retrieved the small crystal.

The dragon hissed. 'Fallen brother.'

'There! Could we not... could we not move the dragon's power back to this stone? It would weaken Aciel, save the dragon's life, restore her strength...?' Moroda asked, her voice quavering at the realisation of a possible solution.

'Well... it is... such a long way...' Topeko mused, taking the stone from Kohl and scrutinising it.

The dragon spoke again. 'Rhea herself kept me alive. Gave me the strength to live on through pain and anguish. This is the reason.' Moroda could hear desperation in her voice. 'This girl speaks truth. I know of your magic, Samolen. What she asks of you is hard... but it will work... it must work.'

'Topeko?' Morgen asked.

'I fear there would be nothing to stop Aciel finding and killing more dragons to undo this effort.' Topeko said.

'There are so few elders remaining, do you think it truly

likely?' Moroda asked.

'We have his ereven sphere. He'd have to be real lucky to find one.' Morgen added.

'There is chance to take main source of his power. Take the risk.' Palom said.

'Topeko. What do you need us to do?' Amarah asked, stabbing her weapon on the floor again.

'Light a fire, provide light and warmth. This may take some time.' The Samolen said, sitting cross legged on the ground, his robes billowing around him. He took a deep breath, raised his hands, and began to work.

Chapter Twenty-Four

Topeko worked long into the night. While the fire crackled and the blizzard howled outside, the dragon seemed to sleep, closing her eyes and resting her jaw on her chest, almost motionless save for a little steam rising from her nostrils.

Moroda sat beside Topeko and watched the drake's stone carefully, waiting for any sign that the magic had worked. She had spent some time studying the dragon, amazed at how close she was to one of this age and power. The dragon's scales were a dull grey-green colour, but the bulk of her body lay hidden in shadow, for she could not move save her forelegs and head. Even her wings drooped lifelessly at her side.

Morgen bound up the worst of Kohl's injuries, while Amarah and Palom kept watch at the cave's mouth. Moroda hadn't seen Palom so angry before, and the Ittallan kept his distance from Kohl. She hated conflict, but knew he could not find it in him to forgive the Arillian for his betrayal, no matter what his reasons were.

Most of Kohl's strength was focussed on keeping the blizzard going; Aciel's scouts were unlikely to be found so high up, but no-one wished to risk being discovered now, at such a critical time. Moroda found the howling wind strangely comforting, as though no one could pierce their little bubble where inside the most incredible thing was happening.

'What's happening at the palace, I wonder.' Morgen said. He sat beside Kohl, his back against the cave wall, sword across his knees. 'Those poor souls. Against Sapora and Isa.' He shook his head.

'Isa sounds like she's got things under control.' Amarah said, leaning on her scythe near the mouth of the cave. 'Guess she'd have to. With a brother like Sapora.'

'But the ones he killed... They couldn't even fight back, he was so fast. And the servants who had to tidy everything up after.' 'Feel bad for them, you know.' Amarah said, scratching her cheek. 'I know what it's like. Tried to get a job properly once, when I first came to Corhaven at twelve. Pah. It's why I hate Goldstones—worked for three different families. They all shared the same dismissive view of anyone beneath them.'

Morgen nodded, though he fiddled with his sword's scabbard.

'I cooked, cleaned, clothed, bathed and served them, and the best I ever got was a sneer! If they weren't barking orders, they were complaining about me and what I did or didn't do; changing from one day to the next. One day I'd work too quickly, the next, too slowly. I kept changing to suit, but it was never good enough. After the third family brought me to tears, I vowed to get away from it— to one day have them serve me! Laughable, really, but it drove me to get out. Hah, that third family was my first theft in Corhaven, come to think of it. A diamond necklace with a single opal in the centre. Pretty little thing. Worth fifty crowns; what I'd earn in a year cleaning up after them.

Theft itself was easy enough; I dusted the cabinet it was kept in every day. Getting close was too easy, even taking it off the rock it sat on was simple. Strange thing was it took nearly six weeks before the woman who owned it realised it was missing! I'd long since sold it and made enough coin to get me through. After I stopped working for 'em, a notice went up in the local tavern: five crown reward for the return of the stolen necklace.

Made me laugh it took that spoiled bitch so long to realise—she had so much money and so many jewels that she didn't notice one go missing! But I guess five crowns is pocket change to a Goldstone.'

'It's not her fault, you know,' Moroda said quietly.

Amarah snorted and shook her head. 'Just watching them palace servants and how they reacted to the Varkain reminded me of what it was like for me. But there's ways out of it if you don't like it. Always is. Most servants say there's no other way of life, but I escaped and do alright for myself. They can do the same.'

'Wonder how easy it is for a royal servant to leave, though.' Morgen said, looking up at Amarah. 'Not quite the same as working for a rich family, I bet. Probably kill you if you leave. Sapora doesn't seem to care.'

Moroda thought to Andel. Though he wasn't a servant as such, he did cater to Topeko's needs and acted every bit a wonderful host when they had spent time in Berel. Andel had seemed very comfortable in his role, even if he didn't say a single word to them. If it weren't for Andel, they never would have realised an ereven sphere would lead them to the situation they were in now. Fate was funny sometimes.

You couldn't help where you were born, what life you were handed. You had to make the best of it, and hope that things would work out, didn't you?

'Kohl...' Moroda said, deciding to address him. 'I know you didn't want to... behave as you did. I know you didn't intend for anyone to be hurt.' She swallowed, thinking about her words and trying to hold back tears. 'Jato actually left us. She left us with the other Arillians. You could have stayed, you know. I don't think she wanted to fight. She seemed more interested in getting back to Aciel.'

Kohl looked up, grimacing. 'She... she didn't attack you?'

'Not then, no. Maybe... Maybe just wait and see how things pan out before you decide whether to stay or go. I guess we will see more of her, or Aciel, or the other Arillians before this war is finished. We really need you with us.'

She heard Palom's growl from somewhere to her left, but ignored it, her attention on Kohl.

'Surely you wish for me to die, Moroda. What I did was deplorable.'

'No, of course I don't wish that. You dying would not... bring... Eryn back. Or Anahrik. I'd feel even worse, if anything.'

'Moroda, you don't still trust him, do you?' Morgen asked.

'I know you were fearful. We all were. If I had a pair of wings, I'd have flown away, too. But it was an awful situation you were in, one you tried to avoid.' Moroda said.

Kohl took his hat off and held it over his chest, his scars clear in the firelight. 'You honour me, Moroda. But I do not deserve your kindness.'

'Everyone deserves kindness.'

Morgen shook his head with a grunt, but did not say anything.

'Moroda. I've met a lot of people in my time but I can't say I've met anyone like you. I told you before and I'll tell you again. Your nature will get you killed.' Amarah said.

'Well I don't know how to be any other way, Amarah. I don't think I can be any other way. I'm doing the best I can.'

'You're doing just fine, Moroda.' Kohl said, placing his hat back on his head.

A snore from the dragon reverberated in the cave and Moroda returned her attention to Topeko. He rocked slowly where he sat, silent and deaf to all but his work. She could see sweat beading on his brow and she did not think he was aware of anything outside his own magic.

Palom was sullen and silent, and Moroda was happy to give him as much space as he needed to. She'd not noticed quite how emotional he could become, and found him a little intimidating, even though his rage was directed at Kohl.

She wanted to speak more with Kohl, to find out about Jato and what happened with Aciel to cause his exile, but she had no energy left for a deep conversation, nor did she think Palom could listen to much more of it.

Moroda supposed they were all behaving the same way as

she. They were all being themselves, doing what they thought was the best thing to do. Rightly or wrongly, none of them knew, but they couldn't be any different. Even Sapora, with his brutal behaviour, and Aciel, in his justification of his takeover. She shuddered at the memory of him. Regardless of his justification and Topeko's earlier words, Aciel's behaviour was wrong.

She thought to Eryn, and wished her sister could be with her now to offer comfort, conversation, and company. She thought back to her former home in Niversai, half a world away, and wondered what was left of the great city. If the castle had fallen, the city itself would not have fared well, either.

*

Moroda slept a little, drifting in and out of sleep throughout the night. No-one said anything else for the rest of the evening, and the fire remained lit to provide heat and light while Topeko worked.

In her dreams, she and Eryn were in Niversai, fleeing from some unknown hunter. A shadow followed their every step, getting closer whenever they turned to look behind them. Suddenly, it shapeshifted into a great dragon with glowing green eyes, but instead of fire, it breathed smoke that froze everything it came into contact with. Rosecastle was turned into an enormous statue of ice, people all around it frozen solid as the shadow-dragon flew over and breathed more and more freezing smoke with each pass.

She held Eryn's hand as they ran, rounding a corner and racing past lines of grounded airships, their wooden hulls rotten and falling apart. Eryn screamed and Moroda let go of her hand. She looked over her shoulder as she continued to run, and the shadow-dragon descend on her sister, smothering her in smoke and ash.

Moroda woke with a start, her cloak bundled up around her, and it took several moments before she remembered where she was. Licking her lips, she yawned, piecing together what was real and what was a remnant from her dream. A wave of sadness passed over her as she remembered Eryn's death, and she whimpered quietly.

The crackle of the fire turned her attention back to Topeko. Though it was almost morning, it appeared the Samolen had hardly moved a muscle. 'Topeko?' she ventured, knowing full well she'd not get a response.

Kohl and Morgen seemed half asleep, but Amarah and Palom's backs were to her, so she could only hope they were awake. She returned her attention to Topeko and the small crystal sat in front of him.

Shuffling over, she knelt beside him and looked at the crystal while he continued to mumble through his incantations. She wondered what their purpose was. It was not something she had been taught or shown during her brief time in Berel, and she was again reminded of how little she knew. Moroda clutched her ring as she watched the stone, trying not to blink, until her eyes watered and her vision blurred.

Then, as the dawn sunlight trickled into the cave, it finally began to happen. She had been drifting in and out of sleep, and it happened so slowly at first that she thought it was simply her tired eyes tricking her, but the crystal began to glow. It was a bright, pinkish-purple, rich in hue, and shimmered in the firelight. Moroda was in awe at Topeko's abilities—she had not dared to truly hope it could be done, but the dragon herself had agreed, and now the fruits of the Samolen's work were beginning to show.

As Topeko drew to a finish, Moroda saw the exertion of the work beginning to take its toll on his body. Sweat drenched the top half of his robes and he hunched forward like an old man. She wanted to comfort him somehow, but was scared to distract him in case she affected the magic.

Finally, he opened his eyes and raised his hand to the crystal laid on the ground. At his touch, the stone ignited and burned a bright, violent purple, flickering for a few seconds, before extinguishing itself. 'It's warm.'

'You have done it, Samolen.' The dragon breathed, her eyes twinkling in the low light.

'You have?' Morgen said, getting to his feet and hurrying over. 'Amarah! Palom! Look!'

'Kohl, you drew this stone from my blood brother. You will now give it to me.' The dragon said, shifting her position so the open wound on her chest was visible.

Moroda stood up, exhausted, though she had slept and done nothing to aid Topeko with the crystal. She was excited and nervous, eager to see what would happen.

Though weak, Kohl picked up the stone from Topeko and made his way to the dragon's side. The cave rumbled with her breath and growl, a dormant power that set everyone on edge. Moroda shivered. This was myth and gods, meddling and magic, and she wasn't quite sure whether it was the best thing to do. But it felt like the right thing to do. Stopping Aciel was important to bring peace to Linaria. Helping this dragon was one essential part of that. 'The crystal is now full of your sacred power.' Topeko said, as Kohl carefully rested his hand on the dragon's side, clutching the stone in his other hand. 'I have moved all the energy from Aciel's stone, to this one... and now Kohl returns it to you.'

Moroda held her breath as Kohl gripped the stone and plunged it into her chest.

The roar of the dragon shook the cave, her primal bellow a fearsome sound, made more terrifying by the sudden flames she released from her gaping jaws—straight through the cave mouth and into the blizzard outside. The dull scales on her back shifted immediately to bright, vivid coppery-green, her horns thickened and turned black from the dirty grey they had been, and her eyes; before a pale yellow, were now the brightest of gold, flecked with red and chips of silver, burning brightest of all. The scar on her chest was pronounced, and glowed bright orange, but her strength had been fully restored.

'Samolen, I am in your debt.' She hissed, once the intensity of the fire had passed.

Topeko returned to the floor, too exhausted to stand any longer. 'No, not me... Moroda. She is the one who thought of the solution. Aciel... the bulk of his power will have now left him. No matter how many dragons he has killed, it would never compare to that of an elder such as you.'

The dragon growled, a low rumble which Moroda felt in her bones. She dropped to her knees again and lowered her head. 'I thank you... Moroda.' The dragon spoke, closing her eyes to Moroda's bow. 'Arillian, lower your blizzard. I wish to fly.'

'The battle is not yet over.' Topeko said, his voice croaky between breaths. 'Aciel will be furious. He has many followers now, removing his power will have done little to change that. This has been a damaging blow, yes, but to secure victory, we need a Sevastos. Please help us.'

The dragon, who had been making for the cave entrance, paused in her step. 'They would be most unwilling to give their lives to help those who have brought nothing but destruction to Linaria.'

'The Samolen have always stayed out of war. We used the original Sevastos stones for healing and restoration only.' Topeko replied.

The dragon swayed slightly. 'Yet here you are. Acting in war.'

'Please, Archon.' Moroda said, using Topeko's earlier honorific. 'Returning your power was the first step. Won't you help us save Linaria from Aciel? We have crossed the world looking for you.'

'The Samolen have indeed been guardians. But the combined strength of the dragons Aciel and others of this world have killed may be stronger even than the power of a Sevastos.'

Moroda did not let the warning faze her. She had lost too much, worked too hard, to give up now. 'We have no time to lose. Aciel will be looking for a Sevastos, and once he finds one, he'll stop at nothing to take the stone. If he was able to trick you, he could trick a Sevastos! We must find one first! I ask this of you.'

Smoke continued to pour from the elder's nostrils as she

considered Moroda's words. 'You do not bargain with your gods, Moroda. All dragons are linked. We know when hatchlings emerge from their eggs and when others die. We feel nothing but pain from the deaths of dragons slaughtered in pursuit of power... the Sevastos will not be so easily found. Many of our number are already turning on towns and cities in revenge.'

'This destruction isn't needed! It's Aciel who needs to be stopped! Then peace can return!' Moroda cried.

'Beware of any dragon you see, for they may already be on the attack. But there are three Sevastos still living—the red, the gold, and the white. Sevastos are wanderers, they do not keep territories as we lesser dragons do. I fear the time of dragons, deities of Linaria, is coming to an end.'

'That they still live is something.' Amarah said, shouldering her scythe and putting her other hand on her hip. 'But how are we supposed to find one?'

The elder shook her head and ruffled her folded wings in irritation. 'That, I cannot help you with.'

'After everything we did for you and you can't tell us where one is?' Amarah said. 'Seems a crappy deal. We saved your life and you're not going to help us?'

The dragon snorted, steam rising from her nostrils. 'They are far greater in size than any dragon you have seen. They rival the size of your giant airships, and have four wings, to better soar the skies. But I cannot tell you anymore. My power is returned, and I must see to clearing the skies of Aciel's filth.' Saying no more, the dragon exited the cave in one, swift leap, extended her wings and was lost to the sky.

'Archon! Wait!' Topeko called, his voice hoarse, but his words fell on deaf ears.

Moroda followed him out of the cave and stood by the entrance. The snow was deep all around them from Kohl's blizzard, but the skies were clear and the morning was bright. 'All that... everything... for nothing?'

'Always agree the terms of the deal before you do any work.' Amarah said, folding her arms. 'Of course I've never done a deal with a dragon. Guess if they don't like you they can just bite your head off.'

'Topeko... What... do we do now?' Morgen asked, turning to the scholar.

'Go back to the palace and take matters into our own hands. At least Aciel is weakened. Might be closer to a fair fight now, if he challenges the city?' Amarah said.

'The dragon... She...' Moroda whimpered.

'She is starved. She is wounded, pride and body.' Kohl said. 'She has been beaten to an inch of her life and left to rot in a cave on a mountainside. I am not surprised she left.'

'Another trick.' Palom snapped, glaring at the Arillian.

'We have the same goal of defeating Aciel. This is a strong blow, one we'd not have been able to make without her.' 'So what're we going to do?' Morgen repeated. 'We could wait for her to return?' Kohl suggested. Moroda sat down in the thick snow, legs stretched out in front of her. 'I can't face walking back down the mountain just yet.

Let's wait.'

Amarah crouched down beside her, stomach growling. 'Make sure you don't let Palom kill Kohl while I'm gone. There's food on Khanna. I'll see if I can rustle up some breakfast.'

Moroda nodded, amazed Amarah's unique sense of humour never faltered despite their circumstances. Morgen sat beside her again, though Topeko and Kohl lingered in the mouth of the cave.

She watched as Palom stalked off to the side and stood on a large rock protruding from the snow. His anger seemed to have receded a little through the night, but she knew it simmered just beneath the surface. She wasn't quite sure what she could do to stop him if he chose to attack Kohl, but hoped he would remain still until they could set off again.

Moroda didn't know how long they'd have to wait, but she was prepared for as long as it took. She looked up into the bright morning sky and exhaled slowly. 'I miss you so much, Ryn. If only you were here with us, you'd know what to do.' She sobbed quietly as overhead, lesser dragons circled.

Chapter Twenty-Five

Sereth was much as Sapora recalled, though the Varkain in its capital, Timin Rah, had not grown quite as lax here as they had for Isa in Taban Yul. Still having a ruler probably had something to do with it, he supposed. Timin Rah was a city in the loosest sense of the term; a cluster of caves and tunnels deep below the surface of Linaria, unmarked on the land and hidden from the world.

Sapora had not been born in the bowels of the ground like his Varkain brethren. No, he'd been born in the luxury of the palace in Taban Yul, surrounded by Ittallan, like his mother. The two races did not always see eye to eye, and mixed bloods were not unheard of, but it had always been seen as a weakness in him.

He strode calmly through the tunnels as around him, Varkain shuffled and leapt out of the way, and others stalked him from several paces back. He knew they would not harm him, not immediately on his return, but he would have to prove his worth before the day was up.

Closing his eyes, Sapora smiled. Day and night merged into one in the depths of the tunnels. It was one thing he did not miss about Sereth. The everlasting darkness and murkiness. While many tunnels were wide and well ventilated, it did not detract from the loss of time or claustrophobia that set in after several hours.

Most of Sereth was underground, a labyrinth of tunnels

stretching many leagues into the depths of Linaria. They would cluster together near places of interest—a forest, a river, or near natural ore. Torches were fixed to brackets in the wall down the wider tunnels, but many remained in darkness, however they were all, for the most part, fastidiously clean.

The cities of Sereth were little more than underground labyrinths – a maze of intertwining tunnels connecting one town to the next. Shielded from the worst of war and weather, the Varkain thrived underground; though it took some getting used to. Sapora had never felt more at home than in the wide, smooth tunnels of Timin Rah, and felt he had been away from his people for too long.

Timin Rah was the largest settlement, and had adopted the moniker of capital city, though there were no buildings as such, although gateways and passageways had been built to distinguish permitted areas. Various caves and dens had been dug into the earth and rock, and different areas were used for different activities, but to the untrained eye, it all looked much the same.

As Sapora clambered up a particularly steel slope, he remembered struggling as a child. Everything seemed the same, and it was only after almost a full year that he was able to learn his way around. Being confident enough to wander through the tunnels unescorted was something he'd wanted to learn as quickly as possible, though it meant getting lost for hours, sometimes days, at a time.

He reached the crest of the slope and paused, looking at the expansive hall before him. Perhaps two dozen Varkain milled around, some carrying cloth bags full of food or weapons,

Cerastes—guards—standing watch by the edge of the cave. One spotted Sapora as he appeared, and immediately headed for him, the metal on his shoulders gleaming in the torchlight.

'My liege.' The Cerastes dropped to one knee as in front of Sapora. 'We have long awaited your return.'

'Take me to the king and queen at once. I have urgent matters to discuss.'

'Of course.' The Cerastes replied, rising once again. 'Clear a path at once, prepare food and drink. Prince Sapora returns immediately.'

Sapora followed the Cerastes along the winding tunnel, pleased with the quickened pace. It had been so long since he had been among his own kind, and he studied the Cerastes carefully. They were second only to the Naja in strength, and served as the guards for not only the ruling family, but all Varkain. They rarely left Sereth, and ensured no enemy ever reached the people of his country. He saw the longsword sheathed at his hip and smirked. They were all armed, but a bite from any Cerastes would lead to death faster than one of his own.

Here, his kind was home. On the surface, they were looked upon with disdain, disgust, and even fear. Sapora had come to relish the fear—the terror he held over most people of Linaria. What other way was he to react to being excluded and shunned?

Almost two years had passed since he had last been in Sereth, and had he been a pure Varkain, he would have stepped into power without question. But like many on the Ittallan Council, there were those here who thought his mixed blood would weaken his senses or physical prowess, and his errantry had been set to prove himself to all doubters. He knew his greatest test was yet to come, however. Though his father still lived, if he passed the final test, he would assume power now he was twenty-one.

He had abhorred the idea at first. He was the blood of the Varkain and could transform, why did he have to prove himself further? However, as he had traversed Linaria, he began to realise there was power to be learned from others, and the journey had strengthened him. Yes, it was a great pressure, and many believed he would be an unfit ruler if he returned early or was killed on his travels, but his eyes and mind had been opened. Having experienced Aciel's wrath, he knew what had to be done to ensure the survival of the Varkain, and have them benefit from the Arillian's treachery against Linaria.

'How is Vasil?' Sapora asked as they pushed deeper into the city.

'Your father is well. With things as they were, they were considering having Tacio crowned!'

Sapora snorted in response. 'I'd have killed him the moment I returned, had he done so.'

'Well you are your father's son.'

Sapora didn't respond to that—he wasn't sure whether it was a compliment or an insult—and remained quiet until they arrived at his father's keep. It was on top of a huge cliff that jutted out from the side of the cavern, resting above a deep lake. The water was still and cloudy, suitable for bathing and little else, but it was the most spacious part of Timin Rah, and Vasil had claimed it as his own keep many years ago.

To the side of the cliff, several paces from the water, the ground fell away sharply. Sapora glanced towards it, but the scent of blood and sweat distinguished it from any other part of the city. It was the scent of home, and further confirmed what action Sapora needed to take. It also reminded him of what he had to face.

The Varkain had long ago done away with formalities. Your standing was based on merit, which was strength, more than blood or birthright. Anyone could approach their king if they wished, and the Cerastes left Sapora to wait while he informed Vasil of his son's arrival. Sapora shifted his weight and folded his arms as he waited, and he could sense excitement all around him as the crowd grew. He could feel eyes peering out at him from the edges of the cave, or just hiding behind the corner of a tunnel. He had been trailed since he first arrived, and now he was stood in full view before their king, the entire country would be aware of his return within a few hours.

'Sapora, Sapora, Sapora. Where oh where have you been?'

Sapora looked up at the drawling voice, narrowing his eyes when he recognised the speaker.

'Come to take the Jade Crown, have you? It was so close to being mine!' The Varkain sauntered down the sloped cliff, hands in his pockets. He wore silver necklaces draped long and loose around his neck, which clinked together with every step, and a black, perfectly tailored overcoat embellished with silver buttons. Tacio grinned, his golden eyes squinting at the breadth of his smile. His skin was grey, the same as any Varkain, but it was pale and smooth, almost white, matching his ivory fangs on display every time he spoke or smiled, contrasting his dark, reddish hair.

Sapora eyed Tacio, blinking slowly as he approached, but made no move to greet him. 'My timing was impeccable then. Where is Vasil?'

'Here.'

Sapora and Tacio dropped to their knees at their father's voice. Sapora held his position for several long seconds, before looking up. The Cerastes who had brought him here now led his father down the slope. He was not old, by any means, only in his late forties, but his black hair was thinning and had receded, giving way to grey. He wore a circlet of gold, adorned with jade stones carved straight from the ground, the only outward sign of his wealth. Behind him, Savra strode. She was tall, younger than his father, with the same red hair and graceful, arrogant walk as Tacio.

'Isn't this a wonderful family reunion?' Tacio smirked, flicking at one tooth with his tongue. 'Snows started a few days ago. We were only going to give you another day or two.'

'You doubted me?' Sapora asked.

'Heard you were captured in Rosecastle. Thought you were killed when the mad dragon burned Niversai.'

Sapora blinked.

'Is this true? You were captured?' Vasil asked, bearing down on Sapora with his larger frame.

'What of it?'

'A little foolish, don't you think? They are quick to execute our kind in Corhaven. Savra sneered.

'Insulting, too. You didn't tell them who you were?' Tacio

asked.

'It wasn't necessary.'

'We can't get involved while you're on errantry.' Tacio said, removing a clawed hand from his pocket and picking at a piece of dirt on his thumb. 'We wouldn't have been able to come help if they'd done anything to you.'

'I don't need your help. Never have.' Sapora narrowed his eyes and took a step back, increasingly aware of the crowd of Varkain that gathered by the waterfront. 'What do you know of Aciel?'

'The Arillians have been seen patrolling our borders, no doubt looking to pick off those travelling alone.' Vasil said. His voice was cool and calm, belying the anger which bubbled below the surface.

'But no direct attacks on the city?'

'Correct. They are unable to breach Timin Rah.'

'Good. I have news of what fuels Aciel's power, and how we can respond to his show of strength. The Varkain will take advantage of this and we will emerge triumphant. I will not have us cower in our tunnels like rats cornered.'

'You speak like you are a king already.' Tacio laughed. 'The pits have been waiting for you for a season now. You've not forgotten what you must do first?'

Sapora glared at his brother. 'It will give me the greatest pleasure to slaughter them to keep you from power.'

'Sapora. Mind yourself. Tacio has been in charge of the Cerastes. He is ready to step in should you fail.' Savra said, ever defensive of her son.

'You have such confidence in me.' Sapora stepped forward, approaching the stench of the pit beside the water. 'You're prepared to cast me aside as your ruler for Tacio, and here I am, spoiling all your fun. I shall certainly put on a great show for you.'

'Prince Sapora, a moment.' The Cerastes stepped out from Vasil's keep, holding a large stone mug, and hurried down the cliff to where they waited. 'You are to be dry for this.'

'Dry?'

'We thought it'd be a better test of all you have learned while traipsing across Linaria.' Tacio grinned, one hand on his hip.

Sapora exhaled through his nose, his pride stung again. But there was a crowd gathered, and he could not, would not, lose face in front of his father. 'Very well.'

The Cerastes handed Sapora the mug, and he turned to face Vasil, Savra, and Tacio. Sapora continued to ignore the dozens of expectant faces and licked his fangs. He extended his front four and raised the mug to their tips. Pressing down, he filled it with his venom. 'Not a warm welcome, but I did not expect anything else. Have any other rules changed in my absence?'

'We've had a lot of Ittallan sign up, you know.' Tacio said, wandering across to the lip of the pit. You've got four of those ready and waiting. The rest depends what they have left. It's been busy these last few weeks.'

'All at once, I suppose?'

'Of course not. We're not savages!' Tacio grinned, his pointed teeth glistening in the darkness.

'It is your time to show them.' Vasil said.

Sapora felt a wave of nausea in his stomach, but drew his scimitars and approached Tacio. 'You'll be bowing to me before the night is over.'

'We'll see, Sapora. We'll see.'

Taking a deep breath, Sapora stepped off the edge of the pit and dropped twenty feet to the bottom. The ground had recently been churned up; it was sticky and damp with congealed blood. The stench threatened to overwhelm his senses, but he remained focussed on the far wall of the pit.

'The first of six rounds. Prince Sapora fights for his right to the Jade Crown.'

Sapora heard Tacio's voice from somewhere above him, and moved across the floor of the pit to drier, firmer ground. One final test. He saw creatures waiting for him at the other side. A gila. An eagle. A great monitor lizard.

He heard a deep bellow from the darkness, and he locked in on the noise. Definitely an Ittallan. Sapora took another step. Then another. This was all part of what had to happen. Another obstacle to overcome to obtain the greatness he desired.

When the bear lumbered into view, Sapora tightened the grip on his blades. One final test to take his crown and demand the respect he deserved.

*

The morning air was crisp and cool, the mountain below them covered in a fresh blanket of snow. Moroda looked out into the infinite whiteness, her breath forming in the air before her.

Everything seemed so surreal—in Niversai, the most snow she would ever see would be gone before the day's end. Here, the world seemed so incredibly vast and open. She thought it was vulnerable, and mirrored her own feelings about the fighting to come.

'Do you think there's a chance Aciel will back down? Give up now his power has been lessened?' She asked Morgen, hardly daring to hope.

'You met him. What do you think?' He replied, drawing shapes in the snow with his fingers.

'No, I suppose not. Wishful thinking?'
'Too right it is. He's on the brink of bringing Linaria to its knees. Rest of the world probably doesn't even know his strength has halved.' Amarah said, sat away a little, her back against a rock. 'I wish he would stop, too.' Topeko said. He was stood by the mouth of the cave, resting against the bare stone. 'I fear your idea to restore the dragon's power has not offered us any boon.' 'Everyone wants something. Shame is we gave it to that damned snake and she flew off without a second thought!' Amarah said.

'I have not met a dragon like this before.' Topeko said, straightening his robes. 'I did not expect her to be so dismissive of us, after we spent all night to save her.'

'Tough old bird. How long has Aciel been around now? She must've been waiting to die a long time.'

Moroda looked to Topeko. 'How did she survive without her stone?'

'I don't know, child.' The scholar replied with a sigh.

'Perhaps there is an explanation in one of the books you have. Perhaps she holds a magic deeper and greater than I realised or understood. Perhaps she was simply fortunate and slumbered, waiting.'

'I don't think she'll be back any time soon.' Morgen said, getting to his feet and dusting snow off his clothes. 'It's midday and there's been no sign of her.'

The dragon had been gone almost four hours, and Moroda was beginning to give up hope of her returning that day. She hated to be negative, but she couldn't ignore Morgen's words. That, and as the day drew on, the temperature dropped.

'No reason for us to stay here on this freezing mountain.' Amarah said at length. The sky was overcast, fading between dirty white and dark grey, with the thin sun struggling to break through.

'Hopefully Isa's done her job and my warship is ready. Come on. We don't wanna sit out here all day and freeze.' She stepped onto the snow-covered path back down to where Khanna had been parked haphazardly the evening before.

Moroda heard Amarah, but remained where she was, watching the clouds darken and writhe in the distance.

'Arillians.' Kohl said, catching her gaze. 'Not an attack… just their presence.'

'Do the others have the… cold powers, like you?' Moroda asked, curious.

'No. They can all control the wind and lightning, in various amounts and strengths. But the ice touch is unique.' Kohl replied, dropping his gaze as Palom shouldered past. 'We best get on the way.' He limped after the others.

Moroda had been about to ask after him, but stopped at Morgen's sudden cry.

'Moroda! Look!' Morgen said, pointing into the distant clouds. 'They're coming back!'

Following his line of sight, Moroda squinted against the bright whiteness, when she saw a sudden flash of light. Blinking, she tried to find the same spot in the clouds again, when another flash of light caused her to look away.

'Phoenix?' She asked, shutting one eye and peeking out of the other, protecting her vision against the gleam of bright, yellow light when it appeared intermittently between clouds. Keeping her eye open until it began to water, Moroda finally distinguished the tiny, bright flame as the distant bird approached the mountain.

'Yeah. Looks like this dragon's power really is back, if the phoenixes have found her. At least you did some good, here. Even if she's not grateful for it!'

Moroda held her breath, mind racing as she thought of how they could potentially track down one of the three remaining Sevastos. Time was against them, even with Aciel's strength diminished, and she did not know whether a Sevastos would even help their cause, if they were to find one. The Archon earlier had been less than willing. What was to say a Sevastos would be any different? Wouldn't one be worse?

Lost in thought, she followed Morgen down the trail, retracing the footsteps of Amarah and the others as they wound their way down the mountain to the small plateau where Khanna waited beneath a blanket of snow.

'I dunno what we'll find when we get back to Taban Yul.'
Amarah said as they boarded one-by-one. The steps on Khanna's
side were half frozen, and Moroda readjusted her grip to keep from
slipping as she clambered on board.

'I hope that warship is ready. I'll have a fighting chance
when Aciel comes. Khanna isn't cut out for that kind of battle.' She
shouldered her scythe and swiped at the snow on deck as she
spoke, nerves showing despite her fierce words.
'I'll fight with you on the warship.' Palom said, breaking his
silence.

'We've come too far to stop now. We need to do something
to help.' Morgen added.

'Before you return to the capital, please leave me in Feoras
Sol. I wish to visit Sereth.' Topeko said, as Amarah started her
engines and unfurled her sails, great clumps of snow falling from
them.

The sky pirate nodded. 'Dunno why you'd wanna go to that
damned hole in the ground, but if that's what you want. Hah. I've
always been one to do alright when things get rough. Let's face Aciel
and make him pay for everything he's done—everyone we've lost!'
Pushing all three engines to full power, Khanna rose swiftly, shook off
the last remnants of snow, and flew back to Taban Yul.

Chapter Twenty-Six

'What? Why is Sapora not with you?' Isa snapped immediately after Amarah disembarked. Amarah had flown Khanna to the palace docks in Taban Yul and found the princess waiting for them.

'I hope you didn't leave him on the mountain!'

'No, princess. Though perhaps I should have.' Amarah retorted. 'He's back in Sereth now, I'd guess. He said he didn't want us to wait for him.'

Isa paused for a moment and Amarah took the opportunity to press forward. 'My warship. Is it ready?'

'Not yet. The final touches are still being made. Aciel himself is on his way to the city. He was spotted by one of our scouting parties just north of the city. Seems he's burning everything with his wind and lighting, stripping trees and destroying the earth below. The whole city is on full alert.'

'How much time do we have?' Palom asked, pushing his way to the front.

Isa shook her head. 'We don't know. The Arillians rush forward in spurts then disappear, only to reappear at another village. Could be days, could be weeks. But soon. Definitely soon. The scouts are trying to keep up with him and report back to what's left of the Council. Seems like Aciel has a few warships, too. But if

Sapora has returned to Sereth for his coronation, I will be able to get everything sorted much faster.'

'How so?' Moroda asked.

'He will make me a queen. And instead of these useless councillors who dither and delay until the enemy is upon us, I will act. If I am to be queen, my city will stand strong and the people will stay safe.'

'Isa… princess…' The raven had appeared, wringing his hands and looking paler than usual. His robes were bunched up around his neck, his black sash in disarray.

'Another attack?' Isa asked. 'Where was it this time?'

'Cora Keb.'

Isa narrowed her eyes. 'How many dead?'

'Still unknown. At last count it was approaching two hundred.'

'Where is that? Is that near here?' Moroda asked, panic rising.

'Eighty leagues away, maybe? North of here, along the coast.' Isa said.

'It is big trading city.' Palom said. 'Second in size to Taban Yul.'

'Supplies for the capital usually come from there. He's trying to turn it into a siege. Make it so we can't leave. Starve us out.' Isa growled, her pupils dilating.

'Good plan.' Amarah said.

'And whose side are you on?' The princess asked.

'My own side. But right now, I fancy my chances better

with you.'

'Isa, please. The Council wishes to gather to continue with preparing for the city's defence.' The raven said, shuffling closer.

'Alright. I'm on my way. I presume the guest suites are still available?'

'Indeed.'

'Good. If you are on our side, Amarah, get yourself and your friends settled and armed. The battle is coming to us. I'll send for you when the ship is ready.'

Moroda could hear her heart thumping in her chest as Isa followed the raven out of the hangar. This was it, then. A great battle on the horizon and no dragon to speak of.

'It is best I show you now Topeko has gone.' Palom said, stepping forward.

'Show us…?' Amarah tilted her head.

'I had some things left here in palace the night we got to Taban Yul.' He said, strolling down the corridor. 'Now we have real need of it. Your gift, Amarah, is one such thing. Come to the rooms now and I will show you. It will help us.'

*

Blood trickled down Sapora's arm, but it was not his own. The bear that had stood tall and formidable only a few minutes before now lay gasping on the edge of the pit, its throat slashed open. As it died, it transformed back, but Sapora paid the Ittallan no mind—the Gila was already lumbering towards him. At six feet long, Sapora could see it weighed a fair amount, and what it lacked in speed, it made up for in power. He widened his stance, ready, when from the pit's other side, the giant monitor lizard trundled forward, too. The lizard was more than twice the size of the Gila, its bulk shaking the pit with each step. Both flicked out their long forked tongues as they approached.

Sapora gripped his scimitars, planning his next move. The thick hide of the lizards would render his weapons ineffective, and if he was caught and pinned by one, he'd be finished off pretty quickly.

The monitor lizard charged at him before he had time to think. Sapora darted back, using his speed to get him out of trouble before the monitor's attack could connect. He heard jeers above him as the onlookers voiced their excitement and annoyance, but drowned it out.

The Gila lunged, it's flat, wide head suddenly at his side. Sapora slashed down with one blade, deterring it more than harming it, and leapt back again. His feet were slow on the soft, damp earth, and he cursed Tacio for making him fight in the smaller pit. Behind him, the monitor hissed, and he whirled round and stabbed at its nose. Another glancing blow. But he overreached, and the great lizard opened its jaws and clamped down on his wrist.

Sapora dropped his blade at once and brought his other hand round, plunging the scimitar in the soft flesh of the monitor's ear, just behind its head. The great lizard roared and released his wrist, toppling over with a crash. Sapora darted forward to pick up his blade, losing his footing on the sticky round and landing face-first in the dirt.

The Gila was on him in moments, pinning him down with

its strength, jaws open as he bit down. Sapora lifted a knee, digging it into the Gila's belly, while he held its throat away with his good hand. Sapora grimaced as drool spilled from its open mouth, laden with venom, but he was unable to push the creature off him or attack with his wrist bleeding.

The stench of the creature made it hard to focus, but he would not let the Gila—no, Tacio—beat him. He had first claim to the Jade Crown and he would not give his brother the delight in seeing him ripped apart by an Ittallan. Overhead, sniggering rippled though the crowd, fuelling his anger. With a hiss, Sapora transformed.

'Seems like he is a true Naja, father.' Tacio said as the enormous cobra wrapped himself around the great lizard. 'Even has your markings, see? On the front of the hood?' Tacio was more interested in rearranging the long, silver chains that dangled around his neck than seeing the end of Sapora's fight. 'Still taking him a while, though.'

'Hush, Tacio. This is his chance. Your time will come in due course.'

Tacio rolled his eyes. 'If he succeeds, I doubt that. He's just as bad as Isa.'

The crowd grew as more and more Varkain approached the edge of the pit, all calling down insults and praise, both.

Sapora's coils covered the Gila's mouth, forcing it shut, as he smothered it with his weight. He squeezed, cutting off the air to the Gila, and suffocated it.

'He is doing well. I know you cannot bear to admit that.'

Vasil said.

'We'll see. Three more rounds to go. Great numbers always break them.'

They looked down as Sapora released the limp Gila, but remained in his cobra form. Across the pit, a gate opened, and from it poured twenty men and women. They were a mixture of ages in various forms of dress; some had armour, some had weapons, some had shields.

'Thralls always love a go at freedom.' Tacio grinned, caressing the jewelled rings he wore. 'Let's see how he handles them.'

*

On the outskirts of Timin Rah, Topeko hurried along the tunnels. He was escorted by one of the Cerastes on guard in Feoras Sol. She had been most unwilling to permit him into Sereth, but after he produced a black onyx with Sapora's seal engraved, she relented.

It had been at least eighteen years since he had last visited the Varkain homeland, though under vastly different circumstances. When he was last in Sereth, the Crown Prince lived in Val Sharis with his infant sister, both far too young yet to transform, and King Vasil's third child, a pure Varkain, had just been born. Topeko had come to pay his respects to the new child, and though everyone had behaved as if all was well, it was clear that strong emotions simmered among both Ittallan and Varkain. When he grew, Sapora would have first claim to the Jade Crown by right of age, but there were many who believed the newly born Tacio had better claim to the throne than the half-breed Sapora.

Vasil had conquered the Ittallan by force only a few years prior, yet retreated to his dark tunnels to allow the Ittallan to rule themselves with their own Council, so long as they paid homage to him. His takeover had been so vicious that by the time anyone realised what was happening, it was all over. An uneasy truce grew between the Imperial allies of Corhaven and Val Sharis, and the Varkain of Sereth.

In his prime, Vasil had been formidable. Topeko had been in awe of the Varkain when he met him, and was thankful he had brought such a large gift to remain in favour with him. Vasil had led an assault on the palace in Taban Yul and taken it in a single night of bloodshed.

While in the palace, and on subsequent visits, Vasil and his Cerastes dined in their balls, drank of their wine and ale, and lay with the men and women of the court. Sapora and Isa were born to two such women, and though Sapora's true form was a Naja—a cobra—befitting his royal lineage, Isa could only transform into a wildcat, like her mother. The laws of the Varkain forbade her from entering Sereth, leaving her to be raised by the Ittallan who never quite saw her as one of their own. All three of his children had a lot to live up to, with the elder two having the odds very much stacked against them. Sapora, in particular, had something to prove, and it was most apparent now he was on the cusp of becoming a ruler.

'Looks like you're right about Sapora's return.' The Cerastes said as she led him down the winding tunnels, suddenly darting down another to the left or right. Still tired from his evening's work with the dragon, Topeko lagged behind, and the Cerastes stopped to wait for him. She flicked out a forked tongue and tasted the air as they reached a large cavern where many tunnels joined. 'Fresh kills. There are no fights planned. It must be Prince Sapora.'

'Am I too late?' Topeko asked, panting.

'You may not be. Quickly. Come.' She checked a tunnel and darted off, and Topeko hurried after her as quickly as he could.

*

Corpses littered the pit, the floor swimming in blood. Sapora had lost one scimitar, but he still had one strong blade to see him through the last two rounds of his final test. There was no food or water between bouts; no resting or chances to re-arm himself. This was a brutal fight to survive, a fight to claim his crown. His wrist throbbed from the monitor's bite, and he bore wounds of the fighting he had endured, but Sapora remained on his feet, determined.

Another Ittallan stepped forward, an older man with white hair and a crooked back. His hands were chained behind his back, his robe caked in years of grime and dirt. Sapora narrowed his eyes, wondering how a thrall had lived to such an age in the bowels of Sereth.

Sapora did not wish to transform any more than was necessary, and readjusted his grip on his scimitar. Opposite, the Ittallan picked his way past dead bodies and pools of blood. He was engulfed in light as he transformed, and Sapora snorted as he saw an eagle, almost seven feet tall, stood before him. His wings were ripped apart, feathers torn from the bone, but the talons on his feet were easily as long as Sapora's own weapon. In contrast to his white feathers, the eagle's beak and eyes were coal black and piercing.

The eagle lashed out with talons extended; four huge blades on each foot. Sapora danced around the eagle as much as he could, but with the pit getting full, the ground soft underfoot, and the injuries he had sustained, he could not move with the speed of the earlier battles and felt fatigue taking hold. The eagle's beak was also deadly—it was hooked to pierce and tear through flesh, and Sapora was nicked by it several times as he continued to dance around his enemy.

He jabbed at the eagle with his blade, but was deflected and thrown away by the sheer strength of its head and beak, and it forced him backwards to the corner of the pit. The crowd's chanting and cheering were louder here than in the centre of the battlefield, and Sapora heard their disdain for him. How could he, a mixed-blood bastard, ever hope to survive the trials?

'It should be Tacio down there.' 'Vasil should rule another two years.' 'Send the half-blood back to Val Sharis.'

The eagle struck, the force of its attack shoving Sapora back into the wall. Is talons tore through his coat, but missed his flesh, and Sapora pressed himself flat against the wall to avoid another strike. The jeers grew louder.

Sapora crouched and switched his hold on his scimitar so the blade pointed towards himself. He mustered his strength and pounced as the eagle extended its talons again, shooting past the bird's neck as he drew his blade along the length of it. When he landed a moment later, all time stilled around him. He used his incredible speed for strikes more than anything, but he could also use those same muscles to move faster than most could blink. It was faster than the eagle could strike. It crashed to the ground in a heap, its head severed.

The booing above turned to cheers as Sapora straightened. One round to go.

'Tacio. Prepare my crown. I'm ready for it.'

'Don't be so sure of yourself, Sapora. The best is yet to come!' Tacio called back in his lazy tone.

At his brother's words, his final opponent fell into the pit from above. Sapora stepped back, getting the measure of his new target, and grimaced. It was a Varkain, one of the old guard—a constrictor with dark coils thicker than tree trunks, almost double the length of Sapora's transformed state.

Another faceless, nameless opponent. Another life to be taken. Sapora was expected to transform, too. To face his opponent Varkain to Varkain. But without his venom, he'd be crushed. He had to show them all what he was truly capable of. It was the only way to silence his doubters.

Instead, he gripped his weapon and darted forward, slashing at the huge snake, but doing little damage against its hardened scales. The constrictor, while enormous, did not have the speed of a Cerastes or Naja, and Sapora managed to evade the few strikes it attempted. He heard the whisperings above him, and knew they expected him to wear down his opponent, getting in an attack here or there, turning it into a battle of stamina more than skill. But Sapora wanted to shock them, to prove that he was a worthy ruler. That he was indeed his father's son, but greater.

With one hand still limp from the bite, Sapora inhaled sharply. The snake took up most of the pit, its bulky form pushing away bodies to create the space it needed to move freely. It was now or never. He darted forward, expending all his remaining energy in boosts of speed as he clambered onto the snake's body and darted up higher and higher until, in a few heartbeats, Sapora crouched on the top of its head. Flicking his scimitar out, Sapora plunged it through the constrictor's skull, right to the hilt.

'It looks like we are to have our last meal at the keep, Tacio.' Vasil said, leaning forward to his son as he joined the crowd in applause. 'Perhaps you could beg Sapora to remain, if you're particularly attached to this place?'

Tacio trembled, his eyes on the fallen constrictor that filled the bottom of the pit. 'I think we need to get some stronger challengers. Maybe double thrall recruitment?'

'Do not show your displeasure so openly, son. You will pay your respects to the new king, as will we all. Law is law. Sapora fought well. A worthy successor to the Jade Crown, and I can rest.'

'Well fought.' Tacio said, clapping slowly as Sapora pulled himself up the side of the pit and out into the open cavern having retrieved his second scimitar. Blood and sweat dripped from him, but the smile he wore was nothing short of triumphant. Tacio dropped to his knee, as his parents did beside him, and one by one, so did the other Varkain gathered.

Sapora tried to slow his breath as best he could. Whether the adrenaline coursing through him was a remnant of the fighting or excitement at what was to happen, he couldn't tell. He looked up as Vasil stood and removed the circlet of dark silver from his head. In the low light of the tunnels, the jade jewels glistened, and Sapora's mouth went dry.

'King Vasil speaks to those of you gathered here. You are in witness of the passing of sovereignty to Sapora, the Crown Prince of Sereth and Val Sharis, who will be the ruler of these lands and protector of the Varkain now his errantry is complete.'

Vasil took three steps until he was stood in front of Sapora, who dropped to one knee before his father. Their eyes met as Vasil placed the crown on Sapora's head, and bowed to him.

'I receive the Jade Crown, symbol of my people, and all the powers and holdings that come with it. Vasil shall remain an advisor to me, as will Tacio as our world is in the midst of war. This shall remain so, until such time as I have no need for counsel. You are witness.'

Sapora stood up to an eruption of noise and hissing, applause and cheering, as he became the new king. 'To the keep. I wish to dine.'

He brushed past Vasil and Savra as they kneeled, and paused by Tacio, who was still mid-bow. 'Put your hatred to one side and we might come out of this war better off.' Sapora said, continuing up the overhanging cliff and into his new home.

*

'My King, you have a visitor. A Samolen.' A Cerastes

announced, entering the large, inner-room of the keep where Sapora dined with his family. Four Cerastes stood at the door, all in matching livery.

'A Samolen?' Sapora hissed, glancing up from his meal, the first he'd eaten since returning to his homeland. He'd had no time to rest or prepare before his battles, and did not wish to stop now, when he needed to replenish his energy and venom. 'Send him through.' Now he wore the crown, those seated with him ate only when he did, and kept wary eyes on the visitor as he was brought in.

'King Sapora. May I offer you my felicitations on your new title.' Topeko said, bowing his head to the table as he entered the inner keep. When he raised his gaze, he carefully took in the new King and his entourage. Sapora could feel his unease, and broadened his smile. 'Thank you, Topeko. It is most kind of you to travel all this way.'

'New kings in Sereth do not come about often.' Topeko nodded, keeping his attention only on Sapora. 'May I have a private word?'

Sapora considered the request as he chewed his mouthful of food. His people were watching him as closely as Topeko, and he had no intention of appearing weak considering the trials he'd endured to claim his crown. 'We may not. You can speak freely here.' Sapora pushed his empty plate away and drank deeply from his cup, watching Topeko all the while.

The scholar cleared his throat. 'I have come to tell you of the elder dragon we found, the one in the mountains bordering Val Sharis.' He licked his lips. 'It was the very same dragon whose power Aciel stole at the beginning of his conquest—still alive, but barely.'

Sapora remained silent as Topeko spoke, his pupils slightly dilated.

'We were able to restore her power. We took it from Aciel, moved it into the stone of the drake Kohl had with him, returned it to the elder dragon and healed her wound. It was the most astounding thing I have witnessed. Aciel's power will have suffered immeasurably.'

'Listen to this magician. The threat is over now!' Tacio said.

'They could never reach us here anyway.' Vasil shook his head, pursing his lips together.

'Would you have wanted to risk it? Ridiculous birds.' Savra replied.

Sapora remained silent as he digested Topeko's words. 'You stole his power?'

'Yes, we did.'

'Then he will be most desperate to reclaim it.' Sapora said, voice measured. 'His Arillians have invaded the skies above Sereth. For the moment, we are well protected by our land, but I'm sure it will not be long before he finds some way into our tunnels. I do not like hiding, like a rat, but I am unwilling to sacrifice myself or my soldiers in a fight we cannot win.'

The chatter stopped around the table at his words, and all eyes returned to their liege. Despite the gravity of what Sapora said, his voice was calm—there was no fear or anger in his tone.

'King Sapora, I fear the war will end with a bloody battle

between Arillians and dragons, and it is the dragons that will end up burning the world and reducing all peoples to ash. From dragon fire begun, from dragon fire undone.'

'Spare me your prophecies, Topeko. Tell me. Why did you visit Sereth? To spread misery? Get us to leave the safety of our homes and fight back? I've just gotten hold of my kingdom, surely you do not expect me to risk it all on day one?'

Topeko paused a moment, his cheek jewels glinting. 'I seem to recall some sealed tunnels here, Sapora. Rumours that a sleeping dragon is buried here, deep within the earth.'

The Cerastes closed in on the Samolen at his words, mouths agape and fangs extended as they began to transform.

'Halt!' Sapora ordered, getting to his feet. 'How did you come to hear such a thing?'

'Why did you not disclose the location of the sleeping beast before? You have known since you left Berel that you sought a Sevastos!'

'This is an ancient Varkain weapon. For the Varkain alone to know and use, no other!'

'So it is true, then. How did it come to be?'

'Enough! I permitted you entry to my country so you could pay your respects, and you insult me? You have walked willingly into the snake pit. Your boldness is your failing! Get rid of him.'

Two Cerastes turned to Topeko, their weapons raised. 'We will escort you out.'

As the footsteps of his guards died down, Sapora realised he trembled and his stomach churned. It was the most well-kept secret among the Varkain. Had there been some spy who had let information slip? Had Topeko's magic somehow given him the ability to learn of it?

'It appears you do not have the same ruthless touch as father after all.' Tacio voiced, leaning back in his chair. 'Trials sapped all your strength? None but the Varkain are to know about the weapon, and you have let—'

Tacio was on the floor a moment later, so swift and sudden was Sapora's strike. He withdrew his scimitar into his sleeve immediately following the attack, stunning the whispers into silence. Sapora allowed the gurgle of blood on the floor to echo in the room for several moments before speaking. 'I do not take kindly to being called weak, Tacio. The Samolen is a friend who I have allowed to live. I am your king. Question me again and you won't live to do anything else.'

Clutching his chest, Tacio staggered to his feet.

Sapora continued. 'Even if Topeko spreads the information, it does not matter. I will unleash the weapon on Linaria soon enough, and then Aciel will have a real fight on his hands.'

Chapter Twenty-Seven

Palom pulled the first sword from his satchel once the door to their suite was closed. A scythe followed the sword, and then two daggers. The bag still held weapons—half finished blades and axe points, but they were rusted and blackened, failed attempts from the forging of the dragon's weapons.

'Palom!' Morgen gasped, stepping forward to take one of the swords. He unsheathed his own weapon and held the blades against one another. 'What... what is this?'

'Dragon-forged weapon.'

'D—Dragon-forged!?'

'Anahrik learned how to do this from the book Topeko provided. We needed to guess at a few bits. My workshop is half burnt from the attempts and you can see many weapons did not work. But these weapons are done.' Palom rested his broad hands on his hips.

'You bastards, you did it!' Amarah grinned, picking up her new scythe. 'No silver?'

Palom dropped his eyes. 'There was... no time.'

'This is incredible!' Morgen said, holding a sword in each hand, weighing them against each other. 'It's so light. Perfectly balanced.'

'Is not just the weight. The power.' Palom shook his head.

'Is unlike anything you have seen before. We cut the Arillians down with these. Nothing can stand before the blade.'

Moroda looked to Kohl, and saw he remained stoic. He stood off to the side, gazing out the window, uninterested in Palom's bounty. He and Palom would never see eye-to-eye, it seemed; the Ittallan had no tolerance for secrecy. Moroda could understand it, after all, he lost his trading partner because of Kohl's actions, but holding onto a grudge? What good was it going to do? She remembered the Arillian's words back in Burian, that grudges were a poison better forgotten. She wished Palom could see that and push his hatred aside, but it did not seem likely.

'This is incredible, Palom.' Moroda said, picking up one of the blade tips and gently running a finger over it. 'Are these what you wanted? The legendary weapons?'

'It is.'

'You must be very proud to have created them from your own hand.'

'This is my gift then?' Amarah said, twirling the scythe. 'You're too kind.'

Palom straightened up and looked at the sky pirate. 'Is gift for you all. The Arillian is taking over. We must fight, we must protect ourselves. With these weapons, you can do this.'

Moroda tilted her head. 'You... you're fighting too, aren't you?'

'Yes, of course.'

Moroda nodded, but couldn't help but question his words. It sounded like he was going away more than anything else. 'These are incredible!' She held the blade up to the light, marvelling at the colours emitted from the metal. 'How did you do it?'

'The dragon ore did most of the work. Unlike any weapons I have crafted before.'

'The ore?'

'From Berel. I do not think Topeko would be pleased to learn what I have done. This is why I waited until he left before I showed you. But with these, we have good chance to survive the coming battles. No more losses.'

'Damned good idea. Why not use whatever weapons we have? Who knows what tricks Aciel and his generals will have up their sleeves!' Amarah laughed. She passed the scythe from one hand to another, marvelling at her new weapon. 'You're a useful guy to have around, Palom.'

Moroda laughed as the Ittallan glared at Amarah, who did not retaliate. For all his anger, words had, for the most part, left him. Moroda knew he was still coming to terms with the loss of Anahrik, as she was for Eryn.

'I promised to protect you. If I fail again, these weapons will not.'

*

Morgen stood watch at the balcony on the far end of the palace guest suites. The night was clear, for once, and the moons shone brightly down on the sleeping palace. Taban Yul was certainly not asleep, and even at five or six floors up, he could hear the laughter and chatter of the townsfolk as they enjoyed the night. Shouts rang out, footsteps clattered on the stone paths, and carriages charged through the winding streets.

He held his dragon-forged sword—Palom's gift—and held it loosely. He'd little time to practice with it, but it was of a similar length and weight to his normal swords, and he felt comfortable wielding the new blade. Whenever he held it for more than a few moments, it glowed blue, and he loved watching it shimmer in the moonlight.

'With this, I can avenge her.' He lunged at an invisible target, swung round and brought it down as though to cleave through a skull. 'I can avenge Anahrik, too.' The blade flashed in response, a light in the darkness. 'Aciel doesn't stand a chance—'

'I'm sure the Arillians will cower in fear.'

Morgen dropped the sword with a clatter and looked up at the sudden voice. 'P—Princess Isa! How long have you been there?'

'Since you started muttering to yourself.' She was lounged on the sloped roof above the balcony, her arms behind her head as she fiddled with her hair. 'That's some blade you have. I've never seen one glow before.'

Morgen bent down to pick it up, and sheathed it to dim its light. He wanted to give her the answer she desired, but she'd not asked the question directly, and he held his tongue. Palom hadn't sworn them to secrecy, but he'd kept their armoury quiet. 'Why did Sapora do that?'

'Do what?' She bit her thumbnail and looked down at the city.

'After the ball...'

'Bit of spring cleaning. Winter cleaning, I suppose.'

'But why? Why the violence? Eryn... She... She...' 'She and Moroda should have left when I warned them. They didn't seem the type to enjoy a cleansing.'

Morgen balled his hands and looked away. He leaned on the balcony and looked over the edge. 'I don't know what's wrong with you. Why you kill so willingly...'

'Fodder are weak. If they won't listen, they must be made to. I tried to make them listen but they're too stubborn. Sapora simply showed his fangs to set them in line.'

'Set them in line... Sounds like Aciel.'

Isa laughed, her voice singing. 'If anyone does anything you don't like, you always compare them to your worst enemy. Sapora has the right to rule. Aciel does not. Sapora wishes for peace in Linaria. Aciel does not. Sapora shows mercy, and then kills those who continue to defy him. Aciel steals lives for his own gain.' She stood up and leapt from the roof to the balcony.

Morgen lowered his gaze as she approached. She moved with silence and skill, and he could tell she was related to Sapora. Out of the corner of his eye, he saw her reach into her pocket, and he tensed. His dragon-blade had yet to taste blood, and he would use it against her if she gave him reason to.

'Relax, Morgen.' She purred, darting to his other side. 'It's not too late for you to leave. Go back where you came from. Leave dragons and monsters to the real kings and queens. Some of us have grown up beside the nests of vipers. You don't belong in this world—your world is cosy and peaceful—you've no idea what it feels like to be robbed of your birthright, and hated by your own kind. I have learned the art of silence. Of stealth. It's quite remarkable what you hear when people don't know you're watching from the shadows. Some of the things the councillors got up to… I fed the information back to Sereth, but Vasil had none of it. When Sapora takes his throne, I shall finally have the respect I deserve. These dances are written in blood. Go home, Morgen. It's not your world.'

'No! I need to avenge her!' He shivered at her words, but he could not quit, not now.

Isa giggled and jumped up onto the edge of the balcony, balancing on the narrow wall. 'So sweet. I suppose you want to keep little Ro safe, too?'

'Little Ro…?' He watched her pace along the balcony, turn, and pace back. The fall would kill her, no question, but she stepped as confidently as if they were on the street.

'If you're staying with us, you must give it your all. Here. In case you need anything.' She pulled out her hand from her pocket and tossed him something small and dark.

He caught it with both hands and looked down. It was an onyx stone, engraved with a crest—the same one that adorned many of the shields and tapestries throughout the palace. 'Princess, what is this?' When he looked up, she was gone. 'Princess Isa? Princess?'

'Remember whose side you're on, Morgen!'

He looked up and saw her back on the roof. She waved at him before transforming and racing off into the darkness.

*

Moroda was awakened in the early hours three days later by

armoured feet charging up and down the hallway outside her room. She had spent the majority of the wait in a state of heightened anxiety, practicing the Samolen magic as best she could, and training with Morgen so she knew how to hold a sword, block and attack. All around her, the palace rumbled as it shook, thunder rolling around outside. 'Arillian storms!'

She raced to the window of her room and peered out. It was light outside, but thunderclouds gathered ominously above the city. She could see ripples of sheet lightning streaming across the sky, and as they lit up the clouds, she saw warships. Her heart pounded. This was it. Aciel was here, with all his strength.

The Council had sent Ittallan scouts to Corhaven in the hopes of bringing back reinforcements, but with the recent fall of Niversai, Isa did not have high hopes. There were few cities large enough in Corhaven to have enough soldiers to aid Val Sharis, and many of those would be focussed on restoring the country's capital. Any that could be spared would also need to be flown over, a trip that would take several days at best. It was simply too little too late.

One thing was to be said for the Arillians—once they sacked a city, they immediately moved on to the next one. No hostages were taken, but they left few alive. Only those who went deep into hiding survived; everyone who fought back was killed.

Moroda had toyed multiple times with the idea of returning to Niversai. It would have been easy to get home on one of the Ittallan scouting ships, but the thought of returning to a blackened city scared her more than she realised. She did not know, after losing her sister, whether she would be able to stomach returning to a home that may not be there.

She understood Palom's desire for vengeance, but she knew there were other ways. There had to be. Killing in revenge would not bring back their loved ones, and it would not make her feel better, as she said to Kohl. Too many lives had been lost in this war, and she did not wish to add to it.

She wished Topeko was there to guide her in the short time they had before the battle. His knowledge would have been invaluable, but all she could do was pore over the tomes she carried and practice with either her magic or sword.

The weapons Palom had created and gifted them were something quite incredible. Even Amarah was stunned into silence by their ability. Not only could the weapons slice through almost anything, but simple thrusting of the weapon in the direction of a target was enough to send out a wave of power, causing significant damage.

Moroda hadn't quite got used to it. She preferred to prevent damage than cause it, and while she carried a blade at Palom and Morgen's behest, she had little intention of using it except if the situation grew dire.

She quickly shrugged into her thick travelling cloak and hurried down the corridor, following the guard as they raced along.

'Get out of the damned way, you cowards!'

As Moroda rounded a corner leading to one of the large reception halls in the palace, she heard Amarah's savage words—of everyone she had come across in Taban Yul, none rivalled the sky pirate for uncouth language and behaviour.

'I want to get on my warship to defend your damned city! Stand aside!'

Moroda saw Morgen stood beneath an archway, watching Amarah battle against a small crowd of palace guards that blocked access to the passageway leading to the palace hangar.

'Lady Amarah, the warship belongs to the princess. We cannot let you on board.' One pleaded, his brow covered with sweat as he battled with the pirate.

'I don't care what you think! It's MY ship! I'll cut off your damned head unless you move!' Amarah bellowed, drawing her scythe along the marble floor and sending sparks up the blade.

Morgen approached the group, his helm under one arm. 'I have orders from Princess Isa.' Hearing his words, the palace guards lowered their weapons as they turned to face him, finding him suited in full armour, ready for battle.

'Sir, are you certain?'

'I heard it from the princess herself. Moroda, Palom, Kohl, and I are accompanying Amarah on board.' He held up the onyx stone with her family crest, and the guards sheathed their swords.

'Yes sir. Apologies Lady Amarah.' The guard moved out of the way and nodded curtly to the group.

Amarah scoffed at the niceties and brushed past them.

Morgen waited until the guards marched off, and followed Amarah. 'You're really going to fight?'

'What a question.' She tapped her blade on the floor every few steps, the sound echoing off the marble. 'I'm not about to let these Arillians destroy my best chances of riches. I will fight them.'

'I will be fighting too.' Kohl said, gliding down from a stairway to their left, sending out a cool breeze as he landed.

'I thought you didn't fight your kin?' Amarah asked, balancing her scythe on her shoulder.

'I want to face Aciel.'

'How do we know you won't turn tail and run like you did before?' Palom asked. 'Or attack us? If Jato appears? Once a liar, always a liar.'

'I've never lied to you…'

'Please, Palom.' Moroda said. 'Aciel is at our doorstep! Kohl will help us!' In truth, she was worried about the relationship between Kohl and Jato, but, despite the odds, trusted him. She had to trust him. If she didn't, she'd be no better than Palom's outrage.

'You don't have to fight, Moroda.' Morgen said, as the group entered the hangar.

Moroda shook her head. 'I don't want to stand by and do nothing. I'll fight with you all. Whatever it takes.' They raced to the hangar, hearing the intensity of the storms outside and the cannons from airships outside.

The hangar was a flurry of activity; captains looking for their ships, crew both anxious and eager to fight, staff trying to direct events amidst chaos. Orders were barked out, engines were started, propellers turned and the wind picked up as half a dozen ships took to their air. They were large and ungainly, unbalanced, and heavy with ammunition.

The ships were barely out of the hangar before cannon fire could be heard, with smoke billowing back from immediate impact.

Coupled with the heat and steam rising from the many engines, Moroda found herself sweating before she was even on board Amarah's new warship.

'I won't lie, I'm more used to running from a fight than charging into it. But this ship has enough power to hold its own, and I've no plans on going down.' Amarah announced, striding along the wide deck. 'Looks like everything I wanted is here. My Khanna is below deck, nice and safe in the cargo bay.'

Moroda thought to Amarah's words on fleeing from battle and wondered why Khanna had to come along, too.

'Come on big girl, let's get airborne!' Amarah cackled, forcing the ship's engines into life and raising the sails as they took off. 'Palom, Morgen, get the cannons ready—pull every hatch open, load every gun, and get them into position! Moroda! You come up here with me.' She twisted the wheel sharply to the right as she manoeuvred around other docked ships towards the hangar entrance.

Moroda made her way into the cabin. It was surrounded on all sides by thick glass housed in wooden frames. The ship was definitely built to last.

'Fighting is coming, you know that.' Amarah said, keeping her eyes focussed on the sky as it opened in front of her.

'I know.'

'I'm a better fighter than you. Years more experience. I need you to keep this ship out of harm's way while the rest of us fight. Torpedoes are at your control. You remember what I told you about flying Khanna, right?'

Moroda's eyes widened as she realised what was being

asked of her. 'I... remember... but I should, shouldn't I... The Samolen magic—'

'You're no Topeko. Dragons above, we could do with his help now. Hah. If he could even be convinced to fight. We've more chance of pulling through if you stay out the way and keep us near the action. Not too close. Weapons panels are here.' Amarah lifted a flap to the right of the large steering wheel, 'and here.' There were eight buttons in each.

'Centre cannon here. Low power but fast rate of fire. Got it?'

'But... I...'

'We don't have any time!' Amarah wrenched the steering wheel to the left and pushed the engine's thrusts to full, avoiding a surge of lightning—an attack from one of the many Arillians who filled the sky above the palace.

Flipping another lever to pull back the main sail, Amarah turned the ship again and opened fire with the main cannon—a cloud of black smoke rising from the hull due to the intensity of fire.

'Amarah they're swarming the deck!' Morgen cried.

'Dammit! Moroda keep this thing in the sky!' Amarah charged onto the deck. She swung her scythe wildly to fend off their aggressors. It was a dazzling blue, and glowed as it was wielded.

Moroda had no choice but to lurch forward and grab hold of the wheel, her palms slick with sweat. Her heart pounded as fear threatened to take hold once again, and she cast her eyes above her, peering through the thick glass which ceilinged the cabin. Perhaps two hundred Arillians swarmed above, the wind of their attacks tearing into every warship in the air, the clouds thick with electricity, which whipped up Moroda's hair.

They would be overrun, surely. There were fifty or so warships in the air, and countless smaller airships unsuited for battle. It was formidable, though Moroda worried it would not be enough against Aciel's entire army.

Claps of thunder rolled through the sky, crushing smaller airships as they were overwhelmed by Arillians. Spinning the wheel and pushing forward, Moroda tried to position the ship away from the thick of the fighting, as Amarah had told her. Though very much on the side of the Ittallan, Amarah's warship was not garbed in the Imperial colours, which, she supposed, meant it was a smaller target.

Moroda heard the clash of steel quieten, and she ran to the edge of the cabin and looked out on deck. 'Well fought.' Morgen panted, lowering his sword as the last of the Arillians flew off, leaving the deck slightly scalded, but otherwise intact. The weapon glowed soft blue, almost green, and smoked slightly now the fighting had paused.

'Where's Kohl?' Palom growled, staring at the clouds above. 'Can't tell him apart from the Arillians up there.'

Amarah raced back into the cabin. 'Good move! Keep us out of danger. We'll pick off whichever stragglers we can.' She patted Moroda on the shoulder and took stock of the battle as it unfolded around them.

Her gaze settled on a small cluster of Arillians, perhaps eight or ten, as they made a beeline for the palace below. 'I don't think so! I'm going to blast you out of the sky!' She flattened one sail and pulled at another, swinging the ship around to face the group with its broadside. It groaned under its own weight, but she held the sailes and pushed the throttles up. When they were in her sights, she flicked two switches and fired twin torpedoes.

The warship jolted with their launch, and Moroda struggled to keep her footing. She watched the two, long grey shapes shoot out of the side of the ship somewhere below deck, a thick plume of brown-grey smoke following in their wake as they honed in on the group of Arillians.

The resulting explosion sent a shockwave through the sky in all directions, fire and more smoke billowing to join the fracas. 'Keep us moving, Ro!' Amarah said, as the attack drew the eyes of surrounding Arillians to them. She raced back out, scythe in hand, to aid Palom and Morgen with the incoming attacks.

Moroda couldn't bring herself to fire on the Arillians—they were just following orders, weren't they? —and busied herself with moving the ship out of harm's way each time they were assaulted by another wave of attacks. She was wracked with guilt at the suffering and death all around her. She didn't want to do nothing, but fighting went against her very nature. Arillians fell like like flies, and three airships had also gone down in smoke. On the ground below, troops of charged forward, clashing with Aciel's followers, staining the ground with blood. Overhead, the skies darkened, and below, fires raged across the city, sending up black smoke. Moroda lost all sense of time.

In the chaos, she saw Palom transform into the stronger, fiercer version of himself; taking out those Arillians who had been foolish enough to land on deck. Morgen and Amarah were also able to fend off their attackers with their weapons, enhanced tenfold by the strength of the dragon crystal Palom and Anahrik had imbued within.

In the thick darkness of the smoke, the crystals glowed. Moroda blinked back tears watching Amarah and Morgen as their entire weapons glowed. They fought viciously, keeping the Arillians away and protecting their ship. After a while, Kohl landed on deck, joining the fray and keeping Aciel's followers from taking the ship or destroying their defenders.

Moroda continued to move the ship around the sky, keeping to the edges of the battlefield, trying to stay away from the thick of the fighting. Visibility dropped as the fighting became more intense—cannons and guns were fired so often from so many ships, and claps of thunder rattled so intensely, that Moroda could no longer distinguish between one blast and the next. The only thing which seemed unchanging was the glow of her friends fighting on deck with their dragon weapons.

Despite the power they had stolen back from Aciel, and the strength they had added to their own repertoire, they were outnumbered ten to one. She trembled, watching as one by one, warriors fell from the skies to their deaths. It had to stop. It had to, else they would all destroy each other. Unless the tide of the battle was turned, everything would perish.

As strong and skilled as Amarah, Palom, Morgen and Kohl were, they could not fight indefinitely. Moroda felt more tears form as she realised they were all who remained from the original party, barring Sapora. She had lost her sister. Palom had lost a brother. They had all lost friends. It was all because of this. They all stood to lose one another in this battle; there was no chance Aciel would surrender. It was the wishful thinking of a silly, naïve girl. He had amassed too much power, too many followers, and his goal was the eradication of all non-Arillians. How were you supposed to fight something like that?

Moroda shook her head at the futility of it all. Talking wouldn't help; none of them would listen. None of them would stop the fighting. There had to be another way. There had to be a way to protect those who remained from perishing. A Sevastos would be able to do that, surely? But what was to stop it from burning everything and ending the fighting that way?

'If I don't do something, we'll all perish. If I do something… there's a chance it may end. I must, must take that chance. That's what Ryn would have wanted…' Moroda breathed aloud, her fingers slipping from the steering wheel. Looking up, she could barely see the glow from the cabin, the smoke and ash was so thick. She had to speak with the dragon again. There was no other way.

Decision made, Moroda pressed another switch on the control panel, and found herself running away from the cabin before her mind realised she had come to the conclusion. In a daze, she made her way down, into the depths of the ship, past the loaded guns, past the steaming engines, past the supply storage, and into the cramped cargo bay where Khanna lay resting.

She clambered aboard, by now, the side steps as familiar to

her as her ring, and hurried to the controls on deck, each step reaffirming her decision and strengthening her actions. She brought Amarah's pirate's ship to life and felt the familiar noise of Khanna's engines purring. 'I'm sure you'll understand, Amarah.' Moroda whispered. There was no turning back now, as the cargo doors slowly opened underneath Khanna.

Moroda dropped like a stone, and she wrestled with the levers as she tried to control the dive. Arillians and other ships flew past her as she shot towards the ground, before she finally opened the right sails and levelled out her trajectory. Heart racing, Moroda pushed the engines to full thrust, and headed back towards the mountains.

*

In the deep darkness of Sereth, King Sapora was well hidden from the violence on the other side of the mountains. Though he and his people were all too aware of it, Sapora had chosen to keep them underground and away from the fighting while he had been mulling over Topeko's visit. It was a decision that split the Varkain. Some agreed wholeheartedly that they needed nothing to do with what was happening in Val Sharis, others believed as their king, Sapora should send aid. He'd had enough of the debate and had finalised his decision, returning to the keep to ruminate.

'My king, Arillians have made it across the Feor Mountains and into Sereth. They look to be scouts, just two of them.' A Cerastes announced, dropping to one knee as she entered the throne room.

Sapora considered her for a moment before smiling. 'Bring

them before me. They will regret coming onto our land uninvited.'
Getting to his feet, Sapora turned to the remaining Cerastes who
stood guard in the circular room of the inner keep. He brushed
down his front and turned to them slowly. 'Be ready to attack on my
order.'

A hiss echoed around the room as they acknowledged his
words, transforming into their true forms; vipers in grey, brown, and
black scales, the horns above their eyebrows marking them as
Cerastes, their fangs dripping in anticipation of a fresh kill.

'The Varkain find your presence here most unwelcome.'
Sapora said. Both Arillians bled profusely from the leg, their bodies
rigid, paralyzed from the venom of the attacks.

He knelt beside where they were laid on the floor, his
Cerastes surrounding them. 'What are your names?' Sapora
whispered, pupils dilating as the two Arillians shivered.

'S... S... Sable...' One gasped, his windpipe
already beginning to close. 'This... is... Nir... Nira...'

'It appears she is most unwell.' Sapora spared her a glance;
she was suffering from the effects of the Cerastes' venom far more
than Sable. The king leaned forward, listening to her breathing
quicken at his closeness. Her heart still beat, but it was fast and
fluttered, only her chest able to move as the venom took hold. With
incredible speed at such close range, Sapora struck; the bite barely
grazing her skin, yet leaving venom potent enough to quicken her
death.

'This is the penalty for your kind trespassing.' He stood up
and looked down at Sable. 'But, seeing as you have come all this

way, I will show you one thing,' He grabbed the Arillian by one, stiff wing, and dragged him across the rough stone floor to another passageway.

'I will be fair to you. I will show you mercy, by allowing you to live.' Sapora said, as he led his Cerastes deeper into the labyrinth of Timin Rah, still dragging the stiffening Arillian along behind him. 'You Arillians have always bemoaned your status in Linaria. Complaining about your unfair treatment and banishment from the main continents.' Sapora made his way down a flight of stairs, crudely carved into the earth. 'Whinging how you've been shunned and mistreated. Fussing and howling about how much you are owed by the people of Linaria...'

The darkness grew around them as they descended. 'So you fought back, tried to take what you thought was yours.' He continued. 'How dare anyone speak ill of you? You have the gift of flight, of Rhea herself. Doesn't that make you better than everyone else? Prove you're owed more, hmm? Isn't that what you all shriek?' He yanked the Arillian forward and stopped by a tall, wide door of metal, built directly into the cave wall.

'Life is unfair. I detest people who complain about it yet do nothing to improve what they have. For his willingness to try, I give your Aciel a little respect.' He brought forth a small, silver key from his outer coat, and unlocked the door. 'But he, like all of you flying creatures, is misguided. The Arillians had their time. You've had your chance. You ruined the harmony of Linaria in forcing this war, and we Varkain, left to slink in caves and hide out of sight, are going to fix your mess. I'm going to have to clear up after your wanton destruction.'

He shoved the door open, and thrust the Arillian inside. Hardly able to breathe, and no longer able to blink, Sable had little choice but to look upon the deepest cavern of Timin Rah; upon the sleeping Sevastos, with gold encrusted into his scales.

The heat emanating from the beast was enough to melt rock; indeed the texture of the blackened walls was almost liquid— superheated rock which cooled occasionally enough to solidify once again.

'Tell your leader that I wield the power of the Sevastos.' Sapora gazed at the dragon. It filled the vast cavern with both its body and its horde of gold crowns; the wealth of the Varkain. 'If he does not cease the fighting now, I will use all the fury of this dragon against your kind. So he does not get any ideas of somehow overpowering it and stealing that power—he seems to have a knack for doing that—I will use this beast to take the five Sevastos crystals from Berel and enhance its strength, and my own. With six crystals at my fingertips, it is a power too great for any army to threaten, wouldn't you agree?'

Sable began to tremble as he lay on the floor, his skin steaming from the heat.

'Release him from the venom. Let him deliver this message, while we ready ourselves for a victory like the Varkain have never seen before.'

Chapter Twenty-Eight

'I told you before that I could not help you.' The dragon snarled at Moroda, lashing her tail like an angry cat. Moroda had hoped against hope the dragon had returned to her lair, something the ereven sphere confirmed, and managed to land Khanna in one piece a short way from the cave. Without Kohl's blizzard, visibility was far greater, and she found the dragon resting outside, sunlight glinting off her scales.

'You can help, I know you can.' Moroda said, her hood pulled up to protect herself from the wind. 'You said yourself you know when other dragons die, when they are born; when they fight… you all have a connection you can tap into. It's just energy, isn't it?'

The dragon let out another snarl but said nothing.

'So you can find the Sevastos, but you don't want to. I understand you don't want to add to the fighting.' Moroda tried again. 'I just want the Sevastos to protect us. Not power. Not to destroy Aciel and his armies, that would just lead to a never-ending war… I just… want to protect those I love from being taken away from me!

I've lost my father, my sister, my home. Anahrik, too… so many friends… On my way back here, I saw Aciel himself, he leads another wave of fighters towards Taban Yul, with airships, too!

How many lives must be lost today?' She fought to keep desperation from her voice, but as things stood, she had no choices left.

'You restored my power so I will not kill you.' The dragon said, getting to her feet and striding along the mountain away from Moroda, flexing her wings. 'But you are trying my patience.'

'Archon.' Moroda bowed her head, hoping the use of the honorific would placate the dragon. 'The people of Linaria worship you. You are a god to many. Please, I beg you. If there is anything else I can do, just name it!'

'The Sevastos are wanderers. They do not settle.' The dragon said at length, pausing to look out at the land. 'But they feel the ache I feel. They feel the pain of Linaria acquiring more scars because of this war between you all. The life of Linaria is a concern to the Sevastos.'

'It's my concern, too!'

The dragon laughed, shaking the mountain. 'Offering power and knowledge has always been a risk.'

A flash of bright gold captured Moroda's attention, and she looked up to see a phoenix fluttering above them, trying to cling to the side of the mountain with its talons and letting out a shrill cry. It scrabbled to get hold, and Moroda could just barely see a tuft of straw on a rocky ledge. The phoenix sent small stones and snow falling, along with a handful of feathers.

Moroda reached into her cloak pocket and brought out the ereven sphere. 'Archon, this is what I used to find you to seek your guidance as Topeko instructed, and to help restore peace and balance to Linaria. Please.'

'Hmm, an ancient sphere?'

'Aciel used it to find and kill other dragons and steal their power. We took it from him, and then moved his power back to your stone. I do not want a Sevastos for more destruction and death, as Aciel does. I want to stop the war. I want to end all that!'

'Your intentions are indeed different to the Arillian. He sought to use my power and that of my brothers and sisters for his own gain, not to help Linaria.' The dragon said. 'It may end the battle. I do not think it will end the war.'

'What about the fighting?'

'The fighting will cease… But war is not always fighting.'

Moroda whimpered and looked at the ereven sphere. So close to the dragon, the feather and liquid both quivered, and the whole sphere vibrated. She turned it in her hand, looking at it closely, but it couldn't point in any direction because she stood right beside the thing it was designed to find.

All the effort they had gone through to obtain such a simple, yet powerful item. For nothing? When they had finally found this old dragon, this powerful creature, they had moved Aciel's power back to her. They had returned what was stolen, and the thanks they received was simply not being burned alive. Tears threatened at the futility of it all. She had abandoned her friends in the middle of the battle in the hopes she could stop it in one last, desperate attempt. She was still a silly, naïve girl. She was still a Goldstone with no understanding of the world and the unfairness everyone endured.

Moroda sat on the snow, her cloak covering her legs, and held the sphere to keep her hands warm. Somewhere along the way she had lost her gloves—on Jato's warship, perhaps—and hadn't obtained replacements. Her bare skin was numb in the cold, and she wondered whether it was fitting she remained on the mountain and froze, before she did anything else stupid.

The dragon lay down and the snow melted where it touched her scales. Moroda put one hand in the pocket of her cloak, and paused as she felt something sharp against her thumb. Bringing it out, her eyes widened at the thin shard of crystal in her hand. It was from one of the Sevastos stones back in Berel. She'd forgotten it had splintered off at her touch and Topeko had told her to hold onto it for good luck. Moroda held it up and watched blue and green light emanate from the shard and reflect on the white snow all around her. In her other hand, she still held the ereven sphere, and in a heartbeat, another idea hit her.

Moroda twisted the top and bottom halves of the ereven sphere, splitting it open and exposing the contents to the air. Clutching the crystal shard, she placed it into the centre, on top of the phoenix feather, and closed the sphere. She shivered, watching as the droplets danced around as though unsure what to do. 'Please... please work...' After a moment, it settled, and Moroda felt the sphere grow cold.

'What are you doing?' The dragon growled, but Moroda was too engrossed in the sphere to respond.

'It's just energy. It's just moving energy.' Could she... Would it be possible to summon the Sevastos' energy to her, instead of the other way around? The crystal in her ring was a conduit. The ereven sphere had the ability to seek dragons, and now she had given it a very specific target with the shard. 'It's just energy…' The wind picked up as she focussed on what she had learned from Topeko and his books, from what she had been practicing while waiting for Aciel to attack.

The dragon raised her head to the skies. 'How can you do this? It is not possible?'

Moroda rocked where she sat, feeling her own strength leave her as she summoned the Sevastos. She could hardly understand what she was doing, how she had managed to flip the puzzle around, but it was working. She could feel it, and the dragon's words solidified that.

Minutes dragged by as she continued. She felt like Topeko, and prayed she had a more favourable outcome than the Samolen had.

'It comes.'

She did not need the dragon's words to know that. She felt an enormous energy approaching, and the temperature of the sphere rose. When the heat of the sphere became too much, she dropped it onto the wet ground and looked up.

Moroda saw a dark shape looming in the distance, and her mouth went dry. She swallowed, unable to speak, and got to her feet. The shape drew closer and closer, crossing leagues of distance with every second. It was surrounded by dazzling gold light, and she saw dozens of phoenixes flying beside and behind the Sevastos.

Moroda held her breath, and it was suddenly on top of them—a dragon of immense size. It had deep, silvery-blue scales and black horns, and its wings blotted out the sky. The phoenix that had been trying to land on its mountain nest took off, shrieking wildly as it circled the Sevastos with the others. The heat radiating from the group melted the snow, leaving the rocks wet and slick. Words failed her at the sight of the Sevastos, and she understood why they were called the gods of Linaria.

The dragon bowed her head and spoke with the Sevastos in a language Moroda could not comprehend—guttural noises and rumbling—and after their greeting, she switched back to the common tongue. 'Archon, are you truly willing to give this woman your strength? Am I mistaken in my judgement?' The dragon's eyes remained closed as she spoke.

'You wish to seal away the bringer of war.' The voice of the Sevastos reverberated through Moroda herself as much as the mountain she stood on, and she shook in his presence. 'You have summoned me with old magic, yet you are not a daughter of the Samolen. Commendable.'

Moroda struggled to breathe as the Sevastos spoke, and could hardly bring herself to look upon him.

'I have felt across the dragons who have seen Aciel. Fought him. Succumbed to him. Been destroyed by his greed for power. To seal this Arillian, I am willing to give you the crystal I have carried for over a thousand years and join my brethren in death, leaving only three Sevatos remaining. This is my burden.

My crystal will allow you to keep Aciel sealed away. You would not have him destroyed, but sealed away he is no threat, no influence on Linaria. Your own life force will be drained to keep him sealed. Your own life force is the price you have paid to request

I sacrifice mine. This is your burden. Will you pay?'

Moroda shivered, forcing herself to look up at the great creature. She licked her lips again. 'If, in death, the lives of everyone I know will be safe... every parent, every child... then I would gladly die.' She took a deep breath and looked at him, his golden eyes burning. 'I will do anything to end this.'

'So it must be.' The Sevastos tilted his head towards the sky and let out a roar of such intensity, Moroda thought the world would split. His scales burst into flame, the fire licking up his wings and legs, engulfing his body. The Sevastos dropped to the ground and landed heavily on the mountain. The flames burned violent purple, covering his body and peeling away the flesh.

Horrified, Moroda jumped back. In only a few minutes, there was nothing left of the Sevastos except a blackened skeleton. She trembled from head to toe, and it took all her strength just to walk over to where the skeleton lay. She could not fathom this creature, the strength it held, the suddenness of its arrival and depature. A beast that had lived for countless centuries, a god among men and dragons, willingly gave its life at her request. She sought its power, true, but did not want more death. Her cloak flapped around as the wind picked up and snow began to fall.

'The decision was made willingly. You have little time, if you wish to stem the deaths.' The dragon said, bowing low over the skeleton. 'I did not think the great one would listen to you. You are no Samolen, but you have skill in their ways.'

Moroda ran a hand over the Sevastos' skull, and as she touched the blackened bone, her fingers began to glow. She tried to wrench her hand free, but she could not pull away from the bright, writhing light which enveloped her skin. 'What is—?'

It engulfed her arm and moved to her chest. She squeezed her eyes shut against the brightness, only daring to reopen them when the light dimmed. She looked down and saw the blue-green light swirling on her hand—no, her ring.

Lifting her hand, she saw the stone on her ring glowed a bright aquamarine, and her whole body warmed despite the coldness of the mountain and the falling snow. She had the power of the Sevastos at her fingertips, and knew what had to be done. Calm determination washed over her, as everything became clear.

'Moroda. You have no time. The Sevastos sacrificed himself and his power to you. I will take you to the battle to fulfil his wish.'

*

In the midst of the battle above Taban Yul, Amarah had taken the wheel of her warship, worried Moroda had been thrown overboard during the attack. Chips of splintered wood and broken glass lay about the cabin and on deck, but the ship was afloat, and everyone on board was alive. The sky pirate had to hand it to Palom, the weapons he had created were nothing short of sensational. Simply flicking the blade in the direction of an aggressor sent forth a blast of energy that seemed to do more damage than the blade itself. It had removed the Arillian's flight advantage and levelled the battlefield.

But she was not in a celebratory mood. Moroda was gone, without a trace. There was no blood or ripped clothing, there had been no screams. She'd simply disappeared. Amarah wondered whether an Arillian had targeted the cabin and flown off with her while she and the others were in the thick of fighting. She was barely aware of what was happening five feet away, let alone keeping an eye on the cabin. Keeping Moroda there was her best chance at keeping her safe, but it seemed to have backfired.

She strolled out of the cabin and to the deck, where Palom, Morgen, and Kohl were sat, taking a break after the intense wave of fighting had passed.

'These weapons of yours saved us, Palom.' Morgen said. He was bleeding from a scrape to his cheek, but was otherwise uninjured. 'They couldn't even get close to us. Thought it was some sort of trick, but we're proof it's not! I can see why these things were so powerful in the war. Need to arm the whole guard with them!'

'We needed to survive. We have done that.' Palom held his right shoulder, and glanced up as Amarah steppd out on deck.

'I think we did well, considering how outnumbered we were. I suppose numbers count for nothing when those who are fighting are undisciplined. But I didn't see Aciel or his generals.' Kohl said, sitting down next to Morgen.

'Know who else I don't see?' Amarah said, stopping in front of them. 'Moroda.'

'Moroda?' Morgen said, getting back to his feet, sword in hand. 'I thought she stayed in the cabin?'

'Well she ain't in there now. Did any of you see any Arillians land? Did one grab her?'

The three shook their heads.

'Did she go below deck? Hide there, maybe?' Kohl said, lifting his wings and taking to the air. He flew overboard and circled around the ship, while Amarah led Palom and Morgen into the ruined cabin.

'Nothing at all.' She snapped, pulling at a lever to straighten one of her sails as they hovered on the edge of the battlefield. 'Damned if I know what happened to her.'

'She's escaped.' Kohl said, landing by the cabin a moment later. 'Cargo hold doors at the bottom of the ship are open. Khanna's gone. She must've fled.'

'On Khanna!?' Amarah raced out the cabin's rear door and down into the hold. 'On my damned ship!?' She threw open the doors to the cargo bay and stopped in the entrance. It was empty. 'Moroda! Dragons above, what are you thinking?'

'I can't believe it!' Morgen said, joining Amarah. 'You really did teach her to fly, didn't you?'

'If she's damaged a single panel on Khanna...'

'But where would she have gone?' Morgen asked. 'Back to Niversai?'

'And how the hell would she know the way?'

'I don't know. Where else would she have gone?'

'Damned thief!'

'Get up here now!' Palom shouted from above them. 'Dragon approaching!'

'Don't we just have all the luck?' Amarah growled, charging back to the deck. Palom and Kohl were stood outside the cabin glaring towards the sky.

Amarah brandished her scythe as she walked out. 'I don't believe it.'

'It's the dragon from the mountain!' Morgen exclaimed. 'She changed her mind? She's here to help us?'

Across the emptying skies, the dragon flew closer, its bright scales dazzling in the sun. Smoke still rose from burned airships, and many wreckages littered the plains below. Taban Yul glistened behind them, a shining city of wealth and strength, in juxtaposition to the scorched battlegrounds. Troops on the ground saw to their injured and dead, but as they began to notice the dragon, many stopped to look up, raising their shields in defence.

'That is... That is Moroda?' Palom said, squinting up. 'On dragon's back?'

Kohl was in the air the moment he heard, flying across the battle-strewn sky to the dragon. 'Moroda! What? Where did... How did you...?'

'I don't quite know how to explain!' Moroda cried back, digging her knees and hands onto the dragon's neck so as not to fall off. 'The fighting has to end. Now!'

'We've already won! Reinforcements from Princess Isa arrived not long ago, look.' He hovered beside the dragon and waved an arm to show off the influx of Imperial ships, now numbering nearly eighty, floating the sky. 'I reckon the trick you and Topeko did was enough to stop Aciel. He's too weak to fight.'

'No, it's not finished! This was just the first wave! I've seen Aciel himself leading more Arillians and a fleet of warships! It's far more than you all can handle!'

Kohl flinched. Aciel leading reinforcements? Perhaps Jato and Fogu were with him then? He flapped his wings and flew vertically, climbing almost a league high. He scoured the horizon, and in the distance, near the Feor Mountains, he saw the ground covered with thousands of soldiers on foot. He backed off a little, eyes widening as he realised the darkening sky overhead were not gathering clouds, but more Arillians in their air, along with a collection of airships. 'Is this every Arillian living?'

He dove back to Moroda.

'All this against what remains of the Imperial fleet... If we don't have any more reinforcements, we don't stand a chance.' Moroda said. 'I have to get to Aciel before the second wave can begin their attack. I don't want anyone else to die.'

'Moroda, get back to the palace and take cover! You don't need to see this. Don't need to be a part of this!'

'It's too late, I've already made my decision.' She raised her left hand to show her glowing ring. 'The Sevastos.'

'It can't be...'

'It is. I thank you for everything you've done, and I forgive you for leaving when Jato appeared. But I can't stand this anymore. I promised Ryn I'd keep her safe, and failed. So I will do what I can to protect all Linaria. It's not fair you having to take on your daughter, your people. It's not fair what Aciel is doing. It's wrong.'

'Moroda...'

'The girl has made the pact with the Sevastos, Arillian. Clear the air, if you can.' The dragon growled.

'Moroda, this is not your battle. You've been caught up in it. Aciel could take control of you again, and if you truly wield this extraordinary power, we shall all be at risk. Aciel is mine to take down. I won't flee any more!' Kohl left Moroda and the dragon no time to respond. He darted off in a wave of freezing air, intent on taking down Aciel.

'Kohl, no!' Moroda called out, but he ignored her. It was his fault Aciel was even in Linaria. He should have stopped him a long time ago, while he'd had the chance. As he soared across the sky, Aciel in his sights, anger rose within him. He had blamed himself for what happened to Jato, for not protecting her from Aciel's compulsion, but she was immune, too. She truly believed in him and what he stood for, to the point she'd killed in his name and enjoyed causing pain and misery to those who were against them.

Fogu and the others were just following orders. Perhaps they didn't even realise they were. He could not hold anything against them. No, the root of it all was not his mistakes, it was not caused by something he did or didn't do. It was Aciel. It had always been Aciel. He was going to make him pay.

Thunder roared through the sky as Kohl let out waves of icy air. Aciel was in his sights and he would not let up. Not this time.

'Kohl, what are you doing? You are trying this again? You'll fail. Like you did before.'

Aciel's voice rang in his mind, but Kohl drowned him out. His tricks had no effect, and Kohl had no intention of failing again. Aciel hovered in front of him, his arm heavily bandaged and covered with thick armour. Kohl smiled at the sight, remembering

Amarah's attack on the Arillian leader. He was not going to be so lucky, this time. Kohl raised his hand and sent out another wave of freezing wind. It bit into the group of Arillians hovering nearby, and scattered them. Only Aciel remained.

'Fool. You had your chance to live.' Aciel spread his wings and raised his arms. 'Your life and legacy ends now.'

The two clashed with each other, their attacks sending shockwaves out into the air. Aciel was faster, and dodged most of Kohl's attacks, but he was not powerful enough to do any real damage to Kohl. His attacks, when they connected, stung, but Kohl bore the brunt of them and retaliated in kind. This was why he had Fogu and Jato as his generals. This was why he resorted to using compulsion. He was a weakling. Kohl shot another wave of freezing air at Aciel, knocking him back towards the main battle.

'Attack him…' His voice echoed in the sky, and Arillians who had been targeting Imperial troops or ships turned their focus to Kohl. They flew towards him, hands outstretched, and Kohl readied himself for another bout.

'You're a coward, Aciel. You cannot take me on. You've never been able to fight for yourself!' Kohl roared, sending the Arillians flying with his icy wind. He was sure to only deflect their attacks, but for Aciel, he increased the intensity, slowing him down and weakening him. 'Stand and fight me, Aciel! Coward!'

'I am no coward! You fled our homeland! You left Jato!' Aciel said, darting in close to Kohl and grabbing him by his cloak. 'You fled death. You fled our law. I was also told you fled a battle and left your friends for dead… Who is the real coward?'

Kohl screamed, freezing the air around him as Aciel responded with another wave of electricity. He whirled round and grabbed Aciel's collar, pulling him close. 'Without your compulsion, you're nothing!' Holding on to Aciel, Kohl flipped over and shot towards the ground. 'You will pay!'

*

'Amarah, land the ship! Kohl has Aciel on ground! I will rip him apart!' Palom roared, preparing to transform.

'Palom, be careful!' Morgen said, his sword at the ready. 'He can control you!'

'Hold on!' Amarah yelled, pulling back the sails and engaging the throttles. Though the warship was not as fast as Khanna, the sheer weight of the vessel enabled them to drop at speed—she pulled up the nose just as it was about to kiss the ground, allowing the tiger to leap off the deck and sprint towards the two Arillians locked in combat.

Aciel fought back viciously, punching and blasting bolts of electrical energy at point blank range. In his peripheral, Kohl saw orange and black race towards him, but Aciel deflected Palom's lunge with a bolt of lightning. It sent Palom flying backwards by the sheer force of the attack, and he lay still and stunned.

Amarah's warship deck was swarmed by Arillian reinforcements now their leader was under direct attack; they blasted the ship with lightning and wind, bringing it to the ground. Amarah let go of the wheel and sails, allowing the ship to crash land. She grabbed her scythe and raced out to join Morgen on deck to fight.

'I have heard of you. You are the woman with the scythe!'

One Arillian said, his hand extended towards Amarah. 'I am General Fogu. You'll regret what you did to Aciel.'

Amarah flicked the blade of her scythe towards him, a wave of energy surging forward. 'You'll regret taking me on!' She did not let up, and charged forward, spinning her blade like a carriage wheel. Sparks and energy flew in all directions, slicing through the Arillians and toppling them.

Fogu dodged her attacks and raised his hand, sending a sharp blade of air through Amarah's thigh. She yelped and dropped to her knees, her scythe clattering in front of her. 'Bastard!'

'Now I have you where I want you.' Fogu sneered, flapping his wings to hover above her. He sent wave after wave of attacks, the air slicing into her, cutting through to the skin.

Fogu splayed his palms open, summoning up a ball of electricity to finish her off, when he was knocked out of the sky by a flash of blue-green energy.

'Great shot, Morgen…' Amarah winced.

'Back on your feet, Amarah.' Morgen rushed forward and grabbed her by the elbow, hauling her up. He leaned forward and picked up her scythe. 'Can't lose you, too.'

'So… kind…'

'Let's finish this.' Spinning his sword, Morgen rushed forward, the downed Fogu in his sights.

*

'This is our chance!' Moroda cried out, watching the Arillians fight on the ground. 'We have to dive! Now!' Her ring pulsed with light and energy, guided by the Sevastos who died for her cause, to protect Linaria. 'This is the only way I can defend those I love. This is all I can do, everything I can do, to help.'

She held on as the dragon swooped down, her great wings casting shadows across the battle. The nerves and fear that had plagued her since leaving Niversai were eased away as she focussed on the heat in her hand. It would all stop. It had to stop. She had bet her life on it. 'Thank you, Archon.'

When Aciel was in her sights, she extended her hand and called upon her magic, not to seek out or move energy, but to contain Aciel's energy where he stood. It felt like the Sevastos had enhanced her strength a thousand fold, and a beam of light poured forth from her crystal.

Brighter than a thousand suns, the magic lifted the darkness and smoke of the battlefield, and called a halt to the fighting. Shielding their eyes, Arillians and Imperials alike turned away from the light as it enveloped everything below. The explosion shook the ground and shattered airships, bringing about a silence to the plains.

'Aciel?' Palom coughed. 'Kohl?' He staggered to his feet, all energy gone, as he gathered his bearings and looked around. When the dust settled, his mouth dropped open. Aciel was encased in a pillar of stone easily as tall as the Sevastos stones of Berel.

The dragon who had carried Moroda landed on the scorched grass, her head bowed. 'She truly committed to her cause. That's the only way the Sevastos could be called.'

Leaderless and in shock, the remaining Arillians scattered. 'Aciel's spell and hold over them has been broken, it seems.' Kohl said, looking up at them for a long moment. They grouped together and flew north, hardly sparing a glance his way. 'Moroda. What were you thinking?'

'It's over?' Morgen shivered, watching the remaining Arillians drop their weapons and fly off into the clouds. 'Amarah? You alright?'

'Moroda!' Amarah yelled, hobbling out of the cabin, using her weapon as a crutch. She and Morgen stood at the edge of the deck and looked over to where Kohl approached the dragon and the stone pillar.

He reached a hand out and grasped the stone, cooling it with his touch. His fingers trembled, and he sank to his knees. 'Moroda! What did you do?' Tears spilled down his scarred face. 'You wanted no more deaths but didn't care if you died yourself?'

'The Sevastos's power. She harnessed it.' The dragon said.

'How did she?' Palom asked. Too weak to stand any longer, he sank to the floor. 'How did she die? If she… If she had the Sevastos's power?'

'Sacrifice. Do you not listen to what your Samolen teach of lore and dragons and powers?' The dragon asked, her voice cold. 'I suppose you are only interested in the strength we can give to your weapons and little else. I see the weapons you wield. Thief of stolen power. You will understand sacrifice soon enough if you continue to use them. You are the same as Aciel. You should be dead, not this one.'

'Where is the Sevastos's crystal?' Amarah asked, limping towards the others with Morgen and Ittallan soldiers in tow. Ground troops began to gather around the pillar.

The dragon spat a little flame into the air. 'The Sevastos gave her his crystal and it went into her Samolen ring.'

'Moroda...' Morgen whispered, kneeling down next to Kohl.

'Her life force went into this magic, as payment for the Sevastos's death. You people cause so much damage to Linaria.' The dragon said.

Around them, the Imperial soldiers erupted into cheers and stamped their feet.

'We must report back to Princess Isa of our great victory!' 'You will be heroes for all the ages to come!'

Kohl shook his head. 'The Sevastos gave his power to Moroda. Such incredible strength.'

Imperial soldiers praised them, and chatter descended through those who gathered. One soldier shook Morgen's hand and pulled him to his feet. 'We must get the wounded back to the city at once. Val Sharis is indebted to you all. You have saved us.'

*

Topeko could not be more thankful to see sunlight when he finally reached the end of the tunnel. He had been escorted out of Timin Rah, and four Cerastes had tailed him until he was a league or so away from Feoras Sol and getting out of the dark tunnels. It had taken almost two days to work his way back out of Sereth, though all sense of time was lost in the deep darkness.

He was met at the gate to the tunnel by two of the Imperial Guard, and he bowed to the Ittallan when they permitted him through.

'What news of Taban Yul? Is the city safe?' Topeko asked, adjusting his robes.

'The city stands. There is some damage to the outer walls but our defences protected the people from Aciel's battle.'

'He attacked?'

'Indeed. Victory was ours this morning. Would you believe a Sevastos helped us!'

'A Sevastos? Truly?'

'Truly, scholar. At least, the power of one, the beast itself was not present. We were on guard here, but a messenger arrived not long ago. They say a woman summoned it. She arrived on the back of a dragon and sealed Aciel away in a pillar of stone.' The guard adjusted his helmet and shifted his weight. 'No more damned Arillians about, that's for sure. You heading to the palace?'

Topeko shook his head. 'No. No. I shall return to my homeland. I've been away from the University too long. Thank you for the news.' He bowed again and strode past.

If the Ittallan spoke the truth, it was Moroda he spoke of. He could not imagine Amarah taking it upon herself to speak to the dragons or find a Sevastos. Nor the princess. No. Moroda was the one who had managed it. It had to be. Quite how, he wasn't sure, but she did have a knack for ideas and understanding theory. What a student she would have made if she had studied with him in Berel.

If the Sevastos had willingly sacrificed itself to give Moroda power, then she would have paid a hefty price for it. All five previous Sevastos had been the same, and Topeko knew it was the way Linaria was balanced. Why would this one be any different?

He walked through Feoras Sol, and the villagers acknowledged him with low bows and cheerful smiles. They had every right to be happy, of course. Aciel and his Arillians were no longer destroying their lands and killing their families. They were safe. Moroda had put an end to it, somehow, but Topeko's heart was heavy at what it would have cost her. No-one should have that burden, no matter how well intentioned.

Palom had said Feoras Sol was his hometown, and indeed, his name was on the lips of many. Stories of the small group Moroda travelled with had reached the village, and a tiger Ittallan was a rarity. The villagers believed it was Palom, and celebrations of the war ending were underway.

Topeko smiled back and greeted those who spoke with him. He declined many invitations to food and drink, instead pressing on to get back across the sea to Ranski. There was much to consider.

With Sapora's Sevastos in hibernation, and two other Sevastos still wandering Linaria, he was unsure how long the peace would last, and the Imperial victory over Aciel was bittersweet. Topeko knew the threat to Linaria was not Aciel, or any race, for that matter, regardless how much power they amassed. No, it was the dragons themselves. While a Sevastos had aided Moroda, he could not believe it would be without a long-term consequence. With the age of dragons coming to an end, Topeko believed Moroda's sacrifice would be in vain. He worried the peace would be temporary, that the worst was yet to come.

He left Feoras Sol for the path to Taban Yul, where he could find a ship to charter back to Ranski. His red robes billowed out behind him, in stark contrast to the barren, white landscape, ancient words in his mind. 'From dragon-flame begun, from dragon-flame undone. In the end, everything burns.'

End

NOTE FROM THE AUTHOR

Thank you so much for reading *Moroda*, I hope you enjoyed it! It would mean the world and more if you would be kind enough to leave a review on Amazon and Goodreads.

Book reviews help readers find new books, and they help indie authors like me find new fans. They also let me know what I'm doing right and what could be improved for subsequent books.

Book two in the World of Linaria series, *Palom*, is due to be published in summer 2018.

If you can't wait to get back to the World of Linaria, sign up to my mailing list and you'll be the first to hear news, announcements, and special offers. You'll also receive a high-res digital map of Linaria just for signing up!

www.llmcneil.com/contact

Moroda is now available as an audiobook on Audible and Amazon. Buy your copy now and hear the World of Linaria brought to life by Georgie Leonard!